Deception OF A *Highlander*

MADELINE MARTIN

DIVERSIONBOOKS

Diversion Books
A Division of Diversion Publishing Corp.
443 Park Avenue South, Suite 1008
New York, New York 10016
www.DiversionBooks.com

For more information, email info@diversionbooks.com

First Diversion Books edition April 2015.
Print ISBN: 978-1-62681-632-9
eBook ISBN: 978-1-62681-631-2

This book is dedicated to my parents—
thank you for raising a bookworm.
And, no, we're not going to read this aloud as a family,
but I appreciate that you support me enough to offer.

Chapter One

London, January 1604

The drug had taken effect. Mariel Brandon caught the young earl as he slumped forward in a state of unnatural relaxation and eased him back against the lush velvet settee. A familiar ache tightened in her chest.

Aaron was wrong. She would never grow used to this.

The earl's silk doublet was cool beneath her fingertips and far superior to the fraying skirts she wore.

She averted her gaze, unable to bear the weight of her own shame. He was younger than she had initially presumed. Not any more a man than she was a woman.

His face would haunt her dreams. As the ones before him already did.

Like all the others, he had fallen prey to her flirtation and allowed himself to be pulled into the private, sumptuous room in the bowels of Hampton Court Palace. The information he'd been entrusted with fell from his lips with a few kisses and a bared shoulder. The laudanum laced wine kept her from having to make good on false promises.

A lock of dark hair fell across his forehead. It was a reminder of why she did all this, of why she endured her lost morality, of why she let part of herself die when she coaxed men's secrets. And every time, she slid deeper into the shadows of sin.

Jack. Sweet, innocent Jack with laughing blue eyes and silky black hair. He was but a pawn in the cruel game Aaron played. They all were.

How many more men would she be forced to betray until her brother would be released? Until the threat on his life would dissipate and she could be free from this hell?

She reached without thinking and brushed the black curl from the earl's brow. *Forgive me.*

"Are you growing sentimental?" The voice laced with sarcasm sounded from the shadows behind her.

The heavy odor of Aaron's perfume filled her nostrils and the familiar wave of nausea rolled her stomach. Mariel fought the flare of emotion that rose within her. The fear for what his presence represented and the hatred for what he had done. The helplessness he confined her to.

"Don't be silly." She let her hand fall to her side. "He's just a boy."

Aaron emerged from the dark corner of the room as she turned to face him. His breeches and jacket were midnight blue velvet, far more subtle than his usual attire.

She gave him a coy smile and sauntered in his direction, playing the game that had been forced upon her. "To what do I owe the pleasure?" Revulsion threatened her composure as she pressed her lips to his dry powdered cheek.

"I wanted to watch you work. I have to say, I'm most impressed." He glanced to where the earl snored softly behind her. "How long will he be like that?"

"He will not wake until morning. And with a wicked headache, poor man."

Aaron regarded her with obvious suspicion. "So long as he can never recognize you."

Mariel pulled the heavy blond wig from her hairline, revealing her black tresses beneath. The cool air was heavenly against her scalp. "He leaves tomorrow."

"And you never leave the house. I swear you are becoming a recluse, poppet. If you killed these men, you could be shopping and dancing like the rest of the girls."

"You know what I want." Keeping the malice from her voice was becoming more difficult as time went on.

"Yes, yes—your brother." He rolled his eyes heavenward.

"He is not yet ten," she added with great patience. "I haven't been allowed to see him, and no one gives me word of his welfare. Have you given him my letters?" She pursed her lips to stop her desperate words. Aaron would only use them against her.

A slow smile curved his thin lips upward and raised the hairs on the back of Mariel's neck.

"You will be most delighted with my news. I have one final job for you. The benefactor paid enough to cover the remainder of the fees you and your brother have accrued."

Despite her wariness, her pulse raced at the prospect of their freedom. Never before had she been offered the hope of immediate release. Mariel waited for him to continue, but a thick silence settled between them. No doubt intentional.

Aaron ran his gloved finger over the glossy top of a marble table beside him. "There's a Scottish barbarian at court presently. You need to compel him with your..." His gaze slid down her body. "...talents." He rubbed his fingertips together with a look of disinterest. "You must discover the location of two people: Blair and Dougal Hampton. If you can't do this, you must kill him."

"I don't kill," Mariel reminded him gently.

"And I am not refused." The threat glinted like ice in Aaron's pale blue eyes. "Do you really think I would fund your training if I only needed you to lure men to private rooms and slip them a sleeping draught?"

Heat touched her cheeks and she hated that he would see her discomfort, that he would know she had been so naïve.

Under his insistence, she had been educated in foreign languages and customs. With honeyed lies served on a silver tongue, he had prompted her to learn the art of weaponry along with the ability to defend and kill using only her hands, skills taught by Aaron's famed Chinaman. For her protection should something go awry, he had said. And like a fool, she had believed him.

His bark of laughter rang out sharp in the heavy silence of the room. "For one so intelligent, you can be so foolish, poppet." He shook his head. "Any whore can garner secrets, but you…" He drew a deep breath and his eyes widened, "…you are something special."

His face eased into a wide smile that revealed one crooked bottom tooth. "Besides, you need not kill him. You are given three months to obtain the information you need. After what I witnessed tonight, I doubt you will need even half that."

"Why so much time?" Her cheeks flared with heat. Asking questions would only prolong the inevitable.

He gave a derisive snort. "Those Scottish beasts are always wary of strangers. I've held the manor for years and still the ghastly creatures don't trust me enough to do my bidding without question. Do you have any idea how much it costs to staff a household with English servants so far from home?" A sound of annoyance rolled from the back of his throat. "Even you might need the full three months to gain his trust. You'll need to travel to Scotland with him as I can assure you he won't stay in London long. You've perfected your Gaelic, I assume?"

Before she could answer, Aaron waved his hand dismissively. "Of course you have."

"What is the barbarian's name?" The crude question sat bitter on her tongue, but she knew to reference the Scotsman otherwise would give Aaron cause to question her sympathies.

"His name is Kieran MacDonald. You need to seek him out tonight." He glanced around the room. "Jane is with you, correct?"

Mariel bit back a grimace. Jane had been sent to act as her lady's maid. For appearance's sake, or so Aaron had claimed. But Mariel knew the truth. He wanted her watched at all times, especially after she had discovered where they were keeping Jack. He'd since been moved, and Jane had become her permanent shadow. As much as Mariel hated it, she knew Jane hated it more and considered the task beneath her.

"She is outside the door. While she may follow me at your bidding, I work alone." She lifted her chin, her heart racing with the boldness of her challenge.

He studied her carefully for a moment. "Very well, but she

will travel with you to Scotland. That is not up for debate."

"Of course, I wouldn't suggest otherwise."

His bony knuckle rested beneath her chin and tilted her face up toward his. "Heaven help the man when he looks into your violet eyes and falls prey to the words whispered from your sweet lips."

She met his gaze and silently willed the impossible. "Let me see Jack before I go. Just once."

Aaron dropped his hand and sighed with impatience. "You are wasting time. Go find the savage and secure a place for you and Jane in his party as they travel back to Scotland. I don't care who you have to kill or seduce to get there."

Her heart sank low into her belly. Of course she wouldn't be able to see Jack. That she should have known better did little to ease the burn of disappointment.

"I'll make sure to give your regards to your brother when I see him next." The edge of warning in Aaron's tone was unmistakable.

• • •

Mariel's gaze swept over the crowded room once more, but to no avail. Several Highlanders stood out in King James's new court, but not one in particular looked approachable to question about Kieran MacDonald. Concentrating on the task at hand was impossible with the heat of so many bodies in one small area. The air was thick with heavy perfumes and left little room for breathing. White spots dotted her vision and a cold sweat broke out along her brow. She needed to get outside, to breathe fresh air. Fainting would call far too much attention.

She threw open the heavy glass door and found herself submerged in the quiet dark of night. All traces of the party were shut out as the door snapped closed behind her. The late winter air nipped her heated cheeks and turned her breath to white fog. Shadows stretched over the garden below and shrouded various shaped hedges.

Did Aaron lurk in the darkness?

A shiver slid down Mariel's spine as she imagined his eyes trained on her. Would she ever live a life where she was not constantly watched?

Doubtless Jane stood just inside the door—waiting, spying...

Jack would be free once she betrayed Kieran MacDonald... or killed him. Doubt niggled her conscience. Could Aaron be trusted? Would he really free them when this was done? She drew a deep breath of the frigid air in an effort to steady herself. Women had been released from his clutches before; she'd seen it with her own eyes. Besides, what choice did she have? He had Jack, and if this was her only opportunity, she had to take that chance at freedom.

Aaron had been correct in his reason for the length of time she had been granted. The Scottish did not take well to strangers, especially English strangers.

Winning a Highlander's trust was a most impossible feat, and if she managed it, her betrayal would be all the more painful. No longer would her victim be someone she knew only several hours.

A hard knot balled in her throat. Completing this task would tear away the final vestiges of her morality.

To kill a man...She gripped the coiled iron railing and let the metal bite into her damp palms. No, the option was hers and she refused to kill. The truth would be found, no matter what the cost to her conscience.

Who were these people being sought? Blair and Dougal Hampton. Obviously brothers or perhaps father and son. Most likely political refugees. Whoever they were, they had caught the attention of the wrong people.

"If ye squeeze that bar any harder, ye may snap it from the wall." A man's voice sounded behind her, startling her from her reverie.

"What?" she gasped and spun around to face him. She had not heard the door open.

Dark brown hair grew past the stranger's shoulders, and he stood a head taller than any man she'd seen in London. His eyes were black against the darkness of night as he studied her. "Why do ye cry?"

Had she been crying? She touched her cheek and met the cold wetness of her tears.

The hard lines of his face softened as he regarded her with a tenderness that made her long for the ability to speak candidly to him, to be comforted by him. But she was no ordinary woman with ordinary fears that were able to be soothed.

She dragged her gaze from the warmth of his stare, severing the delicate connection between them and kept her silence.

"Will ye tell me yer name?" He moved closer, and a subtle breeze carried the light masculine spice of his scent toward her. She breathed deep before she realized what she was doing.

"Mariel Brandon." Her response came automatic and without thought. Her heart slammed erratically within her chest. She had given her real name. For the last two years she had maintained an alias, her own name nothing more than a memory. Yet here, in the face of a foreign stranger, she had announced her true name without hesitation.

"Mariel," he repeated in his hypnotic burr. The corners of his lips tugged up in a ghost of a smile.

Something about him gave her a reassuring sense of comfort and made him feel somehow trustworthy. Doubtless he could help her find Kieran MacDonald. She drew a slow breath around the sudden tightness in her chest. Like so many before him, she would have to use this kind man to her benefit. And she hated herself for it.

"Perhaps you might help me." She stared up at him, keeping her gaze innocent.

The golden glow of the lights from inside the palace spilled onto the balcony and highlighted his strong features. His jaw was hard, too sharp for his sensual mouth, and his nose appeared bent as if it had been broken before. He wore a kilt belted around his waist and a simple jacket over his plain white leine, the garb of a Highlander.

His eyes searched hers; his thoughts were impossible to discern from his impassive expression. "What is it ye need?"

"I'm looking for Kieran MacDonald." It was a direct approach, but Highlanders were a direct sort of people.

His face did not reflect any kind of recognition. "Why do ye seek him?"

"I heard he returns soon to Scotland and hoped to secure passage with his party." She glanced down, unable to meet his gaze. "I cannot stay in London any longer, and I have nowhere else to go."

"I hate to add to yer sadness, lass, but I dinna think he will take ye."

Mariel's heart raced. So he did know him? "Why do you say that?"

"Because I'm Kieran MacDonald." His eyes narrowed. "And I'm curious how ye came to know my name."

Chapter Two

Kieran regarded the dark-haired woman with a hard stare. Her mouth fell open, and he regretted the bluntness of his demand. She was a courtier, not a prisoner of war.

Some habits were difficult to leave behind.

Still, she had asked for him by name. He could not leave that be.

Color spread across her cheeks. "I overheard several Highlanders speak of you earlier." Her voice was soft with a huskiness to it. While most English spoke in harsh, clipped tones, her words sounded almost melodic.

She lowered her eyes demurely and tucked her lower lip between her teeth. He was being ridiculous with his suspicions. She had not sought him out. She hadn't even seen him when she came onto the balcony.

Irritation bristled along the back of his neck. Coming to London always set him on edge, but even more so now given the circumstances.

Still…if Colin and Alec were discussing their plans in full earshot of the court, he would have some choice words with them.

"I dinna remember seeing ye earlier. What did the men speaking look like?"

She tilted her face toward him, and the light spilling from inside the palace caressed the smoothness of her skin. "Would you have remembered me?"

Her wide mouth curved into a coquettish smile. Almond-shaped eyes the color of heather gazed up at him from beneath a veil of thick, black lashes. He did not have to glance down to know her breasts swelled enticingly above her gown or how her bodice hugged her slender waist. He had noted those features earlier. No, Mariel was not the kind of woman any man would miss.

He grunted in response and turned his attention to the garden below. He didn't have the patience for flirtation, not when this unwanted trip to London had been such a waste of his time. Subtle questions had rendered far too little information and thus far, no one had seen Hampton at court. Kieran ground his teeth against the angst of his frustration.

She shifted closer, and the smooth fabric of her skirts brushed his naked calves. He turned his attention to her and found her wide gaze fixed on him, her expression earnest.

"I'm afraid I've upset you. This was not how I wanted my introduction to be." Her brow furrowed. "Perhaps we might start over?"

Before he could respond, she offered a brilliant smile that would have felled the most stoic of men. "I'm Mariel Brandon."

Though he felt ridiculous, he played along with the charade. He inclined his head in her direction. "Kieran MacDonald, laird to the MacDonald clan."

The back of her hand was white as cream against the darkness of night. He glanced around to the neighboring balconies. If Alec saw him acting like some frilly courtier, he would never live it down. Her tiny hand all but disappeared in his grasp as he placed a kiss above her knuckles. Her skin was warm silk beneath his lips, her delicate rose scent enticing. His gaze shifted to her mouth. He knew without a doubt her lips would be soft and sweet and hot.

Mariel's hand lingered in his as he straightened. "It's a pleasure to meet you," she said. "You're from Scotland, correct?"

"Is it so obvious I'm no English?" He teased.

She gave an exaggerated stare that dragged from his chest up to his face. "Quite. I assure you, no Englishman was ever so tall as you." Color rose in her cheeks, and she pressed her hand against the side of his arm. "Nor so strong."

Kieran never had been one to fall prey to flattery, yet he felt himself warm at Mariel's words.

Tempting though it was, he was not fool enough to think she was wholly interested in him alone. Beautiful women flirted when they wanted something, and clearly this one wanted to go to Scotland. He eyed her warily. "Ye said ye want to accompany me back to Scotland. Why?"

The playful grin melted from her lips. "I have no ties to keep me here." Her gaze dropped to the garden below. "Everything I held dear is lost to me, and everyone I love is either gone or out of reach. I have no friends, and no one to care for me or about me. Not anymore." The sadness he'd seen before burned deep in her luminous stare. "Going to Scotland will allow me a freedom I can never have here; a chance to start over."

"Ye can go anywhere in England to do that. Why Scotland?"

She leaned closer to him, her mouth softening, and her gaze pleading. "I am in danger if I stay in England," she whispered.

The lass's head barely came to his chest. What kind of danger could she possibly be in? He took in her wide-eyed desperation and furrowed brow.

"Please," she said softly. "I'm not safe anywhere in England."

"What is it ye've done to bring on such danger?" He held his hands at his side, fighting the urge to reach out to her.

Her fingers pinched one another, and she inhaled what seemed to be a pained breath. "I owe a man more money than I could possibly pay, and he's ruthless in his pursuit to collect what is owed." Her head lowered as she glanced down at the ground. "Perhaps I shouldn't have told you that, but there's something about you." She met his gaze once more. "Something I trust."

Her smile was apologetic and suddenly shy. As if proving his point, Mariel waved her hand in the air, and the shy smile became too broad and bright to be heartfelt.

"Enough of me. Tell me of Scotland. I've heard no other beauty compares to the Highlands." A wistful note tinged her words.

"Aye," he said. "It's verra lovely. What ye see depends on where ye are. Skye, where I live, is on the coast, and there are deep blue seas lined with jagged cliffs. The wind blows so fiercely that the waterfalls on those cliffs flow upward and rise to the heavens." He looked down at her and winked. "Ye'd probably blow away."

"Skye," she repeated. "Even the name is beautiful. Like one could spread their wings and fly into the crystal blue nothing."

She drew an invisible pattern on his forearm with her slender finger. The movement was subtle and surprisingly intimate. No longer did his thoughts linger on the beauty of his homeland. Instead he found his gaze fixed on her parted lips. He wanted to feel her full mouth beneath his, and her slender body against him.

His finger rose of its own volition and stroked the hollow of her cheek. She tilted her face up toward his.

"Take me with you," she whispered.

"What would ye do on Skye?" His voice was deep with desire.

She rested her hand on his chest, her fingers burning his flesh through the layers of cloth. "I could be your mistress."

. . .

Mariel waited for Kieran's ready acceptance, but it did not come. Had she misjudged his interest?

"I dinna need a mistress," he said and eyed her warily.

Frustration pricked her. She had acted too quickly, was too blunt, and now she would lose him if she didn't smooth this over.

Her eyes swept over his powerful frame. "I don't doubt your lack of need," she said with a smile. "But I know I could make you happy." Her finger trailed down the smooth fabric of his leine, following the carved planes of his chest beneath. "Very happy."

His hand folded around hers and stilled the teasing gesture. "I said no."

He was slipping away. She let her hand drop to her side and regarded him with a composure she did not feel. "Are you newly married?"

Kieran gave a snort as though he found the prospect distasteful. "I am no married."

"You have a mistress already, then?"

"I have no mistress either," he replied.

Her heart tripped with fear. "You are in love."

The corner of his lip lifted in a sardonic smile. "I dinna have time for love. Nor do I have time for a wife." He gave her a pointed stare. "Or a mistress, aye?"

His rejection stung no matter the reasoning. She was suddenly grateful for the allotted time. There might be need for it after all.

If she had not already pushed him away, that is.

Mariel forced a chuckle to lighten the heavy mood. "Then perhaps I can console my broken heart with your friendship. Come. Let us go inside before my dear maid becomes anxious over my absence." A statement all too true, unfortunately.

If he did not come now, she instinctively knew she would lose his interest forever. His rejection was not an option; her failure was not an option. Not with so much at stake.

No longer was Jack's life the only one at risk, but now Kieran's as well. If Mariel could not perform the task, the sympathetic Highlander would lose his life rather than his secrets. She met his dark eyes, and her heart flickered with sorrow.

Despite his obvious suspicion, Kieran pushed open the glass-paned door and motioned for her to walk ahead of him.

The uncomfortable warmth of the room was stifling as they left the cool silence of the night behind them. Yawning hearths glowed with red-hot embers on either side of a room lined in green silk; an opulent expense meant to block out the cold. Mariel's palms tingled with sweat.

She covertly scanned the crowded room for familiar faces. A habit borne out of necessity.

Jane appeared at her side and held out a plain metal goblet of wine. Her cheeks were flushed, and her amber eyes sparked with what could only be rage. Apparently she had been informed of the new assignment as well.

"Thank you, Jane." Mariel took the goblet with a smile, but

would do no more than put the cup to her lips. It was never wise to lose one's head while on assignment. "Kieran, would you like Jane to get you something to drink?"

"I dinna care for English wine." His response was curt, an indication that he still bristled from her folly outside. She may have lured him to her side, but she was still far from her goal.

Jane bobbed a curtsey and disappeared into the crowd, doubtless to find another of Aaron's men to relate Mariel's progress.

Several unoccupied chess tables stood near a large window, and an idea came to her. "Do you play?" she asked, nodding toward the table.

Kieran's eyes followed the direction she indicated. "Aye." His response was flat, and his face unreadable.

"Then let us play." She grabbed his hand to pull him in the direction of the table. His palm was calloused and hard beneath her fingers. For all his noble status as laird, the man worked hard with his hands.

Mariel sank with careful grace into the dainty chair. "Jane has my purse. Perhaps we could wager something of a different nature?" She did not meet his gaze as she positioned the board, setting the yellowed ivory pieces in front of her and the chipped onyx before him. Would he take the bait?

"What did ye have in mind?" Caution laced his tone.

"If you win, I'll leave you alone since I fear that is what you desire."

He did not protest. "And if ye win?"

Mariel settled back in the chair and surveyed the board. "If I win, you take me to Scotland. Both myself and my maid. All expenses covered."

A frown tugged at his lips. He would need a little goading.

"Afraid I'll beat you?" she challenged playfully.

Kieran's eyes narrowed as he settled in the seat opposite her. The delicate chair looked like a child's toy beneath his massive frame. "Yer move."

The tension in Mariel's shoulders eased. Once she won the game and secured her passage to Scotland, she would have to come up with a way to win his trust enough for him to speak openly with her. That would be the difficult part. She knew from experience men did not part easily with their secrets. Their innermost thoughts were shared with other males of close acquaintance or the women they slept with. As Mariel was not a man, that left only one option.

She pushed her pawn forward two spaces. Kieran was not completely disinterested. She had not imagined the desire in his eyes. Her pulse fluttered with unaccustomed nervousness as she waited for him to make his move.

She must win this game.

"I hear King James is trying to establish his own Bible," she said. Men typically liked to talk when they played chess.

Kieran grunted and pushed his pawn forward. He kept his large, tapered fingers planted on the piece and surveyed the board.

Mariel let her gaze wander over Kieran, noting the small creases lining his brow. He was a serious man, one with heavy responsibility. Though the clothes he wore were not ornate, they were sewn well and with fine material. He was a proud man of simple taste.

"Shakespeare is going to be presenting one of his plays for the king tonight." She fingered the smooth indentions on her knight and moved it into position.

Kieran shifted his rook forward and did not respond.

Mariel slid her bishop across the board.

The dark wool of Kieran's jacket stretched over his powerful arms as he nudged another pawn forward. Several white scars slashed across his hand.

She breathed out a sigh and captured his rook.

With a start, she realized the intensity of his stare was fixed on her. Not on the tops of her breasts like most men were wont to do, but on her face, carefully studying her.

She returned her gaze to the board and tried to focus on the game for the next several moves. One final nudge of her rook placed the piece within reach of his knight. The very knight that protected Kieran's king.

"Ye can take the piece back if ye like," Kieran said and indicated to the piece.

The move looked like a mistake on her part and left her rook open for capture.

She smiled sweetly. "That wouldn't be fair."

He was hesitant when he captured the sacrificial rook as if he somehow felt bad for playing on what he assumed to be an error she had made. His fingers curled around the defeated piece, and his eyes widened slightly. No doubt a realization of what he'd done.

Victory surged through Mariel like a balm for her ragged nerves. She'd accomplished her goal and won her passage to Scotland. Jack would be safe.

She slid her queen into position and lifted her fingers from the smooth chess piece. "Checkmate."

Chapter Three

Kieran stared down at the chessboard in amazement, studying the pieces in an effort to discover an error. He found none. No one had ever beaten him at chess and certainly not in only nine moves.

Mariel appeared disinterested in her own incredible victory as her extraordinary violet gaze skimmed the room once more. She had done that throughout their game. Being in full view at court left her on edge.

Despite her distracted state, his guaranteed win had become his greatest defeat. And to a most unexpected opponent.

He had underestimated her and that arrogance now placed others at risk. Frustration tightened the muscles along the back of his neck. Bringing her to Skye was dangerous, not only for her but also for his people. Too many secrets filled his home. Too much balanced on the edge of discretion to make a stranger welcome.

Honor pressed Kieran. While he had agreed to take Mariel to Scotland in the unlikely event that she won, he had also made another promise to his people. One of greater import and severity. One that would be jeopardized by her presence in his home.

His ready trust had once been abused, and he paid for it still on a daily basis. He would not repeat that mistake again.

"I canna take ye to Scotland, Mariel." He stood to leave, hoping she would not press her hand.

Hoping, but not expecting.

She rose quickly from her chair. Too quickly. Her look of nonchalance could not hide her anxiety. "Oh?" She folded her arms over her chest. "Did I not hear you correctly when you agreed to play?"

"Nay, I did agree to play chess with ye." Though it had just begun, he knew the conversation would not go well for him.

"And did you not hear me when I told you the wager?"

"Aye, I heard the wager." He'd heard but had not expected to have to honor it.

She motioned to the board. "Do you think I have in some way cheated?"

He gritted his teeth. "Nay, I dinna think ye cheated."

"Then the men of court were correct." She turned away from him. "Highlanders are not honorable men." Her eyes met his as she glanced back over her shoulder. "I confess I thought more of you."

Pride squeezed against reason and shoved common sense from his thoughts. He caught her hand and pulled her to face him once more. "The English are the ones who are nae honorable."

One perfectly groomed eyebrow lifted at his words. "I've never had an Englishman lie to me the way you just did."

"It isna lack of honor that keeps me from agreeing to this, but fear for yer safety. I dinna think ye understand how difficult life on Skye can be." He eyed her soft, milk white hands and continued. "Ye would need to work hard to earn yer place."

Mariel's gaze wandered to the chessboard. "Perhaps you underestimate me, Kieran."

He regarded her with silence. She was full of surprises, he would give her that.

Kieran studied her upturned face and, for the briefest of moments, allowed himself to entertain the idea of accepting her as his mistress. Having her in his bed would make him the envy of the Highlands. He kept his gaze from trailing down to her bodice, but he knew what lay there. The very idea of having her be his, of being able to pull her into his arms, of being able to kiss her, touch her—it was too damn tempting.

Kieran folded his hand around his defeated king and let the sharp edges of the chess piece bite into his palm as he tried to clear the images fogging his mind. Wanting her was a waste of energy. She could never be his.

He would never allow her to buy his protection with her body. Too recently he had seen what the abuse of man could do. And it made his body burn with rage.

He gave her an appraising look. "If ye are able to work for yer keep in Scotland, then why did ye offer to become my mistress?"

"Working for my keep in London is not possible. There are no options for a woman, save marriage." Mariel rose up on her tiptoes and peered over the elaborate hairstyles of several women to where King James stood with his bushy beard and velvet frippery.

"King James and Queen Anne were married by proxy," she said. "However, when our queen tried to depart for Scotland, she encountered storms and was unable to travel. King James was beside himself with misery and wrote sonnets in her honor. Unable to take her absence any longer, he gathered his men and set sail for Oslo where he plucked her from its barren shore and bore her safely to Scottish soil." Mariel gave a little sigh. "Is that not the most romantic story you've ever heard?"

Kieran didn't bother commenting on her diatribe. What a man's passionate notion toward his wife had to do with Mariel's offer to be his mistress made no sense. Besides, the king's chivalrous effort seemed like a waste of men, time, and funds, but some fools considered themselves romantic. That James was such a fool came as little surprise.

"There is a woman by the door with blond hair in a pink gown." Mariel continued without turning her head. "Did you notice her when we came in?"

He glanced toward the door and immediately spotted the woman. The frivolous gown framed a curvy figure and drew attention to her heavy bosom while the arrogant tilt of her chin indicated how very important she thought herself.

He had not noticed her when he entered, but then what man would see the haughty blonde when he had Mariel on his arm?

Kieran felt her eyes on him, and he realized she was waiting for an answer. "I dinna see her when we came in," he confessed.

"Then you are the only man who did not." With a wry smile, she leaned closer to him. Her light scent tickled his senses and coaxed the arousal he fought to keep at bay. She spoke softly, her words meant only for his ears. "Do you see how King James looks at her?"

He turned and found the king staring at the blonde as though she were spit-roasted game and he a starving man.

"That's his mistress, Lady Glamis," Mariel explained. "His wife, for whom he'd made such a production of loving, is in another palace while Lady Glamis travels with him." She tilted her head to the side, musing. "Not so very romantic, is it?"

"No all men are that way," he replied carefully.

Mariel gave a small shrug that suggested she did not agree with what he'd stated but hadn't the desire to argue. "Lady Glamis is free to come and go as she pleases, and when our king tires of her, she will do well for herself with the gifts he has bestowed upon her. Queen Anne, however, is doomed to a loveless marriage with a faithless husband. No," she said with finality, "I'll take a mistress's freedom to a wife's unloved misery any day if those are my only options."

"Besides," she added while he absorbed what she had told him. "Is it such a bad thing for a woman to want a man without the attachment of marriage?" She lowered her head and slanted her eyes up at him from beneath her long lashes.

•　•　•

Mariel knew her brazen question had been a risky move. However, she had not imagined the glint of interest in his eyes or the subtle way he glanced down her body when he claimed to have not noticed Lady Glamis. If she were going to seduce Kieran, she would have to slowly break down his hardened exterior.

Judging from the heat of his gaze, it had just been chipped.

Her question did not need a reply when the answer hung so heavy between them.

"It's warm in here," Mariel said in a soft tone. "Perhaps we should continue our conversation outside."

Without waiting for his answer, she slid her hand against his elbow so the curve of her bosom brushed against his arm. Kieran took a step back and his broad shoulder bumped against the back of a man with cropped blond hair behind them. The slender courtier whipped around to face Kieran. His throat was so crowded with a stiff neck ruff that he had to turn his entire body.

Mariel's blood ran cold. She knew the man's face. Worse still, he would know hers.

"You made me spill my wine," the courtier slurred. He pointed to the ruby drop that beaded on his ornate doublet. Kieran cast the thin man a look of rude nonchalance before turning back to Mariel.

"I was speaking to you, barbarian." The man pressed a lazy finger into Kieran's cheek, and his bleary gaze drifted to her face. Recognition flickered in his unfocused eyes. "Hey," he murmured. "I know you."

Her stomach clenched. Her heart slammed against her chest. She was caught.

Chapter Four

Several courtiers nearby eyed Mariel with interest. The drunk man's finger lay pressed against Kieran's reddening face still.

"I think ye should remove yer finger before I break it," Kieran growled.

The man pulled his attention from Mariel to Kieran. He loosed a high-pitched laugh and placed his free hand next to his ear with an exaggerated motion. "What's that? I don't understand Erse. Perhaps if you spoke English—"

Kieran's fist slammed into the man's bony chin and sent him crumpling to the ground.

The chatter of voices ceased, music fell away midnote, and the clink of coins from the card tables stilled. A roomful of hundreds of people skidded into unnatural silence. Every eye was drawn to the out-of-control Scottish beast and the hapless courtier he'd brutally assaulted. To make matters worse, the man did not rise from his pile on the floor.

While Kieran did not seem to notice the commotion he'd caused, Mariel did. Any attention drawn to him was aimed at her as well, something she could ill afford in a court where she made naught but enemies.

"Kieran," she said in a quiet voice and placed her hand on his forearm, "perhaps it's best we go now." She caught Jane's shocked gaze from across the room and nodded her head toward the door.

"And I was finally starting to enjoy myself," Kieran muttered under his breath. A white-haired dowager gasped and stared incredulously at him. He turned away from the unconscious man and tucked Mariel's hand in the crook of his arm as gallantly as any gentleman.

Mariel dropped her eyes to the floor and tried to keep her head turned toward Kieran to shield her face. Her heart beat wildly and every nerve was on edge. Where one person knew her, there could be more.

The heavy thump of Kieran's boots on the polished wood floor filled the tomblike silence of the room. Upon their exit, a wave of voices roared to life behind them. It was not difficult to guess what they were saying.

Relief eased the tension in her shoulders. Though he would never realize it, Kieran had saved her by accosting the man. Were the courtier not so drunk, he would have doubtless recognized her more quickly.

Too many things could have gone wrong.

"You've created quite a stir," she said as they strode through the quiet hall. Candles flickered on either side of them, illuminating prized pieces of art and furnishings. "I'm afraid you may not receive a warm welcome at court tomorrow."

"I dinna intend to be at court tomorrow, or London for that matter." They rounded the corner to the final few steps that led to the sprawling front lawn.

Jane waited by the doorway with Mariel's sable cape in her hands.

"We leave for Scotland so soon?" Mariel allowed Jane to drape the fur over her shoulders.

Kieran did not reply as they stepped out into the frosty night once more. Mariel glanced behind them to ensure no guards followed. For either of them.

Thus far the hall behind them was clear, but she steered them toward a shadowed corner of the lawn just in case.

"Yer maid isna a verra good escort." Kieran looked over his shoulder to where Jane stood against the door with her back facing them.

Mariel pulled in a deep breath of icy air to calm her nerves and offered him her most seductive look. A look that left her gaze heavy lidded and her mouth soft. She took a bold step closer so her body whispered against the heated wall of his chest.

So close that his scent tugged at her awareness. A sensation fluttered in the pit of her stomach and bumps of excitement prickled her skin.

"Jane understands when I want to be alone."

His indifferent stare held her gaze. "Ye want to be alone?"

In the soft glow of the moon, his eyes gleamed like inky pools. They captivated her, drew her with the power of her own seduction, the challenge of his resistance, and the success of earning his affection.

Her hand rested on the fine wool of his simple jacket. "I want to be alone with you." She wanted the heat of his lips against hers and his strong arms wrapped around her body. In a world of feigned lust, the heady rush of the true emotion left her reeling.

Intoxicating though it was, she did not know if she liked it.

"Mariel…" Kieran gently removed her hand from his chest and stepped back. "I canna take ye to Scotland." His lips thinned into a stubborn line—a silent command not to be questioned. The command of a man who did not know the persistence of a woman like Mariel.

Kieran took one look at Mariel's set jaw and knew she would not accept his decision easily.

"We had a deal, Kieran." She lifted her chin and her eyes flashed in the muted light of the moon.

"We did, and now I am saying I canna take ye. It is far too dangerous a journey and life on Skye is harder than anything ye've been exposed to here."

"You don't know what I have lived through, what cruelty I have endured. Surely nothing on Skye can be so vicious as what lays in the shadows of London." She caught his hand with icy fingers. "Despite your hesitation to honor your agreement and take me to Skye, I can sense you are an honorable man. There are far too few in this world we live."

She gazed up at him with the naïve hope of a child as if silently pleading with him not to disprove her trust. Something in his gut twisted. He had been correct. She had been subjected to the abuse of men.

He wanted to give her his trust, to allow her to come with him so he could protect her against the sadness that never left her exotic gaze.

"Please." Her voice was soft in the semidarkness. "If I become too much of a burden, you can leave me along the way."

"I would no leave ye," he said firmly.

She gave him a slow smile. "Thank you, Kieran."

He stilled. Had he just agreed she could come? He muttered a curse under his breath. Damn his arrogance. It could cost him more than he was willing to pay.

How could he have agreed to let her come to Skye? The wager had been agreed upon under the assumption his win was guaranteed. It was supposed to have released him from her company so he could continue his search. Thus far he had been unable to locate Lord Hampton and was starting to question if the whoreson was in London at all. Perhaps Alec and Colin had been more successful.

Mariel closed the distance between them once more and drew his attention with her heated gaze. "I promise you won't regret this."

He wanted to step back from her, but the tone of her voice lured him like a siren's song. She tempted his curiosity.

Her slender hand settled on his chest once more, and the pressure of her fingers sparked a heat in his veins.

Kieran gazed down at the dark-haired beauty, torn between drawing her to him and walking away forever.

Unbidden, his hands slid down her back and circled her narrow waist, neither holding her to him nor pushing her away. He should release her and leave, yet found he could not. Not when he wanted to trace the delicate curve of her neck with the tip of his tongue to sample if she were as sweet and soft as he'd imagined.

Mariel eased her body closer against his so her supple breasts pressed against his chest and swelled over the top of her bodice, milky white in the light of the moon and tempting as hell.

Her red lips were moist and parted, teasing his resolve with unspoken promises. "Kiss me, Kieran." Her breath was sweet against his mouth and her black lashes fluttered closed.

White-hot desire flashed through him and singed the fraying edges of his control.

The woman could tempt a damn saint.

He trailed the back of his hand down her cheek and his resistance cracked. Her skin was silk against his calloused thumb. He lowered his head to hers and let the heat of her lips whisper against his.

The scent of roses tugged at his crumbling resolve and baited his lust. She would be soft and luscious beneath his mouth.

It was only a kiss, but he knew without a doubt the heat of her mouth against his would only serve to whet his desire further. He would not be able to still his hands from gliding over what was hidden from view or from pulling her against the parts of him she made ache.

With an incredible act of willpower, he straightened, released her, and took a step back to address her from a safer distance lest he give in to temptation.

"If ye still want to come, meet me here tomorrow morning at nine o'clock, aye?"

He turned to leave when her hand on his forearm stopped him.

"Why did you not kiss me?" she asked.

Kieran studied her face and desire tugged at him once more. "Do ye always get what ye want, Mariel?"

Her eyes trailed the length of his body with a shrewd expression. "Only if I know how to get it."

With a swish of her skirts, she turned and walked away, leaving him staring after her with the hollow ache of regret.

•   •   •

Mariel's gaze scoured the crowds swarming the manicured lawns of the palace while she waited for Jane to bring the two small traveling bags. Nervous anticipation churned her stomach. She would see Kieran soon.

Excitement had been the culprit of her lack of sleep the

night before. She had been haunted by the way he'd brought his lips so close to hers, and the way he'd teased her with a kiss that did not follow. His scent lingered on her skin and tangled with the memory of his warm hands around her waist.

Mariel shielded the sun from her eyes with the flat of her hand and looked over the sea of faces once more, confirming what she already knew. Kieran was not there.

A young, gawky squire strolled past her. She waved her hands. "Oh, excuse me," she called.

He wheeled around and gazed at her through a fluff of blond hair. "Yes, my lady?"

"Have you seen Laird MacDonald?" The boy probably didn't know who Kieran was, but perhaps he could direct her to someone who did.

The boy's brow furrowed for a moment. "Do you mean the man who punched—" He cleared his throat. "Er...yes, I have."

"Marvelous." She breathed. "Can you direct me to him, please?"

The boy rubbed the back of his thin neck. "I'm sorry, my lady. He left an hour ago."

Chapter Five

Kieran quickened his pace along the narrow cobblestoned streets as the bells tolled the nine o'clock hour. Despite all he had accomplished that morning, agitation crept along his muscles.

Last night's discussion with Alec and Colin had not gone as well as he had hoped. In fact, had he not made the damned wager with Mariel, he would have been out of London before the sun even rose.

His assumption had been correct. Lord Hampton was not at court. Kieran gritted his teeth. His trip to London had been for naught and now Caisteal Camus was left without its laird. Doubtless that had been the bastard's intention the entire time.

The last minute preparations for two additional people had taken longer than Kieran had anticipated, and now he was running late. He cursed himself for accepting that ridiculous bet in the first place.

He approached the wide lawn and spotted Mariel's slender back amid the throngs of people. Her maid was with her, as well as a young page who pointed in Kieran's direction. Mariel spun around in a graceful swirl of skirts and beamed a devastating smile at him.

"Kieran," she said in a breathy voice as he approached. "I thought you'd left me."

The glare of the sun streamed against her face and brought out sapphire blue flecks among the brilliant amethyst of her eyes. Her hair was bound again, this time twisted beneath a cap with an absurd feather thrust through it.

The gray jacket she wore looked stiff and her skirts were overfull for the narrow saddle. She would be uncomfortable on their journey wearing her ridiculous English attire.

Mariel bent to retrieve the leather bag at her feet, and her full, creamy breasts strained against the low neckline, threatening to burst free of their confines.

Of course, if she insisted on wearing such clothes, who was he to stop her?

A slight crease appeared between her eyebrows when she straightened. "The page said you had left an hour ago. I thought..." she trailed off and sank her teeth into her full lower lip.

Kieran let his gaze settle on her mouth. He had dreamt of those very lips last night. "There was much to prepare for two unexpected riders. Skye is a long distance away and will take a significant amount of time to reach, aye?"

Her cheeks colored as she seemed to notice for the first time the laden horses behind him. "Of course, I didn't even realize..." The smile she gave him lacked the finesse of the previous ones and appeared almost shy. "Thank you for the purchases. And for letting us join you."

Kieran accepted the note of gratitude with a grunt. He preferred the women not come at all and tried to ignore the prickle of guilt associated with the selfish thought. Haste was necessary if they were going to leave within the hour.

"The others are waiting for us at the stables." He eyed the satchel in Mariel's hand. "I trust ye are ready?"

He did not wait for her to respond before taking the bag from her and two additional bags from Jane. For their small size, they weighed more than a sack of grain each. He hefted them over his shoulders and started toward the stables.

"The weather is perfect for travel, isn't it?" Mariel said, appearing beside him. He felt the weight of her gaze on his face.

The sky was clear blue through the milky haze shrouding London and the sun shone down on his back despite the icy gusts. It was a good day for travel indeed. Although any day that marked his departure from London would have been a good day for travel.

He slowed his pace so she would not have to rush. "We

will need to travel with more haste than I had anticipated. There have been…developments that have made it necessary for me to return home as quickly as possible."

If Mariel was apprehensive, she did not show it. But then perhaps she did not truly understand how grueling fast-paced riding could be.

"Kieran," Colin called from the stables. His eyes immediately fixed on Mariel and a wide grin split his face.

Kieran gave an irritated groan and steered the women to where Colin and Alec prepared the horses. Colin would waste no time introducing himself to Mariel. Or trying to get her into his bed.

Perhaps Kieran should have kissed her last night as it was no doubt his last opportunity to have done so.

• • •

Mariel smiled as the red-haired man with kind green eyes approached her.

"Colin MacKinnon at yer service, my lady." He bowed as low as an overzealous courtier and grasped her hand.

Through the corner of her eye, she noticed Kieran's jaw clench. Regret lodged a bitter seed in her stomach. She would have to use that jealousy against him.

"It is a pleasure to meet you, Colin." She let his name roll off her tongue like a dainty sweet. "I'm Mariel Brandon."

Colin's hand lingered on hers longer than was necessary. "Ye look bonny this morning, Mariel."

"Are the horses ready?" Kieran demanded, cutting off the conversation before it began.

Rather than answer, Colin gave Mariel a lopsided smile that revealed the deep dimple in his left cheek and winked at her before turning back to the row of stabled horses.

Kieran nodded to a man with long black hair and a wild glint in his ice blue eyes.

"That's Alec MacLean."

The large Highlander met Mariel's smile with a

narrowed glare.

"Is he always so friendly?" she teased.

"Highlanders dinna like the English." Kieran cast a pointed look down at her. "This is what ye will face on Skye, so ye'd better get used to it. Of course, ye can always stay in London."

She smirked. "You can't get rid of me that easily."

To prove her point, she waited by the horse strapped with her bags in the hopes Kieran would lift her onto its back. While he appeared otherwise engaged, Colin was more than eager to assist. He cradled her waist a moment before he lifted her to the saddle with ease.

Colin was not as tall as Kieran or as large, and he carried himself with less of a stiff-backed silence. While remarkably attractive and charismatic, he did not hold the quiet, brooding mystery that drew her to Kieran.

Nor did he possess the information she needed.

Mariel drew a steadying breath. She was doing this for Jack. All she needed to do was obtain the location of Blair and Dougal Hampton and she could be free without anyone having been physically harmed.

She patted the glossy brown neck of her steed and regained her composure. Kieran had gone to great expense to purchase their horses, especially considering the exorbitant prices in London.

Once everyone was in their saddles, she urged her horse to his side to express her gratitude and appreciation.

"You have purchased very fine horses for us. Thank you." No one had bought a gift for her in years and certainly none so grand as the steeds. The idea of accepting such an expensive gift made her uncomfortable, but also gave her a glimmer of hope that she might succeed in her assignment. After all, no one would gift something so costly and not expect anything in return.

"A cheap horse is no a good horse, and we have a verra long distance to travel." He gave an indifferent shrug and rode ahead to join Alec, leaving her alone as they departed the palace grounds.

The horses' hooves clacked loudly against the dirty, cobbled streets and echoed off the tired buildings that housed man and business alike. Mariel was leaving London, leaving the overwhelming presence of Aaron, and the power he kept clutched in his bony fist.

Nothing held her to the filthy city; at least nothing she cared to remember. Nothing except Jack, with his silky black curls and precious smiles. The very thought tightened in her chest. The memories hurt more as time passed, but she did not shy from them. Coupled with the guilt she harbored for her actions to free him, the pain of her memories kept her human.

She turned back to her former home, facing the ugliness of the city. Somewhere in the filth and fog was her one reason for living, and she basked in the ache that pulled at her heart. She did this for a purpose, a reason more important than her own life.

Determination flared within and filled her with a renewed energy. She would be successful and when she returned, Jack would be free.

She glanced to where Kieran rode ahead of her. Even from her vantage point, she could make out his exposed forearm where he'd rolled up his sleeve. Though he maintained a relaxed hold on the reins, the strength beneath his tanned flesh stood out with sinewy muscle that would have left the Greeks desperate to sculpt him.

Seducing him would be easy enough. She'd seen the desire in his eyes, felt it in the warmth of his mouth when his lips almost grazed hers. Almost.

She could lose herself to a man like Kieran MacDonald.

Trepidation crept into her chest and squeezed the air from her lungs. She could lure the man into her bed, but would she be able to keep her own heart protected?

Chapter Six

Mariel swayed in time with her steed's gait and her breath fogged in front of her. Pine trees crowded the narrow trail, scenting the air with a sharp tang.

The deep intake of breath did little to quell the anxious churning in her stomach. A fortnight had passed since they'd left London and not once had she had a chance alone with Kieran.

Not that Mariel hadn't tried. True, he spoke to her often. His banter bordered on flirtation, and he seemed to seek her out for conversation, but all her suggestions to lure Kieran from the others had been thwarted with his petty excuses. As if he did not wish to be alone with her.

A disheartening fact echoed in the razor edge of Jane's glare.

Mariel studied her maid's childlike profile. The woman was not as old as her harsh words made her appear. Jane was similar to so many of Aaron's other whores. Young, pretty, full of bitter self-loathing, pushed forward with the futile hope of rising above her station.

Like most of Aaron's girls, she had doubtless been a street urchin lucky enough to clean up well and keep all her teeth to adulthood. Mariel, however, had a different beginning.

After her parents had fallen victim to the plague and neighbors turned her and Jack away in fear, she had become his sole caretaker. When hopes for employment found fruitless reality, they were forced onto the streets. They survived well enough for a few months by scavenging for food in the stinking masses of filth piled outside homes and shops. Then Jack got sick.

No doctor would look at him when she had no coin to pay,

and all declared the same dismal fate—he would be dead within the week and wasn't worth the expense.

Aaron had approached her then, elegant and handsome in his velvet breeches and fashionable brocade doublet. She was penniless and desperate to cling to any scrap of hope she could grasp. His words were soothing, delivered with a confidence she wanted to trust no matter how wary she had become. She knew better, but she'd had no other options.

Mariel glanced once more to where Jane rode beside her. How the woman had been pulled into their dark life was of little importance. They were both among the many on Aaron's shelf of broken dolls, and for that Mariel could not help but feel sympathy toward her wayward companion.

• • •

Kieran watched Mariel's straight back ahead of him. Her maid's complaints had carried on throughout their journey thus far. Mariel, however, had tolerated the brutal pace in silence, even though her stiff-backed walk hinted her obvious discomfort.

Truth be told, he had enjoyed her companionship and was glad for her presence. It'd been a long time since anyone had really made him smile.

He edged his horse beside hers and tried to ignore the way the heady perfume of roses caressed his senses and coaxed his arousal. "We draw near Edinburgh." He pointed to the buildings evident through the tree tops in the distance. "Can ye see it?"

Mariel craned her neck and a childish grin touched her lips. She turned toward him, her eyes alight with excitement. "Will we sleep there tonight? On beds?" The question held a note of excited hope.

"Beds? Ach, no. We got rid of those flimsy things years ago. We Scots prefer to sleep on the floor, but...," he added straight-faced, "it'll be a warm floor."

The tinkling sound of her laughter warmed his chest. "Oh, Kieran, you're wicked."

"Aye, lass, ye get to sleep in a real bed tonight," he conceded.

"I'll even let ye sleep late if ye ask nicely."

"Is that an invitation?"

The light had faded with the setting sun, but he could still make out the slanted look she gave him. Desire dug her claws deep, leaving him overly grateful for the cloaking shadows blanketing the forest.

"Who's being wicked now?" Kieran shifted in his saddle for a more accommodating position.

Resisting her affection was becoming more difficult by the day. She wanted to be alone with him. Her desire was evident in the way she remained by his side at camp, and the way her fingers lingered against his chest when he helped her down from her horse each day.

But he did not trust himself to be alone with her. Not when he knew a kiss would lead to so much more. Not when pain shone through in her eyes when she thought no one would notice. Not when his secrets were not his own to share. Women asked too many questions, and he could not afford to betray Blair and Dougal.

The heavy forest parted ahead and gave way to the high stone walls of Edinburgh. The aroma of baking bread and roasting meat wafted toward them and set Kieran's empty belly snarling with anticipation. They would eat well that night.

Kieran had no difficulty locating Sheep's Heid Inn. The food was good, the ale was fresh, and the beds were comfortable and free of vermin. A barmaid with brown hair winked at Colin as they entered.

Though they'd only been there a handful of times, something about the whitewashed walls and low, wood-beamed ceiling gave Kieran a feeling of home. Casual conversation murmured around them and the heavy spices of simmering stew hung in the air.

"Back now, are ye?"

Kieran turned to find a sturdy blonde making her way toward him. Her low-laced bodice displayed the tops of her full breasts. The smile on her face was as genuine as her purpose.

Gaira was always happy to see him.

Chapter Seven

Mariel tried to ignore how the voluptuous blonde's gaze lingered on Kieran as she addressed them.

"Welcome back, gentlemen. I see ye found a couple companions along the way." Her gaze settled pointedly on Mariel. "Ye know we've always got the extra ale and rooms available…if necessary." She began clearing off the table nearest them. "Will ye have the same three rooms, then?"

The subtlety of the question did not mask what she was asking, at least not to Mariel. Especially when the woman paused from her task and looked up at Kieran with her eyebrows raised in silent demand for an answer.

Kieran, however, seemed oblivious. "Aye, Gaira, with an additional one for Lady Brandon and her woman if ye have it."

Lady Brandon. He had never called her that before. Again, she felt Gaira's critical stare sweep over her and hated the flicker of self-consciousness that made her want to smooth a hand over her hair or pull at the bodice of her rumpled riding habit. She must look a mess after all the time spent on the road.

Mariel chanced a look at Kieran and found his face impassive. He did not stare back at Gaira with the same interest in which she gazed at him, nor did he appear to be overly glad to see the woman.

"I'll get the rooms set up for ye," Gaira said with a satisfied grin. "Ye hungry?"

While Mariel had discovered an immediate and profound dislike for the owner of the Sheep's Heid Inn, she had to admit the woman knew her business. Within minutes their rooms were prepared, fresh ale foamed in the mugs, and a steaming tray of food was heading in their direction.

"Ye're back sooner than I thought ye'd be," Gaira said as she passed around their trenchers.

Kieran's face darkened. "We werena able to find what we were looking for."

"Well, whatever brings ye into my doors and gets ye into one of my beds always pleases me well." She patted his cheek and sauntered off.

Jane arched her eyebrow at Mariel from across the table. Apparently the intimate gesture between the woman and Kieran had not gone unnoticed. Aaron would hear about it.

Mariel looked down at the contents before her. While the food was not what she was used to back in England, it smelled divine. A large piece of sausage-looking meat glistened on the tray, and the scent of cloves and other herbs rose with the wisp of steam. She sliced off a piece and slid it daintily into her mouth. The meat wasn't cold cheese or gritty bread. No, it was moist and hot and flavorful and she almost moaned out loud as she ate it.

Jane, however, picked at the food with a slight curl of her lip, a clear indication of how she felt about the fare.

"Ye like that?" Kieran asked Mariel, his face skeptical. Colin and Alec, she noticed, also watched her carefully.

She drank deeply from the mug of sweet ale to wash down a mouthful of food before speaking. "I've never had anything like this. It's delicious."

"Ye dinna meet many English who have an appreciation for fine haggis, do ye?" Colin asked Gaira as she brought Mariel a second helping.

"It's true," the woman agreed and tossed a flirtatious smile in Kieran's direction.

Mariel looked down at the food on her plate. "Haggis?"

A small, rare smile quirked on Alec's lips. He wasn't bad looking when he wasn't scowling. "Let's just say ye wouldna find this on yer plate at court."

Considering some of the things Mariel had been forced to eat in order to survive years ago, haggis was a delicacy—

whatever it was.

With a small shrug, she said, "What do English nobles know about good food?" She grinned and slid another bite into her mouth.

Alec nodded appreciatively and Kieran looked down at her with what could almost be described as pride. After the food was cleared away, a curvy brunette brought out several more tankards of ale and Colin's eyes lit up.

"A bonny lass bringing me the finest ale in Scotland. Does life no get any better than this?" he asked. His smile deepened and the dimple appeared in his cheek. The woman blushed, lingering longer than necessary under the pretense of clearing the empty trays from the table.

Jane's sharp gaze stayed fixed on Mariel, weighing upon her with an uneasy feeling.

"You look tired, Jane," Mariel said sweetly. "Why don't you go lie down?"

Jane's eyes narrowed, and then dropped demurely to her lap. "I'm not as tired as I seem, my lady," she murmured.

After almost two weeks of constant vigilance, Mariel had little patience. "I confess that it is I who is weary," Mariel said. "I'd like for you to please go prepare the bed for me."

With angry silence, the maid rose off the bench and made her way up the stairs. Mariel waited until Jane's skirts disappeared up the final steps and heaved a sigh of relief.

The serving girl had given up the façade of cleaning and slid into Jane's seat beside Colin. She leaned close and whispered something that raised his eyebrows.

Mariel chuckled and nudged Kieran. "Should we leave him alone with his conquest?" she teased.

"It may be best," he replied with a slow grin and drained his mug.

Alec, she realized, had slipped away as well.

"Do ye want me to show ye to yer room?" Kieran stood and nodded toward the stairs.

"Yes, please," she said and rose from the hard bench.

Across the room, another barmaid slid into Alec's lap. His

hands caught her waist, and her face tilted toward his.

Kieran gave Mariel an apologetic smirk. "They've been on the road a while now. They needed a little distraction."

"No need to explain," she assured him. She knew all too well how men worked.

"Gaira," Kieran called across the room where the woman rummaged in a low cabinet. The woman's head popped up with a smile. Mariel did not miss how Gaira stayed bent over with her ample bosom on full display.

"Can ye be a love and bring me an extra blanket when ye get a free moment?" he asked.

"Of course. I'll be up in a minute." Her eyes shifted to Mariel for a brief second before she turned back to what she had been doing.

A ball of ice hardened in Mariel's stomach. Had he just propositioned Gaira in her presence?

His hand pressed Mariel's lower back and nudged her toward the stairs. "Come on, lass. I'll show ye to yer room so you can get some sleep."

"An extra blanket?" Mariel bit her tongue lest she demand the real reason he wanted the buxom blonde in his room.

"Aye, the ones here are small and my feet stick out." His nonchalant answer failed to ease the harsh squeeze of blatant rejection.

Mariel allowed herself to be escorted up the stairs. "Thank goodness Gaira can bring you another one."

Kieran gave her a long look. "Aye," he agreed slowly, "it is." His brow furrowed for a brief moment. "That is yer room. I imagine Jane already got everything for ye, but let me know if ye need anything."

She nodded and turned toward her door, desperate to escape. Having Gaira witness this moment would only make Mariel feel worse.

His large hand caught her elbow and spun her back to face him.

Her body tensed with the need to defend herself, to lash out aggressively and neutralize an attack before it could begin. Hard won lessons of the body were difficult to ignore. She forced her muscles to relax and met the challenge of his gaze.

"What?" Exasperation laced her tone.

The tips of his fingers caressed her cheek, his dark gaze wandering over her face.

"I shouldna be doing this," he muttered.

His stare settled on her mouth and her pulse tripped.

She swallowed. "Shouldn't be doing what?" she whispered.

"This," he growled and his mouth crushed against hers.

His lips were warm, softer than she expected. A sharp contrast to the cool scrape of his unshaven chin.

Kieran's arms tightened around her, and he pressed her against the door with his solid torso. He caught her jaw with one large hand and tilted her head back so her mouth instinctively opened to the coaxing caress of his tongue. Her nipples tightened beneath her bodice, straining against the wall of his chest as she rose on her toes to deepen their kiss. His tongue dipped into her mouth, savage in its seductive exploration. The sweetness of ale lingered on his lips.

Even with layers of clothing separating their heated flesh, Mariel could make out the hard lines of Kieran's body and the thick column of his desire where it pressed against her belly. The steady pulse of longing between her legs pounded with a need that left her breathless. She arched toward him, nudging the blazing heat of his arousal with her hips. A low moan slid from her throat and melted against his mouth.

He cradled her face in his calloused hands and pulled away from her, his breathing ragged.

"Gaira will be here in a moment," he said in a low voice. His eyes burned bright as he held her gaze.

Mariel took a step back, her mind reeling with the power of his kiss. "What?"

He glanced toward the staircase. "Gaira. She should be here in a moment."

Anger flashed through Mariel, singeing away the coil of desire. Her fingers fumbled with the doorknob behind her back, and she gave a sharp nod.

"I hope ye sleep well in yer bed tonight." The weight of his stare pinned her in place, forcing her to think of an answer.

"I'm looking forward to a break from the forest floor." She turned away with a mixture of disappointment and humiliation and stumbled awkwardly into her chamber before slamming the door shut behind her.

Jane was not inside the small room, but this did not surprise nor disappoint Mariel in the least. Given her current mood, she preferred the quiet reflection her solitude would allow.

A knock at the door startled Mariel from her thoughts and set her heart pounding with hope. Perhaps Kieran had changed his mind. Perhaps he had chosen her.

But it was not Kieran behind the door when she pulled it open. Gaira held out a thick, brown blanket and opened her mouth to speak. A look of confusion flitted across her comely face.

"Oh, forgive me." The woman's face flushed. "This is usually where Kieran…"

Mariel gave a terse smile and slowly closed the door, but not before noticing a few extra laces of Gaira's bodice had been untied.

·   ·   ·

Kieran scrubbed his face with his hands and let his weight sink into the bed's soft mattress. The sensation of Mariel's lips lingered on his mouth and left him aching with need. He should not have given in to temptation. He should not have kissed her, even if he knew Gaira's impending arrival would keep him from taking more than he should.

A gentle knock at his door filled him with a mix of eagerness and trepidation. If Mariel stood on the other side of that door, would he turn her away? Desire throbbed hard and hot against his belly.

Could he turn her away?

He rose to open the door. When it swung open, Gaira sauntered into the room. Not Mariel. The innkeeper did not ask to be invited in as she made her way to the bed and shook out a blanket.

"This is the warmest one I could find. It should do nicely." She draped the heavy wool across his narrow bed and turned back toward him. Her arms clasped behind her back, all but shoving her breasts under his nose. "Is that all ye need, then?" Intent sparkled in her eyes.

His body rose to the blatant suggestion. This was the kind of woman he was used to—one he could take and not feel guilty about. One who would expect nothing when morning came. Gaira took another step toward him and pulled at the lacing of her bodice. Her breasts swelled dangerously over the top of their confines.

"Perhaps it isna a blanket ye need to stay warm tonight." She leaned into him and the bulk of her bosom brushed his chest.

His body throbbed for release. He had no ties to Mariel. He'd made no promises to her. What was one willing woman between friends?

"Perhaps." His answer was intentionally noncommittal as he stared down at her.

But Gaira required little encouragement. She rose up on her toes and pressed her lips to his neck.

Desire that had only moments before pounded through him dulled to nothing. She kissed him with a passion he did not share.

Gaira was not the one he wanted.

The woman he wanted had turned away with a wounded look. She confused him, excited him, and elicited such a visceral response within him that he longed to show her exactly how badly he needed her.

Kieran stepped back from Gaira and struggled over what to say. She regarded him with a nonchalance that suggested her lack of offense.

"Maybe I'm no the woman who ought to be warming yer bed tonight," she said with a good natured wink.

"I should stick with the extra blanket," he murmured irritably.

Gaira pressed a kiss to his cheek and slipped out the door.

Kieran stalked across the room toward his bed. What the hell was the matter with him? He couldn't bring himself to take what Mariel offered, and yet he couldn't bring himself to do anything with any other woman either? Frustration rattled in his brain and desire ached deep within his bollocks. He settled on his bed and jerked his head back against the pillow.

The night could get no worse.

He heaved a long sigh and pulled the blankets over his chest when a giggle sounded from the other side of the wall. Colin's room. Kieran closed his eyes and turned on his side in a futile attempt to get comfortable.

A groan broke the silence followed by another giggle. Kieran turned to the other side and slapped a pillow over his head. It did little to block the panting and guttural moans. Did they have to be so damn loud?

After enduring several rounds of Colin's exploits, a blanket of darkness soothed Kieran's tired lids and eased the tension along his brow. He had just plunged into the mindless black of sleep when a shriek ripped into his subconscious. He bolted out of bed and was already down the hall when the second scream sounded. The hair on his arms rose with realization.

The cries came from Mariel's room.

Chapter Eight

Mariel lay upon the filthy floor, broken and bleeding. The darkness was like a weight that squeezed against her flesh and pressed into her eyes. Her empty stomach heaved at the rich copper odor in the stale air. Panic hovered on the border of her consciousness.

"You'll learn not to disobey Aaron."

She froze at the low, grating voice of her torturer and swallowed the fear welling thick in her throat. He would not win. Not this time.

Her fingers splayed against the grit of the floor and came away slick with moisture. The room echoed with her ragged breathing as her hands stretched blindly before her toward a nightmare she shouldn't face, yet could not bring herself to ignore.

She brushed something cool, something once supple and now unnaturally firm. Her fingertips patted until she recognized the shape of a nose. The frantic beat of her heart roared in her ears. She traced the rounded edge of a chin and continued further until she reached the neck.

It was too late to stop her hands from moving, too late to stop the horror of her discovery from gripping her in its icy hold. She was at its mercy. Her fingers sank into the gaping slit that had sprayed her with the gore now dried upon her skirts.

Screams filled the small room, raw and inhuman. Her screams. And on the other side of the door, the crescendo of a high, wheezing laugh.

A solid mass locked her arms against her sides. Fear crowded all thought from her mind, and she lashed against the restraint with the final vestiges of her energy.

$$\bullet \quad \bullet \quad \bullet$$

Kieran tightened his grip on Mariel in an effort to still her thrashing. Her slender body writhed with incredible strength.

"No." Her voice was hoarse, but she showed no signs of tiring.

"Mariel," he said softly. "Shhh, lass. It's Kieran. Ye need to wake."

Her struggle ceased, but her arms remained tense beneath his hands, and her breathing ragged. Quivering fingers skimmed his face in the semidarkness. She gave a choked cry. Her slick palm rested against the center of his throat and she went still.

He wrapped his arms around her trembling form, drawing her against him as her soft sobs filled the silence, and the warmth of her tears tickled his naked chest.

"It's all right now," he crooned, "everything is all right now." He had said those words before when he cradled a body too thin, too battered. His heart flinched from the thought.

Five years had passed since Brennan's death. Kieran's mind shied from the thought of his brother's name and the pain it bore. Clan MacDonald had lost more than a laird the day he died. They'd lost a true leader. Though no one pointed a finger, Kieran had been at fault.

He would not make the same mistake twice. His heart burned with determination as the image of Blair and Dougal surfaced in his mind. He had sworn he would protect them, and he would not let them down.

A shadow appeared in the dimly lit doorway and Colin's voice sounded in the darkness. "Is she all right?"

"Aye, she had a night terror," he answered in a hushed tone.

Colin remained a moment longer and if he spoke, Kieran could not hear what was said before the door clicked closed.

He was fortunate Colin had come to the door and not one of the other occupants of the inn. Doubtless the situation would not appear innocent with Mariel screaming and him trying to restrain her while wearing only his plaid.

The wetness of her tears upon his skin had begun to dry, and her sobs slowly quieted. The ropes of the bed groaned beneath them as Kieran settled back and pulled her against him so her head rested over his heart. Her hair was unbound and spilled across his naked flesh like a gossamer cloak.

He put an arm around her slender waist, and she relaxed against his body with a sigh. Her hair was cool silk beneath his hands. Before he realized what he was doing, the dark strands were threaded between his fingers as he stroked the length of her shimmering tresses.

He didn't know how long he lay there with the warmth of her curled against him, but eventually his body began to ache from lack of movement. Sleep would not be possible. Mariel's deep, even breathing indicated she was not suffering from the same insomnia as he. Perhaps he could ease from beneath her without her waking.

He eased his hips toward the edge of the small bed, hoping she wouldn't notice.

Her hands clutched his arms. "Please," she whimpered. "Stay."

Her voice was small and laced with unmistakable desperation.

"Aye, I'll stay." He shifted back in an attempt to relieve the stiffness of his joints. This time she did not protest his movements.

The room fell silent once more and filled with her slow, steady breathing. Despite the days they had spent on the road, her hair was clean, and her skin still held that enticing rose scent.

She sighed in her sleep. A sound so feminine and intimate, his body jerked awake. The thin fabric of her nightgown hid her from him, and it was all he could do to keep from tracing her curves through the gauzy fabric. Her hand rested against his naked chest, rising and falling with each breath he took, tormenting him with the most innocent of touches.

He wanted to roll her beneath him and caress her until she woke with a need as intense as his own. Instead, he endured the whisper of her breath across his flesh and tried to turn his mind from the burn of desire.

There was so much more to Mariel than what she let him see. So much more than what lay beneath the beautiful, polished surface.

His arm curled around her waist, and he breathed deep her

intoxicating scent. For this one night, her hair was unbound, her body free of its confines, and her soul vulnerable.

She was a woman in need of a protection he could afford to give this one night, but no longer than a few more minutes for surely he could not stay.

Chapter Nine

Sunlight streamed through the slatted wood shutters and cast a lazy, filtered light into Mariel's small room. Something warm wrapped around her. Arms. There were arms around her torso and a leg thrown over hers. The spicy scent surrounding her indicated who lay behind her. Perhaps she should have questioned how he'd ended up in her bed, but she found all she wanted to do was melt against his heat and lose herself in his embrace.

"Kieran," she sighed softly.

The prickle of his whiskers rasped the sensitive curve of her neck.

He nuzzled his lips against her ear and sent a delicious wave of chills across her skin.

"I thought ye wanted to sleep in," Kieran mumbled.

Mariel breathed in his scent and let herself fall under the security of his embrace.

Her fingers brushed his arm and found them bare. Her eyes flew open. Had they? Surely they had not or she would have remembered...

Unexpected and harsh reality crashed through the blissful haze of safety. A storm of questions rolled unanswered through her head. How had he gotten into her bed? When did he get there?

Mariel rolled over to face him and felt her mouth fall open at the sight of his bare torso. A light dusting of dark hair sprinkled his powerful chest and accentuated the etched lines of his physique. Banded muscles tightened across his stomach and disappeared into the tangle of sheets around his hips and legs.

Was he naked?

He opened an eye slightly and gave her a lazy, lopsided smile that woke the low pulse of desire within her.

"Ye made it to morning, I see." His tone was light, intimate.

She offered a blithe smile, not quite sure what to say as she scrambled to remember what had occurred the previous night. When had he returned to her room?

Mired in frustration, she came up with nothing more than the memory of falling asleep alone and irritated. She couldn't remember Kieran coming to her bed, but dared not admit it out loud.

Her eyes skimmed over his finely sculpted torso in quiet admiration. Looking at him now, she had no idea how forgetting such intimacy would be possible.

If Kieran noticed her assessment, he did not show it nor did he appear discomfited by it. His dark eyes were both now open and met hers with a quiet comfort.

"Ye dinna remember last night." It was a statement more than a question.

Heat warmed her cheeks and she stammered a reply. "I…I slept deeply and must still be tired. It's not because you weren't memorable or…"

His deep, warm chuckle stopped her and an amused smile lit his face. "Dinna worry, ye dinna forget anything like *that*."

The smile disappeared from around his eyes, and his expression grew serious. He cupped her cheek in a tender caress. "Ye had a nightmare, Mariel. Ye woke up the entire inn, probably all of Edinburgh for that matter, with yer screams. I came in here to quiet ye, and ye tried to fight me off." He arched his eyebrow. "Ye're a strong wee thing. I've half a mind to let ye toss a few cabers at the next games."

The warmth drained from Mariel's face with the realization of what he referred to. *God, not that.*

She had not had that nightmare in over a year. Her mind flashed back to the horror that haunted her dreams. Chills crept across her flesh.

Kieran's arms tightened around her and pulled her from the

memory before it could entangle her conscience. He traced the curve of her neck with his lips until the heat of his breath left chills of pleasure in place of those caused by dread. He brushed her ear with his lips, his voice velvety. "In an effort to defend myself, had we slept together the way ye thought we had, ye wouldna forget."

A shiver wound down her spine, and her eyes raked down his naked torso. The intimacy of their closeness did not escape her. In fact, she was painfully aware of every movement, every subtle shift that brushed their bodies against one another, and every inch of him not covered by the sheets, including his bare feet thrust out from the short covers.

He had not been lying when he'd spoken to Gaira about the extra blanket. Jealousy had gotten the better of Mariel for naught.

All ten toes suddenly wriggled under her observation, and a carefree bubble of laughter burst from her.

"Your feet must be freezing," she said.

"Aye," he said. "Ye should feel them."

His feet disappeared under the covers and icy toes pressed against her calves through the thin nightgown, a shocking contrast to the warmth of their shared bed. She squealed and kicked at his feet to keep them away from her.

Kieran dodged her futile attack and thrust his frigid feet against her legs once more. She laughed and tried to roll out of his grasp. Too late did she remember how narrow the bed was and found herself slipping toward the floor. Before her rump could smack the hard floor, Kieran's warm hands caught her by the waist and drew her back toward him.

He tucked her against his strength and the chilled imprint of his feet upon her flesh melted away in a sizzle of awareness.

"Are ye all right, lass?" he asked.

"I'm perfectly fine now, thanks to my hero." She studied the warmth of his dark gaze on her. His eyes crinkled at the corners from too many hours in the sun, and the relaxed smile on his lips was one she had never seen before. A smile she had put there, she realized with pride.

For all his strength and black stares of intimidation, he was kind and comforting. "You aren't like any man I've ever met, Kieran," she said.

"Ye say that like it's a bad thing." The words rumbled beneath her ear.

She found herself smiling. "I haven't figured that out yet."

Her fingertips skimmed the taut lines of Kieran's stomach and heat blossomed in her belly. Her breath quickened with the force of how badly she wanted this. Not just the feel of his skin against hers, but also the closeness.

She wanted to get to know Kieran MacDonald. It was a desire that had nothing to do with Aaron or his schemes.

Her hand flattened against Kieran's firm chest. His heartbeat raced beneath her fingertips and his flesh was soft and warm against her hand, the muscle solid. The light sprinkling of hair prickled her palm.

"Most men who found themselves in bed with me would try to take advantage of the situation. You, however, seem as comfortable as if we were both dressed in our court wear." She traced an invisible line across the hard lines of his chest.

Kieran rose on one elbow, and the blanket shifted off his hip, revealing the top of his kilt. Pity.

His hand lingered on her shoulder and gently pushed her back. He traced his finger along the neckline of her gown and a playful smile tugged at his lips. His fingertip grazed the sensitive skin beneath. A tremor of excitement trickled down her back.

"Nay, lass, this is far too high for court wear—especially yer court wear."

His gaze dipped lower as if noting for the first time she wore only her night rail. With a subtle arch of her back, she pushed her breasts forward so they stood out proudly. The delicate rasp of the linen left the pink of her nipples strained against the sheer fabric.

The smile melted from his lips.

A low groan sounded deep in his chest, and his eyes met hers, black with desire. Her body responded to the blatant, primitive yearning that sparked between them and left her pulse fluttering.

Her stare dropped to his lips, so sensual and soft against the sharp, hard lines of his face. The memory of his mouth moving over hers, the smoothness of his lips, and the stroke of his tongue—all of it shot forefront to her mind.

How would it feel to have his tongue trail down her neck to her breasts? Her nipples tightened to the point of aching, and she exhaled a long, shaky breath.

"I should go," he said tersely. Contrary to his words, he did not shift off the bed.

"Stay." Her voice was husky and need pounded a demanding staccato through her body.

She shouldn't want this as badly as she did. Certainly she did not deserve it. He sat motionless on the sheets. Yet there was hope.

He hadn't left yet.

He leaned forward and brushed a lock of hair away from her face. The ropes of the bed creaked beneath his weight. Mariel closed her eyes against the wash of pleasure at his caress and allowed herself to be lifted into a sitting position against him. The breath she had been holding eased out in a sigh of longing. She let her eyes flutter open and met his scorching gaze. His heartbeat was strong against her breast, fast and frenzied. Heady anticipation seized her and left her breathless.

"Do ye know what my staying means?" he asked raggedly. His breath was warm and tantalizing where it whispered against her lips.

Not trusting herself to speak, Mariel gave a slow nod. Still, he studied her for a moment more as if giving her time to change her mind. Her heartbeat thundered in her ears.

He lowered his head and swept his lips against hers. She craned her neck toward him, hungry for the searing kiss she now knew him capable of. But he did not oblige.

Her fingers slid desperately along the muscular plane of his back. He was raw power beneath her hands, and yet when his lips brushed hers, they were gentle. Too gentle.

Tepid.

He was holding back. She could feel it in the tightness of his body and hear it in his labored breath. Her invitation to stay had not been enough.

He would not take what she did not offer.

Blood pounded through her veins, demanding action. She didn't wait for another restrained kiss. Rising to her knees, she cradled his face in her hands and caught his lower lip in her mouth. With a greedy moan, she dragged the tip of her tongue across his captured lip and arched her body against him. He grabbed her shoulders, and a spike of anxiety shot through her. Would he push her away?

His hands slid up against her scalp and gripped her head. He jerked his face from her hands and a muscle worked in his jaw. Something sparked in his eyes. Something dark and hungry. A whimper of victory sounded deep in her throat. She couldn't move, couldn't breathe.

His thumb tugged at her chin so her mouth fell open, and the silky caress of his tongue thrust against hers.

He captured control of the kiss with a primal groan that vibrated against her lips. The strength of his arms curled around her waist and he leaned over her, his generous mouth moving restless against hers.

Mariel allowed herself to be laid back against the cool sheets of their small bed, a soothing contrast to the flaring heat of her flushed body. The decadent cadence between her thighs thundered into a pounding need. Kieran covered her body with his welcome weight so only their clothing lay between them. He rose thick and heavy against her belly, a thrilling testament to his desire for her.

A desperate moan escaped her lips. She wanted this. She wanted him. Her hips moved of their own volition, arching and rolling and her legs tangled with his. Kieran slanted his mouth over hers, drawing the sounds of her pleasure into him.

His fingers spanned the fullness of her breast through her night rail and the pad of his thumb grazed the bud of her nipple. A bolt of pleasure shot through her, and his name was little more than a gasp on her lips.

Kieran's knee slipped between her legs, nudging them apart. Teasing her with delicious pleasure. He settled his hips in the cradle of her thighs and pressed the length of his arousal against her throbbing center. Her legs wrapped around his taut waist in an attempt to get him closer, to increase the euphoric friction that left the room scorching.

A groan tore from his chest. His hand on the blanket beside her balled the fabric of the sheet in his fist.

His tongue curled against hers, stroke after frantic stroke adding to the fire burning within her. His hands skimmed up her legs with fingers inching closer, closer to the source of her need. Mariel's mouth went dry.

The heat of his lips trailed down her neck to the top of her night rail. He pulled the silken ribbon from its bow at her throat and pushed aside the thin fabric, baring her breasts for him.

His hot gaze sizzled across her body and a low growl rumbled from deep in his throat. He thought she was beautiful. He hadn't said it, but she knew. And it only served to fuel her lust further.

His mouth closed over her breast, wet heat against soft flesh. His hand moved between her thighs, his fingertips dancing a maddening ring around her sex, teasing but not touching.

Mariel gasped for air she didn't know she needed. His tongue flicked against her nipple, circling the tender flesh as she strained and writhed beneath the exquisite torture of his touch. And then his finger brushed the slick bud of her sex.

Pleasure spun Mariel in a blur of heat and excitement. She cried out in a hoarse voice and ground her hips against his hand, desperate for relief from the building tension tightening within her. Each glorious stroke sent a fresh wave of bliss rippling through her.

She could take no more.

"I want you," she whispered fervently against his ear. Her fingers glided over the rigid plane of his stomach to where his arousal strained against his plaid. He was hard beneath, pulsing with a need that matched her own frantic heartbeat.

His breath hissed between his teeth and his fingers ceased

their teasing pleasure. "I canna do this."

Mariel jerked back and stared up at him. Was he serious?

His jaw was set, his gaze hard. He looked serious.

She fought hard to think of something, anything to say to keep him from leaving. "I don't—"

"I should go." His tone was strained and offered no room for protest. The mattress shifted as he freed the bed of his weight and left her staring up at him.

His face was impassive, but his dark eyes burned with desire when they raked over her once more. He hesitated. His hand curled into a fist at his side. And then he turned toward the door.

"Kieran?" Mariel gasped in shock. Had she heard him correctly?

Without apology or explanation, he left the room and answered her startled question with the hard click of the door closing behind him.

Chapter Ten

Kieran stalked back to his room and cursed under his breath. His resolve had crumbled beneath the lure of Mariel's desire. Somehow he had found the strength to stop before it was too late. Before he led her down a path where she would eventually be hurt.

Alec stood outside one of the rooms wearing the same clothes as the previous evening. With a sly grin, he scanned Kieran's naked chest and looked pointedly down the hall to Mariel's room. "Did ye finally have her?"

"Mind yer own damn business," Kieran growled and burst through the door to his own room. He slammed it shut behind him with a satisfactory bang.

The cold silence of the empty chamber greeted him with bitter solitude. He stood for a moment and drew in a deep breath in an effort to steady himself.

The desire to possess Mariel had been overwhelming. Even still, his loins ached with need of her. She had certainly been willing and ready. God, she had been so ready—slick with need, swollen and pink beneath the thatch of downy hair. Her scent lingered on his fingertips and the ghost of her yearning all but drove him mad with want.

How easy it would have been to cradle her buttocks in his hands and thrust himself inside of her. He groaned aloud at the thought.

Agitated, he began to pace. He should have gone back to his own room last night when she slept. Why hadn't he taken advantage of the opportunity when he could? Damn it, he knew exactly the reason, and it had everything to do with her soft curves pressed tight against him, and the delicate scent of her under his nose. The way she made him feel like an invincible warrior who could keep all her fears away and soothe the pain of her past. He hadn't stayed because she'd asked him. He'd stayed because she needed him, because he wanted her to need to him.

The thought of what the morning would bring had briefly crossed his mind. Not that he hadn't had lusty thoughts the entire night he lay beside her, but he hadn't expected to act on any of them.

She had been so damn tempting with her dark hair tumbling down her shoulders and her lips and cheeks rosy with the warmth of sleep. The sheer fabric of her nightgown hugged the shape of her body and enticed him toward something he should not touch.

His attempt to leave the sensual warmth of her bed was stopped with one small word.

Stay.

The same word she had whimpered the night before when she begged him to remain. The same word, yet the meaning could not have been more different. He had wanted her badly. Hell, he still did.

But he would not allow himself to use her the way others had.

He took a deep breath and let it out slowly. What happened between them could not happen again. The next time he might not have the strength to stop. Letting Mariel go was better for her and better for him.

A change of clothes later, he opened the door to head downstairs when a strange thought occurred to him. Where in God's name was Jane last night?

* * *

No matter how hard Mariel scrubbed with icy water, she could not clear the burn of humiliation from her cheeks. Though the tears had long since been blinked away, a stubborn lump sat in the back of her throat.

She tightened the lacings of her most becoming gown. The small room was absent a mirror, but she did not need one to know how well the pale lavender velvet complimented her complexion and eyes. The cut was flattering and drew attention to all the right areas while still maintaining a level of modesty. With such a gown, how could she feel anything less than beautiful?

Her gaze shifted to the crumpled night rail, and her confidence sagged.

The door to the room opened and Jane sauntered in. Her hair was neatly combed, and she wore a different dress than the one she'd worn the previous days.

"Where were you last night?" Mariel asked with barely suppressed irritation.

"Someplace where I wouldn't have to sleep on the floor like a servant," Jane sneered.

Where didn't matter. Mariel knew exactly what her accomplice had been doing. Doubtless the woman had delivered another grim report to Aaron.

"Kieran slept here last night," Mariel said. If Aaron thought she was failing as badly as Jane portrayed, Jack may not survive the three months.

"Did he?" Surprise flickered in Jane's amber eyes before the cool mask slid back in place. She marched over to the bed and pulled back the blankets. "Looks like that's all he did." She let the covers fall from her hand and glared at Mariel. "Do you need instruction on how to handle a man?"

Mariel straightened her back against the insult. "I'm perfectly aware of how to handle a man."

Jane arched her eyebrow. "Then why hasn't he fucked you yet?"

"Kieran isn't like other men." Mariel pursed her lips to keep from saying more, but the smirk on Jane's face told her she had already said too much.

"Shite," Jane exclaimed. She slapped her hands on her hips and shook her head with obvious contempt. "You actually care about him. And here they all think you're so damn smart, when really you're more stupid than a common street whore."

"Don't be ridiculous." Mariel began to remove the plait from her hair in an effort to maintain control over the emotion threatening to shatter her calm exterior. "I know better than that."

"No." Jane crossed her arms over her chest. "You're foolishly risking everything. I can see it in your eyes when you talk to him." She leaned her torso toward Mariel. "Do you really think they intend to let him live?"

Mariel narrowed her eyes and said nothing to the doubt that flashed sharp in her chest.

Jane sneered, marring any beauty her face held. "He's going to die after this is over whether by your blade or by that of another. I don't know why Aaron coddles you so damn much to let you think you won't have to actually kill him yourself when all this is over."

Mariel gave an impatient sigh, the perfect cover for a much needed deep draw of breath to provide air to her burning lungs. "Cease this ridiculous chatter at once and pack up this room. We leave within the hour."

Jane kicked Mariel's discarded nightdress and sent it fluttering across the floorboards. "I won't be your damn maid anymore. Once Aaron hears about this, he'll see to it that you are removed back to London." She smirked. "If you're lucky."

The blood froze in Mariel's veins. If Jane convinced Aaron Mariel held affections for her target, he would have her dealt with, and she knew all too well what that meant. Fear yanked at her heart. Jack would have no one to save him.

"That's not necessary," Mariel said with a calm she did not feel. "You know as well as I do what you say is a lie. You would condemn me for no other reason than spite." Her fingers curled against the palm of her hand to still their trembling. "You don't speak Gaelic and you know nothing about the culture. How would you assume you could take my place?"

"You don't speak to the rest of us, like you're too damn good for our lot. But if you did, you'd realize you're not the only one learning Gaelic." Jane smirked. "Aaron is smart enough to know there's enough hatred between the English and the Scots to make it worthwhile to train others."

Mariel's heart leapt. If others were learning Gaelic as she

had, perhaps Aaron truly did intend to let her and Jack go free.

Jane backed toward the door, threatening that delicate hope of freedom.

"Where are you going?" Mariel asked sharply.

A cold smile curled over Jane's lips. "Oh, I think you know."

Shirking all pretense of composure, Mariel lunged forward and caught Jane's thin wrist.

The woman's eyes shone with surprise. Her arm cocked back, and her fist flew toward Mariel's face. Mariel pushed her forearm between them so the blow bounced harmlessly off the meat of her arm.

"Let go of me," Jane hissed. Her foot flew out in a desperate kick.

Mariel fell back on an instinct caused by countless hours of brutal practice. She shifted her leg toward the blow and flexed her thigh so the hearty kick could do nothing more than leave a slight bruise. Certainly it did not rock her balance as she assumed Jane meant for it to.

Undeterred, the woman reached forward with a clawed hand and grabbed a fistful of Mariel's hair, fingernails gauging painfully into Mariel's scalp. She caught Jane's hand with both of her own and bent forward at the waist. The woman's wrist snapped sharply upward, but Mariel didn't stop. She jerked herself backward with Jane's hand still pressed against the top of her head, dragging the woman to the ground face first.

Her movements were controlled and practiced. Their struggle created no sound.

"Enough of this," Mariel said in a harsh whisper. "You and I both know we're both better off with me doing the task I've been sent to do."

Jane glared up at her.

Mariel pushed a hand through her hair to finger comb the tangled mass at the top of her head. "I have more at stake in this than I could possibly explain."

In a show of good faith, Mariel knelt down to help Jane to her feet. The woman's amber gaze softened, but only for a brief moment.

She leapt at Mariel, using both their weight to throw them to the ground. "I can't let you ruin this for me," Jane snarled.

There was most likely more she intended to say, but Mariel never gave her the chance. She pushed with her knee, edging Jane from her body and swung a leg over the woman's head, trapping her.

One sharp drop of Mariel's foot to the floor and Jane was on her back, trapped once more. This time in a position that would not fatigue Mariel.

The woman breathed heavily and writhed in protest.

Mariel flexed the muscles of her legs, ensuring Jane would not move. "I'm not—"

A knock sounded at the door.

The calm surrounding Mariel during the fight shattered and sent her heart into an erratic beat. She met Jane's gaze and knew they both understood: no matter who took charge of the mission, discretion was still necessary.

Mariel eased her legs from Jane's body and offered a hand to assist the other woman in standing.

Jane ignored the offer and pushed herself up to her feet. "Just a moment," she said in a pleasant tone.

Her hands swept over her dress, setting her gown back into place before she opened the door.

Relief all but choked Mariel as Colin grinned down at them. "Kieran said we need to leave within the hour." He glanced between them and lifted an eyebrow. "Is something wrong?"

Before Jane could answer, Mariel spoke up, determined to not let the opportunity slip from her grasp. "Colin, I have a favor to ask of you." The words rushed out of her mouth before she even realized what she was saying. "Jane got lost last night and wasn't able to find her way back to the inn until morning. I'm afraid she has a terrible sense of direction, poor dear. Please show her where to put my bags and stay by her side until we leave. It would be a pity for her to get lost again and stall our departure." The blaze of Jane's anger burned against Mariel's face.

"Anything to stay in the company of a bonny lass," Colin said with a wink at Jane. "Let's head to the stables first. I'll help ye with the bags."

"Thank you so much." Mariel beamed a grateful smile up at Colin and purposefully avoided meeting Jane's eye.

The faux maid turned on her heel and stalked down the hall with Colin at her side.

Only when they disappeared from view did Mariel allow herself to collapse against the sturdy wall of the inn and gasp for breath. Her heart still slammed against her chest and her palms were slick with sweat. That had been close. Too close.

Her quick thinking and Colin's unexpected assistance had bought her time, but how much?

. . .

The onset of an overcast dawn lit the sky with a wet, smoky gray that settled into Kieran's bones. He glanced to where Mariel rode several paces beside him. A gust of wind blasted them with air so cold it cut through the heavy fabric of his plaid. She did not so much as wince. Her lower lip remained tucked into her mouth, and her gaze fixed unseeing into the snow dusted ferns layering the forest floor. She had been like that the last four days, since they had left the Sheep's Heid Inn. Ever since he had walked out on her.

He'd meant to apologize but found reasons not to—from the inability to speak privately to the justification that it was for the best for her to dislike him. The thought of being alone with her shot through him in a thrilling mix of excitement and bittersweet trepidation.

Mariel's eyes slid to where Jane rode ahead with Colin and her knuckles whitened where she gripped the reins.

The mood of the party was solemn, as though the loss of Mariel's tinkling laugh somehow dampened everyone's spirit. Or perhaps he'd grown so used to her pleasant conversation that the silence now seemed hollow in comparison.

Time was a bitter mistress, and he realized too late he should have spoken to her sooner. A spike of anticipation shot through him.

That night when they set up camp, he would speak to her.

. . .

Mariel surveyed the bleak surroundings as they rode in silence. Snowfall had ceased, and the struggling rays of sunlight melted the pristine white blanket to a dingy gray. The horses' hooves squished over sodden leaves and thick mud, making a rhythmic *squish suck, squish suck.*

She glanced once more to where Jane rode ahead with Colin, and her stomach clenched against the twisting ball of fire beneath her breast. He seemed to sense the unease between the women and used light jests and quick humor as a barrier to keep the tension from snapping.

Despite the passing of days, Mariel was still no closer to a permanent solution to Jane's very real threat. The familiar swell of panic fluttered in her chest, and her palms were slick despite the cold. She had to figure something out and soon. For Jack.

The weight of Kieran's gaze settled on her again. Her cheeks warmed with heat. For a man who was uninterested, he certainly did stare a lot. Though he often watched her, he had yet to approach her. Not that she minded. While his rejection still stung, she already had enough to occupy her mind.

The trees to her left rustled, and a flash of blue showed behind the red and gold leaves. A warning of unease slipped down her back like an icy blanket. She stiffened. They were being watched.

Kieran eased his horse close to her, and his hand slid intimately over her thigh, accompanied by the weight of something pressed into her lap. Mariel jerked her head up at him and found him smiling affectionately at her. His eyes were serious as he glanced down to where his hand lay. She followed his gaze and caught the glint of a blade nestled in her skirts. As discreetly as possible, she fingered the folds of her dress to assess the weapon. The edge was razor sharp and significantly longer than the dagger hidden in the depths of her travel bag.

"Down," Kieran hissed unexpectedly. His large hand clasped the back of her head and shoved her forward against her horse's velvety neck.

The musty aroma of the animal's sweat filled her nostrils and time held still. The whizz of an arrow sailed past the very spot where her head had been. A feral cry pierced the air and the once peaceful forest erupted into chaos. Terror hovered on the edges of her awareness as men leapt from the trees with swords and axes brandished. Kieran positioned his horse in front of hers and jerked his blade free of its scabbard. With one powerful stroke, he cut the first man down.

Mariel swallowed the scream that threatened to tear from her throat and dug her fingernails into her palms. Losing her composure would mean certain death. She clutched the blade in her fist and assessed their situation.

By her quick count, there were at least ten men. Each was smeared with grime and swathed in plaids like the barbarians from an English nightmare. Their savage cries filled the forest as they swung their large swords with both hands.

The sounds of war raged around them, from the ringing metal of fended blows to the guttural curses uttered by Alec and Colin who valiantly fought back.

Two men ran toward Kieran, their eyes wild with rage. They came at him from both sides and Kieran met them without hesitation. Each blow was deftly blocked with the resounding clang. A third man lunged at Kieran's back.

"Kieran, behind you," Mariel cried.

He turned in his saddle, parried the blow, and sunk his sword into the man's chest.

"Get out of here," he said through his teeth and jerked his blade free.

Before Mariel had a chance to obey, a vicelike grip wrapped around her ankle and tugged. She clawed at her saddle in an attempt to stay upon her stead. Then her eyes fell upon a riderless horse with a body lying face up next to it.

The shock of loss slammed into her and robbed her of breath and thought. The hand around her leg yanked once more, and this time she had not the strength to hold on.

Chapter Eleven

The horrific cries of battle faded in a distant echo as Mariel stared in horror at the body of her fallen comrade. Jane's eyes fixed sightless at the sky above with her head cradled unceremoniously in the thick mud. An arrow jutted from the center of her throat in a wound glistening with blood that had not yet had time to dry. Panic clawed at Mariel, spurring her to fight a battle she already thought lost. Her fingernails snagged the slick leather of the saddle, but the merciless grip around her ankle was too strong and rendered her desperate effort fruitless.

Her fall was broken by a solid torso, and her face shoved against a rough leine that choked off her scream with the acrid tang of unwashed body.

Something wrapped around her, securing her arms against her sides so she couldn't move, couldn't struggle. Her captor began to walk, and her feet swayed in time with his lumbering gait.

She wanted to scream and thrash in his arms until she caught Kieran's attention, but to give in to the panic would only see them both injured if not killed. Mariel squeezed her eyes tight and fought for control of her emotions. The way the Chinaman had instructed. Her training pushed to the forefront of her mind, and the frenzied terror waned. She needed to appraise the situation and form a plan before her captor stopped. Her chest compressed, exhaling the sour odor of the man, and she focused on her surroundings.

Her feet dangled from where she'd been pressed against his fleshy body. He was at least as tall as Kieran. She recalled the grip on her foot that unhorsed her. He was also just as strong.

Her stomach churned with disgust. Men pulled women

from battle for one reason, and it had little to do with her safety. She squeezed her eyes tighter to force her concentration.

The wheeze of labored breathing nearby suggested another presence. She had fought two men at once in her training, but never ones as large as her captors. Taking them on would be difficult, but not impossible.

"I like that ye dinna struggle." Her captor's breath fogged hot and sour against her neck. His hand slid against the curve of her bottom. The unmistakable scent of whisky caught her attention. If the other man was as drunk as this one, she stood a better chance at emerging unscathed.

"You don't want to do this," she warned in an acid tone.

His erection pressed into her belly. "I think I do."

Revulsion burned the back of her throat and curdled in her stomach. Her hand clenched the handle of Kieran's blade hidden within her skirts, and she took comfort in the knowledge that she could defend herself. The sound of Kieran and his men fighting could still be heard in the distance, but certainly they were too far away to hear her screams over the sounds of battle.

Good thing she wouldn't be screaming.

Her captor slowed to a stop. If she did not act now, she would lose the element of surprise. Her knee jerked up into the man's crotch. His arms loosened and he uttered a sharp curse. Mariel squirmed free of his hold, and a torrent of energy flowed through her. Acting on practice-honed instinct, she slammed her fist into the center of his neck and crouched low to dodge his awkward grasp. She whipped her leg at the backs of his knees, causing him to fall before he landed even a single blow upon her.

The other man lunged at her with his sword drawn, but she managed to evade his stumbling attack. She threw herself on the fallen man before he could rise again and plunged Kieran's dagger into his throat. Surprise lit his dull brown eyes and a sickening gush of warmth washed over her hands. A moment of shock pierced Mariel's calm as the life drained from his body.

Pain exploded in the back of her head and the forest blurred. She felt herself falling. Brilliant flecks of light clouded her vision and her stomach churned. She gritted her teeth against the pain and focused on gripping the dagger. Her heart tripped with fear. The dagger that was no longer there.

She needed to get up. She needed to fight regardless. Mariel rolled onto her stomach and crouched into a low ball as a massive, two-handed sword sank into the soft ground where she had lain.

"I'll be damned if I let a bitch best me," the barbarian slurred. He yanked his blade from the wet earth.

He advanced toward her and swung his sword again and again with no real precision. Each wild arc easily missing her as she darted and leapt out of its path. She could not escape his sword forever, nor could she effectively attack without a weapon.

It was time to attempt a different approach.

Her skirts swirled around her ankles as she danced away from the swinging blade. "Please stop. I...I know it was stupid, but I had to do it."

The sword jabbed in her direction.

"Please." She hoped the flimsy excuse sounded reasonable in his drunken state. "It was you I wanted the whole time...I saw you during the attack and you just..." She kept her tone low and sultry and met his bleary gaze.

The blade stopped. "Why did ye kill him?"

"He told me he was going to keep me for himself."

Disbelief crossed the man's ugly features.

"But I didn't want him. I wanted you." She took a confident step toward him and thrust her lower lip out in a seductive little pout. "You're not mad at me, are you?"

He gave her a slobbering grin, and his gaze shifted to her breasts. "I'm sure ye could find a way to make it up to me." The tip of the blade dipped toward the ground.

"I'm sure I could." Her eyes trailed down his body with slow purpose. No dagger clung to his belt and none appeared to be stuck inside his boot. Did the man not have a single dagger on him? She would have to search his person.

Mariel choked back the urge to gag and took another step toward him. "I was trained at Hampton court." His waist was thick and soft beneath her hands as she skimmed the worn leather of his belt in a discreet search for a hidden blade. She found none.

"Trained?" His stare was still fixed on her breasts.

"I'm no common street whore," she said, keeping her voice low, husky. "I was trained for royalty. Have you ever been loved by a woman who has brought a king to his knees?"

Slowly, she started to walk backward to where the body lay behind her, to where her dagger lay thrust in the neck of the man who had carried her.

"I canna say that I have." The remaining Highlander advanced toward her, his piggish eyes bright with desire.

Her calf bumped something solid. The body. Mariel widened her eyes in mock surprise and allowed herself to fall over the corpse as if she had tripped. Her voluminous skirts concealed her hands as she jerked the dagger from the man's throat. A heavy metallic odor filled the air and stuck in her nostrils.

She hid the blade within the folds of her gown before a strong hand grasped her arm and lifted her off the body. Her ardent attacker wasted no time pressing his rubbery lips against hers, his tongue slimy where it parted her lips with aggressive determination.

Mariel locked the hilt of the dagger in both hands and thrust it up into his body. The blade slid easily into his fleshy folds, stopping only when the sides of her fists pressed his soiled leine.

He howled in surprise and shoved her back. She took an instinctive step away from him and surveyed the dagger jutting from his side. The stab had been sightless and ineffective. His ruddy face twisted into a primitive rage that stilled her heart with fear.

"Ye'll pay for that, whore." Spittle glistened on his lips, and he lifted his claymore. The muted sunlight shone along the blade's edge.

A sense of danger prickled the hair on her arms, and he ran at her with a savage roar.

Her surrender to fear caused a slight hesitation-one that might have very well been her demise. Skill was sacrificed in her haste to escape the blow, and her feet slid in the slick mud.

Though she narrowly missed the direct path of the blade, she felt the force of it collide against her hip and fell beneath the weight of its impact. She could only hope the layers of her gown had been thick enough to protect her flesh.

The man leaned so close that the stink of his sweat stuck in her throat and permeated her nostrils. If she lived through this, she doubted she would ever be free of his odor. His large, grimy hand curled into a brutal grasp around her neck.

"I'm going to enjoy this." His breath was sickly sweet with rotting teeth and alcohol where it fanned across her cheeks.

His grip tightened against her throat, and he lifted her from the ground. The rasp of her own choked breathing echoed in her ears, and her feet kicked against air for a split second before he threw her into the mud. She gasped mouthfuls of clean air despite the burn of her raw throat. Her hands and feet slipped and sloshed across the soggy grass as she floundered in an attempt to get to her feet.

He stood over her with a sadistic smile on his face and slid his claymore into its scabbard. His weight crashed down on top of her, pinning her. He pulled a dirk from somewhere she had overlooked and raised it over his head. Mariel struggled helplessly beneath him with one resounding thought racing through her mind: *Forgive me, Jack. I have failed you.*

● ● ●

Kieran raced across the sodden earth, heedless of its pull against his boots. His eyes scoured the dense trees for a flash of lavender velvet, and he strained to hear the sounds of the forest around him. She hadn't screamed. What woman didn't scream?

The last he saw was the MacLeod bastard ripping her from her horse and dragging her out of sight. Kieran had tried to fight more quickly, desperate to be free of the troublesome lot so he could find where they'd taken Mariel before…

He gritted his teeth. He refused to allow himself to finish the thought.

Damn it, he should have protected her, kept her from being

abducted. His gut clenched.

He stopped and held his breath, listening to the natural sounds of the forest. The man was on foot, he could not have gotten far. Kieran took a cautious step forward when a rustle of leaves sounded to his right. He held the position and waited to see if the rustle sounded again. Nothing. And then...

A man's grunt.

Kieran's fist tightened on the hilt of his sword until the worn leather burned against his palm. By God, the whoreson would pay for what he did to her.

Kieran crashed through the brush, sending twigs and branches snapping against his thighs. And then he saw them. His heart seized against his ribs.

The MacLeod was sprawled on top of a crushed pile of velvet. Mariel flailed beneath him, her legs bare and smeared with mud. The bastard's hand moved beneath her gown.

Rage exploded into insanity. With a savage roar, Kieran charged forward and used his body as a battering ram to knock the dirty MacLeod from Mariel. The man stared up at him in surprise from the flat of his back and opened his mouth. Kieran didn't wait to hear what the man intended to say. His blade swung with powerful vengeance and connected with the MacLeod's neck, severing head from body.

He turned with disgust from his fallen foe and sank to his knees at Mariel's side. She had smoothed her skirts down and now looked up at him, her eyes wide with horror. Blood speckled her skin and soaked her dirt-smeared gown.

He cradled her sweet face between his hands. The grit of filth across her flesh could not mask its silken warmth, nor could the stench of death outweigh the gentle scent of her rose perfume.

He gathered her in his arms and got to his feet. She weighed almost nothing. How easy it must have been for the MacLeod bastard to carry her away. Rage simmered once more, but Mariel's head nuzzled Kieran's chest and called him back to the present.

He reveled in the heat of her body against his and in the

soft, feminine sigh she gave as she nestled closer against him. Holding her was a heaven he almost feared he'd lost. Relief crushed his chest. She was alive.

And right now, he needed to get her away from the horror of death to a place where he could safely ensure she had not been injured. He strode away from the dead man with Mariel curled in the protection of his arms, and then gently set her on the ground where she wouldn't be able to see the carnage.

Kieran stroked the strands of hair from her face and held her gaze. "Did he hurt ye?"

A choked cry escaped her lips. "Kieran…oh, thank God…" Her voice was raspy, strained.

A single tear slid down her cheek, leaving a trail of exposed porcelain skin beneath the mask of gore. "You're safe," she said.

Were the situation not so serious, he might have laughed. *She* had been worried about *him*.

He settled on the wet ground beside her. Mud caked her hair and soaked her once fine dress.

She leaned against his chest, clinging to him. "I didn't think I…" her words tapered off and she shook her head. After a deep breath, she continued. "They are both dead now."

Both? Alarm pricked Kieran's senses and suddenly he was alert once more. He hadn't remembered seeing a second one. Was the second man really dead?

He gently pried Mariel off him and stood up to survey the area. Almost twenty feet away lay a fallen MacLeod with a gaping hole in his throat. Startled, Kieran looked down at Mariel's wide gaze. "Did ye…?"

"I c…couldn't let him touch me."

Kieran's stomach churned. In his absence, she'd had to complete the grisly task on her own in a feat that left her clearly shaken. He sank beside her and pulled her against his chest once more. "Ye did what ye had to do. If ye hadna killed him, ye would be dead right now, aye?"

She nodded and kept her stare fixed on him.

God, it felt so damn good to be holding her. For the briefest of moments he had feared he might never have the opportunity again. The level of desperation he'd felt surprised him. He cared for her.

Mariel pursed her full lips, and Kieran's blood surged as the effects of battle wore off and left white-hot desire in its stead.

She was smooth and beautiful under his rough, calloused hands-an amorous balm to soothe the ugliness of war.

He wanted to beg her forgiveness for failing her, for leaving her at the mercy of the MacLeods. He wanted to confess his feelings of affection and gently kiss away her hurt. God help him, he wanted to sate his lust with the warmth of her body and find salvation in her arms.

He pulled her tight against him and smoothed a web of tangled hair from her cheek. Her quickened breath was warm against his lips.

She needed him as much as he needed her.

With a strangled groan, his lips came down on top of hers, and his tongue plunged into the sweetness of her mouth. She melted against him and yielded to his hunger.

His conscience tugged at him through the haze of desire. She was stained with the blood of men who meant her harm, who had intended to force themselves upon her. He could not take what the men had so aggressively sought.

Kieran broke the kiss and pulled away from Mariel. Her hands clutched the back of his neck, and she strained toward him with a pleading gaze.

"Please, I need this," she whimpered. Her lips brushed his, silky soft and hot with temptation.

Kieran clenched his jaw until the muscles ached. "I canna be like them."

Tears glistened in her eyes. "You could never be like them," she whispered fiercely. "Don't you understand? I want your lips to erase the feel of theirs, your body to burn away the insult of their touch." Her fingers against his chest clenched the dirty fabric of his leine and dug into his flesh. "Make me forget, Kieran."

He caught her upturned face in his hands and studied the spark of desperation in her stare. Too vivid was the horror of losing her, and the fear he would never see her again. Too recently had she been locked in the clutches of helplessness without him there to protect her.

She was not the only one who needed to forget.

"Please," she whispered again.

He could not deny her appeal any more than he could ignore the pain in his chest at the thought of her death. His lips came down on hers, and he tightened his grip on her once more.

Her mouth moved against his, frantic and hungry. She slid her hands up his back, her fingers dancing restlessly beneath his leine.

His caught the length of ribbon holding her ruined chemise closed and tugged it free. The fabric parted to reveal creamy white skin unsoiled by the effects of battle.

His hands cupped the velvety curve of her breasts, and she gasped into his mouth. She was so warm, so silky beneath his battered hands. He clutched the back of her neck as her sweet tongue tangled with his while his other hand found the sensitive little nub of her breast. He wanted to hear the soft cry of his name upon her lips. He wanted to make her moan with need.

Her nipple pebbled between his fingertips, and her breathing hitched. The ache in his cock was almost unbearable where it strained against his plaid. He squeezed her breast, his thumb blindly circling the sensitive little bud. Her moan started off low and ended in a breathless whimper as her body ground against him.

Desire clouded his mind and robbed him of thought.

Her fingers left trails of fire against his naked flesh where she explored his chest beneath his shirt. He knew her hunger all too well. She murmured his name against his lips and arched her back so her naked breasts pressed toward the sky.

Her weight shifted as she leaned into him, nudging the heat of her desire against his cock. His breath hissed out between his teeth as her inquisitive fingertips neared his throbbing tip. He needed release, a way to come down from the height of battle. God help him, he needed her.

Now.

"Kieran!" Several male voices called in the distance.

Mariel pulled the warmth of her mouth from his. "The men…"

Kieran snatched her back to him and growled against her lips, "Let them wait."

The voices called again, this time closer. Kieran let out a soft curse and released Mariel. She tied her chemise with trembling fingers as he rose to his feet.

He extended his arm to her. "Are ye sure ye're fine?"

Her gaze met his with bold desire, and her kiss-swollen lips lifted in a languid smile. "Yes, thanks to you."

She placed her small hand in his palm and allowed him to lift her from the thick mud.

"Mariel, ye're safe!" Colin charged through the brush to where they stood. "Are ye all right?" His brow furrowed. "Ye look verra pale."

Kieran looked down to where Mariel clung to his arm. She *did* look pale. How had he not noticed that before?

She wavered on her feet, and her gaze shifted to the body of the man he had killed.

This was too much for her. "Dinna look, Mariel. Come, let's find an inn and get cleaned up, aye?"

"It's all right," she replied in a weak voice. "They are only… bodies…" Her words faded to a faint whisper, and her weight sagged against him.

Alarm flashed through Kieran. He wrapped his arm around her in an attempt to keep her upright, but she flinched from his touch.

"Mariel?" He pulled his hand away from her hip and found it bright red with blood.

"I couldn't move quickly…I didn't realize…he…" She swayed, and her face went white beneath the smears of mud.

Kieran gripped her waist above where she'd been injured and cradled her weight against him as her legs gave way. Fear clenched at his chest. He caught her slender body and held her against him, but she wasn't looking at him. No, her head fell limply in the cradle of his arms, and her eyes fluttered closed with heart-stopping finality.

Chapter Twelve

Mariel awoke to the baritone murmur of voices in the distance. Exhaustion pulled at her, enticing her back to the numbing warmth of sleep. She gritted her teeth and tried to keep a sense of awareness. She had to stay awake. There was something she needed to do.

The scent of herbs hung heavy in the air, pungent with the almond notes of meadowsweet and the acrid tang of juniper sprigs.

She forced her heavy eyelids open and shards of brilliant light stabbed into her skull. She slammed her lids shut against the pain and lay immobile until a roll of nausea eased.

As the muffled voices continued outside, familiarity seeped into her subconscious.

"How did she manage to kill a MacLeod, do ye think?"

The scrap of information danced at the edge of her memory.

"Those men were taken with drink for certain," mumbled another voice.

"The bastard probably tripped over his own damned feet and Mariel took advantage of the situation like the smart lass she is." The voice was smooth and rich, rife with underlying authority. Kieran. Her heart skipped with bittersweet elation.

He had saved her from certain death. The MacLeod had her pinned down, her legs rendered useless beneath the weight of his body. The memory of his hands groping her sent a shudder of revulsion through her.

Kieran had arrived in a flash of chaos that blurred with soggy earth and spatters of blood. And then he'd drawn her into his arms, and her world had slowed. Everything had pulsed with the warm glow of sensuality as they fell into a realm where time did not matter.

Jane.

Oh God, Jane had been killed by the MacLeods, run through with an arrow like a wild pig on a hunt. Mariel's stomach churned.

Colin's voice outside drew her back to the present. "Before ye arrived, had they—"

"Nay, they dinna touch her. No that it's any of yer business," Kieran answered tightly.

"We still dinna know what Hampton meant by luring us to London," Alec broke into the conversation.

"Ye dinna need to remind me of that," Kieran said with a bitter tone to his voice. "I have thought of little else. We need to focus on how we are going to get home."

Their voices dropped low and their words became too difficult to decipher.

An underlying urgency laced their tones. They were restless to return home. How long would their patience hold as they waited for her? She did not care to find out.

Hampton. The name struck a familiar chord, but she could not remember why. Pain gripped her skull in its wicked grasp and kept memories from surfacing.

Mariel forced herself past the discomfort and blinked her eyes open once more. Whitewashed walls reflected the sun's brilliant glare and bundles of herbs hung from the low, wood-beamed ceiling above her head.

She lay atop a hard, unyielding surface covered with a cloth—rough wool from the way it scratched against her body.

She froze. Where was her clothing? She clutched a thin blanket to her naked breasts and tried to turn in an effort to inspect her surroundings. A fierce burn ripped across her hip and sent stars dancing before her eyes.

A soothing voice broke through the pain. "Dinna sit up yet. I need to finish binding ye."

A wrinkled face and soft brown eyes appeared above Mariel. The aging woman was anything but threatening.

Mariel obeyed the gentle command and lay back on the makeshift bed. The woman's hands were warm and dry as she brushed the blanket away from Mariel's side. A neat row of about twenty or so small stitches followed the curve of Mariel's hip. The injury was far more significant than she'd realized.

The old woman had saved her life.

The healer cradled an open jar in her withered hand and rubbed its greasy contents against Mariel's freshly stitched wound. An acrid odor stung Mariel's eyes and nostrils.

At least she wouldn't have to worry about being attacked again. No man would touch her with this foul odor on her flesh. The putrid balm warmed with a soothing heat along the tight ache of her stitches.

Perhaps the scent could be endured after all.

As if reading her thoughts, the woman gave her a sympathetic look. "I know, lass. The stuff stinks to high heaven, but it will help stave off fever." She pulled a strip of linen from a small basket at her side. "Now we'll get ye bound and dressed and ye can be on yer way."

With gentle hands, she stretched the linen across Mariel's waist and drew it around her back. Mariel jerked forward, fearful of what the woman might find, and sick from the thought of someone seeing the price she'd paid for Jack's protection.

The old healer paused, her fingers held aloft. "Ye need no worry about me. I ask no questions, and I tell no more than needs be told."

Mariel gave a terse nod and tried to ignore the brush of linen against her back. She tried to keep from remembering the pain.

The kind voice broke through her concentrated silence. "I'm finished, lass. Ye only need to bind it while blood still seeps. After that the wrapping isna necessary."

The burning tension in Mariel's muscles waned. The worst was over.

The healer helped her rise to a sitting position and motioned to a shapeless bundle on the table near a small bed. "It's no much, but I have a dress ye can wear. I dinna want ye putting on that wicked corset again and dinna think ye can get yer dress on without it. No with that wound so freshly stitched, aye?"

"You are too kind—" Mariel began, but the woman held up a hand.

"I also have some poultices for ye to place against your wound when ye change the bandage, as well as the balm I just used. Ye need to rest for at least one week. I say I want ye to be in bed the whole time, but I'm no daft enough to think ye'll listen to me. Rest at least the night in a proper bed, and be careful when ye ride, aye?" She placed several bundles of linen bound herbs on top of the clothing.

The healer looked out the window to where Kieran paced and shook her head. "The toughest men are the most helpless when their women are ill." A wry smile spread over her wrinkled lips. "I'll leave ye to dress while I go speak to him."

The woman slipped from the room and let the door close soundlessly behind her. Nervous excitement fluttered in Mariel's belly. Once she was dressed, she would see Kieran. She reached for the dress and caught sight of her mud-smeared arm. Her fingers crept over her gritty hair, still riddled with leaves.

And then a realization slammed into her like a punch to the stomach.

The breath left her chest and her heartbeat slowed to an aching throb. With the liberation from physical pain came the burden of memory. Her giddiness faded at the prospect of seeing Kieran.

She remembered why she was there.

•   •   •

The healer leaned so close to Kieran, the tip of her long gray braid brushed his forearm, and the sweet scent of herbs hovered in the air around them.

"It's no my place to say this, Laird MacDonald, but the lass has been ill used. Ye be good to her, aye?" Though worn with age, the look in her eyes was fierce and protective.

"Did she say something to ye?" He heard the hope in his

own voice. If he knew the cause of her hurt, he could help ease her pain.

The old woman considered him for a moment before answering. "She dinna have to."

Kieran nodded in silent understanding. There was something in Mariel's past. Something she was not telling him or anyone else.

Before either of them could say another word, the door to the cottage opened, and the world dropped away as Mariel stepped toward him. Golden light from the low setting sun splashed over her in a wash of ethereal essence. Gone were the velvets and silks and ridiculous hairstyles. All that remained was her. The way she had been for him that fateful night at the Sheep's Heid Inn.

A plain brown overdress caressed the fullness of her breasts and accentuated the sweet flare of her hips. Her unbound hair fell to her slender waist and reflected the sun's dying rays like rich onyx flecked with gold.

Her cheeks flushed as she drew closer, a fine display of color on a face deathly gray not two hours prior. Mariel ducked her head, and the color of her cheeks deepened.

"Kieran, you're staring." A nervous smile touched her lips. Without a word, the healer slipped away, leaving them blissfully alone. "Am I such a mess?"

"Ye look different, Mariel. Verra, verra different." A slight breeze rustled the leaves overhead, and an errant lock of hair fluttered across her cheek. Before he realized what he was doing, he reached out and tucked the tresses behind her ear. "I dinna think I've seen ye look more beautiful."

He trailed a finger down her cheek. Her skin was always so soft, so smooth. Heedless of others, Kieran drew her against his chest and wrapped his arms around her slender frame, careful to avoid her injury.

Her familiar, heady scent enveloped him. For a moment he had feared he might never breathe deep her tantalizing perfume again. But now the danger had passed, and she was there, safe in his arms.

He wanted to press his lips to hers, to make up for all the time he had fought his attraction toward her. Awareness sizzled between them, bewitching him and making his mouth hungry for the taste of her.

Colin materialized beside them and cleared his throat. "We should most likely find the inn the healer recommended before dark."

Kieran dropped his arms and stepped away from Mariel, irritation coursing through him. "Mariel, ye ride with me," he said, more harshly than intended. "And dinna try to argue. I'll no have ye riding a horse on yer own with that wound."

Her mouth opened and then closed as the protest died on her lips. Disappointment pricked at him. He'd been looking forward to finding alternate methods of silencing her.

* * *

Kieran ushered Mariel to her rented room. The furnishings were typical of most inns with a bed in the corner, and a short wooden table holding a simple basin and ewer. Though small, the chamber was clean and would allow Mariel the restful night of sleep the healer had insisted on.

The innkeeper's two sons followed close behind with a large tub held between them. Kieran set Mariel's bags on the floor and then straightened. "How do ye feel, lass?"

"Better than I expected," she said with a wry smile. Her coloring had paled slightly after the ride, but other than that she appeared to be faring well.

The boys disappeared out the door. Their feet were heavy upon the stairs as they went to retrieve water for Mariel's bath.

"I plan on bathing as soon as they finish filling the tub." Her gaze turned pointedly toward him.

Kieran sat down on the bed. It was comfortable despite the aged ropes that groaned in protest beneath his weight. "Aye, I figured ye would."

The boys entered the room again and emptied their large buckets into the tub before dashing out to get more water. Once they had left, Mariel lowered her head and gave him that slanted look that set him on fire. "You intend to stay?"

"I do, but no for the reason ye think. With no woman to help ye, I dinna want ye by yerself when ye're injured."

She tucked her lower lip into her mouth, and her brows knit together. Immediately Kieran regretted having brought up her lack of a maid and the memories it no doubt procured.

Mariel heaved a deep sigh and lifted her chin with stubborn determination. "I'm perfectly capable of bathing, even in my battered state." She sauntered toward him. "Unless," she amended, "you want to help…"

Once more the boys entered the room to empty their buckets before disappearing for the final time.

Kieran settled back on the bed with his arms folded behind his head and closed his eyes in an effort to clear her smoldering look from his mind. "Nay, I'll be here in case ye need me."

Keeping his eyes closed was a bad idea. The sound of lacing sliding through fabric, however, stopped him from opening them. Wool and cotton rustled like a seductive whisper as it slipped from silken flesh. Kieran swallowed thickly and tried to ignore the insistent pulse that beat an erratic thrum in his swollen cock. Did wool always create so much noise as it pooled at a woman's feet?

Just when he thought he could take no more of the torturous sounds of her undress, the gentle lapping of water against the wooden side of the tub filled the room. He didn't need to open his eyes to know she was in the perfumed water— naked, slick, and wet.

Chapter Thirteen

The water's intense heat left Mariel's flesh rosy where the gentle ripples licked her calves. Spirals of steam curled above the mirrored surface in silent temptation to sink into its liquid embrace. The neat stitching at her side, however, would not do well under water. Experience had taught her that much. Her wistful sigh disturbed the languid ascent of perfumed mist rising around her.

A quick glance at the bed confirmed Kieran lay in peaceful slumber with his arms crossed behind his head. Regret was a slow burning flame lodged in the pit of her stomach. Were it not for the gash at her side, this would have been the prime opportunity for seduction. Not that it had gone well in Edinburgh.

Armed with a clean strip of linen, a chunk of soap, and a small bucket, Mariel set to work ridding her body of the ravages of battle. Blood and dirt ran in murky rivulets down her legs and clouded like swirling smoke in the water below her knees. She scrubbed her skin pink, but could not remove the filth that embedded itself in the cuticles of her nails and ridges of her fingertips. Nor could she remove the memory of the man's face whose life she had taken.

Had she not killed him, he would have killed her. She knew that, yet somehow it did not ease his death from her conscience.

Nor could the guilty ache of Jane's death be so easily removed. Much as Mariel hated the heartlessness of her internal admission, with Jane's death came the opportunity to devise a different plan.

No longer was Mariel watched. No longer would she be reported. She cast a sidelong look at where Kieran lay stretched out on the bed.

How would he take her confession if she told him?

Her gaze settled on the claymore he'd set aside, and the hair on the back of her neck stood on end. The blade had been wiped clean of the blood from their recent battle, but the massive sword did not appear any less dangerous.

Her thoughts were thick, muddled by the pain at her side and the exhaustion pulsing in her skull. There had to be another way.

Mariel squeezed her eyes shut against her churning mind and lifted the heavy bucket into her arms. She would think more on it tomorrow when her head was clear and her body rested. For now she needed to focus on washing her hair or Kieran would never want her. She raised the bucket overhead and an unexpected sting knifed through her side.

"Mariel?"

Stars flashed before her eyes and nausea threatened to consume her. The act of lifting her hands over her body had pulled tight at the freshly stitched wound and left her paralyzed with pain. She gripped the damp wooden edge of the tub for support.

She would not faint.

The bed ropes squeaked against one another. "Lass, do ye need help?"

"No," she whispered. "No," she repeated a little stronger. "I...I don't think I'm going to be able to wash my hair." Was that a quiver in her voice? She swallowed the knot of helpless frustration.

Silence followed her admission before he finally spoke, his voice terse. "Get dressed. I'll wash yer hair for ye."

"What?" Had she heard him correctly?

"Just get dressed," he snapped.

Mariel patted herself dry gingerly and reached for something to wear. A fresh tear of pain ripped through her side. She gritted her teeth and considered her options. The brown dress was being washed, and all her dresses required a corset. She had no choice but to wear a night rail.

The thin cotton fabric slid over her body like a breath of cool air against skin flushed from the heat of the bath. She turned to find Kieran in all his hard masculinity kneeling by the crude tub, waiting for her. His gaze was black, unreadable where it slid down the length of her night clothes.

He cleared his throat and motioned to the leg he had propped against the edge of the bath. "Lean against me to ease the pain."

"It's nothing I can't handle." Despite the stab of fire, she straightened her back in an effort to look stronger than she felt.

His jaw clenched, and he gave her a long look that indicated he was not in the mood to argue. Mariel settled on the floor and leaned her back against the hard muscled wall of his thigh. His spicy scent mingled with the humid haze of steam from the bath and lulled her into the slow, steady pulse of languid arousal.

Warm water poured over her scalp and all thoughts but those of pleasure washed from her mind. Kieran's battle hardened hands were gentle where they ran through her hair, working out the bits of leaves, mud, and God only knew what else. Heat radiated from his solid torso, mere inches from her face. The slightest lean forward and she would be close enough to press her lips against the warm skin of his neck.

His nearness consumed her. She was intensely aware of every move he made, no matter how slight. Sweat prickled her palms, and the lazy pulse thrummed between her thighs as she surrendered to his gentle ministrations.

Stroke after sweet stroke, he ran his hands through her tresses with such tenderness it could only be considered a caress. A bucket of water washed down her hair once more, and, with disappointment, Mariel knew he was finished.

He supported her back with his arm and helped her to her feet. His black eyes fixed on her with a look that made heat pool low in her stomach. His hands lingered against her lower back longer than was necessary. The sun had long since set, and the candlelight cast a flickering golden glow against his face. Jagged shadows etched across the sharp edge of his jawline and cheekbones. He looked fierce, darkly handsome—

almost dangerous.

Droplets of water snaked down her back, and yet she barely noticed. Having him wash her hair had been a strangely intimate act. An act whose poignancy she knew was not lost on him either.

A gentle rap on the door shattered the unspoken connection between them. Kieran turned away from her with a look of regret lining his face.

Her senses came hurtling back. What was it about him that made her lose her wits? Was it his powerful presence? His handsome, rugged features? His size?

A shiver wound down her spine. No. It was the way he looked at her. The way she responded to him, and the way she melted under his touch.

Her hand balled into a fist in an effort to shove away her feelings. She was there to gather his secrets. She was there to save Jack. No matter how badly she wanted Kieran or how significant he made her feel, she needed to do this. For Jack. And for Kieran.

Jane's warning echoed in the back of Mariel's mind. It was a nagging burr that had been lodged there since it'd been uttered. *He's going to die after this is over, whether by your blade or by that of another.*

If what Jane said was true, then why would Aaron give Mariel the option? Her thoughts were a haze of fog and pain.

Kieran returned carrying a small mug of steaming brown liquid. "This posset came from the healer. She said to drink it tonight to ensure ye get good rest before we press on tomorrow." He eyed her for a moment before adding, "If ye feel like continuing with the journey. If ye need another day or two for recovery, we can always—"

"No," she replied quickly. "I'll be fine. We need not to delay on my behalf." The sooner they arrived in Skye, the sooner she could begin her discreet search for Blair and Dougal Hampton. The sooner she could be free of the heat of his stare and the overwhelming guilt that inevitably followed.

She reached for the cup and paused. Aaron had praised her

determination in the past. Countless times. She had always been the sort who focused on the prize and did not stop until she attained it. And he knew that.

Her heart slammed hard against her ribs.

Aaron gave her the option because he knew she would do whatever was necessary to get the information rather than kill.

She gripped the scalding mug with her fingertips and gave a murmured thanks before settling in front of the fire.

The flames licked against one another, prancing with rapacious speed over the crisscrossed logs. If she was right and Aaron had given her the option to ensure success, he was indeed crafty. Fortunately, she was crafty too.

Mariel set the posset aside to cool to a drinkable temperature while she combed the snarls from her hair carefully lest she injure herself again.

Aaron was right, not only about her determination but also her uncanny ability to gain trust. She would earn Kieran's trust and find the location of the Hamptons as she'd been instructed. But once Jack was safe, she would go back for Kieran before Aaron's assassins could ever lay claim on him.

She could save them all.

A quick dip of her finger into the brown tea confirmed it would not scald her.

She held the rim of the cup to her lips and inhaled the musty scent before tilting the liquid into her mouth. Bitterness washed over her tongue and clung to the back of her throat with such potency she could not stop the unladylike gag that followed. Perhaps only one sip would be enough.

Kieran was unsympathetic to her plight. "I dinna care what it tastes like, Mariel. Ye need to drink all of it so ye can be well rested. That wound will pain ye tonight otherwise."

Mariel whirled around with a sharp reply on her tongue and stifled a gasp. Kieran's naked back faced her from where he stood beside the tub. His kilt was still belted around his narrow hips, but would not be for long as his hands were tugging the belt free.

Her breath caught in her throat, and she turned away lest he catch her staring at him. She brought the cup to her lips, hoping to ease the sudden dryness of her mouth. Holding her nose as she had done as a child, she drank the remainder of the tea. She hoped it would be worth the effort.

From the safety of the silky curtain of her hair, she peered through the ebony strands to where he stood. His back was still toward her, but that didn't mean there was nothing to see. Good Lord, the man was glorious.

Broad, powerful shoulders framed the strength of his back and the seductive play of shadows along the tantalizing plane. Smooth skin stretched taut over well-honed muscle from years of battle and practice with the sword. Indulgent, Mariel let her gaze slide lower, past his tapered waist to the enticing curve of his buttocks. Heat flooded her cheeks at her brazen observation, but it did not stop her as she shifted her eyes lower still to take in his long, sculpted legs from the bulging thighs to where his finely wrought calves disappeared into the glassy surface of the bath.

She was just about to turn away when he lifted a bucket overhead and let the water run down his shoulders. Droplets clung to his naked back and trembled as each subtle movement sent the muscles along his back rippling. A single bead rolled along the length of his spine and glided down the powerful lines of his body. Mariel moistened her lips and watched its seductive descent, overwhelmed with the temptation to trace its path with the tip of her tongue.

Heat tingled at the base of her skull and wound down her back before exploding through her limbs. The sensation moved too quickly for comfort and set her heart racing.

What had the old woman given her to drink?

As quickly as it had come, the intensity of the heat faded and with it the throbbing pain of her wound. The relief did not last long, however, before the room began to spin. Slowly at first and then faster and faster until everything blurred together and threatened to swallow her whole.

Panic wrenched the air from her chest and blackness wavered before…She meant to cry out for Kieran, but the word came out as little more than a whimper.

The echo of water splashed as his voice called to her from far away. Her tongue grew thick in her mouth and no matter how hard she tried, she could not answer.

Darkness curled her into its embrace and she felt no more.

• • •

Kieran rushed to where Mariel lay sprawled upon the floor and gathered her into his arms. The healer had indicated Mariel might appear addled, drunk even, but had said nothing about fainting.

Panic lurched in his chest. Mariel was still. Too still.

Her flushed cheeks burned beneath his fingertips. He had never seen a fever occur so early after an injury, but it did not mean such a thing was not possible.

"Mariel," he called sharply. He needed to rouse her from the frightening slumber.

Her lashes fluttered, and her beautiful eyes opened and focused on him. Confusion wrinkled her brow and then a languid smile spread over her lips. "I don't know how I ended up in your arms, but I'm glad I'm here."

Relief released the iron grip of fear in his chest. Mariel's words slurred ever so slightly, but the small lines of pain around her mouth had faded. Despite the strange effects, the healer's posset was obviously working.

"Are ye feeling all right?" God, did she have to stare at him like that? He eased her into a sitting position and kneeled beside her.

She gave a throaty laugh. "I've never felt better." Her hot gaze crept down his body. "And I've never seen you in such a state of undress."

In his haste to reach Mariel, he had not bothered with so much as a scrap of linen to wrap around his waist. A detail his aching cock already made him regret. To think her thin cotton night rail was all that separated him from her silky flesh…again.

Kieran stretched over her to reach his discarded plaid when Mariel's small hand settled on his arm, stopping him.

"No. Please." She shook her head, and her hair brushed his naked flesh. "I want to see you."

He rose to his feet and held his arms out for her observation.

She looked up at him from where she sat on the floor, and a corner of her luscious mouth lifted in a coy smile. "Should I kiss you?" Her gaze traveled up the length of his legs to where his arousal was beginning to show. "Should I tease you?" She got to her knees in front of him and met his gaze with a heat that left him rock hard. "Touch you?" Her lips were a whisper away from the head of his cock.

"Then should I leave abruptly?" She gave a satisfied little smirk and settled back on the ground.

The minx. So her silence before *was* due to his quick departure. "My punishment is to be naked?" Frustration and lust clouded his mind.

She tilted her head to the side so the delicate line of her jaw was displayed in the soft glow of the fire. "And to be at the mercy of my inspection."

Anticipation coiled low in his stomach, but he immediately crushed it. Mariel had just fainted, and her words were garbled with the effects of the tea. She was not in her right mind and he'd be damned if he would allow himself to touch her as she was. Ignoring her pout of protest, Kieran belted his plaid and knelt beside her.

"Ye can inspect me another time. Right now, ye need to be in bed, aye?"

She watched him with a wide-eyed, luminous gaze. She reached out for him, hesitant at first before gently stroking his naked chest with a feather light touch that singed his flesh. Her fingertips grazed a crescent scar below his collarbone.

She drew in a shallow breath through parted, glistening lips and let her touch skim down his torso. Her finger ran over his stomach and caused all the muscles there to tighten against her caress.

Kieran couldn't speak, couldn't move beneath her study of his marred flesh. Women had marveled at the scars before with exaggerated gasps as they begged for stories of war. Mariel, however, gazed upon him with a pensive expression on her flushed face.

Her fingers dipped low to a hairline scar below his navel, and his cock jerked to attention, stretching for the heat of her hand.

Somewhere he dredged up the strength to take hold of her wrist and still her maddening exploration.

"This must have been the most painful." She slid her hand from his grasp and lightly touched an uneven scar along his ribs where a blade had caught him several years before. The recovery had been considerable.

"Women must ask you about your scars all the time," Mariel murmured thoughtfully, tracing the outline with the delicate tip of her nail.

Small bumps rose on his flesh in pleasant response to her touch. "Some," he answered carefully.

Would she ask him? He hated the curious glances and notable admiration. Mariel, however, seemed different from others. And he didn't want to be disappointed.

Her eyes met his, bright with the effects of the tea. "I won't." She turned her gaze to his exposed chest once more and, regretfully, removed her hand from his body. "A scar carries secrets, memories, and lessons. Asking you for an explanation would be like asking you to bare your soul to me."

Her hand glided up his chest, and she gave him that slanted look she was too damn good at.

"You like the way I touch you." Her mouth curved in a slow smile. "I know because I can feel it."

She slid into his lap, straddling him with her long, smooth legs. Her lips tickled his neck as she whispered in a husky tone, "I like the way you touch me too."

She pressed a kiss to his neck. "I like how your body is so solid against mine. So strong…" Her fingers curled around his arm, and she sighed next to his ear. "I like the way you burn me with a desire unlike anything I've ever known." Her hips rolled against his straining arousal.

She rose up on her knees so the swell of her breasts hovered invitingly in front of his face. "I like the way you caress me…" Her eyes fluttered closed, and her hand slid down her neck, splaying across the expanse of milky flesh like that of a lover. "…the way your touch leaves a trail of fire."

She dropped her head back. Her face was relaxed and

serene as her tapered fingers skimmed the rounded tops of her breasts. His cock lurched.

"Touch me, Kieran." The words came out in a breathy moan. "Burn me with pleasure as only you can."

She leaned into him, pressing her breasts closer. The pink of her nipples showed through the thin fabric. The slightest nuzzle would part the gown and give him access to the sleek warmth she so readily offered.

He groaned aloud and pulled her into his lap once more, freeing his vision from a temptation he had not the strength to resist. Too late did he realize his mistake as she arched her hips against him.

Her face relaxed in a veil of pleasure and her glossy hair was cool against his fingers where it hadn't yet dried. His cock throbbed to the rapid beat of his heart. A slip of his finger between her thighs would confirm what her expression already told him—she was wet, ready, and willing.

And then she swayed. It was a jarring reminder of her heavily drugged state.

"I think what ye really need is a solid night of sleep, lass, no a solid night of loving." Using every ounce of will power he possessed, he got to his feet and pulled her into his arms. She did not resist, even when he carried her to the bed.

She snuggled against him and gave a wistful sigh. "You always protect me." He could hear the smile in her voice, and the throatiness of her remaining desire. "I feel safe with you, like nothing could ever hurt me."

Her candid admission startled him. Did he truly make her feel that way? He paused beside the bed, reluctant to let her go.

She seemed to sense his hesitation and burrowed against his arms. "Please hold me. I haven't felt so safe since…" Her eyes widened as though she suddenly realized she'd said too much.

He shouldn't press her. She was not lucid. Her secrets were her own. She had granted him that courtesy when she examined his scars.

Yet this was an opportunity for him to understand her intention, to clear the suspicion that clouded her presence.

"Ye havena felt safe since what?" He ground his teeth, half regretting having spoken the question and half relieved to have done so.

"Since my parents died," she said solemnly. "The plague." Her teeth caught her lower lip.

He would not press her further. He did not need to. She stared off into the distance and continued on her own. "I was nineteen when it happened. I was still so young then." A mirthless smile touched her lips. "I had no one to guide me or reassure me that I would have a meal that night or a safe bed to sleep in. Everything we owned was burned to prevent the plague from spreading further. I had…nothing."

He could imagine her as a young girl, naïve and vulnerable, thrust into the cruelty of the world with no one to care for her. How had she managed to survive?

Something painful and dark twisted in his chest. He knew how women and girls survived the streets.

"Until you," she added quietly. Her distant gaze focused on him. "I've not ever spoken of this to anyone." Tears shimmered in her eyes. "You are an unexpected ray of sunshine warming my face in an otherwise hard, gray world."

Kieran shifted awkwardly. She spoke again, saving him from speaking. "What was in that posset? I sound like a bard."

He chuckled. "Ye need to sleep, Mariel."

She nestled deep under the covers without protest and let her eyes flutter closed.

He should push her now. There would never be a better opportunity to urge her for information.

And yet, she was so vulnerable, so innocent and hurt.

Her breathing became even, and he knew she was on the verge of falling asleep. Her face was smooth and peaceful. If he did not do it now, he might never have the chance.

Tamping down the guilt of taking advantage of her, Kieran spoke the burning question on his mind. "Why do ye want to go to Skye?"

"For Jack," she murmured, a tender smile lighting her lips. "Everything is always for Jack."

Chapter Fourteen

Icy spray pelted Mariel's cheeks like needles. Waves rolled and heaved against the roughhewn hull of their crude boat as they pushed through the violent ocean toward Caisteal Camus. Kieran's home.

Mariel squinted through the dense gray fog toward the blurred landmass ahead of them. If there was a castle on its surface, it was impossible to see in such conditions. Salt-laced air burned a path down her raw throat, and the frigid wind tore through her clothes. Warmth seemed a fleeting memory. One she would not soon relive.

In the last week of travel they had pressed through ice storms and trudged through drenching rains. Cold, miserable days were followed by bitter, unbearable nights spent with little more than the thin batting of her bedroll to separate her from the frozen ground. The only heat she experienced was the blazing hot stab of pain from her wound.

A gust of wind slammed into her with such impact, it stole the breath from her chest. Her hands clutched the fine wool of the plaid wrapped around her. The soft rasp of the fabric was no longer noticeable against her numb fingers. She burrowed deep within the sturdy folds in a futile search for warmth. And then she caught his smell buried deep in the tightly woven fibers. The familiar scent left her with a wild need to bury her face against the muted greens and blues of the plaid and breathe deep.

Then she felt it again, the weight of his gaze fixed upon her, as cold and unyielding as the ocean that churned beneath them. His face had been as hard and emotionless since the morning at the inn.

The burden of his scrutiny was crushing, but Mariel refused to turn away. Something flashed in the depths of his black eyes, vulnerable and brief. The muscle in his jaw leapt, almost imperceptibly, and he turned away. His features were fierce with discernable rage.

Frustration gripped her. What had been said that night at the inn? After the attack, he had been passionate and tender; the moments between them had been poignant. And then she drank that blasted tea.

She woke the next morning and found him sleeping on the floor with his back propped up against the wall. He stiffened when she approached to rouse him. The movement was slight but unmistakable, nonetheless. His silent rejection stung, though not nearly to the extent as the glaring accusation in his eyes.

What had she done? The memory was lost to her, as if it had never existed at all.

Initially she had feared she disclosed her true purpose. Those fears were slowly assuaged throughout the week as she found herself treated with the same respect and comfortable freedom she had enjoyed prior to that night.

But if she had not spoken of her task, what could she have done to warrant his sudden disinterest?

She didn't have to be there, not anymore. Not with Jane gone. Mariel could have left Kieran and gone back to Aaron's manor. If Jack were there, she would find him and save him.

But nothing was that easy. It would be a suicide mission. Aaron always had men teeming over every one of his manors. That's how they'd caught her searching for Jack the last time.

This time they wouldn't be so lenient.

A wave slammed into the boat with a force that pulled Mariel from her thoughts and made their small vessel shudder. Kieran was staring at her again. He drew in a breath as if he were about to speak. Her pulse raced with anticipation. Was he actually going to talk to her?

"We draw near Caisteal Camus."

Mariel forced a smile despite the anxious knot in her stomach. "I am eager to arrive."

His eyes narrowed. "Have ye given any thought to what ye plan to do when we arrive?" His cool tone informed Mariel now was neither the time for flirtation nor teasing retorts.

"You've made it clear that you don't want me, Kieran, in more ways than one." If he was surprised by the bold declaration, he did not show it. Nor did he object. "I do well enough with a needle. I was hoping I could find work as a seamstress and establish my own residence."

"Ye need no find another place to live. Ye are to stay at Caisteal Camus…as my guest." His arms folded over his chest. "While ye heal."

He welcomed her readily into his home with the trustworthiness of an honorable man. Although he did not seem eager for her arrival, nor did he indicate he planned to have her stay long.

She did not deserve such hospitality.

Mariel looked miserably into the churning water and wished it could swallow her up.

Perhaps staying within the castle walls would allow ample opportunity to eavesdrop on servant's gossip. If the information she sought could be gleaned through overheard conversation, perhaps she would not have to betray him at all.

"You are kind to offer me a place in your home. Thank you."

He looked toward the hazy shore looming in the horizon with his mouth set in a grim line. "Are ye expecting to meet someone here? Someone ye know?"

His face was unreadable, yet somehow she felt he was pressing her for information.

"I don't know anyone in Scotland, save the men you've introduced me to." She eyed him warily. Her nerves were frayed from waiting for a noose to drop around her neck. She was tired of carefully worded games and grasping assumptions. "Is there something you wish to ask me, Kieran?"

The gauntlet had been thrown. With her back straight, head lifted, and heart guarded, she waited for his response.

The menacing look he gave her was one meant to intimidate, but she refused to cower. In silent response to his challenge, she arched her eyebrow.

"Have ye ever dyed wool?" he asked. The lines on his face eased and a slight smile lifted the corner of his lips.

"No," she replied, confused by the change in his demeanor.

"Ach, it's easy. Ye will learn it quickly."

The boat bumped against something solid below. "Here ye are, lass. Caisteal Camus."

A shadow loomed over their vessel so expansive and great, it blotted out the sun. A jagged cliff rose from the swirling waters stoic, as white-capped waves crashed against it, shielding the fortress that rested atop its crown. Stone walls followed the rock-faced plane and ascended toward the heavens where it crested in fashioned turrets. From where she sat, Caisteal Camus appeared cold and ominous.

"How do we get there?" Mariel asked, eyeing the churning water.

"Ach, ye dinna need to be concerned about the ocean, lass. It's only deep enough to come to yer knees."

The thought of plunging herself, albeit only to the knees, into the frigid sea was not a pleasant one. Letting Kieran see her bested by something as petty as cold water, however, was even more unpleasant.

"Is that all?" She gripped the hull of their boat and leapt deftly over the edge.

A thousand daggers broke her fall as she crashed into water so cold it burned. The exhausted muscles in her legs locked against the freezing temperature and refused to move. Idle waves rolled to life and clawed at her heavy skirts. The wind shrieked its rage in her ears and tore at her hair, shoving her back with powerful gales.

And then he was there. Kieran's strong arms wrapped around her, and she was free of the water's sucking grip. His chest was dry and warm beneath her cheek as she nestled closer against him in an effort to free herself of the wind's wrath. Heat. Finally.

Kieran's chuckle rumbled deep in his throat and vibrated against the top of her head. "I dinna think ye'd jump overboard.

I had planned to carry ye."

There was a smart retort on Mariel's tongue, but her teeth wouldn't stop chattering long enough for her to speak. Instead, she clung to him and allowed herself to revel in his comforting strength.

Once they arrived on land, Kieran lowered her to the ground. A chill spread against her body where he'd held her and seeped into the warmth he had created.

"Welcome to Caisteal Camus," he said, his voice low in the roar of the wind.

Mariel looked up to behold her new home, and a gasp stuck in her throat. Grassy hills tinged with the dormant gold of winter rolled as far as she could see. It was a startling contrast to the brilliant blue sky stretched above. The glowing sun sparkled majestically and burned off the last vestiges of mist from Skye's lush landscape. Without turning to look, she knew the fog behind her had closed around them like a heavy curtain, as though it were a shroud masking the magnificence of the island from those not worthy enough to glimpse it.

In the sunlight, the castle was not so imposing as it had appeared from its menacing perch atop the cliff. The large, rectangular building ran along the curve of the sheer-faced cliff with its walls made of smooth cut stone. Several windows looked out toward the turbulent sea and winked in the sun's light. Chimneys lined the peak of the roof and thick, dark smoke coiled briefly above the stone columns before being whisked away by strong winds. It didn't look like the impenetrable fortress she had heard others describe it as. Caisteal Camus looked like a home. A magnificent, beautiful home where one could feel protected and warm.

"What do ye think?" Kieran asked beside her.

"It's magic," she breathed. Heat flooded her cheeks as soon as the words were spoken out loud. Had she really just said that? "I mean, it…looks like something from a bard's tale."

Kieran gave her a knowing grin and led her up the hill toward the large iron gates where throngs of people stood in wait. As they neared, the idle chatter among the awaiting clan fell away and a tense silence hung in the air.

The smile froze on Mariel's lips at the hostile glares. Caisteal Camus may look like a home, but she knew she would receive no welcome there.

• • •

Kieran had been so damn eager to get home. Too eager. He had not allowed himself to dwell on the ramifications of his clan's feeling toward Mariel.

Then again, he had hoped to have found another place for her to stay prior to their arrival on Skye. Her injury and the ill-timed death of her lady's maid left him in a position where he had to allow her to come to his home. Something he'd regretted ever since she uttered that other man's name. *Jack*. Kieran gritted his teeth against a rage he had no right to feel and focused his attention on his clan's unwelcome reaction to Mariel.

Highlanders always carried a level of disrespect toward the English, and Brennan's blood drying on an English blade only served to encourage that hatred.

Kieran stood tall and met the angry faces of his people, suddenly grateful for Mariel's inability to speak Gaelic as the malicious insults hissed forth from the crowd.

English.

Witch.

Murderer.

Whore.

Mariel turned her face to Kieran. "I hope it will not be inconsiderate of me to beg introduction from you?" The smile on her face was genuine, and he almost allowed himself to believe that she had been blind to such blatant hatred.

"Mariel will be a guest in our home," he announced in Gaelic. "She is to be treated with respect as any guest would. If you are unable to obey this simple request, you will face punishment."

Several people shifted from one foot to the other, but the cruel names ceased and several glares were cast downward. In the awkward silence, Mariel stepped forward as regal as any queen with her back straight and her head raised. Mud spattered her sodden homespun gown, and her hair hung in tangles down her back, yet the confidence she exuded could not be ignored. Glares softened to curious glances.

Mariel sank into a magnificent curtsey and rose in a fluid movement. "Thank you," she said in Gaelic.

So, she had picked up some Gaelic on their journey. A prickle of unease crept along the back of his neck. She was too intelligent for her own good. She might ask questions he would not be able to answer.

Kieran motioned Colin to his side. "Show the lass around, but keep a close watch on her, aye?"

Colin flashed him a grin. "Ye know I willna let anything happen to her."

"And Colin," he added, unable to swallow the bitterness he felt toward his friend's all too eager compliance, "keep yer hands to yerself."

*   *   *

Kieran sank into the overstuffed chair in his solar and breathed in deeply. The familiar, musty odor of the ancient books lining the wall gave him a profound sense of home. He was grateful to be here, away from the filthy streets of London.

He was grateful to discover Blair and Dougal safe upon his return. There was little doubt in his mind Hampton had intentionally placed a rumor he would be in court, knowing Kieran would run to London in the hopes of finding him. Hampton was definitely up to something.

Sunlight streaked across the desk, illuminating the parchment in front of him. A similar beam of light had moved over Mariel's face when she'd gazed upon Caisteal Camus and lit her heather colored eyes as they'd widened in awe. Her response had been so unabashedly honest it brought a smile to his face.

It's magic.

He almost laughed out loud at the memory.

A strange ache twisted in his chest and wiped the smile

from his lips. The past week had been difficult for him to travel in such close proximity to her as he'd tried to distance himself. If this man, this Jack, was someone she loved and intended to reconnect with, who was Kieran to stop them?

He was too busy with his clan to fret like some fool over matters of the heart. Other things occupied his time.

Things like the accounts in his hand for example.

He shifted the paper so the light did not caress it. He needed to banish Mariel from his thoughts. There was no sense in worrying after a woman who wanted another man. A woman whose very presence in his home threatened everything he held dear. God willing, she would heal and leave quickly, and Kieran would never have to think of her again.

A knock at the door pulled him from his thoughts. "What?" he barked.

Though the interruption was irritating, he welcomed the distraction. Not only against the accounts he couldn't focus on, but also the woman he could not stop thinking about.

Alec strode into the room and closed the door behind him before assuming a wide-legged stance in front of Kieran.

"I have news that concerns Mariel."

"Is she gone?" Had she left so soon? Unfounded disappointment flooded him when he should have felt relief. He should be grateful for Jack taking Mariel from his life.

Alec furrowed his brow in momentary confusion. "Nay, Laird. I've uncovered a plot to kill her."

Chapter Fifteen

"Someone wants to kill Mariel," Kieran said with a note of bemusement. "And how do they intend to accomplish this?"

Alec crossed his arms over his chest. "Take her from her room tonight and throw her over the cliffs."

Kieran nodded. The brutish plan was simple but would have been effective. "I'm surprised it took so long," he said. "She has, after all, been here for several hours."

The warning Kieran had issued to the clan earlier had clearly not been taken seriously by everyone, and he had a strong idea who dared defy him. "Do ye know who was behind it?" he asked.

"Hamish."

Hamish. Young, oversure Hamish constantly overstepped his boundaries. When Brennan had been alive, he'd acted as a father figure in Hamish's life and had been the only person able to control the lad. Brennan's death had been difficult for the clan, but Hamish had taken it especially hard.

"Very well, I'll deal with him in the morning. Hamish has been allowed to do as he pleases for far too long. It is time he learned a lesson." Kieran was not certain what he would do, but such blatant disregard for his direct order would have to be publicly acknowledged and reprimanded.

"And Mariel?" Alec crossed his arms over his chest and narrowed his pale blue eyes.

Kieran knew what Alec referred to. Even after teaching Hamish a lesson, others might still plot against her. His people had always been loyal to him, even in the trying time following his brother's murder. Hatred for the English, however, could overwhelm even the most loyal of hearts, and he was not willing to risk Mariel's life.

"Keep her company at all times. If ye are unable to do it, then leave Colin in yer stead." Doubtless Colin would not mind that duty. "And have her placed in the room nearest mine. Keeping her close to me will dissuade attacks."

The corner of Alec's lip twitched upward.

"Dinna give me that. I dinna have time for a lass." To prove his point, Kieran lifted a stack of account books and let them slam back down onto the worn wooden surface of his desk, sending dust motes frantically swirling in all directions.

"She wants ye, Kieran. She's bonny enough, even if she is a wee thing. I dinna understand—"

"That's enough." It came out harsher than he'd intended.

Nonplussed, Alec rose with ease and a wide grin spread over his usually serious face. "I'll have her placed in the room next to yers."

Kieran turned back to the ledger in front of him without responding and waited for the door to close behind Alec.

The neat row of numbers occupied Kieran's eyes, but his mind filled with the memory of Mariel arching her back so that her breasts stood out beneath her thin gown, and the way her fingers had caressed her own creamy flesh. He remembered how her cheeks flushed when she begged him to touch her. His cock throbbed to life.

Kieran cleared his throat loudly and focused on the parchment in front of him to no avail.

In placing her out of harm's way, he had left himself without the defense of multiple walls of stone between them. He hoped he was strong enough, disciplined enough, to resist what lay sweet and tempting in the room beside his.

.   .   .

That evening, Kieran sat at the head of the table in the large, intricately carved chair that had belonged to his brother and their father before him. The scent of venison and freshly baked bread hung among the scents of home.

He refused to touch the food before him, not when Mariel had yet to arrive.

Out of concern for her discomfort among strange people in a strange place, he had offered her the opportunity to dine alone in her room. She had politely declined and insisted on eating in the main hall with his clan. Truth be told, he had been pleased with her resolve to join the others. Coming to Skye had been her decision—nay, her insistence. She would do best to deal with the repercussions of her choices rather than hide from them. He could not protect her from everything.

Within seconds of being considered late, the large wooden doors to the great hall swung open and in stepped Mariel. A blue velvet gown hugged her shape like a second skin despite the modest cut. The fabric fully displayed every sensual curve, from the generous swell of her breasts to the sensual dip of her lower back.

Women stared with spite, men gawked with open lust, and Mariel ignored every one of them as she strode to the table, her brilliant gaze fixed on him and him alone. Despite his determination to remain cold and distant, he warmed beneath her gaze and was about to stand to offer her the place beside him when Colin rose smoothly to his feet.

Kieran gritted his teeth. Damn Colin. Kieran glared at his old friend and watched Mariel sink gracefully into the seat between them.

Dinner was a long, torturous process. The warmth of her body blazed beside his, a constant reminder of her closeness. Her sweet scent hovered over the aroma of food and teased him with memories he could no more ignore than the woman beside him.

"Don't you agree, Kieran?" She arched her eyebrow in expectation.

"Ach, he's far too humble to agree to the like," Colin said, saving him from having to admit he had been staring at her and not listening.

"A true gentleman if ever I did see one," Mariel

acknowledged with a flirtatious smile. Her hand rested on his forearm for the briefest of moments, but it was long enough for the heat of her touch to linger with a slow burn.

She turned her head to say something to Colin, and her long neck arched gracefully. A silky black tendril of hair trailed down the white expanse of her throat and clung to the sleeve of her dress. He ached to smooth the errant lock back into place as he'd done before. To let his fingertips caress the softness of her skin, and to slide his hand around the back of her neck and tilt that beautiful face up toward him so he had access to her full, promising lips. She would be sweet to the taste and passionate in her response.

He knew that much from experience.

Colin's voice traveled toward him. "Mariel, ye look exhausted. Would ye like me to show ye to yer room?"

Kieran shot up abruptly before he realized what he was doing and sent the heavy wooden chair grinding into the rushes below. "That willna be necessary, Colin." He shot a challenging look toward his friend, a silent warning to stand down. "I'll do it."

"Thank you," Mariel said with a weary smile. "I confess, I am rather tired, and the thought of a warm bed is tempting indeed."

It was the closest thing to a complaint he had heard from her since they'd began the trip over three weeks ago. She'd endured the freezing cold, soaking rains, and even an unexpected attack without the slightest issue. Now she sat before him with dark smudges under her eyes, admitting only to the enticement of bed. If only it were his bed.

Kieran exited the great hall, not looking back to ensure she followed. He did not need to. After over an hour of sitting beside her, he was all too aware of her searing presence.

The wind howled outside and filled the comfortable silence between them as they wound through the narrow halls. They passed the plain wooden door of his room before stopping at hers. If anyone passed down the hall where she slept, he would hear them.

He leaned over her and pulled the handle on the door so it swung open with a great groan of protest as unused hinges ground against one another.

Golden light from the fireplace spilled out into the hall and pulsed around them with an aura of warmth. She looked up at him, her gaze no longer confident or flashing with the merriment she had displayed only minutes before in the great hall. Exhaustion dimmed the light in her eyes and exposed the hint of vulnerability he had glimpsed on the balcony when they'd first met.

"Thank you, Kieran." Her voice was soft even in the tomblike silence of the stone hall.

"I'm more a gentleman than Colin would have been had he shown ye to yer room." It was meant as a jest, but the very thought of Colin touching her made him want to punch something.

"I…" she hesitated as if searching for what to say. "I know your people are not happy with my presence here. I also know you anticipated this when you allowed me to come and still you brought me. You took a chance in welcoming me into your home." Her brows knit together in an earnest expression. "Thank you."

Her shy smile and obvious trepidation were disarming. He had seen her carefree attitude throughout the day and wondered how she could be so oblivious to the cold welcome. Now he understood that she was not oblivious, yet nor did she succumb to her own ambiguity. For all her quiet strength, she was wounded by their hatred.

And she trusted him enough to let him see that.

"It isna that they dinna like ye. They dinna trust yer people. The English have caused…much pain among my clan. Dinna worry though, they will grow to like ye." He doubted he spoke the truth, but the way her brow smoothed with relief made him glad for the lie.

Unable to resist the temptation, he ran his fingers over the velvety softness of her cheek. She turned her face toward the palm of his hand, encouraging his touch. Her skin was warm, smooth, enticing.

He brushed her full lips with the pad of his thumb, and her lashes fluttered closed. A warm sigh bathed his finger.

The moist heat of her mouth tempted him to sweep the digit against the tip of her tongue, to feel the pressure of her mouth close around him. Desire tightened low in his belly, the same way her lips might wrap around his cock, which now jutted uncomfortably beneath his plaid. The bed in her room was large enough to accommodate them both.

His breathing had grown deep as he stood like a fool staring at her, hungry for what he would not allow himself to take. He needed to go, lest he give in to a temptation he would not allow himself to sample. Not again.

Kieran let his hand drop to the side and rubbed his fingers against his thumb to obliterate the sweet sensation. Her presence at Caisteal Camus unnerved him, and it had little to do with the clan's reaction to her arrival. There was too much at stake. His hand tightened into a fist. And then there was her confession of Jack...

"Good night, Mariel," he said in a voice terse even to his own ears.

Confusion and hurt flickered across her face, but she did not protest. Wordlessly, she entered the bedroom and let the door close behind her, plunging him into total darkness.

●　　●　　●

Mariel finished lacing the simple bodice of her homespun gown the next day, careful to leave it loose to account for the slow healing wound. Wearing her corset the previous evening had aggravated the gash considerably and now the white-hot stab was a constant reminder of its existence.

The look on Kieran's face when he saw her made the pain worthwhile. His obsidian gaze had fallen on her throughout the night, burning with interest. Heat warmed Mariel's cheeks at the memory. She was not so indifferent herself.

He had been handsome and proud at the head of the table-the obvious leader to his people. His hair had hung loose to his shoulders, and his sharp jaw was clean shaven. He'd donned the garb of a Highlander and wore a fresh white leine with his plaid belted around his tapered waist. The combination had been overwhelmingly masculine and left her pulse racing at his nearness.

Shouts from outside trickled into her room, muffled by the shutters on the lower portion of her window. Though tightly locked, a chill seeped through the slats and spread cold against her waist when she looked through the warped glass to the scene below. People circled something she could not make out. Their jeers were carried away by the wind. Mariel strained to make out what they had gathered around. A flash caught her eye. A glint of sunlight as it glanced off the blade of a sword, followed by the distinct ring of metal on metal.

Something was not right. She spun away from the window and ran out her door, right into Colin's wide chest.

She backed up and mumbled a feeble apology as a charming smile slid over his handsome face.

"Good morning to ye, Mariel. I was just coming to see if ye'd broken yer fast yet."

"What transpires on the lawn below?" Even as she asked the question, she had a sinking suspicion he would not answer her.

"Nothing ye need to be seeing." His lighthearted wink was obviously meant to dissuade her questions.

A savage cry drifted in through the window at the end of the hall, followed by a chorus of cheers.

"Please, Colin."

His arm slid around her shoulder and pulled her tight against him. "I'd rather have yer company in the hall." The smooth tone of his voice made the suggestion behind his words all the more blatant.

The great hall was downstairs. Mariel knew how to leave the castle from there. Perhaps going to breakfast with Colin was not a bad idea.

She gave him a bright smile and ducked out from under his grasp. "On second thought, food sounds enticing, but I'm afraid I don't know my way around the castle."

"Then I'll show ye. First we'll start with the hall and where we'll end…" A wide grin spread over his face.

Mariel playfully laughed off his implication and followed behind him. She committed the path they took to memory this time. There might be need of it later. If everything did not go according to plan, and she had to escape to Inverness to fight for Jack's life, her mental map of the castle would need to be flawless.

Once downstairs, Mariel spied a door off to the side along the back of the castle. If her estimation was correct and it led outside, she would be exactly where she wanted. She slowed down and edged toward the door. Colin's wide back continued ahead. He did not seem to notice she was no longer behind him and disappeared around a corner.

The unlocked handle opened easily in her hand, and she slipped from the quiet darkness into the blinding brilliance outside. Stars danced before her eyes as her vision adjusted. The wind slapped against her, ripping at her hair and tearing at her skirts.

Mariel pulled the shawl around her shoulders and regretted not having grabbed a heavy plaid instead. The MacDonald clan stood a stone's throw away, still clustered together.

No one noticed her approach and for that she was grateful. She stood on her tiptoes in an effort to see over the towering clansmen and frustration pulled at her patience. Were all Highlanders so tall?

And then the crowd broke for one brief moment, long enough for her to see Kieran, his expression fierce, focused as he drew his sword over his head.

People leaned closer, inadvertently clearing a spot for her. Mariel stepped into the open space lest it fill again and observed the melee before her. A young man lay on the ground, his dirty blond hair disheveled around his flushed face. Kieran stood over him, body tense and sword held aloft in warning. Though bested, the blond man held his weapon bravely before him, ready to ward off the bite of the threatening blade.

Kieran spoke in Gaelic as he growled, "Ye dare defy me?"

The defeated man's voice was harsh with barely contained fury. "If ye would so easily forget the crimes the English have committed against us for that whore, then aye, I do defy ye."

The wind sucked the air from Mariel's chest, and the bitter sting of icy air dulled against numbed flesh. This was about her?

A barbaric cry erupted from Kieran. He whipped his blade through the air toward his opponent's neck and stopped a hair's breadth away from the tender flesh. The young man did not even flinch. "Dinna call her a whore," Kieran said between clenched teeth.

She froze, stunned by his words. Kieran had defended her. In front of all of his people, he had defended her honor. No man had ever done such a thing. Why would they? Her deeds did not warrant the respect of any man.

Self-disgust rolled through her stomach. Certainly she did not deserve the respect of a man as honorable as Kieran.

He held his blade over the man's throat, and the muscles of his arm bunched under his leine. While Kieran was a solid wall of strength and authority, she remembered how gentle those powerful arms could be and how they'd cradled her when she had been wounded.

Guilt crowded her heart and breathing became difficult. She was not worthy of the affection he bestowed upon her.

Kieran looked pointedly at the crowd. "She stays at Caisteal Camus as a guest and is to be treated as such…by all of ye. Am I understood?"

The crowd murmured quietly. In the excitement of the fight, no one had yet noticed her presence among them.

Kieran clasped the man's forearm with his own and helped him to his feet. "Hamish, do ye understand?"

The man, Hamish, balled his hand into a fist, and then unclenched it. "Ye stake the lives of yer people on her being here. After centuries of rape, treachery, and murder from the English, I ask ye again—do ye trust her?"

Kieran's eyes sifted through the crowd and settled on Mariel. A jolt shot through her. The world paused, held in a span of unrelenting time as she waited for his answer, daring not to breath for fear she might shatter.

She wanted to cry out that she was not worthy. She wanted

to collapse on her knees before him and beg for something she did not deserve.

But she did neither. She stood perfectly still. Her palms were moist with cold sweat and her heart hammered in her chest as she waited for his answer.

Chapter Sixteen

The wind slapped Mariel's heavy skirts against her legs and pulled her hair free from its braid. Her fingernails bit into her palms in an effort to keep her face impassive as she held Kieran's dark gaze.

"Aye," he said finally. "Aye, I do trust her. As should every one of ye."

Heady elation at his acceptance warred with the self-hatred that balled like ice in the pit of her stomach.

Satisfied with their laird's declaration, the MacDonald clan began to disperse. The few who did take notice of her quickly shifted their gaze away and widened the path between them.

Though sentiment warred within her, Mariel plastered a look of confusion on her face and stood off to the side. She had not confessed her knowledge of Gaelic to anyone, nor had they bothered to ask. People spoke without restraint when under the assumption they could not be understood. It was an advantage she could ill afford to lose.

Kieran brushed some dried grass from the man's back, and his voice traveled with the wind toward Mariel. "It's no that I dinna miss Brennan. I dinna let the grief rule my life. Grief willna feed our people or clothe them or protect them."

The young man looked sheepishly up at Kieran. "I suppose I dinna think of that."

"Aye, ye dinna. I am laird here, Hamish. If ye have concerns, ye should speak with me." Kieran gave him an appraising look. "Ye've got a strong arm there, lad. With proper training, I can make ye a warrior yet."

"Aye?" Hamish grinned. "When can I start?"

"When ye make the decision to be a man and leave off boyhood games." Kieran turned him in the direction of the castle and gave his back a final thump. "If ye find yerself a man by morning, ye know where we'll be training."

Hamish strode past Mariel and gave her a nod of acknowledgment, his chest puffed with obvious pride.

Witnessing Kieran's intimate discussion with the rebellious adolescent made her wonder how he would handle Jack. A smile threatened to break her composure as she imagined little Jack standing in Kieran's massive shadow, listening with similar wide-eyed adoration. Her brother had been too long without a strong man to look up to, and Mariel had a sneaking suspicion Kieran would not turn down the chance to help him.

She clenched her fist against the weight of shame lest it overwhelm her. Kieran strode toward her, and it was all she could do to rein in her emotions. Not only was Kieran MacDonald a good, honorable man, but he was also a leader admired by his clan.

"Mariel, ye werena supposed to be here." The corners of his lips pulled down into a frown. He looked toward the castle. "Did no one try to stop ye?"

"If you mean Colin, he did try. My curiosity, however, outweighed his good intentions." She looked pointedly at the hilt in Kieran's hands. "What happened?"

"Ach, nothing to worry yerself over, lass." He swung the sword over his shoulder. "No when there are more important things for ye to be doing."

"Dyeing wool?" she guessed. Idle hands were wasted hands. Apparently, Scotland was no different. Truth be told, she looked forward to honest work.

"Exactly." He grinned. "Let me introduce ye to Innes."

After a few inquiries, Mariel found herself in front of a dour looking woman with snarls of gray hair stuffed under a cotton bonnet. She peered down a crooked nose at Mariel with a sneer that evidenced the woman's clear distaste for being stuck with the English stranger.

Innes waved a hand at Mariel to follow her and stalked

through the heavy castle doors. Her shoulders hunched forward, and her grumbling Gaelic was impossible to ignore. "No that the likes of ye will be of any help. Ye look like a slight breeze might carry ye off. No that I'd mind."

Just over the swell of a hill lay a dense copse of trees, streaked with gold and scarlet amid the splashes of emerald green.

"Here," Innes said and motioned to the narrow stream several feet away.

Carved into the landscape like a silvered ribbon, the crystal clear water moved swiftly through the naturally cut path, gurgling with an excited babble. Were it not for the foul-smelling pots lining the grassy bank, the area would be a very peaceful setting.

Innes grasped a handful of fluffy wool from a large wooden basket. "Take," she barked in English followed by an additional mutter in Gaelic. "If ye even understand me, ye silly chit. It's been years since I've had to speak this damned language, and I dinna like it."

Innes thrust the wool into a vat that reeked of rotting fish. "Put," she instructed as she lifted a thick log and poked the buoyant clump until it sank. "Leave." The old woman then lifted the top off the pot closest to Mariel and pointed. "Done."

Mariel held her breath and peered over the rim to where the snow white wool showed through the murky liquid. It certainly did not look dyed. Perhaps the Highlanders purchased their vibrant fabric from England.

Innes thrust her hands into the noxious liquid and pulled up wads of sodden wool. To Mariel's amazement, the downy white shaded to a dingy pale green and darkened further into vivid blue. She continued to stare in wonder, waiting to see if any additional colors showed.

Innes glanced at Mariel and rolled her eyes before throwing the mass into the empty basket at her feet. She lifted a clam-like shell and looked at Mariel as though she were daft and said, "Woad."

At least that explained the smell.

"Out," she commanded while performing a scooping motion. Without waiting for acknowledgment that she had been understood, Innes turned her back to Mariel and began stuffing fistful after gnarled fistful of wool into a fresh pot of the foul woad concoction. Her grating voice rose over the wind. "We'll see if the cosseted English whore can get her hands dirty like the rest of us. Pampered little brat with her rounded fingernails and milky white skin that have no ever seen a hard day's work."

Mariel shrugged off the bitter grumblings and rolled her sleeves up despite the chill. Holding her breath, she slid her hands into the warm, putrid bath. The wool was spongy against her fingertips, clinging to her flesh like wet hair when she drew it from the pot. She suppressed a gag as a strong wave of the noxious odor washed over her, and then tossed the bluing ball of wool into Innes's basket with a soft *splat*.

Once the vat was emptied, another lay ready, and after that another until the day passed in a blur of gray green and brilliant blue. Mariel's stomach growled fiercely in protest of her skipped meals, and her body was stiff from lack of sufficient movement.

The sun sank low in the sky, cradled in the bosom of the hills beyond. Its crimson light splashed against the drying wool and lent it a purple essence.

As though sensing night settling upon them, Innes rose and stretched her back. She nodded in Mariel's direction. "Done."

For all the misery the woman had obviously intended to inflict, Mariel's chest swelled with the sense of accomplishment. She had completed a day of true, honest work. Her livelihood had been earned with the strength of her body, not the twisting of words and manipulation.

•   •   •

Later that evening, Mariel sat on the edge of her bed, fed and exhausted as she waited for the sound of Kieran's return. The cloak of night had long since snuffed out the sun's golden rays, and yet still he was nowhere to be found.

She had changed into a simple dress for supper that evening and taken great care with her appearance. The subtle hues of the dress complimented the color of her eyes, and her hair had been twisted back in a simple braid. She sighed and looked down at her blue tinged fingers. There had been little she could do for her hands. Not that any of her effort mattered. He had not shown.

No one mentioned where he was, nor did they seem concerned by his disappearance, or so she had gathered from the multiple conversations she had overheard. Her heart thudded in her chest in a frenzy of excitement and regret as she accepted the only assumption remaining. Kieran was with Blair and Dougal Hampton, the men she had been sent to find.

Her gaze slid to the scrap of ice blue silk draped unceremoniously over the wooden chest at the foot of her bed. The tissue thin night rail had come at sufficient cost. Her hand slid under the sheer fabric, letting the coolness of the silk soothe the ache of her overworked fingers. It was a gown made for the bedroom. A gown meant for seduction.

Breathless anticipation filled her chest, and the throb of desire slowly pulsed to life. She closed her eyes and imagined the brush of his warm lips against hers, and the gentle caress of his hand upon her breast and his fingers as they crept up the sensitive flesh of her inner thighs.

The heavy tread of footsteps thudded down the hall. Mariel's eyes flew up. She straightened. Her ears strained for the sounds of movement. If the footsteps retreated, they were those of a guard. But if the door next to hers opened, she knew Kieran had finally returned.

She listened with her breath held, lest she miss anything. The creak of a door opening echoed off the walls of her room and released the air she'd been holding. She curled into the searing burn that twisted in her stomach, the squeezing grip of guilt and weight of remorse that kept her human through the years of deception. She would never shy from its wicked embrace. It was her punishment.

But guilt would not save Jack.

Mariel shrank inside of herself and let the dress whisper down the length of her body, sheathing her in the silky fabric.

The time had come to seduce Kieran MacDonald.

* * *

Kieran released a heavy sigh and sank into the large chair beside the fire. His gaze settled on the smoldering peat, watching smoke curl over the black slabs of earth in billowing plumes. The day had been long, and his dealings with Hamish had been easy in comparison.

Crop fields had needed to be set, and the farmers had argued like old women over the exact day. The kitchen had begged his instruction on meals with questions better left to the lady of the castle. Of course there was no lady, but why the cook insisted on playing that argument over and over with Kieran was beyond him. So long as the food was warm and unspoiled, he cared little what graced his trencher.

Then there was his trip to see Blair and Dougal. His heart wrenched angrily in his chest. To know how they were treated made his iron stomach churn with disgust.

No, he couldn't think of that. It made him too damn angry.

Doubtless Mariel's day had been difficult as well. He absently noticed the smile spreading over his lips as he imagined her elbow deep in those foul-smelling pots. Perhaps she would wish to leave Skye after he found a replacement lady's maid for her.

He took a sip of the whisky and leaned his head back against the chair. The amber liquor slowly burned a path down his throat until it pooled like fire in his empty stomach. While Mariel's departure was necessary, Kieran was not as eager to see her go as he should be.

Pressing the cup to his lips once more, he idly mused if she had worn her hair twisted up or plaited back in a long braid. Perhaps she had left it loose. That was how he liked it best, with ebony stands flowing like a waterfall down the length of her slender back.

A soft knock interrupted his thoughts. He lifted his head and glared at the back of his door, willing the intruder to leave him in peace.

The knock reverberated against the solid wood door with

more force this time.

"Who is it?" he barked.

In response, the door opened and Mariel stepped in, her curvy body clothed in a gown of liquid silver that displayed more of her body than it hid. She pushed the door closed behind her back, and her lips lifted in a little half smile. "I thought you might enjoy some company."

Chapter Seventeen

Kieran swallowed thickly, letting the burn of alcohol sear a path to his loins. The dying embers of the fire flickered against Mariel's shimmering dress. God help him, he could see right through the thing. His gaze slid lower to where her body was visible through the sheer fabric. Her full breasts rose high and round and her nipples were rosy as they hardened beneath his stare.

He was unable to turn away, unable to stop the path of his stare from trailing down her taut stomach to the shadow of dark hair between her legs where her slender thighs met. Where she would be liquid heat and temptation.

He shifted forward in an effort to ease the discomfort of his aching cock and the chair creaked. "What are ye doing here? Ye should be asleep."

She appeared unperturbed by his gruff tone and met the challenge of his glare with indifference. "You were not at dinner."

The burn of jealousy tightened the bands of his stomach as he raked his gaze down the dress once more. Had she worn that into the great hall? Did his men see her thus?

Kieran clenched his hands into fists. Did they follow the lines of her body with their stares? He gritted his teeth. Did they imagine touching her? Possessing her?

"Is that what ye wore?" he ground out with more rage than he intended.

The corner of her lip lifted in a slow, sensual smile. "Of course I didn't." Her hand smoothed over the swell of her hip. "I didn't think you had noticed."

Was she daft? He hadn't been able to pull his eyes from

her since she stepped inside the door, and she hadn't thought he noticed?

"I canna help but notice." He smirked. "But ye already knew that, dinna ye?"

She pulled a pin from her hair and rich, black waves spilled down her back. He hadn't even realized her hair was pulled up.

"It's just my night rail." Her voice was husky, low. The way it had been at the inn.

The gown glided across her skin, caressing what his hands longed to savor. One slim, perfectly shaped leg was unveiled by a long slit in the dress. His fingers itched to follow that tempting cut of the gown, to brush the smooth warmth of her thighs. He swallowed a groan. She would be so slick...so hot.

With each step toward him, her breasts moved ever so slightly with a firm bounce that made his mouth water. All hesitation fled his mind as his cock squeezed with bittersweet tension, and his bollocks ached with want. Her. He wanted her.

And judging from the glint in her eyes, she wanted him.

He shouldn't let her be there. His gaze trailed down the length of her body and desire hammered his brain into thoughtlessness. She approached the back of his chair and slid her fingertips against the expanse of his shoulders with a feather light touch that sizzled across his flesh like lightning. She stroked with light pressure against the taut muscles. The hair rose on his arms and unexpected pleasure tingled across his neck.

Her movements were fluid, continual, so her two hands felt like a dozen, all stroking and easing the tension from his body.

"You look tired," she said in a soothing voice. Her magic fingers worked their way up his neck. Knotted muscle melted into hot butter beneath her ministrations.

He groaned and dropped his head forward. Whatever she was doing, he hoped she would do it to the front of his body... and soon.

"I could go..." She left the statement hanging, but her hands continued to sweep against the back of his neck.

Go? Kieran blinked, momentarily pulled from the heady relaxation. Why would she go?

"Mmm-mmm…stay," he murmured and tilted his head to the side to give her access to his right shoulder where Hamish had landed a solid blow that morning.

As if reading his mind, her fingers moved deftly toward the sore area and eased the gnarled ache residing there. Never in his life had he been given such relaxing pleasure. Never did he realize such satisfaction could exist when both people were still fully clothed—her significantly less than him, of course. A grin lifted his lips. He'd have it no other way.

"What is it ye do to me?"

Her fingers did not stop moving. "Something I learned in London." He could hear the smile in her voice. "Although I have to say, you are significantly stronger than any Englishman I've ever seen."

The compliment would normally roll off his shoulders. Instead, it seeped into his thoughts and widened his grin. Women had admired his physique before, but it sounded different coming from Mariel. Like warm, sensual strokes of flattery—so much like the movement of her hands.

"I ought to be scolding you rather than pampering you right now." A playful slap landed on his shoulder.

Scolding?

"Mmm?" he mumbled. "Why do ye say that?"

"Innes." She paused from her task and rasped in a shrill voice, "Come. Put. Done."

Kieran gave a lazy laugh at her impression of the old woman. "I dinna think anyone has ever dared mock Innes before."

Mariel's hands slid across his back. "I don't think I'd be brave enough to do it in front of her."

He imagined Mariel bent over one of those foul-smelling pots with Innes snapping orders at her and remorse niggled his conscience. Perhaps having Mariel dye wool with the hard old woman had been cruel.

A thought suddenly occurred to him, and a smile curled his lips once more. "Let me see yer hands."

She gave him another little slap. "You cur. You have to earn it."

His mind flashed with the various ways he could do just that. "Did ye have something in mind?"

She was quiet for a moment, hesitant almost. "Tell me what was so important that it drew you from my company this evening."

Her response was not what he had expected.

The tension she worked so hard to ease from his shoulders crept up once more as he remembered his visit with Blair and Dougal. Telling Mariel where he had been would draw her deeper into the clan, make her one of them. It would make her belong when she was so far from a home that did not want her.

But it was not his secret to tell. Could she be trusted?

Guilt tugged at his chest. That morning he had ordered his clan to trust Mariel. He had claimed he trusted her. Yet when faced with the opportunity, he realized the disheartening truth. He did not.

Not when his trust had been so brutally betrayed in the past, and not when that misguided trust had cost him so dearly.

Mariel's soft voice interrupted his thoughts. "I can feel the tightness in your body. Forgive me for asking."

He heaved a sigh of frustration. Mariel was not the spy from his past. She was genuine and kind. She was worthy of his trust.

He either needed to force her to leave Skye, or he needed to allow himself to let her in. Not just for her, but for proof to himself that he had not wholly lied to his clan.

"Have ye ever seen someone so ill-treated that it puts violent thoughts into yer head?"

Her hands stilled on his back. Was she horrified by the question?

"I have." The words were spoken softly.

She understood. Of course she did.

Trust her.

"And when ye see the product of that abuse, it tears at yer soul and leaves ye feeling…empty." Would she know what he spoke of? A glimmer of trepidation rippled through him. Would she think him weak for it?

"Yes," she whispered.

Vain relief coupled with the rage tightening in his gut. "And for all the power and strength ye possess, ye canna do a damn thing to help them?"

"All you can do is bide your time until salvation becomes possible…then take your chance before it's gone…" Her voice caught on the last word and pulled his attention away from his own darkness.

He turned in his seat and saw the pain burning in her wounded gaze.

He rose from his chair and approached her, eager to feel the softness of her body wrapped tightly in his arms, to ease the hurt of her eyes.

But she did not rush into his arms as he had expected, as other women would have done. She took a step back and shook her head vigorously.

"No…please…"

He paused, momentarily confused, and then a realization tore through him like the jagged blade of a dagger. He knew the reason she didn't want his comfort.

"Yer pain…Jack is the cause, aye?" His hands clenched at his sides. Did he truly want the answer?

Shock reflected in her wide eyes and drained the color from her face. "How did you—?"

"Ye spoke of him in yer sleep. Everything ye do is for him, ye said." The days of wondering drew to a tumultuous peak and bitterness seeped into his voice.

Her gaze hardened, but she did not look away. "You are correct, but not in the way you think."

"And ye know what I'm thinking?" Deep down he knew she did. Yet he was fearful to hope and afraid of having the splinter of trust tamped down.

She took a step toward him and closed the cold gap she had widened between them. She rested against his forearm, hot against the chill on his skin. "I do and it's not what you suspect."

Mariel let the comfortable quiet fill the space between them and waited for a stream of questions. They never came.

He gave her a courtesy she had not allowed him, could not afford to allow him. Silence and pleasure had been the weapons she'd used to draw the words from his lips. She had not counted on such a raw confession of emotion, nor had she been prepared for the intensity of the bond growing between them.

In a game where he was supposed to unveil his secrets, they had both inadvertently bared their souls.

Mariel wrapped her arms around the flimsy dress and shifted her gaze to the floor. Had he seen her for who she truly was? Had she revealed too much?

She wanted to look up, to confirm her fears, and yet she found she was afraid of what she would see.

"Blue always has been a fine color on ye."

Startled, she jerked her head up and found him staring at her hands with a boyish smile.

She glanced down at her hands and laughed, giddy with the reprieve from the break in a conversation that ran too deep for comfort.

"We'll have to have a dress made for ye with the wool ye dyed. The color suits yer eyes nicely."

Mariel laughed again and allowed him to pull her woad blue hands against the roughness of his palms. "Who knew you were such a flatterer, Kieran?"

"I'm sure flattery is something ye're verra used to." He paused in his inspection of her fingers and raised an eyebrow.

His hand closed over hers and heat blossomed in her cheeks. "Not from you." She glanced shyly up at him through the veil of her lashes.

He grasped her chin and tilted her face toward his. "Ye are the most fragile wee woman I have ever laid eyes on."

Mariel's brow furrowed. That was flattery? The compliment of her hands suddenly looked like a courtier's praise.

"I'm no finished." The grin that hovered on his face indicated he knew full well what she thought. The rogue. "Ye are the most fragile thing, and yet ye have a strength within ye that I've seen only in my warriors. I've no seen such spirit nor unyielding determination in any other woman."

She had been expecting admiration of her fair skin or her unique eye color. Isn't that what men usually praised? But the compliment he offered took her aback.

He saw more in her than she saw in herself.

"Ye're no so bad to look at either." His gaze swept over her, unabashed with obvious appreciation.

His thumb brushed against the line of her jaw and Mariel found herself smiling up at him.

"Yer skin is smooth as silk." A ripple of excitement raised the hair on her arms. "Everywhere." His voice was a strangled groan that tightened her nipples.

Mariel felt herself sway toward the hard wall of his chest, as if physically drawn to his strength, his warmth. The pad of his thumb brushed her lower lip, sending an insistent thrum of desire humming in her core.

He stared down at her and a muscle leapt in his jaw. "We canna do this."

Frustration coupled with the sting of hurt. His face became impassive and the wall he so often put up rose between them once more.

"You want me," she insisted. She could feel the proof of his desire pressing against her belly.

"I dinna need a mistress, Mariel."

He stepped away, and the chill of the room crept across her scantily covered flesh. His rejection burned deep despite the comfort his words had brought only moments before.

He strode to his chair and sank into it before resuming his stare into the smoldering fire.

But Mariel did not move toward the door.

This was not over.

She would not give up so easily.

Chapter Eighteen

The floor was cool beneath Mariel's feet, a balm for the searing heat flaring through her.

Kieran stared into the flames of the fire, his gaze unfocused. She knew he expected her to leave, but she would not. She could not be rejected again, not with so much at stake.

Mariel drew a deep breath in an effort to gather the strength to sever herself from the newly formed bond between them. If she stayed, she could not allow herself to deepen that connection or she might never succeed at what she'd been sent to do. No, this needed to be an act of a physical nature. An act aimed at his pleasure.

One that omitted her feelings and thoughts. They were far too dangerous.

She did not ask his permission to stay. Instead, she knelt beside his chair. His gaze turned to her, startled no doubt by her lack of obedience to his firm command. The wooden floor was smooth beneath her knee as she leaned forward and trailed her finger along the side of his strong calf.

"Mariel…" His tone held a wary note, and he tensed beneath her fingertips.

Her hand skimmed over his knee and brushed the hem of his kilt. Were Kieran a typical target in the usual setting, he would have succumbed to the effects of the laudanum by now.

She inched toward the edge of his plaid and higher still to reveal the middle of his thigh. Her fingers trembled in their ascent across his legs, hard with muscle despite being relaxed and sprinkled with dark hair like his chest. She had never proceeded this far before.

Kieran's eyes were inky black with desire, watching. Waiting. She bent over his knee and swept her lips across the coarse hair. He did not move to stop her.

A languid thrum of longing pulsed low in her belly. She slid her palms up his thighs and focused on his knees in an effort to pretend he was another man, one she did not respect and admire. One she did not care for.

His fingers threaded through her hair and sent a ripple of pleasure tingling down her scalp to the base of her neck. The heat of his arousal whispered against her fingertips, and her heart slammed in her chest with overwhelming anticipation.

Kieran's hand tightened into a fist against the back of her head with a pressure firm enough to bring her actions to a standstill.

She drew a deep breath and held it in preparation for what she knew would inevitably come next. Rejection.

•   •   •

Kieran held Mariel pinned in front of him, torn between taking her back to her own bed and carrying her into his. His thighs burned where her fingertips had explored, where her lips had scorched. He should have let her continue her way up his legs, let her mouth wrap around him, hot and wet. His loins throbbed in painful reminder, cursing him for interrupting her once more.

Now she knelt before him with her eyes averted and her mouth soft and trembling. Tense silence filled the room as desire warred with honor.

"Ye dinna belong to me, Mariel." His words were choked with the yearning he'd fought too long to deny.

Her eyes flashed with hurt. "I want to," she whispered.

There it was again, the offer to become his, the permission to take what he wanted. And this time he couldn't bring himself to say no.

His fingers tangled in her hair and his mouth came down upon hers, before he changed his mind—before he talked himself out of it again.

The intoxicating scent of rose enveloped him and drove him to the brink of madness. He grasped her slender arms and pulled her from the floor into his lap.

Her long legs straddled his hips as she sank against him, pressing into his cock. He caught her face with his hands and dragged his mouth to the softness of her lips.

With a breathy moan, her lips opened ever so slightly, a sample of what he craved.

The flick of her tongue against his sent a jolt of desire through him. He tugged her head back farther, forcing her mouth open to accept the full extent of his desire. His tongue swept aggressively into her sweet warmth as he spiraled the kiss to a place from which there was no return.

Mariel's hips rolled against his swollen cock, and she met the hungry thrust of his tongue with her own seductive parry. Still holding her in place by the hair, his other hand cupped the weight of her full breast. Her flesh was like silk beneath his hands-supple, firm silk. She arched her back toward his touch until her supple flesh strained against the low cut of her night rail.

The flimsy fabric shoved easily out of his way, and the firelight played across the smooth expanse of her taut skin. This time, there was no abrupt end to his observation, no untimely weighing in of conscience. This time, she would be his.

Her breasts were full and round, absolute perfection. A small pink nipple hardened in the soft light, stretching toward the warmth of his mouth.

Kieran lowered his head and flicked his tongue over the tip of the right bud. Her sharp intake of breath echoed off the stone walls, encouraging him. He glanced up and circled the tender little nub with his lips before sucking it hard into his mouth, his tongue gently stroking. Her kiss-swollen lips parted and she made a sound somewhere between a whimper and a moan. It was the kind of sound that stroked a man's confidence.

She pulled at his leine and drew it over the top of his head. Blue fingers trailed over his stomach, and she began a maddening descent to where he lay hard beneath his plaid. His muscles tightened automatically at her touch, and his cock jerked toward her hand. A slow grin spread over her lips.

She was not the only one who could tease.

His fingers eased beneath the provocative slit in her dress, skimming smooth flesh that seemed to go on forever. Caress by intentionally slow caress, he made his way up the softness of her inner thighs to the thatch of downy hair.

With a lazy motion, the length of his finger grazed the heat between her legs. She gasped, and her hips gave a reflexive lurch. Desire tightened in his stomach. If she reacted with such passion to his hand, how would she respond with him buried inside her?

Anticipation tightened his bollocks and he stroked her again. His fingertip traced the outline of her slick cleft before gliding down its hot center. A groan sounded deep in his throat. God, she was so wet.

He cupped the sweet mound with his hand and probed lightly inside of her, teasing before he followed the natural trail of her slit toward the hardened little nub that would give her incredible pleasure. She buried her face against his neck, her breath hot against his ear. He stroked her again and was rewarded with a breathless moan.

If she kept making those sounds against his ear, he would be unmanned long before he even had her.

With languid, purposeful movements, he massaged the tender bud. She arched back in his arms and ground her hips against his hand, her breathing frantic now. She tensed beneath his touch, and he knew she was close to her release.

His cock strained painfully at her high whimper as she stiffened in his arms. He sucked a nipple into his mouth.

He felt her telltale spasm against his fingers and heard his name on her lips as she cried out.

She opened her eyes and blinked slowly, her lips parted. One look at her dazed expression and a realization slammed into him. This woman may have loved other men well, but it was evident she had never been well loved.

He would see an end to that.

Her gaze trailed down his torso like fire to where his arousal thrust up beneath his kilt. Kieran swallowed. Her fingers glided down his sweat-dampened body to his thick belt. The breath hissed out between his teeth in an effort to rein in the desire that threatened to overwhelm him.

She slid her finger along his belt and a languid grin lifted the corner of her lips. The metal prong clanked against the flat edge of his buckle, and the belt went loose. Kieran gripped the smooth wooden sides of his chair to keep from reaching out to her. Her gaze flicked up to his face, and she tugged the belt from his waist so his kilt lay folded, unsupported, across his lap.

Kieran shifted his grip on the chair and focused on the cool wood against his damp palms. Her hand brushed his thigh as she peeled back the top flap of his kilt. Sweat prickled along his brow. She went too slow. He was so hard he might burst beneath her measured movements before she even unveiled him.

She pulled the plaid away from him, inadvertently letting the wool rasp against the sensitive head, until his cock thrust into the blessedly cool air of the room, freed from the stifling heat of restraint.

Mariel's eyes widened, and her mouth parted in a silent gasp. An arrogant grin spread over his lips before he could stop himself.

His hands caressed either side of her legs, gathering the shimmering silk around her hips. Her legs spread wider, and her wet heat rubbed against the length of his shaft, slick...hot... wanting. His hands balled into fists as if squeezing the delicate fabric might take the edge off the painful level of desire that hammered through him.

His mouth was dry, his blood scalded his veins, and his brain thundered—all with anticipation for what he'd put off for too long. He wrapped his shaft in his fist and nudged the tip against her, teasing her, savoring her, preparing to enter her.

He nudged against her entrance and a primal groan tore from his chest as she gripped the sensitive head of his cock.

One slight shift of his hips, and he would be sheathed within her tight, slick heat.

Chapter Nineteen

Heat raged through Kieran, consuming him in an intoxicating swirl of pleasure and tingling expectation. The blunt edge of his cock pushed gently against Mariel's moist center. He eased his hands to her narrow waist and shifted his hips back in preparation to thrust into her.

Wet. Her waist was wet. No…her hip. His fingers spanned the damp fabric. A dark stain against the dress ripped through the fog of his desire. He stilled.

"Please, Kieran…don't stop." Her words were breathy, frantic. She arched against, him and the stain grew larger.

Fear slammed into him. "Stop. Yer wound has reopened."

She leaned forward and brushed her lips against his earlobe. Her breath was hot against his neck. "I don't feel it. Please…" She rolled her hips against him, grinding with a wild need he too had felt only seconds before.

Kieran caught her face in his hands and gently pulled her back so he could meet her gaze. Her eyes were hazy with unmistakable desire, her cheeks still flushed. All good signs that she had not lost too much blood—yet.

"Mariel, ye're hurt." Carefully, he eased her from his lap and tried to ignore the gut churning ache of his need. "I need to see how bad the injury is. Ye can look away if ye want." He hoped she would. Seeing the torn flesh might frighten her.

He eased the gauzy silk up to better inspect the wound. Her long legs were shapely, lean, and completely distracting. Kieran staunched the desire to let his hands sample the sensual curve of her thigh and fixed his attention on her hip.

Several stitches had ripped out and half the gash had

reopened. A steady trickle of blood streamed down the curve of her perfectly rounded arse.

Damn it. How could he have been so careless with her? He knew she was injured, and yet he'd pawed at her like some randy adolescent.

"The wound is going to need to be restitched. I'll call someone to fetch the healer." Kieran got to his feet and grabbed his kilt off the floor.

Her hand rested on his forearm. "Please don't, Kieran." Her brows knit together with obvious concern. "One look at us and they will recognize why I was here. I don't want your people to know you've been with me…" She lowered her eyes. "…and think less of you for it."

Kieran stared at her, unsure of what to say. Were the hurt in her voice not so apparent, he might have laughed at the thought of her marring his honor. But she did not jest, and the words she whispered bothered him far more than if someone else had said them of her. "Mariel—"

"You can sew it," she said quickly.

Kieran frowned. "I'm no healer. I've stitched war wounds on the battlefield, no the flesh of a lady." The very thought of punching a needle through her petal soft skin made him uneasy. Hadn't he hurt her enough for one night?

"Need I remind you that this was a war wound obtained on a battlefield?" When he did not respond, she stuck her chin out in stubborn defiance. "If you don't do it, I'll do it myself."

Needle and thread lay in his sporran should it be required after a bout of rough training, but many years had passed since he had need of it.

Blood flowed from the wound and for all her stoicism, she was beginning to pale. Even if he wanted to get the healer, by the time she was roused and had traveled the length to his room, Mariel could very well be…

Muttering a curse under his breath, he snatched his sporran off the mantle. "Staunch that," he snapped. Did she know nothing of wounds?

Mariel clutched the shimmering fabric in her hand and

pressed it tight against her side while he threaded the needle. He filled his discarded cup and passed it to her. "Drink this," he commanded. The spirits would at least help dull the pain.

She would have to lie down for him to do this, and the only place she could do so was his bed. His mouth went dry.

"Ye need to lie down," he said in a gruff tone and nodded toward his bed.

He held her slender arm, bracing her as they walked to the other side of the room. She was delicate in his hand, as if squeezing his fingers into a fist would shatter her bone. Apprehension knotted his stomach.

He helped lower Mariel to the bed, her wide gaze fixed on him. Did she have to look at him like that? Kieran clenched his jaw and tried to ignore the way her hair splayed over his pillow, the way her long legs lay across the sheets.

He focused on threading the needle. "Ready?"

She balled her hand into a fist and gave a short nod.

Mariel did not so much as flinch while he stitched the gash closed. He hadn't expected her to weep, he knew her better than that by now, but he had expected her to at least react in some way to the pointed bite of the needle. Instead her eyes had focused on the ceiling, unseeing, and her face remained expressionless throughout.

Men had stronger reactions when sewn on the battlefield than did the gentle woman beneath his fingers. He understood then that Mariel's indifference did not stem from bravery, but was the product of a life of incredible pain and the necessity of endurance. He tied off the string and his gut churned.

In a world where she had been forced to abandon herself to escape any sense of feeling, he had caused her further injury with his overzealous lust. Was there any wonder she did not trust him enough to tell him of her past?

"I'm finished." His voice was loud against the silence.

Dark lashes swept over pallid cheeks as she examined his work. "Well done, Kieran." She let the ruined night rail fall back into place. "Almost as good as the healer."

Her eyes met his, and the memory of their shared intimacy

hummed between them as the room fell quiet once more. Her lips were swollen with the force of their kisses. His desire was still hard and pulsing beneath his plaid.

His body longed for what his mind would not allow. She had been injured too much in the past, and she didn't trust him enough to tell him how. He refused to be another man in the list of those who hurt her. He would cause her no more pain.

As though sensing him pull away, Mariel stepped forward. "Kieran." His name was a whispered sigh on her lips.

He did not open his arms to her. "Ye should return to yer room." She needed rest, she needed to heal.

And he needed to think.

•   •   •

Tufts of wool slid from between Mariel's fingers into the turning wheels of the wooden contraption and emerged as coarse thread winding against a spindle. Kieran spoke to Innes in low tones several paces away. The chattering gossip around her coupled with the noise of the spinning wheel kept the conversation blocked from Mariel's ears, no matter how hard she strained.

Desperate to catch Kieran's gaze, she looked up, silently willing him to glance in her direction. He shifted his weight and clenched his hand at his side, but did not look her way.

Her sigh sent the small fibers of wool fluttering. A fortnight had passed from the evening of her botched seduction, and he had not spoken to her since.

Doubtless he was angry with her for disobeying his orders to cease her work and stay in bed until she was recovered from her injury. She had thought he would get over the offense quickly, that he would realize the necessity of her disobedience. She would never earn the respect of the Highlanders if she allowed herself to be coddled.

While no one had threatened her or harmed her, Mariel was not well liked. With Kieran avoiding her, she had only Colin's misguided friendship and Alec's toleration.

She fed the wool with ease and realized she was frowning.

Why did being ostracized suddenly bother her so much? Wasn't she used to living alone? After all, she had spent the last two years in voluntary solitude.

Without so much as a glance in her direction, Kieran turned and strode from the room, leaving Mariel immersed in a room of strangers and hate.

"Did ye see how he dinna even look at her? He's already moved on." The woman behind her spoke out loud in Gaelic.

Mariel kept her face impassive, but the cruel words found their mark and lashed against her heart. She grasped another wad of wool and layered it between the wooden gears.

"Ach, do ye blame him? Look at her! With his virility, he'd break her." Another woman snickered behind her.

Mariel's back straightened unnaturally as she spun the wheel and worked the clump into fine, blue thread.

"I think it's good he's making the whore work with her hands instead of keeping her on the flat of her back."

Mariel did not have to turn to see their angry stares as they pierced into her back from every angle, like an assault of vile daggers. No matter how wicked their words, she could not let on that she understood them. Instead, she lowered her head and focused intently on the endless blue fluff slipping between her fingers.

"Ye're verra pretty." The words were spoken in Gaelic, the voice little more than a small, timid whisper.

Mariel looked up from her work and found herself face-to-face with a cherub. Golden hair curled around an angelic face that had yet to lose the plumpness of infancy. Large, brown eyes stared up at her, curious. A smattering of freckles dotted the little upturned nose and rosebud lips pursed with a seriousness that should not belong to one so young.

"Are ye a princess?" The girl's chubby hands twisted against one another as though she knew how whimsical her question sounded.

In a world of hatred, this one little girl was brave enough to offer kindness as if there were no boundary between Scottish and English, as if fear and anger had never existed. The way it should be. Mariel smiled down at the child.

"Coira!" Innes growled and grabbed the little girl by the arm. "Dinna talk to her. She canna even understand ye."

"Yes, Grandmother," Coira said as Innes began to pull her away from Mariel.

The little girl looked up and studied Mariel with a furrowed brow as though unsure what to make of her.

Mariel met the girl's wide-eyed stare and mouthed the words, *"Tapadh leat." Thank you.*

A brilliant smile spread over Coira's lips and lit her small face.

A bittersweet sensation filled Mariel's chest. Jack had been about that age when she saw him last. Although the two years of growth since they had seen one another would have stripped away the remaining vestiges of the chubby-cheeked boy she remembered. Nostalgia stung at her heart. Were he with her now, she would be able to take the ridicule with the nonchalant stride she'd maintained in her youth. They could be happy.

Though exhausting, this was the life she had envisioned for Jack and herself. A humble living earned by the hard work of her hands. A life where she went to bed tired, but honest. A life where Jack had everything he needed and was not subjected to the darkness of Aaron's underworld.

The women's sharp words gave her an idea, one that would have made the old Mariel smile. The Mariel who would have never let herself be so hated. She would have taken the slights of the clan and turned them into jests. The life she lived would have been embraced and cherished. As it should be.

If she had the acceptance of the clan, Kieran would not be able to ignore her.

A slow smile quirked on her lips as a thought came to her. She knew the Highlanders did not care for King James despite his Scottish blood. Likewise, the peasants of England bristled against the jeweled hand that lay heavy over their heads. As a result, she had learned quite a few interesting ditties during her time in the streets of London.

She hummed softly for a moment, remembering the tune and then sang the first line.

"King James, so powerful and great,
   With mighty stance and graceful gait.

Several women cast her angry looks.

"Dressed in silks and jewels and pearls,
   Decadent fans and lots of curls.

Brows furrowed and eyes narrowed.

"He wins at cards as only king can,
   And rejects lady love for that of a...

The few women who spoke English gave shuttered smiles as their friends asked for translation. After a quick glance to ensure Coira was not within earshot, she sang the last word.

"Man."

One woman laughed out loud, and a couple others grinned at her. Mariel cast them a glance and winked before turning back to her wool.

Perhaps she could win them over yet.

• • •

Mariel hefted the weight of the basket off the tender scar on her hip where the bothersome wound had finally healed. The sun shimmered like a medallion of gold in the clear blue sky, and the pale green grass spread before her. Perfect weather, were it not for the gusts that whipped against her with such force it lifted her braid from her back and threatened to pull the basket from her tightly clenched fingers. While Skye was not as cold as the rest of Scotland, the wind was merciless.

The sight of the stables in the distance caught her eye, and she quickened her pace. She was almost to the small building they used for storing dyed wool where she would get a reprieve from the merciless gusts.

She knew the surrounding area well. In the time since she'd arrived, she'd spent hours combing through the area, plotting out an escape if necessary. Just over the hill opposite the stables is where the boats were kept. Small ones she could operate. She already knew the one she would take if need be.

Excited shouts came from the stable, muffled by the howling winds. Her step faltered.

"Coira!" Innes's voice rang out.

A shrill cry laced with fear answered the call. "Grandmother!"

Coira raced through the field. Her little legs blurred with her speed, chubby arms outstretched as she screeched in panicked wails. Mariel dropped the basket and was already darting down the steep hill when she saw the large horse thundering behind Coira. He matched her turns and dodges, easily closing the distance between them as breath steamed from his nose like billowing smoke.

Mariel charged across the field, her feet barely touching the ground in her determination to place herself between Coira and the beast before it was too late.

Mariel streaked across the stretch of grass to where the powerful horse charged. The little girl stumbled over the hem of her plain brown dress and tumbled to the ground in a pile of small arms and legs, flailing and shrieking pitifully.

The horse's shadow loomed over her. The beast reared back on powerful hindquarters, his front legs savage as they slashed the empty air.

A burst of energy propelled Mariel forward, driving her burning muscles onward as she dove toward the ground. She threw her body over Coira, wrapped the child in the shield of her arms, and rolled them both away. Hooves slammed into the soft ground where Coira's head had been and the earth shuddered.

Without waiting for a second attack, Mariel scrambled to her feet with the little girl still clutched against her. A crude wooden fence lay on the other end of the field. Its slats were crooked and leaned against one another, but it was their only hope for escape.

Mariel did not hesitate. She darted forward with the girl cradled against her chest, focus aimed on the high fence. The horse thundered closer, and the grass shivered under Mariel's feet. Almost there. Her legs quivered with exertion, but she refused to give up.

Using the last of her energy, she leapt into the air toward the fence. Her feet kicked against the wooden planks and shot her higher. She didn't think about what needed to be done, she fell back on her rigorous training. Her hand darted out automatically, bracing their weight and pushing them over the top of the fence to where they landed safe on the other side.

Through the visible gaps of their barrier, Mariel saw the horse rear back in anger. His hooves stomped the worn soil and his eyes rolled. With a toss of his head, he charged toward the rickety fence.

Mariel's heart sank. He would burst through the aged wood without issue. Her muscles trembled with such exhaustion she could barely stand. Outrunning him was impossible.

In a desperate move to protect the girl from as much impact as possible, Mariel crouched to the ground with her back toward the fence and wrapped Coira tight one final time.

Mariel waited for the crack of rotted wood as the fence splintered apart. She waited for the victorious snort of the beast as it charged at them in their vulnerable position. She waited and yet they never came.

"Mariel." Colin's voice sounded overhead. "We've caught him. Ye can let her go."

Her eyes flew open and glanced to the empty field beyond the slatted fence. A whimper sounded from her arms. Coira. Mariel released her grip on the girl and scanned over the delicate face and tiny limbs. Aside from bits of grass and dirt clinging to her dress, the girl appeared unharmed.

Mariel's chest burned with the breath she hadn't realized she'd been holding. The air rasped from her tight chest and sent her heart hammering anew.

Had the horse not been caught, he surely would have broken through the rickety fence.

They would have been killed.

Then Jack would have no one.

The strength drained from Mariel's body, and it was only the bones within that left her standing upright by some miracle.

Innes appeared beside her and grasped Coira by the shoulders, inspecting her as Mariel had done. Innes's gnarled hand patted one chubby cheek before she straightened and faced Mariel.

The old woman's face was flushed.

"Thank ye." She spoke in English thickened by lack of use. "I dinna know how ye did it. I dinna care. Ye risked yerself to save my Coira." She looked down, her translucent lips pressed against one another. When she looked up, unshed tears shimmered in the depths of her icy blue eyes. "I willna forget this."

Mariel's mouth fell open, yet nothing came out. Innes did not appear to want a response. She turned, gathered the softly sobbing Coira into her arms, and shuffled away.

"Ye saved her." Colin squeezed Mariel's shoulder, breaking her from her trance.

She watched the little blond head nuzzle into Innes's sturdy chest, and Mariel's heart swelled with a lightness she had not known in some time. She had saved a young life with the very skills she had been taught to kill with.

Mariel turned toward Colin's charming smile. "It was just luck," she said, brushing off the compliment and heading back toward her fallen basket with Colin at her side. "Anyone would have done the same had they been closer." Her legs wobbled with the exertion of her feat. And with the fear of everything she almost lost.

Colin edged closer to her as if sensing her depleted strength. "I've no ever seen someone leap a fence like that. Where did ye learn how to do that?"

Mariel lifted the discarded basket to her hip and regarded him from of the corner of her eye, suddenly wary. Was he asking in true curiosity or suspicion?

"I played with boys when I was younger. If you couldn't jump a fence, you got left behind." She gave him a playful wink and added, "I never got left behind."

He grinned down at her and stopped in front of the small hut. "I can see that. I bet ye gave those lads quite a challenge."

Before she could grasp the handle, Colin tugged the door

open for her. Mariel shifted the basked to the front of her hips and angled her way into the doorway. The room was cold inside. Cold and dark and reeking of soggy wode. The sudden loss of sunlight left her momentarily blinded. She patted her hands around for the baskets of wool until her fingers skimmed the smooth braiding of wood, and she knew she had the one she sought. She lifted it and felt its weight pulled from her hands.

"I'll get that for ye," Colin said in the darkness.

She glanced at him as they exited the narrow building, noting the lazy lopsided smile and the flash of a dimple.

Almost two months had passed, and she had made little progress with Kieran. That he was no longer speaking to her only exacerbated the issue. Colin, however, seemed willing and eager to accommodate her in any way possible.

Guilt churned in her stomach and left her palms damp. She did not have the luxury of being fair. Time was running out and Jack was counting on her.

If she could not use Colin to make Kieran jealous enough to speak to her again, then perhaps she could glean the information from Colin and bypass Kieran all together.

If neither plan worked, she would be on her own to save Jack.

Mariel rested her hand on Colin's bulging forearm. "You're very strong. I'm sure the basket weighs nothing to you." She tilted her head to the side so he could glimpse the smooth expanse of her neck.

The proud puff of his chest let her know the seed of seduction was already beginning to grow. Certainly it took almost no encouragement.

Mariel swallowed the bitterness of her shame and pressed her control. "I've never told you before, but your friendship means a lot to me." Her hand lingered on his arm, a quiet indication to let him know that by friendship, she referred to something more. "I don't have many friends here, but I'm glad I have you."

He eased the basket into one arm and slid his free hand around her waist. "My friendship is always yers to be had, my lady."

They stepped into the courtyard, and she allowed herself to be pulled closer to him. "I look forward to seeing you at supper tonight, Colin." She lifted the weight of the basket from him and let her hands caress his.

His green eyes burned a path of interest down the length of her body. "No as much as I do."

.   .   .

That evening at supper, Mariel positioned herself beside Colin and in the direct line of Kieran. By the end of the meal, Colin's eyes were bleary, and his speech garbled with drink. It had taken a considerable amount of whisky and persuasion to get him to such a state. He leaned the side of his head against his fist with an arm propped against the table and gave her a crooked smile. Doubtless many a woman had fallen for that charming grin.

But Mariel was not interested in love or flirtation. Her prize sat at the head of the table, silent and brooding—and completely oblivious of her presence.

"Ye're beautiful, Mariel," Colin slurred.

She smiled in response to the compliment. Considerable care had been taken with her appearance. A simple violet gown of silk had been chosen for the way it hugged her body and complimented her smooth skin. Her hair was left unbound and cascaded down her back in glossy waves. The way Kieran liked it.

"And you are a handsome man. So strong, intelligent," she purred, "important." She waited for her words to take effect through his whisky infused haze. "I bet you know everything there is to know about Skye...even things you shouldn't." A well-placed giggle took the stark questioning from her words. Men were more apt to disclose information when they assumed a woman was harmless and silly.

His eyebrow cocked arrogantly. "That I do. I help Kieran with all of his private business. There's no one who knows more, save Kieran himself."

Her heart flinched at Colin's obvious pride. She swirled the remnants of wine in her cup, but did not drink it. Everything soured in her stomach, churned into bitter disgust. She hated this questioning, the use of people's trust. She wanted to run away from the hall and not stop until she was somewhere dark and cold. Somewhere her skin could prickle and ice the way her insides did.

But she could not. Instead she smiled at Colin and pressed further. "Then you are the perfect person to help me understand things here. Does the entire clan live here in the castle?"

"Ach, no! There are many more people living throughout the island, just no so easy to find."

That was exactly what she had assumed. "I bet you know where to find each and every one of them, don't you?" She leaned closer, her leg brushing his beneath the table.

His hooded gaze dipped to the low neckline of her dress. "We should go somewhere more private, aye? There are more important matters I'd like to…discuss."

"If we prolong it, you will enjoy it more." The caress of her lips against his hair added intimacy to her whispered words. The drink would see him to dark oblivion before he ever had a chance to touch her.

Her gaze flicked back to where Kieran sat at the head of the table and her heart sank. He was locked in deep conversation with Alec, his face turned away from her.

Jealousy, it appeared, did not work on him after all.

. . .

"If ye dinna get Colin out of here right now, I'm going to kill him," Kieran growled at Alec.

"Ye never laid claim to her." Alec rose from the table despite his words. "I'll find Bess to see to him."

Before Kieran could bark a scathing reply, Alec was already walking out the great hall. Mariel's laughter drifted to where he sat, on the dais—alone. The feminine, melodic tinkle pulled his attention toward the couple. Mariel's slender fingers brushed Colin's forearm, and Kieran's hand knotted into a hard fist. To those around them, their conversation did not appear out of the ordinary. From the way her eyes slanted in Colin's direction to the subtle touches shared between them, Kieran knew better. He took a swig of whisky, his knuckles white against the stem of his goblet.

Among his fellow clansmen, Mariel had changed from the hated outsider to the welcomed, honored guest, and from pressing him for his affection to falling prey to Colin's charm.

Grudgingly, he had to confess he had been impressed at her success with winning over his clan. It was a task not easily done. One presumed impossible for an Englishwoman.

Several people had stopped to speak with her throughout the evening with genuine smiles on their faces. Even Innes. Old, impenetrable Innes had actually bid her good evening as she'd passed.

Colin's hand slid beneath the table and a telltale blush colored Mariel's fair cheeks. Any sense of humor dissipated from Kieran's.

Where the hell was Alec with Bess?

Mariel leaned forward so her breasts brushed Colin's arm. Her lips were too close to Colin's ear. Kieran did not know what she said, but judging from the look on his old friend's face, he could damn well guess.

His heavy chair slid against the fresh rushes on the floor and sent the aroma of hay and herbs wafting up to greet him. He stalked forward, muscles taut with anger.

Colin glanced up at him with eyes red rimmed and bleary. He was as drunk as Kieran had ever seen him.

"Kieran! Will ye have a drink with us?" Colin slurred.

Mariel's smile was brittle, and he could not help but notice she did not join Colin in extending the invite. The familiar scent of rose caught him off guard, bringing with it a surge of feelings and unwelcome memories: the sweetness of her mouth beneath his tongue, the heat of her body against his, and the whimpering moan of her release. Kieran's hand clenched at his side.

She had promised herself to him and yet here she sat with his best friend and rival. Colin slid his hand around Mariel's waist and regarded Kieran. A silent indicator of his claim on Mariel.

Colin was drunk indeed.

Kieran's fist slammed on the table with such force, Colin's empty mug leapt up and clattered to the floor. "Get yer hand off her," Kieran growled.

Colin's eyes went wide, and he shifted his hand away as instructed. Mariel opened her mouth, doubtless with some sharp tongued retort. She never got a chance to speak.

"Ye will come with me to my study," Kieran demanded.

Her arms crossed defiantly over her chest

"Now!" he barked and turned to leave. She would follow. Of that he had no doubt.

• • •

Mariel shifted her weight from one foot to the other and waited in tortured silence. She scanned the room for the tenth time in an effort to avoid the stormy rage glinting in Kieran's black eyes. Several ledgers rested on the surface of a large desk that took up half of the room. Soft light glowed in metal sconces around the room, the subtle odor of oil thick and warm, but not unpleasant. Shelves of books lined the back wall and tempered the severity of the otherwise stark chamber.

She returned her gaze to the man in front of her and found he stared at her, his face unreadable as usual. The room was quiet, still. It frayed her nerves. She locked her hands on her hips and glared at him. "What is the meaning of this, Kieran?"

"What were ye doing with Colin?" His voice was unnaturally calm. If he meant it to cause her further unease, he'd succeeded.

"We were talking."

Kieran narrowed his eyes. "Why Colin?"

She arched her eyebrow. "You aren't speaking to me. He is."

"What did ye speak about?"

Mariel's unease grew. Did he suspect her? "What are you getting at, Kieran?"

"Dinna ye understand what ye do to me, Mariel?" His eyes flashed like chips of cold onyx in the soft golden light.

"No, actually, I don't." It was not a lie. Never before had she required so much effort to keep a man's attention.

Kieran closed the distance between them with a single step so that the heat of his torso scorched her. The intensity of his gaze burned a path down her body. "Ye wear a dress like this and ye dinna know what ye do to me?" He caught her against him, and his hand glided down to the curve of her bottom. When he spoke again, his voice was deeper, more sensual. "Ye kiss me with blatant desire and ye dinna think I crave more?" His fierce expression softened and he leaned forward, nuzzling her neck. His lips moved against her ear. "Ye come apart in my arms and ye dinna think the image willna haunt me?" His breath was warm against her sensitive skin, tempting.

Frustration knotted with the thrill of pleasure, and she backed away from the lure of his touch. "You refuse me time and again." She tried to swallow her anger and failed. "You haven't spoken to me in weeks, and yet you expect me to realize you still want me?"

"Ye dinna understand." A muscle worked in his jaw. "There is much ye dinna understand."

She searched his eyes, desperate to know his secrets, to obtain a trust she did not deserve. To end this before either of them would have to hurt more than they already would. "Make me understand."

He shook his head. "I canna."

Part of her was glad for his steadfast determination to keep his secrets, and yet the other part of her felt the hurried desperation of a ticking clock. Her time was running out.

Mariel gave a heavy sigh, as if the deep breath would cleanse her chest of its mounting pain. He made her feel like a better person than she was, and he held a tenderness that warmed a corner of her soul she never knew existed. Yet his repeated rejection stung that newfound vulnerability. The walls closed around her. She could take no more of his excuses.

She needed to get out of the room. Away from him lest she expose herself to more hurt.

She pushed past him and headed for the door. "If you'll

excuse me, Colin is waiting."

An iron grasp locked onto the crook of her elbow. "Damn it, Mariel," Kieran growled and spun her around to face him once more. "Ye belong to me."

Her heart skipped a beat. He wanted her. Mariel wrenched her arm from his hold but did not back down from the heat of his stare. "Then be a man and take what's yours."

The words flew out of her mouth without calculated thought or pause, the challenge borne of passion. Kieran's eyes darkened into pools of ink, and his muscles visibly tensed. He closed the distance she had put between them, his chest almost touching her face. His face hardened, his eyes flaring, and suddenly he resembled the fierce warrior he was. The flickering light of the fire danced shadows against his chiseled jawline, and, for the first time since she'd met him, Mariel felt the icy fingers of fear trickle down her spine.

"What did ye say?" he growled.

Mariel met his hard gaze, refusing to withdraw her challenge. "Take what's yours, Kieran."

His breath brushed her face, the spicy scent made her hunger for the caress of his tongue against hers, and her heart pound with anticipation.

He jerked her against him so her breasts pressed flat against the hardness of his chest. His hand caught her lower jaw and firmly forced her face up toward his. The rough calluses of his fingers rasped her cheek. His eyes burned into hers for one soul stopping moment before his lips crushed down on hers. His tongue slipped into her mouth as he pulled the length of her body against him.

It was a kiss of insistence, demanding payment for services promised.

It was a kiss of possession.

Chapter Twenty

Kieran slanted his lips over the silky warmth of Mariel's mouth. Rage powered his hunger to an overwhelming pitch. She had challenged his manhood.

He held her tight against him and urged her backward until he felt her bump against his desk. She claimed she wanted to be his.

She arched against him and gave a low moan.

His cock pulsed in time with the slow, rhythmic grinding of her hips until it strained between them. God, he never wanted a woman so badly.

Restraint lingered in the recesses of his mind even while his hands glided across the cool silk of her gown, memorizing her shape. If he had her, she would stay on Skye.

Her tongue stroked his, and her hands teased the flesh beneath the waistline of his plaid. If he had her, he would have to trust her.

One sweep of his arm cleared the desk of its contents. He grasped her round bottom and slid her up onto the smooth desktop.

His fingers raked up her naked legs, pushing her skirt to her hips. Her creamy thighs opened for him, and with one swipe of his finger, his decision was made.

Mariel's legs tightened around his hand and her breath came in shaky gasps. Gritting his teeth against the insistent throb of his cock, he rolled the pad of his thumb against the delicate little nub. Her cries echoed off the stone walls, and her hooded eyes sparkled with desire. His mouth fell upon her kiss-swollen lips once more, hungry to devour the sounds of her climax. She was so close to coming for him. The slightest touch and she would unravel in his arms.

But not yet. She did not understand the pain she had put him through. The haunted nights of longing, craving the feel of her skin naked against him and the relief only she could provide. Nor did she understand the rage her flirtation with Colin roused in him.

No, he would not let her off so easily.

Kieran withdrew his hand despite her whimper of protest. Muscles taut with restraint, he pressed himself against her, letting her feel the force of his erection through his plaid. Her long, shapely legs wrapped around his waist, and her heels pressed into his buttocks.

Her breasts heaved with the force of her labored breath, swelling lusciously above her gown. Unable to resist the temptation, Kieran tugged her bodice downward and groaned his victory as her breasts bounced free of their confines. He buried his face against the fullness of her bare bosom. His lips brushed the bud of her nipple and drew it deep within his mouth.

Her hands skimmed his stomach, burning a path of uncontrollable desire down to his loins. Her fingers dipped inside his kilt and closed around him. The coolness of her grasp against the raging heat of his cock was an excruciating balm for the lust that had preoccupied him since they met. Kieran groaned at the intense pleasure of her touch before he gripped her wrist and pulled her hand away.

"Enough," he said, his voice terse. This was his game and he was not about to relinquish the power.

"Please," she murmured against his ear.

"No yet," he growled.

His finger traced the slick cleft between her legs. Mariel moaned helplessly and trembled beneath him.

He released her hand and lifted his plaid. His stomach knotted in anticipation, his body tight as a bowstring. He rubbed the blunt edge of his arousal against her slick core. God help him, there was no stopping now.

This was what she wanted, nay demanded, and he would give it to her.

With a savage push, he sheathed himself completely inside her tight, wet heat and froze.

•   •   •

Mariel gasped sharply as her maidenhead tore beneath Kieran's powerful thrust. She thought she had prepared herself for the pain, and that she would be able to mask its existence, but the sting had been far more acute than she had expected. Desire melted away and left the ugly truth of reality in its stead.

She had deceived him, forced him to believe she was someone she was not. Thinking she could play the part when necessary. His body was taut beneath her fingertips, every muscle locked as he cursed low under his breath. He looked down at her, his black eyes wild.

"Ye were a maiden?" he asked incredulously.

She wanted to shrink under his gaze, cover her breasts, and hide away from him. Not trusting herself to speak, she gave a short nod.

He pulled out of her, the slight movement causing a wave of unwanted pleasure to roll through her. Evidence of her virginity smeared across his hardened phallus, glistening like a flag of shame before he covered himself with his kilt.

"Damn it, Mariel!" His fist slammed into the shelf beside him. A book fell to the floor with a hollow thud and broke the silence following his outburst. "Why did ye lie to me?" He turned his accusing stare on her.

She pulled her bodice over her exposed breasts and pushed off the desk onto shaky legs. Her skirt fell like a heavy curtain, shielding her disgrace from view.

"I didn't lie. You assumed," she hissed. The need to defend herself overwhelmed the burn of humiliation.

"Ye kept this secret from me, and ye're the one who is angry?" he roared, his accent thick with fury.

Heat flooded her cheeks. "You don't know a damned thing

about me, Kieran MacDonald. You don't know the life I have lived or what I've had to do to survive. You know nothing. You don't know what I sacrificed to keep my virginity, saving it like some... some..." She faltered. Unease overwhelmed the humiliated rage coursing through her. Too much had been said already.

She shoved past him, and this time he did not stop her as she wrenched the door open and fled into the hall. The soles of her shoes tapped against the stone floor, a slow steady rhythm that called attention to the erratic beat of her heart. Her vision blurred and turned the hall into a smear of grays as she blindly made her way to her room. She did not stop until she had the door bolted behind her, and she lay upon the bed with her cheeks pressed into the pillow. The cool surface soothed the heat of her face and helped clear her head enough to think.

Emotions raced through her, filling her with sorrow, shame, and the sad reality she had been too stubborn to admit. She was falling in love with Kieran MacDonald, the very man she had been sent to betray. A man of honor and value; one she had begun to look up to. And the more she learned about him, the more she respected him. He was everything she had wanted in her youth and everything she did not deserve now.

How foolish she had been for guarding her maidenhead as if it held any worth. The cost of keeping it had been higher than anticipated, and Jack was still paying the price. She had always resisted the ridiculous sums offered to her under the assumption that perhaps someday she could choose the man to give it to. A foolish girlhood notion a woman should have known better than to believe.

Mariel curled into a ball in the center of the bed. If Kieran shunned her, her options would be limited. The weight of Aaron's threat hung on her conscience and helpless tears pooled under the pillow beneath her cheek.

•   •   •

That next morning, Mariel waited for Kieran to rise and quietly followed him to the stables. It was perhaps a desperate move on her part, taking a chance that he might lead her where she needed to go, but she would rather face the chill of the dark morning than a bed where she tossed and turned in sleepless angst.

She peered from around the large trunk of a tree to where Kieran rode several paces away and tightened the plaid around her, not only for protection against the bitter wind, but also for the blend of colors that would blur her into the scenery.

One quick glance confirmed his ignorance. She moved quietly through the brush and squatted on trembling legs. How long had she been at this? An hour? Two?

The gray light of dawn had feathered into the brilliance of morning and sunlight speckled the sandy dirt at her feet.

Perhaps she had been foolish to follow Kieran on foot when he rode on horseback, but his pace had been slow enough to track, and she would have had difficulty hiding a horse on the sparse terrain.

Kieran climbed a hill in the distance and disappeared from view, giving Mariel an opportunity to dart across the landscape toward a pile of jagged rocks thrusting up through the tender earth. The ocean spread to her left, dazzling blue as it reflected the rays of the sun like a thousand glinting mirrors. The grass near her feet had long since slid away onto the beach and left a short cliff no taller than she. It was the perfect place to keep her presence hidden.

She slipped over the edge into safe obscurity. Though she moved forward with caution, layers of sand gave way beneath her feet. Still she did not stop, not until she could see at least the top of his dark head.

Kieran stopped and dismounted from his horse, his pace brisk as he headed toward something she could not see.

Mariel stood on her tiptoes and peered over the torn earth. He stood before the door of the small hut.

Smoke billowed from the chimney-peat by the rich aroma. The door flew open and a woman with long brown hair stepped out into the sunlight. She was young, beautiful, and eager to see Kieran if the wide, perfect smile was any indicator.

He opened his arms to the slender woman, and she ran

without hesitation into his embrace. His arms folded around her, and he pressed a kiss to the top of her head with an affectionate smile creasing his eyes. Mariel's stomach knotted.

She staggered backward, heedless of disclosing her presence. She had been deceived. Her lips curved in a mirthless smirk at the irony of her predicament. The man so honorable and moral was as much a liar and a fraud as she.

What a fool she was to have thought herself in love, to have thought he might actually harbor feelings for her. And all the while he had a woman here on Skye. Was it any wonder he had not wanted Mariel to come?

The painful throb of her heart echoed in the ache between her legs from the gift she had so foolishly bestowed upon him.

Perhaps killing him would be an easier feat than expected. In fact, at that point she was almost looking forward to it. Almost.

"Momma!" A little voice pulled her attention and caught the tattered remains of her heart.

A young boy's face appeared at the doorway, his eyes black as onyx in his small face.

Kieran had a son.

Chapter Twenty-One

Kieran scrubbed his face with his hands and heaved a deep sigh. The ride home had taken an eternity, and the lack of sleep was catching up with him. What a long damn night, followed by a long damn day.

"Ye asked for me?" Alec gave him a strange look.

"Walk with me," Kieran said and strode toward the castle.

"Get Mariel and bring her to my solar whether she wants to come or no."

"That's what ye need me for?" Alec's eyebrow rose. "Do I need to drag her there?"

Kieran considered Alec's statement for a moment. "Ye very well might. I dinna care what it takes." Their heavy boots fell soundless upon the rushes as they entered the great hall.

Alec gave a nonchalant shrug and stalked off to obey the order he'd been given.

Kieran rubbed the tightness along the back of his neck. Were Mariel not so angry with him, he might have asked her to ease the tension the way she had in the past. Guilt flashed through him.

He turned down the hall toward his solar and found Colin leaning against the door frame with a dour look on his usually cheerful face.

He locked forearms with Colin and narrowed his eyes. "How do ye feel today?"

Colin winced. "Like my head's been split open."

Kieran squeezed his friend's forearm in an iron grip. "If ye touch Mariel again, yer head *will* be split open…with the blade of my sword."

"Ye dinna lay claim to her," Colin protested and tried to wrest his arm free.

Kieran released him with a solid shove that sent Colin sprawling awkwardly against the floor. "I am now. She's mine, and I'll kill any man who dares question that."

Ever the unflappable one, Colin gave an amused smirk. "Consider yer claim laid. Now help me up before I lose the contents of my stomach in front of yer door." He grinned. "And I just ate a whole trencher of food."

Kieran extended a hand to help his friend to his feet. "If ye were anyone else, ye'd already be dead."

"I know, I know." He clapped Kieran on the back and strode down the hall, whistling a jaunty tune.

Kieran smiled in spite of himself and he closed the door behind him. How was it Colin always seemed to slip out of trouble as easily as he found his way into it? Kieran sank into the chair behind his desk.

The ledgers and journals he had swept to the ground the night before had been piled in a neat stack. A cool breeze filtered in through the open shutters and filled the room with the salty, wet tang of the ocean. His gaze wandered to the edge of the desk where he'd held Mariel last night.

Kieran looked out the window to the crashing waves below. He recalled her surprise when he made her come that first time, the euphoric wonder at the pleasure he'd brought her. Damn it, he should have known.

Kieran braced his hands against the wall until the stone bit into his palms.

She had been right. He knew nothing about her life. With the little bit he did know about her past, he could not imagine what she'd had to endure to preserve her virginity but was certain it came at an exorbitant price.

Mariel's voice echoed down the hall and the few words he caught were certainly nothing that would come from a lady's mouth. The door burst open, and in walked Alec with Mariel flung over his shoulder.

Her fists peppered Alec's large back with futile abandon.

"Set me down or I'll…"

"Ye'll no do anything." Alec set her to her feet. "We're already here."

Mariel flung her thick black braid over her shoulder and straightened her gown. Brilliant red cheeks were the only indication of how humiliated her arrival had left her. Her gaze settled on the desk and immediately flicked away as though the very sight of it burned her eyes.

Kieran nodded to Alec, who quickly took the offer to escape and closed the door behind him. Silence shrouded the room and once again Kieran found himself face-to-face with Mariel, lacking the words to express what he wanted to say.

He knew what he wanted to do. He wanted to pull her into his arms and kiss away the hurt he'd caused her, to gently right the wrong he had so roughly done.

Bitter anger laced her glare. What he wanted was not what she needed.

"Mariel, we need to talk about last night," he said more gruffly than he had intended. Apologizing had never been his strong suit.

He recognized the stubborn lift to her chin. She was not going to make this easy.

He cleared his throat, trying to figure out where to begin. "I dinna know ye were a maiden—"

She held up her hand. "Save your petty apology for someone who is willing to listen. You'll find naught but deaf ears with me."

He shifted his weight from one foot to the other in a pathetic attempt to hide the frustration of his failed start. Brennan had always been the stronger of the two when it came to conversation and charisma. What would he have done in this situation?

"Mariel…" he began again, unsure of what to say beyond that.

"Save your lies," she said vehemently and wrenched the door open.

His palm slapped against the heavy wood with a force that

wrenched the latch from Mariel's hand and slammed the door shut. Mariel stared up at him in silenced shock. Her fingers were still locked in front of her where she'd held the door.

"I should no have let ye leave last night, and I will be damned if I let ye leave now."

She backed away from him and let her hand drop. "I don't want to hear what you have to say."

"I hurt you," he stated, trying to let her know he understood.

She did not attempt to hide the raw pain in her luminous gaze. Or perhaps she did. He drew a deep breath to clear the ache in his chest.

"You have no idea how much you've hurt me," she said in a hoarse whisper.

"I dinna know." He moved forward, his hand poised to cradle the softness of her cheek. "But I want to."

She flinched from his touch.

He focused on keeping his voice level. "Had ye told me ye were a virgin, I wouldna have been so rough. Ye have to understand, I dinna mean to hurt ye."

She regarded him with icy contempt. "And what of your wife? Did you mean to hurt her when you took me last night? Did you mean to hurt me when you lied to me and said you had no woman?"

Kieran stared at her for a moment and tried to think around the throbbing in his head. What the hell was she talking about?

"Wife?" He shook his head to clear it. "Mariel, I dinna know what ye mean."

"I saw you." She looked away, but not before he saw the tears pooling in her eyes. "You hugged her and kissed the top of her head while your little boy watched from the house."

Cold realization snaked down his spine. How had she seen that? He had been so careful.

Kieran narrowed his eyes at her. "Ye saw this? With yer own eyes?"

She met the challenge of his gaze. "I did."

"And how did ye see it?" He tightened his fist at his side, struggling to keep his anger restrained.

"I followed you. I felt like you were hiding something from me, and so I followed when you left the castle." Her stoicism faltered, and her delicate white fingers worried the fabric of her skirt.

The dam to his rage broke. "Ye had no right," he began, his voice raising.

"I did," she interrupted. "You said last night that I belonged to you."

Hope and torment mingled in the stormy depths of her eyes, disarming his fury and bringing him back to the reason he had summoned her. Enough hurt had been unleashed in that room.

He took a step closer and lowered his voice. She eyed him warily, but did not move away. "I did say ye belong to me and ye do. What ye saw today, it isna what ye think." Mariel had spoken similar words to him. "But the lass ye saw is dear to my heart, and I'd like for ye to meet her."

Mariel's brows knit together. "I don't understand."

He met her gaze with unflinching stare. "After we eat, I'll have the horses saddled, and then ye can come with me to meet my sister."

·   ·   ·

Mariel's hips rocked with the lazy sway of the horse beneath her. Kieran rode silently beside her as they followed the path he had taken only hours before. Waves crashed against the shore with an erratic rhythm and birds sang out in the distance. The breeze was sticky with moisture from the ocean and ominous dark clouds crowded the sky overhead.

"Why doesn't your sister live in the castle with the rest of the clan?" Mariel asked.

Kieran looked thoughtful for a moment before answering. "She doesna feel safe there."

Mariel waited for Kieran to continue. When he did not, she pressed him out of curiosity. "Why not?"

His hands tightened on the reigns perceptibly, and his

mouth pressed in a thin line.

Mariel shifted in her saddle, sorry to have asked such an unwelcome question. "We don't have to discuss it if you prefer to not to."

His gaze met hers, his expression weary. "Perhaps if I tell ye, ye will understand the hatred my people have for the English and realize why the clan made things difficult when ye first arrived." He relaxed his grip on the reins, his hard stare set on the invisible path ahead of them. "Several years ago, an English noble convinced my sister to be his wife. She fell for his lies and left for England. We didna hear from her for years. Truthfully, after centuries of crimes delivered at the hands of the English, we considered her one of them and dinna think of her often." He smirked. "Sounds cruel, but we are a hard lot, and she made her own decisions.

"Before the snow began to fall this year, I received a message from the MacKinnons informing me that my sister was with them and in dire need of help. I went to her as quickly as I could." His gaze was distant with memory.

"When I saw her, she was..." He shook his head and exhaled deeply. "She had a small boy with her."

Kieran looked directly at Mariel. "My nephew—no my son. I havena fathered any bairns, aye?"

Heat crept over her cheeks, though whether from quiet pleasure or embarrassment, she did not know. She nodded, fearful speaking might shatter the fragile and candid speech he so rarely displayed.

He shifted his gaze toward the road once more. "She dinna want to talk, no at first, but I finally convinced her she needed to. I needed to know what happened." A muscle worked in his jaw. "That bastard of a husband beat her every day she was on English soil. She endured it for years until he raised a hand to their son, then she escaped. No a day goes by that she doesna check behind her back to see if he is following her. She thinks if she lives in the castle, he'll find her and drag her back to England."

The creaking of their saddles filled the silence as Mariel

absorbed what Kieran had told her. Emotion tightened in her chest for the woman she would soon meet.

"You don't like her so far away because you can't protect her," Mariel said softly.

Kieran's shoulders were squared, his body taut with rage. "Maybe ye can talk some sense into her."

He nudged his horse up a steep hill to where the humble whitewashed hut sat. Mariel didn't speak again as he tied off their horses, and they walked the distance toward the plank door.

Her stomach knotted.

Kieran rapped a series of well-timed knocks against the smooth wood. The door opened, and a friendly face appeared in the doorway. Emerald green eyes crinkled with delight as they settled on Mariel, and a wide smile spread over the woman's comely face.

"You must be Mariel." The woman spoke with a melodic lilt that hovered somewhere between Scots and English. "It's so wonderful to finally meet you." Her thin arms caught Mariel in a strong embrace.

Where Kieran was cold and closed off, his sister was warm and open. Mariel smiled in spite of herself and breathed in the clean scent of sunshine and home that seemed to emanate from the slender woman.

"Oh, do come in. I have so much I'd like to say to you."

Mariel allowed herself to be pulled into the small house. Kieran's sister laid a dagger on a table beside the door with a heavy clunk.

Her home was simple, but cheerfully so. A small table sat in the center of the room surrounded by three wooden chairs. Several cabinets dotted the wall and a simple bed was pushed into the corner. Various herbs hung from the rafters and left the air in the small home comforting.

Kieran walked in behind them, followed by the boy she had seen that morning. The boy kept his small, dark gaze fixed on her as he stalked over to his mother with a noticeable limp and stood in front of her, his stance protective.

Kieran's sister ruffled her son's hair and smiled down at

him. "This sweaty little boy is my son, Dougal."

Dougal.

The hairs on the back of Mariel's neck stood on end. *No.*

The air in the cabin grew thin.

It couldn't be.

"I'm afraid I don't know your name," Mariel heard herself say.

"Ach, forgive my terrible manners." Kieran's sister gave a wide grin, her face open and genuinely sweet. "I'm Blair."

Chapter Twenty-Two

Kieran leaned his back against the wall as Dougal sat beside Mariel's feet. The little boy tugged the hem of her dress, his face earnest. She bent to the boy's height with a smile and let him whisper in her ear.

"All right, but this is the last time," Mariel said. She pulled a coin from her pocket, pushed her hands together, and then opened them with dramatic flourish. The coin had disappeared. While Dougal searched her arms for where she had hidden it, she plucked the coin from behind his ear.

His high-pitched laughter filled the room as he clapped his hands. "Again! Again!"

Blair stood up from the table and joined Kieran as Mariel agreed to do the trick "one last time."

His sister grinned up at him. "I like her, Kieran. I like her a lot."

"Ye seem to get along well, but then I knew ye would. It's good to see ye have someone to talk to."

The flush of happiness and the sparkle in Blair's eyes were evidence enough that he had made the right decision in trusting Mariel. He had been a fool for keeping Blair and Dougal a secret from her for so long.

"She would be a very good mother," Blair mused.

Kieran didn't respond as he watched Mariel laugh and allow herself to be pulled to the ground beside Dougal. She would be as patient with her own children and as fiercely protective of them as she had been with Coira. Kieran felt a smile tug his lips at the thought of her cradling his child.

"I think what I like best about her though," Blair continued, "is the way she looks at you." She made a point of peering up at him. "And the way you look at her."

Kieran grunted and crossed his arms over his chest. "I dinna know what ye're talking about."

"You need a wife and Caisteal Camus has been too long without a mistress. Mariel—"

"It wouldna be without a mistress if ye lived with us."

Her smooth brow puckered. "You know why I can't."

Of course he knew. They had this conversation every time he visited. "It's foolish, Blair. If ye lived in the castle I could offer ye better protection. There is no one out here to help if—"

A clap of thunder sounded overhead with a force that rattled the dishes on the shelves. Kieran peered out the small window. Drops had not yet begun to fall, but the dark clouds overhead were angry, and the air crackled with the impending storm. If they left now and pushed the horses, they could arrive at the castle before the rain started.

"We need to go. I need to be back and dinna want to get trapped in the storm. But this conversation isna over, aye?"

"It never is," she said with a good natured smile. "You could stay here. Both of you could." Her eyes lit with a hope that tugged at Kieran's heart.

He knew she was lonely. He also realized that the time she'd spent with Mariel reminded her how lonely she truly was. All the more reason for her to come live in the castle with a majority of their clan. But that was a point to bring up another time. For now, he and Mariel needed to leave.

"I wish we could stay, but we need to return." He lowered his voice. "Mariel and I have a conversation left unfinished. I'd like to speak with her privately." He glanced up at Mariel and caught her staring at him from her spot on the floor. She quickly dropped her gaze and bent over a carved sheep with a feigned preoccupation that didn't fool him.

Blair looked between him and Mariel with an infuriating grin on her face. "Don't let me stop you." She rested her hand on his forearm and looked up at him with a wide, earnest gaze. "Please promise you'll bring her back here again. Soon."

"Aye, I promise." His words were almost drowned out by another crack of thunder, pressing the urgency of their departure.

.   .   .

Kieran squinted his eyes against the driving force of the rain and scanned the horizon through his blurred vision. Lightning slashed through yellow gray skies, followed by another crash of thunder. The spitting precipitation had turned into fat droplets that stung his face and made seeing difficult.

The castle was still quite a distance away. He considered their options to gauge if they could push their horses forward and beat the worst of the storm or if they should seek shelter nearby.

A chip of ice bounced off his knuckle. Several more frozen chunks descended from above and sprang harmlessly from the flanks of their horses.

He had seen storms like this before and knew the hail could reach sizes as large as his fist. The chances were slim, but certainly not what he was willing to risk.

Their salvation lay at the base of the hill in the distance, in the small white building he could just make out. They could be there in minutes.

"Mariel!" he bellowed over the howling storm and jerked his head toward the hut.

She gave a nod from beneath the plaid covering her head and snapped her reins.

The horses needed little encouragement and streaked across the landscape as the chunks of ice grew larger. When the house was a stone's throw away, Kieran halted his horse and leapt from the saddle. A makeshift shelter with a slatted roof sat off to the side.

Mariel slid from her saddle and ran toward the house while he gathered the horses, their reins slick and water logged beneath his palm. Hail popped against the roof of the crude stable.

Once he was satisfied the horses were safe and secure, he darted into the house and slammed the door shut against the deafening roar of the storm. Mariel stood with her back to him, facing the smoldering hearth she had stoked to life. The smoky scent of peat permeated the room with a warm comfort that reminded him of his boyhood days.

Her soft voice was loud in the heavy silence of the room. "Does someone live here?"

"They did, but no anymore. I believe this was Duncan's home. He was getting on in age and moved to the castle for convenience." Kieran strode around the walls, checking for cracks and leaks, the scuff of his shoes echoing in the open room.

Despite the strength of the storm, the thatch roof did not let in any water, nor did the blustering wind appear to be seeping in. Kieran ran his fingers over the smooth wooden shutters to ensure their strength and nodded to himself with satisfaction. Their shelter was in good repair and would do well as they waited out the storm.

He kicked his toe against a pile of hay in the corner and saw no movement. Another good sign. If the hay was free of vermin, they would not need to sleep on the floor if the storm raged on through the night.

He joined Mariel in front of the hearth, and the comfortable warmth of the fire bloomed against his chest. Her damp hair had begun to dry and curled in soft, dark waves against her porcelain skin. Her gaze, he noticed, was fixed on the curl of smoke rising from the glowing peat.

Kieran gently pulled Mariel's plaid from her shoulder to dry. She jerked away and gave a startled gasp, and then a sheepish smile lit her face.

"Sorry," she murmured and handed him the length of sodden wool.

She had turned her attention back to the fire with her lower lip tucked between her teeth. While the storm had been unexpected, he was grateful for the opportunity to spend time with her. Uninterrupted. Alone.

A chill ran down Kieran's back and prickled the flesh on his arms. If he was going to be warm any time soon, he would need to get out of his wet clothing. Heat spread through his groin.

They both would.

Anticipation fired through him as he imagined pulling the clinging fabric from her skin. He kicked off his soggy boots and peeled the leine over his head. Her creamy skin would glow like a pearl in the soft light with every beautiful curve bared for his appreciation.

He glanced over to find her still staring into the hearth and something heavy pressed within his chest.

Her gaze was unseeing, her lips pursed together, and her brow furrowed. Something weighed on her mind, and he knew exactly what it was.

Mariel did not fight the onslaught of guilt. She wallowed in it until the burden exacted the punishment befitting her tarnished soul. Her thoughts filled with the recollection of Blair's gentle demeanor and Dougal's sweet innocence.

He was so much like Jack.

Her heart flinched. Blair and Dougal were not the political refugees she had assumed them to be, and certainly they were not men.

Armed with the knowledge of their history, she could easily guess the client who paid Aaron so handsomely for her to be sent on this assignment. Nor was there any doubt in her mind what Lord Hampton would do once he was reunited with his wife and son. Chills raced down her back despite the blazing heat of the fire.

Jack.

She drew a painful breath and held it, as if the act could ease the ache of her heart. If there were an option between her life and his, she would gladly sacrifice herself. But to surrender a woman and child who had already endured such sadness and abuse—the option was as unthinkable as abandoning Jack.

If she kept their whereabouts unknown, she could save them all, but the cost...

She glanced miserably up at Kieran and her breath caught. His naked torso rippled in the golden light of the fire. Water dripped from the tips of his hair and trailed down his powerful chest.

His eyes shone onyx in the firelight, and he gazed at her expectantly. Had he spoken?

Heat warmed her cold cheeks. "Did you say something?"

"Did ye get distracted by something?" A knowing smile tugged at the corner of his lips.

She wished she could smile, laugh the situation off as easily as his comment was made. But she was hollow inside-a gilded box of dark secrets that housed everything worthless.

The grin slid from Kieran's face, and he regarded her with an earnest expression. "I'm glad we have this time alone. There's much I wish to say to ye." He gave a tired sigh. "I introduced ye to Blair and ye know what they've gone through."

She flinched at his words. She knew all too well.

"That English bastard used her. He hurt her." His jaw clenched. "I dinna want ye to come to Skye because I had promised them my protection." He stepped closer and his fingers trailed down Mariel's jawline. The tender look in his eyes pierced her heart. "If I allowed myself to have ye and then forced ye away from Skye before we arrived, I'd be no better than him." He spoke softly as if he were afraid of scaring her off. "I've no ever wanted to cause ye any hurt."

His hand dropped away from her face. "But I did. I saw it in yer eyes and heard it in yer cry. And then I shunned ye when I was angry with myself." He shook his head, his mouth set in a hard line.

Mariel watched him carefully, so consumed in her own spiral of misery that it took a moment to realize what he spoke of. Last night. Her virginity. That moment seemed a world away, her shame and humiliation so insignificant to the precipice she stood before now.

"Kieran, you could never be like Blair's husband. This pain I feel, it's not anything you've done, it's…" she tapered off, unsure of what to say, of what she could say.

A look of confusion passed over his features, but he remained silent.

"I didn't know all this would happen." The last word caught in her throat, and a hot tear slid down her cheek. "Not that I knew what to expect when I came to Scotland, but it certainly wasn't this. Even you." She looked up at him, silently pleading for him to hear the hidden truth in what she said. "I never expected you to be a man so respected by his people. A man I could admire for his integrity. And Blair...I was so grievously wrong in my initial assumption. Looking back, there is no way I could have known and yet..."

Breathing became difficult as the pain in her chest intensified. "Kieran, how could you ever possibly forgive me?"

"Lass, it was a simple mistake. I harbor no resentment." His thumb brushed her cheek where the tear had fallen. "Ye dinna need to be afraid of anything, especially no me."

She wanted to believe him. She wanted to trust him with her secret as he had trusted her with his.

"It's...complicated," she said.

He smirked. "I know complicated verra well."

His arms came around her, pulling her into the strength of his embrace. The weight of his hand stroked the back of her head and threaded through her hair as the familiar spicy scent of him enveloped her. She tried to resist the tender touch, but his soothing caress did not relent until her head lay against the powerful expanse of his chest.

"I protect what's mine, Mariel." His voice rumbled against her cheek. "No one will hurt ye. No while I'm around."

"There is so much you don't know," she murmured miserably against the cool skin of his chest. Yet she had not the courage to tell him, even now.

She was not worthy of the comfort he offered.

"Why dinna ye tell me ye were a virgin?" The question was sincere and lacked the accusation she'd feared the night before.

A fresh wave of shame brought the burn of tears stinging against her eyelids. "If you knew I was a maiden, you would think better of me than I deserve."

He pulled her back and gazed at her, his black eyes fierce. "Mariel, dinna ever say anything like that. No matter what ye've done in yer past, ye are a good woman." Before she could protest, he continued. "Ye are intelligent and witty, and ye have this way of making people smile, even Innes and she hasna smiled in a decade." He tilted her face up so her lips were a hair's breadth away from his. "And ye are so verra, verra beautiful."

The conviction behind his words coiled her in a sense of security she had not known for a long time. Deep down, she recognized the feeling was a façade, but for that one small moment, she wanted to fall under its spell. She sighed and sank against him so the heat of his naked flesh warmed her icy fingers, and the comfort of his embrace masked the guilt and fear within her emptiness.

The storm howled outside and battered the windows with its rage while the rain whipped against the small house. In Kieran's arms, she was dry and safe.

"I dinna want to hurt ye." His breath was warm against her mouth, and his hand settled on her hip where the wound had finally healed.

"No, you won't hurt me." She closed her eyes against the blister of remorse.

"I've hurt ye verra much already." Sorrow laced his words. "I confess I'm afraid to cause ye more pain."

She blinked her eyes open and found his gaze sincere and shrouded with guilt.

"You won't," she reassured him again.

Relief crossed his features. He nuzzled her neck, breathing deep as he buried his face against her hair. "Ye want this?"

Her body pounded with need in response to the caress. She needed this. For the comfort, for the love, for all the glorious things she did not deserve and yet could not stop herself from wanting. As if the flames of his affection could sear away the guilt and shame from her ugly soul. May God have mercy on her, she could not say no.

Chapter Twenty-Three

Kieran pressed a kiss to the silky warmth of Mariel's neck. Her scent hovered over the pungent aroma of peat. That subtle perfume, it drove him crazy.

"I want this." Her fingers traced the line of his jaw. She pulled his face up and rested her forehead against his. "I want you."

Her lips were a breath away from his. He could restrain himself no longer. He wanted to feel those lips on his, against his skin. Against his body.

He cradled the back of her head in his hand, tangling his fingers in the drying silk of her hair. His chin inched forward and brushed the softness of her lips before gently parting her mouth with his own. He tightened his grip on her, need hammering through him as he swept his tongue into her mouth. A soft moan sounded in the back of her throat and sent a fire scorching through his veins.

God, he loved the little sounds she made.

Cold hands unfurled against his chest as she rose on her tiptoes and stroked his tongue with hers. His bollocks tightened. For a woman who claimed to be ignorant to her effect on him, she certainly seemed to know what she was doing.

"You're so warm," she murmured against his lips.

Her palms skimmed the expanse of his torso, and his skin prickled with heightened sensitivity. One of her fingernails grazed his nipple, and his breath sucked in through his teeth.

He grasped her round bottom. The fabric of her gown was soaked through, cold. "Wet clothes," he murmured. "Ye willna get warm." His own sodden kilt chafed against the strain of his erection. "Ye need to undress." The last word ended on a groan.

Every muscle tensed with a fine thread of self-control. His body ached for what he had sampled the night before. He wanted to rip the gown from her body and plunge deep inside her.

His chest swelled against the breath he locked in his lungs for restraint. With careful deliberation, he plucked the ties of her gown until the overdress hung loose around her. His lips captured hers in a slow, hungry kiss and his fingers brushed the sleeves from her shoulders, peeling the wet wool off her.

He met her wide, violet gaze and saw an open vulnerability there. Gone was the confident seductress, and in her place was a real woman whose innocence could not be contested-one with a shy smile and flushed cheeks.

One whose sark was rendered transparent by rainwater where it plastered against her shapely curves.

Ripples of useless fabric puckered across the smooth skin his fingers ached to stroke. Kieran tried to swallow and found he could not. The baggy underdress meant to hide everything, hid absolutely nothing.

He pulled the delicate ribbon from its bow and ran his finger along the neckline until it widened enough to slide down the length of her body. If it joined the puddle of clothing at her feet, he did not notice.

Her body glowed in the soft light and sparkled like a thousand gems where rain clung to her flesh. Her long black hair hung unbound to her narrow waist and parted over rosy nipples drawn tight against the cold.

His hands skimmed over her curves, icy and slick. She would not be cold for long. He would see to that.

Her hand slid a slow, teasing path down his stomach to where his kilt was belted around his waist. Slowly, achingly, she threaded the leather through the metal clasp and let the belt clatter to the floor. The wet kilt spiraled off his waist to the floor with a graceless splat.

Her frigid skin against the raging heat of his cock was a bittersweet relief that cooled and heated all at once. Desire pounded in his ears and pulsed against her belly, demanding he slake the lust that had haunted him for two months. Two long months.

He would have her this day.

Kieran swept her legs from beneath her and cradled her slight weight in his arms. The pile of hay was not the grand bed she deserved, but in a stark room with naught but wet cloth to cushion them from the hard floor, it would have to suffice.

He lowered her to their makeshift bed and the sweet scent of hay rose up around them. She laid back, her shy gaze fixed upon him. Her breasts rose and fell with each quickened breath. She was nervous. And judging from the unaccustomed pulse in his gut, perhaps he was too.

He stretched his body over hers, enough to feel the heat of her skin against his own, but not close enough to touch. He dared not, lest he lose himself to lust. His lips nuzzled the softness of hers. Once. Twice. She gave a little whimper of protest and lifted her chin toward his mouth. Her efforts were in vain. He would not give in so easily to temptation this time, not until he had seen to her pleasure.

His fingers trailed over the coolness of her damp skin, tracing the heavy fullness of her breast before he suckled the cold pebble of her nipple into his mouth. She gave a sharp gasp and arched her back. Her breasts thrust forward, goading him, begging for more. He circled the warming bud with his tongue and bit back a grin. If she enjoyed this, she would truly enjoy what he intended to do next.

He trailed kisses down her flat stomach until the downy hair of her sex grazed his chin. His fingers stroked the skin inside her thighs, easing higher and higher until her legs parted for him. Sweat prickled his brow.

He let the warmth of his lips brush her inner thigh and her breath caught. She stiffened beneath his touch. He would not be dissuaded.

He grasped the curve of her bottom, holding her captive and he pressed his lips against the heady fragrance of her arousal. His heart raced and he plunged his tongue inside her tangy, honeyed depths.

Heat balled in Mariel's stomach and threaded through her body until her palms burned with it. She moaned and threw her head back in surrender to the waves of pleasure lapping against her molten core. Kieran's finger slid inside of her, gently stretching her. Preparing her for him.

No longer modest, she wound her hands through his hair and cradled his head against her while his merciless tongue of fire flicked against the wild pulse between her legs.

"Kieran," she whimpered. Warmth tingled along her feet, her hands, coiled in her belly. Her muscles tensed in preparation for her impending release.

"Yes," he growled against her. He strengthened his grip on her bottom and pressed her tighter to the exquisite torment of his mouth.

Pleasure exploded around her and the focus of her world shattered into a million pieces. Delicate muscles quivered with spasm after delicious spasm, rolling in time with each wave of bliss. Her hands clutched useless fistfuls of hay.

Kieran's tongue dragged against her one final, breath-shuddering time before the warmth of his lips pulled away. She raised her head and found him staring at her, his eyes black with unmistakable lust.

Her gaze dragged down his naked body where he kneeled between her legs and a whimper sounded in the back of her throat. He was glorious. His arms bulged with power and his chest and stomach were lined with it. Deep indentations trailed over either side of his hips, cut lines of sinewy muscle that traced a path to where his phallus throbbed proudly before him.

He shifted forward, his body graceful in the low light. This time he did not tease her with the whispered touch of his body against hers. This time the sprinkling of hair on his legs and chest tickled her sensitive flesh and the weight of him settled with comfortable ease on top of her. She arched against him until the blunt edge of his arousal bumped between her legs. His back muscles went taut beneath her fingers, and he pressed forward, nudging the moisture between her legs.

His lips brushed her ear. "Tell me if I'm hurting ye."

Before she was able to answer, his mouth was on hers again, the tangy taste of her mingling with the sensual spice of his tongue. He flexed his hips forward beneath her hands and the tip of him edged inside of her.

Mariel arched helplessly against him with a moan of anticipation. The silky heat of his erection pushed again, and he inched deeper inside.

A sharp sensation needled her and rippled the surface of her passion. An unwanted reminder of her inexperience. As though sensing her discomfort, Kieran stopped and held his body motionless over hers.

He trailed hot kisses up her neck, the scrape of his unshaven chin grazing the hollow of her throat. His breath was warm against her ear, his breathing ragged despite his slow movements. He pushed slowly, carefully until he was completely inside of her. He stilled then, and his chest rose and fell with each deep, heavy breath.

Mariel smiled against his neck. She knew it was for her benefit that he forced himself to stop.

She also knew the sooner she accepted the discomfort, the sooner it would fade to pleasure. Ignoring the sting of her inexperience, she slid her hips back and nudged forward again. Kieran gave a choked groan and gripped her thighs.

"Dinna do that…" His voice was low, dangerous.

Mariel arched an eyebrow. "This?" She circled her bottom, and a blissful thrill jolted through her.

A muscle leapt in his jaw. His dark eyes studied her with careful consideration, and then he began to slowly glide in and out of her. Pain tickled the edges of pleasure until it became nonexistent.

His thrusts fell into a smooth rhythm Mariel rose to meet, each grind of their hips more exquisite than the last. His back was slick where she clung to him, his neck salty against the stroke of her tongue. She wrapped her legs around his waist and writhed against him in silent desperation for the impending release humming throughout her body.

Desire prickled her flesh, and his eager thrust sent her to the brink. She cried out in mindless pleasure and yielded to his beautiful strength.

A sublime wave of pleasure crashed over her and robbed her of breath. Her body squeezed against Kieran's arousal, and a deep groan tore from his throat as his buttocks clenched beneath her hands. He grasped her shoulders and warmth rushed against her womb.

She stared into eyes of liquid midnight, riding out the vestiges of pleasure rippling between them. His thumb brushed her cheek, and she found herself turning her face to the comfort of his palm.

"Did I hurt ye?" Concern puckered his brow.

She met his gaze and answered earnestly, "No."

He slid himself from between her legs with a shaky breath and another unexpected jolt of bliss snatched the air from her chest. He did not move off her. With her cheek still cradled in his hand, he pressed a tender kiss to her mouth.

"Did I please ye?" he murmured against her lips.

Did he please her? Her core still quivered from the strength of her release, and her limbs were heavy with the effects of satisfaction. Her answer came in a breathy moan as she remembered the heat of his tongue between her legs.

He leaned back and chuckled softly. "I'll take that as a yes."

Thunder cracked overhead and mingled with the roar of rain as it whipped against the solid cottage. A violent indication the storm still raged outside the cozy warmth of their cabin.

"The weather willna clear for a while still." He grinned down at her. "Looks like we're trapped here until morning."

He rose to his feet and padded to where the plaids were laid by the fire to dry. He wore his nudity with unabashed pride, and rightfully so. Mariel sat upright and took her time savoring Kieran's beauty.

The flicker of the fire cast erotic shadows against the hard contours of his chiseled body. His long legs were strong beneath the muscular curve of his bottom. He plucked a length of plaid from the floor, his powerful back rippling with corded flesh before he turned toward her once more. Her gaze slid toward his semierect phallus, and heat spread over Mariel's cheeks.

He glanced down at himself and then back up at her. His

eyes sparkled mischievously.

"Did I catch ye looking at me?" He knelt beside her and covered her with the plaid.

The fire had dried the heavy wool and left it warm. Mariel wrapped it around her back like a shawl to protect her from the prickle of hay and settled into their makeshift bed.

"I couldn't help myself," she mumbled.

He gave a low chuckle and slid in beside her. His naked arm pulled her close so her head rested on his solid chest.

"Good answer." The smile was evident in his silky voice.

Exhaustion curled around her shoulders and eased throughout her body. The steady thump of Kieran's heartbeat against her ear and their combined warmth lulled Mariel toward the comfort of sleep.

And then a stark thought invaded her dreams, jarring her from slumber.

She was in love with the very man she had to kill.

·   ·   ·

Kieran woke to the graying light of dawn and looked down at the woman who slept with her warm back pressed against his chest. He shifted his hand from her waist and brushed a wave of dark hair from her brow. Her lips curved into a gentle smile.

Sometime in the night she had put on his leine. The front fell open, revealing the rounded edge of one perfectly shaped breast. His mouth watered with the memory of how her skin had been so wet and cold beneath his tongue after he'd removed her chemise and how quickly she'd warmed beneath his attentions.

She had been so responsive, so eager. His cock woke at the memory of how tightly she milked him with each grind of her hips.

Mariel shifted in her sleep, and the curve of her lush rump arched against him, cradling the thick column that rose between his legs. He groaned and tried to nudge away from her. He would not interrupt her sleep with the insistence of his desire.

No woman had ever claimed his interest with as much

intensity as Mariel. In the past, his passions were slaked with women eager to warm his bed, women who departed with ease the next day. Never had their leave bothered him. And yet, here lay a woman who made his chest ache with the very thought of her absence. A woman who called to him from the depths of her slumber even though he'd had her only hours before.

Her bottom ground against him once more and a little noise of pleasure hummed in her throat. His hand rested on her hip with the intent to push her away when he saw the edge of her mouth lift into a slow smile.

The vixen was teasing him.

His hand cupped her fine arse, gently opening her. The little sound of pleasure whimpered into a moan. He brushed the slick center of her desire with his fingertip, and she pressed back into his hand with a readiness that left him near bursting. No further encouragement was needed, not when he was already so hard. He positioned himself against her heat and eased deep inside of her.

They made love as the light of a new day warmed the room. Their frantic breaths and passionate cries melted into the walls, and they reached their climax together.

Kieran gazed down at Mariel, her face cradled in his hands. Her hair was mussed from their lovemaking, her cheeks and lips flushed from it. For all the times he had seen her, she had never looked more beautiful. She had never looked more his.

They were in their own private world, one no one else knew about, locked away in a cabin that smelled of peat, love, and roses. Her skin was silk beneath his calloused fingers, and the way she looked at him made him feel there was nothing he could not accomplish with her by his side. Never had he felt so blissfully happy, so content.

Never had he felt more certain.

"Mariel…" he began. Blood surged in his veins the way it did before battle.

She lifted a perfectly shaped brow and tilted her head up at him. "Hmm?"

He touched her soft cheek with the tip of his middle finger. Yes, this was what he wanted. Forever. "Be my wife."

Chapter Twenty-Four

Silence stretched between them and wavered Kieran's confidence. He'd never asked a woman to marry him before, but surely her lack of response didn't bode well for him.

Sunlight filtered in through the heavy glass windows and streaked across her face, making her violet eyes glow with an emotion he could not name. He sat up in their makeshift bed and hay bristled against his thighs.

He caught her cold fingers in his hand. Perhaps she had not heard him. He waited for her to rise to a sitting position before trying again.

"Marry me, lass," he repeated. "Be my wife."

A mirthless smile touched her lips. "My father is dead, Kieran. You have no one to atone to for the loss of my virginity. It held value to no one." Her cheeks flushed. "Except to me, and I did with it what I wanted. I ask for nothing in return."

She thought he sought her hand through obligation. Sadness coiled around his heart at her own lack of self-regard.

"It held value to me, but that isna why I ask." His thumb traced the delicate line of her cheekbone. "I ask ye because of the way I feel when I'm near ye. Ye're selfless and beautiful, and I love the way ye smile. I want ye by my side for the rest of my life."

Her eyes dropped to their clasped hands, and he felt her hesitation.

"The clan likes ye," he continued. "They will support my decision. I'm probably saying something wrong, but this is how I feel. I want this."

He caught her chin with his fingers and forced her to look

up at him. She had to know how he felt. She had to understand the sincerity of his words. "I want ye. Marry me. Please."

Her teeth sank into her lower lip and that dreadful silence filled the room again.

"Kieran, I…" Her voice faltered. "I…can't."

He dropped his hands and stared at her unreadable expression. Had she not spent the night in his arms with a smile on her lips? Had she not given him her most precious gift and been glad for it?

The heat of anger replaced disbelief. Damn it, he should have known better. There was not a shadow of a doubt in his mind that Jack had something to do with this, regardless of what she'd stated previously. If he ever met the man, he'd have him skewered at the end of his blade.

"Is there someone else?" Kieran demanded, his voice harsh. He would be tortured by the other man no longer. Let her confess and be done with it.

Her brow furrowed. "Of course not. Surely you don't think I'm in love with Colin—"

"Ye know I dinna refer to Colin." Kieran folded his arms over his chest.

"I told you I do not love another man. There is no one else." Her fingers plucked at a loose string along the hem of his leine. "The reason I can't marry you…" She shifted her gaze to her hands. "It's because of who you are. Who I am."

He frowned. What the hell was that supposed to mean? "I dinna understand."

Her voice trembled. "You deserve a woman who deserves a man like you." She swallowed thickly. "I do not."

His fingertips brushed the softness of her exposed shoulder where the leine had slipped low. She did not shrink from his touch. "I dinna like to hear ye say things like that, Mariel. Ye think too highly of me and no nearly high enough of yerself, but I promise to be a good husband to ye."

She tucked her chin to her chest, and her hair fell like a curtain of silk, shielding her face from his view. "You don't know me, Kieran. You don't know what awful things I've done."

Her voice dropped to a whisper. "Or what I will have to do. If you knew…" She shook her head and her hair rippled. "You can't want me, not with the stain I bear upon my soul."

He brushed her hair away from her face and tucked it behind her ear. Tears stained her cheeks. "I want to know what ye've been through, and I want to be by yer side for whatever ye must face. There is no anything that canna be fixed. But ye have to trust me."

"Not even you can help me," she whispered.

"Talk to me, lass," he urged. The sins she spoke of were doubtless insignificant to those of a warrior, but clearly they weighed heavy upon her. Never had he felt more desperate for someone's confidence or more helpless to claim it.

She searched his face for a moment and took a breath as though to speak. And then she hesitated. Her tears shimmered in the sunlight and slid down her cheeks. "I can't," she said miserably.

The lack of trust wounded him far more than he would admit. But he was a MacDonald, and he was as stubborn as he was powerful. He would have her trust, no matter how long it took to gain.

Kieran pressed his lips to the smooth skin of her cheek and let the salty anguish of her tears dissolve against his tongue.

A hearty knock sounded at the door, booming through the intimacy of their discussion. Kieran leapt to his feet and grabbed his sword from beside the bed.

"Who's there?" he growled. His fingers tightened around the pommel of his blade with deadly strength.

"Alec, Laird."

Kieran cursed under his breath and pulled his discarded plaid around his waist. He glanced back at where Mariel sat up in bed. "Get dressed. I'll be back."

He opened the door and quickly closed it behind him in an effort to preserve Mariel's modesty. "There had better be a damned good reason ye are here," he snarled.

Alec's cold blue gaze flicked down to Kieran's half-dressed state, and a slow smile spread over his lips. "That's Colin's horse in the stable. But something tells me that isna Colin in the cottage with ye."

"It's none of yer concern."

If Alec noticed the warning in Kieran's voice, he completely ignored it as he stroked his chin in mock thought. "If memory serves correct, a certain English lass also dinna return after the storm."

"Enough." Kieran glared at him. "What is it ye want?"

The smirk stayed on Alec's face. He reached into his sporran and pulled out a sealed parchment indicating the MacKinnon crest.

"What is this?" Kieran grabbed the letter and cracked the thick wax seal.

"It's from Laird MacKinnon. The messenger said it was urgent. We knew ye were out in the storm and figured ye'd taken refuge." He paused and gave a bawdy grin. "But when morning came and ye werena back, we thought it prudent to find ye."

Kieran unfolded the letter and scanned the scrawled message. His annoyance slid away. "Aye, it is good that ye did. Ready the horses. We return immediately."

He turned to enter the hut and one particular line echoed through his mind with blood-chilling clarity.

Beware an English assassin.

He knew exactly what this meant.

•   •   •

Mariel secured the final tie of her overdress as Kieran burst through the door, his face stern. "We need to leave. Now."

He strode to the fireplace where embers still glowed brilliant red and shoved a bit of parchment into it. The thick paper immediately browned and curled into ash.

"Kieran?" Something was amiss. "What's happened?" She glanced toward the smoldering embers where the parchment had been.

He turned to her with a dangerous glint in his eye. "Are ye ready?" he asked, ignoring her question.

"I am." Her heart thudded in her chest.

Gone was the understanding lover who had only minutes before asked for her hand in marriage. Kieran tugged his leine over his head and tucked it into his kilt with sharp, jerking movements. He pressed a firm hand to her back and led her out the door in an unceremonious exit from their small haven of beautiful memories.

Alec had their horses readied and waiting. He gave her a short nod of greeting while Kieran wordlessly helped her onto the steed.

Within minutes they were galloping toward Caisteal Camus. Kieran's horse rode alongside Alec's. The wind tore their murmured Gaelic across the landscape, leaving Mariel with small snatches that made little sense. And then she overheard one word that made her heart still.

Assassin.

Though she averted her gaze, she felt the weight of Kieran's stare. "Take care of her," he said to Alec.

The bite of the wind numbed against her cheeks, and the scream of the birds overhead died away to a dull echo. Her stomach churned, knotted against the rapid fluttering within.

Had she been found out?

Her heart slammed in her chest.

What would become of Jack?

Kieran broke away from Alec and sidled alongside Mariel with his hand propped on the hilt of his blade. His horse was so close, she could reach out and touch him if she chose to. Doubtless he ensured she would not escape.

They traveled in silence for the remainder of the journey, something Mariel found herself grateful for. She did not trust herself to speak and lacked the energy to do so.

She needed the time to come up with a plan.

Part of her was relieved to be found out and grateful to cease the charade that would harm so many. Blair and Dougal would be safe. Were it not for Jack, she would gladly succumb to the punishment befitting the crimes she had committed. Being discovered as an assassin was no small offense, and Highlanders were brutal in their punishment.

She glanced toward Kieran and her chest tightened with emotion. She had been so ready to divulge her secret to him only minutes before. Perhaps if she'd had the strength to do so, she would not be in this position. Her gaze lowered to his blade. Or perhaps she would already be dead.

A selfish part of her had not been ready for him to discover the truth. Not yet.

Pain knifed through her blackened heart. Did her sin have no limits?

Hardening herself against the hurt, she turned her thoughts from Kieran and straightened her back as they came to a stop before the stables.

Her blood raced through her veins and pulsed in her muscles. She could run. The boat she needed had been pulled to the shore prior and was not yet in the water. A quick sprint would take less than five minutes.

She glanced at Kieran's dark expression.

Five minutes was too long. He would catch her and she would fail.

She had no choice but to see where Kieran took her. At the very least, perhaps she could secure a plan for Jack's life.

Kieran's hands lingered on her waist as he helped her from her horse. A seed of hope flickered within her.

She rose on her toes so her body stretched against the length of his. "Shall I come to your room tonight?" She kept her voice low, ensuring only he heard her.

His eyes narrowed. "I dinna think that is a good idea."

The air squeezed from her chest.

Kieran indicated toward the castle. "Alec will see ye to yer room. I dinna want ye to leave, aye?"

Alec's shadow fell over her and chased away any opportunity to speak to Kieran further.

"The laird will be up to speak with ye later," Alec said. He led her into the castle toward the prison of her room and away from Kieran.

Once they arrived at her door, Alec waited for her to sit on the edge of her bed before he closed her inside her chamber. While there was no sound of a key turning in the lock, she knew leaving would be a poor decision.

Mariel drew a shaky breath and rose to pace the small room. If she were discovered, surely she would be put to death. And Jack would be doomed to a life with Aaron.

She strained to listen. No sounds came from the hall. Perhaps she could sneak out of the castle before anyone came looking for her.

A rap at the door set her heart pounding. "Yes?" she called out, suddenly breathless.

A young red-haired woman entered. Mariel had seen her around the castle in the weeks before. The woman gave a genuine smile. "The laird ordered ye a bath if ye like."

Heat warmed Mariel's cheeks in recollection of why she had cause to bathe. Those stolen hours of passion had almost been forgotten amid the harsh reality she now faced. "Yes, please. I would like that," she replied.

The young woman nodded and disappeared.

Doubt flickered through Mariel. Surely Kieran would not offer a criminal a chance to bathe. Perhaps he did not suspect her after all.

She carefully watched the faces of the servants coming into and out of the room. There was a relaxed ease about them that soothed her ragged nerves. Bucket after bucket of water was sloshed into a massive wooden tub until the bath was filled. The servants all nodded and slipped out the door, leaving her alone.

In an unlocked room.

Paranoia uncurled from her shoulders and the bath beckoned. Mariel wound her hair atop her head and let her soiled dress crumple at her feet. She sank into the hot, scented water and closed her eyes to relieve the pounding ache in her skull. Immediately she saw Kieran's face in her mind's eye, tender and genuine. He had been gentle with her last night, far more kind than she deserved.

Be my wife.

Her choked cry echoed off the cold walls around her. She

scrambled from the tub, desperate to be free of the memory and the guilt. Instead of reaching for the drying linen, she stood beside the tub uncovered. The heat of the fire eased the chill from her dripping body while images of Kieran flashed unbidden through her mind.

The door clicked closed behind her, startling her. How had she not heard it open?

She whirled around and found Kieran staring at her with a look of disbelief on his face. "Mariel." the tone of his voice echoed the horror of his gaze.

Her heart slid like ice down into her belly.

The charade was over.

He knew.

Chapter Twenty-Five

Kieran stared at Mariel's pallid face. Words failed him. How had she managed to hide such a secret from him for so long? How had he never suspected?

He strode forward, disturbing the humid curl of perfumed steam rising from her bath. Her eyes widened, fear evident in the violet blue depths.

She was afraid of him.

Something twisted deep within his chest.

He walked around behind her. Perhaps what he had seen from the doorway would not be as bad up close.

No, he thought, studying her mutilated back, it was far worse. Rope thick scars slashed Mariel's back, marring her otherwise flawless skin. Only a whip would leave such markings, but never had he seen the weapon cause such brutality. How had she even survived? He stroked the abnormally taut skin, and his hand shook with barely contained rage.

She flinched and curled her body forward, away from his touch.

"What are you doing?" Mariel choked.

The tremor of her body was slight, but unmistakable.

"Who did this to ye?" The question came out harsher than intended.

When she did not answer, he came around to face her.

"Wearing my leine last night was no because ye were cold, was it? Ye dinna want me to see this."

Her gaze flicked to the floor and she shook her head. She looked vulnerable standing naked before him with her wounded stare turned away from him. She was too fragile. He lifted the thick robe beside the bath and laid it over her shoulders. She remained motionless, leaving the robe gaping open. Kieran wrapped the heavy fabric around her. Slowly, lest he frighten her further, he placed his hands on her shoulders and drew her against his chest.

She didn't trust him, he knew that. Never did he fault her for her skepticism, but now he understood her hesitation.

"I dinna mean to sound so harsh. I just…" He paused, uncertain what to say. He never was good at this kind of thing. "Seeing yer back made me want to kill the man who did that to ye. I'm no angry at ye."

She turned her face into his chest. "You don't question what I did to deserve it?"

"It doesna matter what ye did. No woman deserves to be treated thus." He drew a deep breath in an attempt to rein in the anger coursing through him.

Certainly he wanted to know why someone would whip her to such an extent, but forcing the truth would only push her further away. He had learned much from dealing with Blair when he first brought her back to Caisteal Camus.

"Ye dinna need to tell me the reason if ye are nae ready."

When Mariel did not speak, he was not surprised. Nor did her silence wound him as it had in the past. She would speak when she was ready, and he would be there to listen, to help ease her hurt.

He released her and kept her hands clasped in his. "We need to talk, lass." The timing was terrible, but the news could not wait. She needed to be told.

The tiny muscles in Mariel's neck stood out. Damn the news for arriving when it did. He felt like an arse for having to tell her now.

"Please dinna be concerned, but I received word that an English assassin has been sent after me. I think ye can understand what this means."

The color drained from her face.

"Dinna worry, I am having Alec collect Blair and Dougal now. I know Blair willna come of her own accord and will need to be forced. With Hampton putting a price on my head, it isna hard to determine who he is really seeking. I'll no stand by and let Blair and Dougal be harmed because she's too stubborn to live in the castle."

He squeezed Mariel's warm hand. Her pulse fluttered erratically against his palm.

"Ye know Blair willna be happy about being made to come here and that is why I am telling ye. I hate to ask this of ye, but I need yer help in making her comfortable here, aye? She trusts ye."

Mariel pulled her hand from Kieran's and secured the robe more tightly around her body. "Of course," she replied at last with a tense smile.

He could feel her discomfort from where he stood. His discovery of her back had unsettled her. "Ye are always so willing to help." His fingertip trailed the delicate line of her jaw.

"And you are always so understanding." Mariel looked up at him, her eyes searching his. "You make me feel like I could tell you anything."

"Ye can, lass." He held his body perfectly still as if the slightest movement would frighten her from speech.

"I want to." She paused for a moment. "You seem like you would forgive anything."

"So long as ye pose no threat to my family, I would forgive ye anything." It was a miserable excuse for a jest in an effort to lighten the mood.

She gave a small smile. "It would be wise not to be your assassin then."

He laughed and drew her against him, grateful to see her playfulness had returned. "It would be verra wise indeed." His hand slid beneath her robe and cupped the silken weight of her breast. "Ye're far too enticing to kill."

"And yet you would keep me from your bed?" Her displeasure was evidenced by her tone.

The weight of the conversation draped heavy on his shoulders. "The easiest way to kill someone is in their sleep. I know I wake easily and can protect myself, but you…" His palm skimmed her glossy hair.

Every part of her was smooth or soft or silky. Her beauty captivated him, but she was so much more than that. If something ever happened to her...

His chest grew tight. No, he would never place her in danger. She was far too important to him, far more than he could ever explain to her.

·   ·   ·

Mariel was grateful for the press of Kieran's chest against her face. She could not bring herself to meet his gaze. The pain would be too great.

She'd had the perfect opportunity to tell him the truth and she had not taken it. How could she be such a coward? He had offered to help. He promised to be understanding.

Yet still she could not risk trusting him.

His hand skimmed down the length of her back. Mariel stiffened against the contact and resisted the urge to jerk away.

Her back was hideous. No matter how kind his words were, she knew what it looked like—a perfect physical reflection of her damned soul.

His hand ran between her shoulder blades and shivers of unease crawled down her back. "I dinna see yer beauty as diminished in any way by this. It only makes me appreciate yer strength all the more." His words were meant to make her feel better. She knew that and yet they did not stop the onslaught of the memory.

The whip whistled as it flew through the air. The leather strip in her mouth tasted of sweat and blood. She clamped it tight between her teeth regardless, knowing she would have need of it. The braided leather found its mark and fire streaked her back. Her body jerked in protest against the pain, but no cry tore from her throat.

"No screams, eh? We'll see how long you keep that up for. Of course, you can end this right now..."

The meaty hand pointed to where a man sat in a puddle of his own urine.

"Kill him."

"Did ye hear me?"

Her eyes squeezed shut, as if the memory could be pressed from her mind.

"Mariel," Kieran said softly. "Did ye hear me?"

She shook her head to clear it of the horrible scene. "I'm sorry. I didn't."

Regret showed on his face. "I have to leave. There are things I must ready for Blair's arrival." His finger hooked the edge of her robe. He leaned closer and the scruff of his whiskers tickled her neck. His rich, masculine scent curled around her and brought with it an entirely different rush of memories. Ones of comfort, affection—safety.

His lips brushed her ear, his breath warm against her neck. "Leave yer door unlocked tonight."

The soft moan that escaped her lips came unbidden as did the rush of heat throbbing at her core. Kieran gave her a lopsided grin and disappeared out the door. He knew exactly his effect on her.

The room roared with deafening silence following his departure. The air was so still Mariel had difficulty drawing breath.

She placed her hand over her chest in an effort to ease the frantic flutter of her heart. For the first time since he'd said it, she allowed herself to believe he truly did not suspect her. Hysteria bubbled in her chest as relief swirled with overwhelming guilt and churned in her empty stomach. Emotions warred inside her aching head, torn between the desire to trust him and the fear that she could not.

So long as ye pose no threat to my family, I would forgive ye anything.

Though said in jest, truth backed those words and their weight settled on her.

She shrugged the robe from her shoulders and pulled on a fresh gown. Blair was being forced to return to the castle against her will because of Mariel. The least she could do was be there to soothe her new friend's fears.

Several minutes later, Mariel made her way down the hall to wait. Perhaps Blair would be more understanding than they all suspected.

Mariel had not gone more than three steps down the stairs when a scream echoed down the narrow corridor.

"Stop! Leave me alone, you brute!" Blair's Scotch English accent was unmistakable, even from a distance.

Mariel raced down the remainder of the stairs and entered the great hall in time to see Alec walk in with Blair slung over his back. A smile quirked Mariel's lips as he set Blair down; she remembered her own delivery at Alec's hands.

"How dare you? Did I not say I wasn't going to come here?" Blair's cheeks were flushed and her chestnut hair tangled over her face.

Dougal appeared behind Alec. He was obviously more confident in Kieran's decision than Blair. "It's all right," he assured his mother. "You know he wouldn't send for us if it wasn't safe."

Mariel approached them with a hand propped on her hip. "I see you are still bullying unyielding women, Alec."

He gave an irritated grunt. "If ye wouldna be so damned willful, I wouldna have to carry ye." He turned his attention to Dougal and ruffled the boy's shaggy brown hair. "Let's go to the stable and leave the women to calm down, aye?"

"Is Colin there too? He promised to teach me a new song." Dougal plastered himself at Alec's side and started toward the main door of the hall.

"Do not let Colin teach him anything," Blair called after them. She cast a weary look at Mariel and gave a defeated sigh. "You know everything, don't you?"

Mariel lowered her gaze, unable to meet her friend's eyes. She understood more than they could possibly realize. "Kieran wants you here to protect you."

Nausea rolled over Mariel. Her comforting words turned acidic in her mouth.

"I can protect myself." Blair pulled the dagger from her pocket.

"Blair," Mariel said gently. "Dougal would never allow anything to happen to you, no matter the cost to himself.

Perhaps Kieran keeps you here to avoid Dougal being harmed in protecting you."

Blair's brows knit together, and the hard line of her mouth softened.

"Ah, Blair, I see ye've arrived." Kieran's booming voice interrupted their conversation. He eyed his sister warily as he approached.

Blair looked up at him and smiled. "I have arrived indeed, brother, on the back of the mule you sent to carry me." She stood on her toes and pressed a kiss to his cheek. "Thank you for seeing to our safety."

"Ye're welcome," he replied slowly. "Now, go on and get settled. Ye know where yer room is."

She gave a compliant nod and strode from the hall with a bewildered Kieran staring after her. He turned his gaze on Mariel. "Ye're helpful to have around," he said in a low voice.

She did not turn away from the heat of his dark stare. Heaven help her, she welcomed it. He offered comfort she did not deserve and yet could not turn away. She needed this. She needed him.

Powerful arms braced on either side of her head, trapping her where she stood. His body crushed against her with a thrilling heat. The length of his desire stood prominent between them and elicited the hungry throb between her legs once more.

His lips brushed the sensitive skin along her neck. His tongue flicked out in wicked invitation and a shiver of anticipation wound through her.

"I dinna think I can wait for tonight, my love," he said raggedly.

My love. Mariel's heart tripped over itself. Had he meant to say that?

"Blair will take a while to get settled," she replied, her voice husky.

Grinning like a rogue, Kieran swept Mariel into his arms and carried her across the great hall.

"Kieran!" She glanced furtively around the open room. "Someone might see."

"Then let them. I am no ashamed of ye, Mariel." His brow furrowed with the sincerity of his words. "Never could I be ashamed of ye."

.   .   .

Mariel lay awake while Kieran napped beside her. His skin was slick with the exertion of their lovemaking. The hard lines of authority on his face smoothed out under the relaxation of his slumber, and she found herself struck with his youth. He could not be older than five and twenty. Still older than she, but not old enough for the level of responsibility upon his shoulders.

The setting sun cast streaks of gold across his cheek, accentuating the dark black stubble shadowing his jaw. She stroked his face and savored the rasp against her palm. He grunted once, but did not turn away.

There was only one thing she could do. Only one option. Her stomach churned. After dinner, once everyone was in bed and they were completely alone, she would take action. She would do what must be done.

This would end tonight.

Chapter Twenty-Six

Kieran's mouth watered at the trencher of roasted meat before him. The smoky tang of crisped fat overpowered the burning grease from the light sconces around them.

Mariel stood by his side in a pale blue dress that made her skin look like cream and roses. He brushed the curve of her lower back with his fingertips before settling into the chair at the head of the hall. A possessive gesture he knew would not be missed.

He loaded his plate with more portions than usual, eager for a solid meal after two days of being too busy to sit and enjoy his food.

"That's quite an appetite ye've got there, Laird." Colin gave him a bawdy grin from across the table. "What would a man need to do to work up such hunger?"

Kieran threw him a dark look in silent warning to still his tongue.

Mariel turned toward Colin and grinned. "Clearly you wouldn't know. Your portions look rather meager."

Laughter filled the table and easy conversation resumed without the suggestion behind Colin's jest.

Kieran smiled to himself. He could not have chosen a more remarkable woman to be his wife. All he had to do was convince her of that. His gaze swept over the ample curve of her breast and desire pulled at his groin.

The convincing would be fun.

An unnatural silence filled the room and drew his attention away from Mariel. A warrior staggered past the long tables of the great hall. Dirt streaked his clothing and blood dripped from a tangled mass of blond hair. Hamish.

Kieran leapt to his feet and would have run to him, but the lad was surprisingly quick and already stood at the head of the table.

Hamish grimaced. "The MacLeod's are attacking."

Kieran uttered a quiet curse. With Hampton threatening Blair and Dougal, this was the last thing he needed.

Shoving aside his irritation, he looked out at his gathered clan. These attacks were not uncommon, and his people knew what was needed. "The MacLeod's want a fight, and I plan to give them one. Let's send them crying back to their wives, aye?"

The clansmen cheered and rose without question to obey his command. He looked down to where Mariel and Blair sat at the table and addressed them. "Round up all the women and children and get to the cellar."

Blair stood and made her way to the nearest table to obey his command, but Mariel faltered, her wide gaze fixed on him.

"Kieran—"

"Mariel, go!" he ordered. Relief swept over him as she jumped from the table and ran after Blair.

He turned to Hamish and noted the large gash over his brow. "Staunch that while we talk."

Hamish ripped off a piece of his leine and tied it tight over the wound. Brilliant red bloomed against the dirty fabric. If Kieran was going to get information out of him, he'd have to do it soon before the lad passed out.

"Tell me what happened."

"Angus and I were standing guard at the cliffs when the MacLeods attacked us from behind. They were verra quiet. Impossible to hear approach. They killed Angus first and left one to fight me."

Angus had been one of Kieran's best warriors. His presence would be missed, but grieving would come later. Right now, Kieran needed numbers, facts.

Hamish continued. "I was able to defeat him and slipped away." The lad clenched his jaw. "I know it was cowardly to do, Laird, but I knew I couldna defeat them on my own. Instead,

I rushed back here to warn ye so we could get the women and children to safety."

"Nay, it was wise of ye to do so, Hamish," Kieran said. "I would have done the same in yer position. There is brave and there is foolish. To attempt to fight them all would have been foolish. How many were there?"

The MacLeods had been causing trouble for years, and the attacks had grown bothersome. Every so often, they would send a handful of armed warriors to Caisteal Camus to cause problems.

Hamish's mouth set in a grim line, and he regarded Kieran with a hard gaze. "At least two hundred from what I saw, Laird."

Kieran kept his face impassive, refusing to let the boy see his shock. The MacLeods had never sent an army of that size before. He would have to round up every able body he could find.

God help them. This was going to be a war.

•   •   •

Mariel followed Blair down the dark, winding stairwell. The echo of dozens of feet shuffling against the stone stairs came at them from all angles of the small enclosure as the MacDonald women and children snaked their way toward safety.

Several sconces lined the walls, but the glowing light did little against the oppressive black. The odor of dank earth met them with an icy blast that burned Mariel's nostrils and stung her throat. One by one, their footsteps fell silent as they descended to the soft, natural floor of the cellar.

Their arrival was met with a darkness so thick, it pressed against her eyes. A torch flared to life somewhere behind her and bathed the room in brilliance.

Mariel fought the cold rush of fear. A solid iron and wood door had been propped open, revealing a stone cell with rusted manacles embedded in the wall and graying rushes strewn upon the floor.

Was this where traitors were taken?

She turned her back from the sight and busied herself with calming the children. An idle mind would return her thoughts to the impending battle above and the dismal future that doubtless awaited her if all did not go as planned.

"It's miserable, isn't it?" Blair's voice was quiet beside her in the dim light. "I used to hate having to come down here when I was a child."

"Did you have to come often?" Mariel asked, scanning the faces of the women and children. They did not appear frightened, as if this were normal to them.

"Far too often. The MacLeods launch attacks on us frequently and have done so for over one hundred and fifty years."

"Why so long?" Mariel asked, alarmed.

Blair smoothed the hair from Dougal's brow and patted his cheek. "According to legend, a MacDonald warrior killed a MacLeod laird by accident. Obviously, the MacLeod's did not believe the act was unintentional, and the clans have been fighting ever since." Her smirk indicated how she felt about the feud. "It's one of the reasons I prefer to live away from the castle. I am not surprised there is an attack the night I return." Blair's hand squeezed Mariel's arm gently. "Don't worry. It will be over within the hour."

"Take up yer arms, lasses!" Innes's cry echoed from the curved staircase.

The old woman's hair flew wild around her face, and a battle axe glinted in her fist. "This isna an ordinary attack. Hundreds of MacLeods storm our shores. We must defend our homes."

Activity exploded around Mariel. Women secured smaller children into the care of older ones. Cries filled the air while mothers and grandmothers left the room and arguments broke out among women who wanted to go and were told they should not.

Amid the commotion of bravery and fierce protection, all Mariel could focus on was Kieran and what needed to be said. She must find him.

"I have to go," she said.

"To fight?" Blair's brow furrowed.

"I have to see Kieran."

Blair considered her for a moment. "That's not a good idea, Mariel." She pursed her lips. "But I don't think you care if it's a good idea or not. Come back quickly, aye?"

Mariel nodded and raced up the stairs. She shoved through the heavy doors of the cellar and left safety behind her. Chaos roared around her as men, boys, and several women rushed about with weapons brandished. Shouts rang out, giving orders and securing positions.

And then she saw the very person who could help her above all others. "Colin," she cried and ran in his direction.

His surprise turned to a frown. "Mariel, ye shouldna be here. Get down in the cellar with the others."

"I can't," she gasped. "I need your help. I have to see Kieran." Several people bumped into her as she waited for his response. None was given. "I'm going to find him with or without your help," she added defiantly.

The corner of his lip quirked up in a lopsided grin. "Ye always know how to get what ye want, dinna ye?" He pressed a dirk into her hand. "If ye are going to be out, ye may as well be protected."

Mariel accepted the blade with a forced smile. Once she was done with Kieran, Colin would doubtless regret his trust.

Colin led her through the throngs of people to the inner walls of the castle where a blast of cold wind stung her cheeks and made her eyes water.

Desperate now, she scanned the warriors until she saw Kieran's proud stance in the distance. Her stomach knotted. Fear spiked her fluttering heart.

He stood at the apex of the wall. The moon etched shadows on his face, lending a darkness she had never seen in him before. His voice was strong and commanded authority as he called out orders with a confidence that would not be questioned or ignored. He looked every bit the barbarian leader she had been sent to kill.

His dark eyes fixed on her and suddenly his expression

became all the more dangerous, if such a thing were possible. He moved forward with a quiet strength, his taut body graceful as a predator as he stalked toward her.

His fist darted out and grasped Colin by the leine. "What the hell is she doing here?" he growled.

Colin shrugged. "Ye know she would have found ye anyway. I simply made her journey quicker and less dangerous."

Kieran shifted his glare to Mariel. A man bumped into her and knocked her off balance as he ran to where the men gathered along the wall of the castle. Kieran steadied her and narrowed his eyes.

Perhaps this had not been a good idea after all.

Colin had disappeared and they were alone. Now was the perfect opportunity.

Mariel's heart turned to ice in her chest and the words she needed to say grew thick on her tongue. "Kieran…"

She swallowed her fear. If she did not tell him now, she might not have the courage to do so again.

She would tell him…everything.

Chapter Twenty-Seven

Mariel stared into Kieran's enraged glare with more courage than she felt. Her pulse raced and left the blood pounding in her ears. "Kieran, I—"

"Do ye have information on the battle?" His dark look rippled her confidence.

Mariel pursed her lips and shook her head. "No."

His gaze bore into her. "Then this is a discussion that can wait."

He turned to go, but she grabbed his elbow. "Please," she begged. If she didn't tell him now, she may not be able to do so later.

He pulled back from her, a deep frown evident on the hard lines of his face. "I havena got a minute, Mariel. I'll be back before dawn. We can talk then."

The lie hung in the air between them. Mariel knew the fight would take him past morning and time was a luxury she did not have.

"You have no idea how important this is." She drew herself closer to him.

"And ye have no idea how dangerous it is to be out here. Get downstairs with the women."

Her voice trembled with desperation. "Let me fight alongside you."

He gave her an incredulous look. "Ye dinna know what ye say. This is no a fight for a woman like ye." He glanced over his shoulder into the darkness and turned back to her. "Ye need to leave. *Now*."

"I need to tell you—"

"Ye need to learn yer place as a woman and listen when yer man speaks to ye. I'm telling ye to go into the cellar with the rest of the women."

Mariel gaped at him, her pride shriveling under the weight of his words.

He caught her around the waist and jerked her against his hard body. "Damn it, Mariel, dinna ye understand?" His hand cradled the back of her head, and his thumb braced against her cheek. "I love ye too much to see ye hurt." He pressed his lips against hers in an urgent kiss that left her reeling.

Before Mariel could react, a clash of swords rang out behind Kieran. He shoved her back toward the castle entrance. "Go and dinna look back!"

He turned toward the sounds of battle but stood his ground in front of her. Defending her.

Dozens of men leapt from the darkness and clambered over the castle walls with swords brandished and crazed looks upon their faces. Mariel stood in place, her mind stunned in horror. Their battle cry rang out over the force of the wind and sent a chill of fear racing down her spine.

Ahead of her, Kieran's body tensed as the mass of men swarmed toward the line of MacDonald warriors who waited at the ready.

There were so many men attacking and far too few defending.

The forces collided with the deafening dissonance of clanging metal and low curses. Her feet were immobile, transfixed as she watched a man with wild hair lunge at Kieran. The wicked blade of his battle axe swung with frightening accuracy.

Mariel tensed in preparation to rush forward in Kieran's defense when a large hand caught her around the waist and forcefully pulled her back.

* * *

The scent of rose mingled with the heavy copper odor of blood, and Kieran knew that despite his warnings, Mariel remained. He flexed the muscles of his arms as though making himself larger would create a stronger barrier between the hell in front of him and the woman he fought for behind him.

Icy wind howled through the battle and added an ethereal element to their world of pandemonium. The moon was a sliver of light in the black sky, hiding her face from the horrors that ensued below. Energy pulsed in the thin air as warriors wrestled in a macabre dance that dictated who lived and who died.

Many would die that night.

Kieran tightened his grip on the pommel of his sword, his palm molding against the smooth leather. The smell of unwashed body pulled his awareness to the massive man in front of him. The MacLeod warrior's shout rose above the sounds of battle as he charged Kieran in a spray of spittle. Kieran deflected the impact with his blade, his hand vibrating with the force of the man's blow.

Had Mariel made it to safety?

Kieran chanced a look behind him and saw nothing in the darkness. A path of fire seared along the side of his arm, and he realized his mistake too late. The MacLeod's dirk caught Kieran in his moment of distraction.

Kieran roared in anger at his foolish error and brought his blade down on the massive shoulder of his attacker. The dirk clattered unseen beneath their feet and left his enemy with only one good hand to wield his sword.

The fight was already won and though they both knew it, the man did not back down. His sword jabbed awkwardly at Kieran who shifted out of its path and swung his blade with lethal precision at the man's thick neck.

Kieran pushed onward, spurred with battle-induced energy. One by one, his foes fell before his feet. Men who would see his people harmed if they were not stopped.

Alec fought at his right, tirelessly wielding the two-handed long sword with its black-purple blade made almost invisible against the darkness of night. A stocky man barreled toward Kieran with a bloodied axe hoisted overhead. The blade came down and Kieran feinted to the left and succeeded in swiping the man's feet from beneath him. Kieran leaned over him for the kill when another MacLeod rushed upon him from the right.

Before Kieran could react, a blade flashed in the miniscule light of the moon and caught the attacker in the chest. The MacLeod crumpled toward the floor. Colin stepped from the shadows and gave Kieran a nod. His sudden arrival meant only one thing.

Mariel was safe.

A steady calm washed over Kieran, shifting him from protector to warrior. The chill of the wind faded away and his vision heightened, seeing clearly into the inky night for the first time since he'd seen her on the battlefield. Every sound filtered through his mind from the low hum of an insect to the ring of metal on metal. His muscles moved with purpose and with the accuracy of well-honed instinct. The stone floor beneath his feet was slick with blood, yet each footstep was anchored and sure.

They would vanquish their enemy. They *would* be victorious.

His men were succeeding in driving the MacLeods back from the walls of the castle and onto the lawn of its perimeter.

Perhaps he had not lied to Mariel after all. Perhaps he would be home before dawn. No sooner had the thought entered his mind than a fresh wave of MacLeods descended upon them, well rested and hungry for blood.

• • •

Mariel cradled Coira's little body in her lap in an effort to offer both comfort and warmth. The lights in the sconces had consumed all the oil and burned out hours ago. The frigid darkness enveloped them, leaving them vulnerable to the echoes of battle overhead.

The clash of swords and shrill battle cries were not so frightful. Those sounds had ceased to unsettle. The horrors that assaulted them came from the meaty *thunk* of a blade as it caught flesh, and the groans of men as they took their last breaths. The clammy air of the cellar grew thick with the silence of fear and sorrow as time ticked by, one slow minute after another.

Younger children wept against their mothers' breasts, their questions long since quieted. The women and older children remained stoic, their faces blank as they attempted to block out the cries of the dying.

"Will it be over soon?" Coira asked, her voice small.

Mariel shifted the girl's weight in an effort to regain some feeling in her legs. They had long since gone numb. Her fingers ached, yet still she clutched Colin's dagger in her right hand.

"Will it be over soon?" Coira repeated.

"I'm sure it will be," Blair said in Gaelic through the darkness. There would be no guilt behind the lie. They had all made false promises in their efforts to calm the children who knew no different.

The deceptive words produced the desired effect, and Coira's tense body relaxed against Mariel.

Thoughts of Kieran pounded in her brain, as did the memory of the large warrior descending on him like a barbarian of nightmares. Colin had pulled her away before she saw Kieran react. He had defended himself in time, hadn't he? He was strong enough to deflect the force of the impact or dodge out of its path.

Mariel squeezed her eyes shut and forced herself to breathe lest she scare Coira. He was strong, capable, and intelligent. Alec stood by his side and would let no harm befall him. Kieran was fine. He had to be.

Of one thing she was absolutely certain. He would not be home by dawn as he had promised.

I love ye too much to see ye hurt.

How could those words be so painful and so euphoric all at once? Mariel swallowed the knot in her throat.

He loved her.

She steeled herself against her fears. When next she saw him, she would tell him—no matter what it took. He loved her and he would trust her. She had to put her faith in that.

Apprehension niggled the edges of her optimistic thoughts. The MacLeod warrior had charged him with such accuracy…

Kieran was fine. He had to be.

A savage cheer sounded overhead, and Mariel sensed the women and children around her give a collective jump.

Though this was Mariel's first experience with an attack, she knew the sound for what it was. A victory cry.

But who had won?

The tension in the room thickened with the unanswered question. The one she knew every woman thought.

Several children startled from sleep and began to cry. Their mothers whispered fiercely in the dark for them to be silent. Heavy boots stomped the overhead floorboards and sent sprinkles of dirt raining upon them.

The acrid odor of fear hung heavy in the thin air. If the MacLeods won, every woman and child in their crowded cellar would face death…or worse. Chills lifted the hairs on Mariel's arms. She would not go down without a fight.

She eased Coira from her lap with a gentle shush and picked her way across the room. Carefully, she crept up the stone stairs, her satin shoes silent against the stone. She pressed her body flush against the rough wall and waited.

The door rattled. A soft cry sounded from below. Mariel tightened her grip on her dagger and forced herself to breathe.

The door swung open and light pierced her eyes, shadowing a great, hulking frame that filled the doorway.

Chapter Twenty-Eight

Mariel tensed in preparation to attack when Colin's voice came from the great shadow.

"Mariel?"

The breath she'd been holding released in a rushing exhale.

The stinging brilliance of light eased against her eyes and Colin's form stood apparent in front of her. "I've never been happier to see you, Colin." She glanced at the crowd of people scurrying behind him. Tentative footsteps filled the stairwell below. "Where's Kieran?"

Colin backed into the hall and motioned for her to follow as the women and children emerged from the cellar with eyes squinted against the glow of the torches.

Before he could answer, Blair appeared with Dougal clasped in one hand and little Coira in the other. Blair gave Mariel a knowing smile. "I'll take Coira to her grandmother. When you find my brother, give him my love, aye?"

Mariel nodded and tried to shrug off the urgency of finding Kieran. Children could sense unease and the two had been through too much already. She bent low and gave them both a kiss on the cheek. "You were both very brave. I'm so proud of you."

Blair translated Mariel's words to Gaelic for Coira and both children flushed with pleasure before disappearing down the crowded hall.

Mariel immediately turned her attention to Colin. "Is Kieran here? Is he all right?" She did a visual sweep of the crowded area and frowned. "I don't see him…"

The throngs of people were mainly women returning from

battle. While many had blood on their clothing, only a few appeared injured.

Colin rubbed his shoulder and rolled his neck in the opposite direction. Weary lines etched his face. "He's fine, but he's no here."

Mariel sagged with relief. She was right. Kieran was fine. But not here? Confusion pulled at her brow. "I don't understand."

"The MacLeods ran. Kieran split us up. Some returned back here to protect the clan and castle, and some are chasing the bastards around the island."

"How long do you think that will take?" She knew her question was useless, but could not stop herself from asking.

Colin gave her a sympathetic frown. "Hard to say. Could be hours, could be weeks."

"That's what I expected." She took a deep breath to still her pounding heart. "I won't keep you any longer. I know you must be ready for bed."

"It's no a problem. I'm waiting for someone anyway."

A voluptuous woman with long blond hair and a suggestive smile peered around the corner.

Colin grinned down at Mariel. "Now I'll be going to bed." He hesitated, his eyes twinkling mischievously. "Ye can join us if ye like."

Mariel laughed in spite of herself at the outrageous invitation. "I don't think Kieran would like that."

"Ye're right. He'd have me strung up by my bollocks. I would say come see me if he ever gets tired of ye, but..." The dimple appeared in his cheek. "I dinna think that will happen."

"Go on," she chided through her mirth and swatted his shoulder.

Mariel's smile faded from her lips. The activity in the hall had dispersed and only a few people remained. Though exhaustion pulled at her, she had no desire to return to her room. Nothing waited for her there but the ghost of regret.

No, she could not go there and lie in the darkness alone. The company she would keep turned her stomach.

A warm hand wrapped around hers, startling her from the

draw of her own despair.

Blair's kind green eyes regarded Mariel with concern. "You needn't worry about him. Kieran is very strong and an excellent warrior. He knows how to protect himself."

Words that had meant to comfort squeezed Mariel's heart like a fist of ice. Blair was a good woman, an innocent caught in a dangerous scheme.

"I'll take you to your room. You can sleep—"

"No." Mariel shook her head. "There has to be something else I can do."

Blair cast her a wary look. "There are wounded to tend to. Are you sure you don't want—"

Mariel touched Blair's forearm. "I'm fine. Please, I'd like to help."

Blair nodded and led Mariel through the doors of the great hall. The long tables had been cleared away and replaced with makeshift pallets. Men lay upon them, some with bloodied bandages and some with gaping wounds.

Mariel shoved Kieran from her thoughts and rolled up the satin sleeves of her dress. These men needed her, and she would not come to their aid distracted.

•　•　•

The wind ripped through Kieran's heavy plaid as if he wore nothing at all. The hard tack he'd eaten several hours ago no longer staved off the gnawing hunger, and his stomach growled in protest. Exhaustion tugged at his heavy limbs, but he sat prone on his horse and pushed onward. What he was feeling was no different than what his men endured.

The sun had begun to rise and speared shards of crimson light through the dense copse of trees overhead, rendering the forest floor a brilliant shade of red. The effect was disconcerting. There had been too much bloodshed over the last two weeks to allow appreciation for the otherwise magnificent sight.

The MacLeods were hiding and had long since refused to fight face-to-face. Kieran and his men were relentless in their search. This was MacDonald land and they would do more than defend. They would punish.

The warriors he lost in defense of the Caisteal Camus had been avenged. Still, Kieran would not cease until every last straggler was found. Scotland would know that Kieran MacDonald was not a man easily taken advantage of, just as Brennan MacDonald had not been or their father before them.

Only a few MacLeods remained. Four by the looks of the tracks they made, and Kieran was on their trail. Like a predator closing in on his prey, he and his men had foregone sleep and hunted through the night with stealth determination. They would bring the last of the MacLeods down and return home to their comfortable beds, warm food, and willing women.

Home to Mariel.

Kieran's gritty hands clenched at the thought of her smooth skin beneath his fingers. He wanted to erase the faces of the dead with her beauty and obliterate the odor of blood with her heady rose scent.

He thought back to the night the battle began and a hollow ache filled his chest. Again. He had not been able to stop reliving it, damn it. She had been so desperate to speak to him, frantic almost. What she needed to say was important. He had no doubt of that. Hopefully she would be as eager to speak with him upon his return.

A patch of blue shifted behind a cluster of bushes. Kieran stilled. His body honed in on the enemy, his muscles tense in preparation to strike. A raw cry broke through the silence and four MacLeods charged through the brush with their swords drawn.

Their efforts were in vain. They were struck down before Kieran reached them. His men outnumbered the fallen MacLeods and yet they had still attacked in a valiant end to their lives, unlike their cowardly brethren. They died with a battle cry in their throats and swords in their hand. A warrior's death.

The poignancy of their courageous defeat struck Kieran's men and rather than cheers of success, their triumph resounded with solemn silence. Too many had died for this victory.

"To home, men," Kieran said in a low voice and turned his horse around. The ride to Caisteal Camus was long and they would arrive late in the night, but the final push through exhaustion, discomfort and hunger would be well worth it. They were going home.

. . .

Mariel wound a length of soft linen around a gash on a warrior's torso as he waited in grumpy silence. Very few men remained in the great hall. Some had healed, some insisted they had never belonged there in the first place, and others had stormed out, muttering about being coddled.

"You did well, Murdoch," she said to the warrior. She pressed a small loaf of still-warm bread into his hand. "For the warrior who can never get enough to eat."

He gave her a rare grin and nodded his gratitude.

Mariel rose to leave and felt the familiar wave of desperation wash over her.

If Kieran did not return soon, she would be forced into action on her own. Her only hope was that she could somehow manage to free Jack before Aaron's men caught her and killed her. But then there was Blair and Dougal to consider. If Mariel left, another assassin would take her place. One who was far more ruthless.

She scanned the room, anxious to start another task in an effort to occupy her mind.

Blair approached, drying her hands on her apron. "You are swaying on your feet. You need to go to bed, and I won't take no for an answer this time."

"There's so much to do. Bandages need to be changed, supper needs to be dispersed, and you know no one can deal with Murdoch but me." Mariel's few attempts at sleep had not been worth the effort. Every time her eyes closed, she saw Kieran's face, his eyes tender, trusting. The image was more than she could bear.

"Murdoch is the one who sent me over," Blair said. She

nodded to the grizzled warrior who clutched the loaf of bread Mariel had given him. Blair caught Mariel's hand in her own cool grasp and gave her a sympathetic look. "I know that something has been bothering you. I don't know if it's Kieran being gone or fear for his safety, but you need to take care of yourself, aye?"

"How did you do it, Blair?" Mariel asked quietly. "How did you manage to escape your past? How did you forgive him?"

Blair's face registered her surprise at the question, but she did not seem offended. "If I did not have my son, I would probably have stayed until he killed me. But Dougal was so small." Her eyebrows knit together. "No matter what happens in life, the young and innocent should never suffer for the mistakes of their elders. As far as forgiving…" She shook her head. "It's not that I've forgiven him, but that I did not want that hatred to follow me here. My focus is what I have in life rather than what I lost. I have been blessed with my sweet Dougal, a brother who cares for me, and a clan that is loyal." Blair gave Mariel a loving smile and squeezed her hand.

Blair released her hand. "Please go to bed."

Mariel nodded and allowed herself to be shuffled in the direction of her room. She trudged up the stairs and tried to convince herself exhaustion would provide a dreamless sleep.

Once the heavy door shut behind her, she fell onto her bed and reveled for one sweet second in the coolness of the sheets against her aching legs and the softness of the rushes cradling her heavy body. Her eyes closed and sleep slid over her like a heavy velvet blanket.

Six days left.

Her lids flew open.

Though her body was fatigued, her mind would not let her sleep. If she did not come up with another alternative soon, she would fail her mission and Jack would pay the price. Her heart raced and her body remained alert in stubborn defiance to the rest she so desperately needed.

The only remaining option resonated within her.

"No," Mariel whispered into the empty room. Tears ran hot down her cheeks.

There could truly be no other way.

Kieran would do anything to protect Blair and Dougal, just as Mariel had done for Jack. Without the opportunity to seek his help in coming up with a plan to defeat Aaron, she had no choice but to comply with the original demands. She sucked in a deep breath of air as though the act could still the pain of her breaking heart.

Kieran MacDonald would have to die.

Chapter Twenty-Nine

The journey home took more time than anticipated, and the moon hung high over Kieran's head long before he and his men arrived at the castle. He fought the weight of exhaustion and trudged up the narrow staircase toward the comfort of his bed. Toward Mariel.

He entered the narrow hall and fixed his gaze on her door.

His arms ached with the need to cradle the softness of her body against him. She would be warm from sleep. The thought was almost more than he could bear.

He stilled. What if she woke and thought he was the assassin? He didn't want to frighten her in the middle of the night, not when she already suffered from night terrors.

Irritation tightened his shoulders. Damn that English bastard for ruining this for him. Kieran would kill the whoreson as soon as he had the chance.

He turned from Mariel's door and entered his room where he was greeted with dark, cold loneliness. The servants had not known to anticipate his arrival and no fire had been lit. Were Kieran not so fatigued, he might have done it himself, but the lure of his bed was too strong to ignore. With a heavy sigh, he lay down, not bothering to pull the blankets back, and fell into sleep's embrace.

•   •   •

Mariel's frantic heartbeat hummed in her ears. The sounds of movement in Kieran's chamber had ceased. The time had come.

She sat up and the room spun. Her stomach lurched

in protest. Despite the chill of the room, a sheen of sweat moistened the surface of her skin.

True, she could flee and attempt to rescue Jack, but that would do nothing for Blair and Dougal. She could not leave them to suffer.

There was no other way. This had to be done.

She knelt before her chest of clothes and pulled a pair of black pants and shirt from its depths. They were men's clothing that had been tailored to fit her small frame. The perfect attire to complete a heinous crime and slip through the night undetected.

Her fingers trembled as she dressed and plaited her hair. Her movements were quick lest she lose her nerve. She squeezed her eyes shut against the pain lancing her heart. If she did not do this, Jack would die. Her darling, sweet Jack who had done no wrong in the course of his short life.

She slid the black mask over her face and nausea threatened her composure. She had worn it to a masque she'd attended the previous year, back when she thought her sins could not slide any deeper. The small mirror caught her reflection. The woman who stared back at her was not Mariel Brandon, but a stranger, a foreign beast borne of desperation.

She turned from the horrific image, unable to stand the nightmare looking back at her. The knife lay on her bed, a silvered glint of moonlight upon her mattress. Were it not for Jack, she would sooner plunge that blade into her own chest than Kieran's.

Mariel wrapped her hands around the hilt of the blade and drew a deep breath. Now.

Soundlessly, she slipped from her room and made her way down the hall to Kieran's door. The metal latch was cool beneath her sweat-dampened palm.

With a slight press of her thumb, the latch gave and the door shifted open. Unlocked. Fear and dread mingled in a bitter, metallic taste in the back of her throat.

His warm, masculine scent lingered in the air and clawed at her tender heart.

Kieran lay on top of his bed fully clothed with his dirty

boots still strapped to his feet. The poor man must have been exhausted. His large arms were folded over his chest, calling to mind not only his raw strength but also the number of times he had cradled her against his warm body. He'd offered her safety and love where she offered him betrayal and death.

Mariel bit down on her lip until she tasted blood. Her hands trembled beneath the weight of the dagger.

One thrust to the throat. Death would come quick and with little pain.

For Jack's life.

To protect Blair and Dougal.

The pale light of the moon spilled across his smooth jaw. Despite the hell he must have been through and the traces of fatigue on his face, he had shaved recently. For her.

She pulled in a breath against the pain in her chest and immediately steeled herself from the onslaught of emotion. Despite her resolve, the hand holding the knife quavered.

A knot lodged in her throat, and the energy coursing through her body went still. Her arms dropped to her sides. She could not do it. She could not kill Kieran.

She backed away from his sleeping form, committing his image to memory before she turned toward the door. If she hurried, she could obtain the necessary boat to leave the island before anyone noticed her missing. A simple note to Kieran while en route to Inverness might provide him with enough time to hide himself as well as Blair and Dougal. She tightened her grip on her blade until the hilt bit into her palm in an effort to bring a sense of reality to the surreal night.

The journey would be difficult, but if she hurried, it would be possible to arrive with enough time to observe the house and monitor guard rotations. In the cover of night, she could launch a silent attack to save Jack on her own.

She reached for the door latch and paused. One last glance to balm her wounded heart, to remember forever the only man she would ever truly love. She looked behind her and froze.

The bed was empty.

. . .

Kieran narrowed his eyes in the darkness, studying the figure in black. Finally, the English assassin showed his cowardly face.

Not visiting Mariel had proven a wise choice. Kieran's blood ran cold at the thought of placing her in danger. He would deal with this bastard as silently as possible to keep from waking her. In no way would he have her exposed to this ugliness, not after all she had been through.

Energy pulsed through his veins, his exhaustion nothing more than a distant memory. Before the whoreson could turn back to the door, Kieran threw his weight against the man and knocked them both to the floor. The assassin grunted as his slender body absorbed the impact of Kieran's weight. Despite his grip, the intruder writhed away with alarming dexterity and darted toward the open window.

He wouldn't get off that easy.

Kieran lunged at him again with arms outstretched and caught the man's ankles. The assassin's head slammed against the floor with a dull *thunk*, and his body fell still.

Kieran smirked. That had almost been too easy.

The man's foot shot out and slammed into Kieran's chest. The impact sent him staggering back. The bastard might be small, but he was tough as hell.

Kieran grasped the man's arm, but the wiry coward twisted free once more and ran toward the window.

Before Kieran could reach him, the assassin swung his legs over the edge in preparation to jump, but Kieran grasped the smooth fabric of the man's shirt, halting the freefall before it could begin. With a savage jerk, Kieran swung the masked man back into his bedroom and slammed the shutters of his window closed.

The assassin stared up at him, his chest rising and falling rapidly. Good, the bastard was scared. He should be.

Caught, but not defeated, the assassin sprinted toward the door. Kieran was faster and headed him off. A savage shove to the man's chest, and he crashed against the wall where he crumpled to the floor.

Unease flared through Kieran. Something wasn't right. That was not a man's chest he'd shoved, nor was it a man's voice that rasped for air.

His attacker was a woman.

She remained on the floor with her back slumped against the wall.

"Lift yer mask," Kieran said quietly.

She did not respond. Her shallow panting filled the room.

"Lift yer mask," he barked.

She flinched as his words reverberated off the walls around them. A slender white hand rose to the base of the mask and peeled the black fabric upward.

Finally, he would see the face of his would-be killer.

Chapter Thirty

There was no way out for Mariel. The time had come to let Kieran view the monster beneath. Her heart raced. No longer would he see a good in her she did not possess. No longer would he seek to offer his protection and comfort. No longer would he love the woman he thought her to be.

Mariel tensed for his reaction and tugged the mask over her head.

Kieran, always so guarded, stared at her now in disbelief. His face was a mirror of everything he felt. The confusion, the shock…the horror as her betrayal hit him full force. The raw emotion in his black eyes tore through her. She should turn away, save herself the torment of his gaze. But no, she must look. She must see the product of her deception.

He loved her and she had hurt him. He trusted her, and she threatened everything he worked so hard to protect.

"Mariel…" Her name was nothing more than a strangled cry.

Desperation seeped from the blackness of her soul, selfishly keening for the loss of the man she loved. She did not deserve him, she never had, and yet to imagine her life without him was not to imagine a life at all.

"I can explain," she whispered.

His agony slid behind a mask of cold indifference. "Stand up."

She staggered to her feet and tried to ignore the empty ache in her chest. "Please, let me speak to y—"

"I dinna wish to hear it."

His calloused hand looped around her wrist and twisted her arm behind her.

The wall of his solid body brushed against her back. "If ye try to escape, I'll break yer arm."

Mariel squeezed her eyes shut against the sting of tears. She wanted to fall against him and let the heat of his quiet strength comfort her. She wanted to soothe the hurt in his gaze with her explanations.

Despair coiled like ice in the pit of her stomach. There would never be comfort from him again.

"Let me explain," she whimpered. The reality of her situation seeped in and her breath came faster.

"No anything ye say can change what I have seen. Now walk." His voice was flat.

She shuffled forward, not bothering to ask where he took her. She didn't need to. Memories of the damp cellar rushed forefront to her mind. Chills raised the flesh on her arms.

Jack.

Her step faltered. He would pay the price of her failure. Kieran nudged her forward, his hand tight on her wrist.

She obeyed his unspoken command and continued on despite the trembling of her legs.

Perhaps she could still save Jack. Not only did she know the rendezvous point, she knew the layout of the manor from the months she had trained there. Information was all she had to bargain with for Jack's life.

Kieran's hold on her loosened, but she did not dare to attempt escape. She allowed herself to be escorted to the bottom of the cellar steps. The entrance to the cold, barren cell stretched ominously before her.

Another nudge against her back urged her toward her destiny. She had no choice but to enter. Her feet scuffed on the hard packed floor and eerie plinks of dripping water echoed off the cold walls. She turned to face Kieran. There was much she needed to say, much he needed to hear.

Her throat tightened. How could she speak if she could not even breathe? From the indifference radiating off him to the way he avoided making eye contact, there remained no question in Mariel's mind that he was no longer her lover. He had become her enemy.

The plea died on her lips and he did not speak. He slammed the cell shut and locked it. He did not look at her before turning away.

* * *

Mariel's rounded shoulders pressed against the unyielding wall of stone behind her and the wet ground left her stiff and aching with cold. She hugged her legs for a warmth that would never come.

Hamish stood guard before her locked door. He did not speak, nor did he attempt to gaze upon her. Instead, his blade whipped in the subtle glow of the single lit candle toward invisible opponents.

The door above the stairs creaked open and a familiar voice spoke in the dark. "Go get yer breakfast, lad. I'll mind her."

Alec.

Hamish did not wait to be told twice and disappeared into the darkness.

Mariel's fists clenched against the wrenching burn in her belly. She wanted to bury her face against her knees and slide from sight. But she could not, she would not. Alec deserved to see her for what she was.

The sounds of his movement echoed around her. She waited in the terse silence of her cell. Each footstep set her heart racing until at long last he stuck his face to the bars of the door and stared at her, accusation hot in his blue gaze. "Is it true?"

"I'd like to speak to Kieran, please." Her voice rasped from thirst and lack of use.

"I dinna think he wants to see ye. I canna say I blame him." Alec glanced to the wall behind her and added, "If it's true that is."

He searched her face in the muted light, his cold eyes skeptical. He didn't want to believe what he'd been told.

"There is so much more than anyone knows," she said quietly. There in the face of one of the few she called a friend, she still could not admit the truth.

His grunt indicated he understood far more than was said.

"Alec, I have to speak with Kieran. He has always relied on your counsel, and I know he will listen to you." She sighed, not sure exactly what to say to convince him. "I know I have no right to be asking this given my position, but if you could speak with him on my behalf, I would be forever grateful."

Before he had a chance to answer, Hamish's footsteps thumped on the stairs. The sound was followed by the mouthwatering salty aroma of cooked ham. "Best get yers while it's still warm," he said.

Alec stared at Mariel a moment longer, his face blank. Without word or promise, he backed away from her prison and took his leave.

Mariel's stomach churned. If she were going to save Jack, she would need to leave by nightfall.

Aaron was not known for his patience and already she had taken so long. She curled up on the earthen floor and allowed herself to wallow in her own misery. Several rounds of guards came and went. Plates of food were delivered and left untouched in the corner of her cell. In a haze of timeless existence, the sounds overhead lessened and eventually fell into silence. Night had descended.

She could not depart for Inverness, and Kieran was not coming.

•   •   •

Kieran sat alone in his darkened chamber. The servants had attempted to light a fire, but he had callously chased them off. He wanted his room black, still, and cold. Like his mood.

His hand clenched into a fist in a vain effort to squeeze out the rage festering within. To no avail. The pounding in his head intensified.

Damn Mariel with her heated gaze and insurmountable beauty. He should have known she was a trap. He'd had his doubts about her the moment they met, and yet still allowed her to force her way onto Skye—and into his heart.

The simmer of his anguish bubbled over. With all the force of his rage, he hurled his cup across the room where it connected against the wall with a satisfying clang.

He was not the only victim to fall prey to her charm. Blair and Dougal both loved Mariel. Trusted her. They would be heartbroken to learn of her betrayal.

With all he had told Mariel, how could she so easily lie to them all?

Kieran leapt to his feet and paced the length of his room.

If she were a man, she would already be dead by his own hands.

With the right words and well-placed moments of intimacy, she'd had him exactly where she wanted him. What a fool he had been.

And still she begged an audience. Did she think he was daft?

Even Alec was not immune to her charms and had pleaded her case. Alec—the coldest warrior in Kieran's army.

Kieran paused his pacing and sat heavily in his chair before the cold hearth. Moonlight spilled into the room with a pearl-like luminescence and fell across his arm. The raised flesh of a vicious scar cast a slight shadow across the crook of his elbow and forbidden memories rushed to the forefront of his mind of the way she had fingered the healed wounds. For the briefest of moments, his bitter anger swept aside. How could an event that transpired only weeks before be so vivid as if it had happened days ago?

A scar is the result of an event borne upon your flesh.

His fingertip traced the pale line across his elbow and recalled the image of Mariel's mangled back. There was much she had not yet told him.

He rose from his chair with a steely determination. She had secrets, and he would uncover every last one of them.

He made his way to the cellar without the aid of light. Below, Hamish stood before Mariel's cell with his sword outstretched in his hand. He straightened when Kieran approached and let his sword drop into the scabbard at his side.

"Practicing," the lad murmured.

Kieran gave him a hard look. "Leave."

Hamish nodded and scrambled up the stairs. Kieran waited for the door to slam shut overhead before he approached the cell. Energy flared through him the way it did oftentimes before battle.

The key grated against the ancient lock, and he pushed the door open. Mariel was on the other side, standing with her back to him. She did not flinch at the noise, nor did she turn as he entered.

"Ye wanted to see me. Here I am." He kept his voice monotone and devoid of his anger, his pain.

Mariel faced him. Exhaustion lined her delicate features. She looked fragile, as if one hard look might break her. A powerful surge of longing swelled within him, unexpectedly and unwanted.

Their meeting would have to be quick.

He crossed his arms over his chest. He would offer her no comfort that night.

"You are still in danger." Her soft voice interrupted his thoughts.

"How am I in danger? Are ye no the English assassin sent to kill me?" He could not keep the fury from seeping into his voice.

"I have information to share with you, but you must agree to two conditions before I agree to help you."

He stared at her in disbelief. Perhaps she was not so fragile as she appeared. "What are yer conditions?"

Her gaze was sharp beneath her fatigue. "When you exact vengeance upon those who have threatened you, there is one person who must be left alive."

"Ye assume I will retaliate."

Her fingers worried the fabric of her black trews. "Catching me will not solve the problem, only prolong it. If you do not kill those who seek you harm, the threat to your life and your family will not cease."

He hated the searing burn tightening like a fist in his gut.

"Ye want Jack left alive."

Her gaze softened, but she did not break eye contact. "Yes," she whispered.

"I have a condition of my own," Kieran said. "I want to know who Jack is. What is the man to ye if no a lover?"

She bit her lip and regarded him with a worried expression he had come to know too well. The look that indicated she was wary of his trust. After weeks of frustrated half-truths, he would know who Jack was.

"Jack isn't a man at all." She swallowed thickly. "He's a boy of ten. He's my brother, and he is in danger because of me."

Kieran narrowed his eyes, unsure of whether he could believe her or not. The tears in her eyes seemed genuine. They'd certainly tugged at a deeper part of him he fought to ignore.

She wrapped her arms around her torso. "I saw how you handled Hamish and how well you rule your clan. Jack needs someone like you in his life. He's innocent of my treachery and needs a home, someone to care for him. He's a good boy." Her voice broke, but she continued regardless. "I know he will listen to you and respect you. Please take him into your clan and make him one of your own."

She drew a deep breath and watched him with shimmering eyes. "Please," she whispered.

If what she said was true, how could he deny her request? Blair would never forgive him if he left a child without a home, and he could never forgive himself to leave an innocent unguarded.

"I agree to yer first condition."

Mariel tilted her head upward and breathed a long, shaky sigh. She turned toward him, and her pale lips lifted in a sad smile. Her nod was more to herself than to him. "Jack will be safe."

"Ye said two things," he reminded her.

He balled his hand into a fist and waited for the request he knew would come.

After all she had done, all she had threatened with her presence—could he allow her to live?

Chapter Thirty-One

Kieran widened his stance in an effort to keep from pacing Mariel's small, miserable cell. Why was she taking so long to answer his question? At this rate, he would be there all night.

Her thin arms were still wrapped around her chest, her brow creased with worry. She looked so damn vulnerable. A stark contrast to the woman who maintained unbreakable strength and determination for the months he had known her. He hated seeing her like this. He hated the raw feelings she evoked with her sorrow.

"The second request?" he pressed. Would she beg for her life?

Mariel lifted her chin, displaying a shadow of the stubborn resilience he had come to expect from her. "I want to come with you."

"Mariel, this isna—"

"You need me. Not only do I know the location of the meeting point, I also know the layout of the property. The manor contains secret rooms and false doors. I know them well. I also know how best to avoid discovery. Together we can catch them off guard and gain the advantage."

He did not bother to suppress his heavy sigh. How like the English to keep a maze-filled home.

His men were used to fighting outdoors or in the solid walls of a castle. Though strong and prepared, the MacDonald men were not used to trickery, especially not with a traitor at their side.

"The men you will face are vicious and lack the honor of Highland battle. They fight dirty." Her gaze dropped to the floor. "They fight like me. I can train your men and prepare them for what they will be up against."

Mariel was a strong opponent, he would give her that. His men relied more on strength than speed. The drastic difference in fighting styles could put them at a disadvantage and cost Kieran lives he was not willing to sacrifice.

Damn it.

Kieran kept her trapped with his gaze. "Where did ye learn to fight like that?"

"The man who sent me here insisted I learn. He had a Chinaman he'd saved from being executed who trained his people for him. I was the only woman to receive such training." Her knuckles went white beneath her clenched hands. "If I would have tried to escape, they wouldn't have killed me. They would have killed Jack."

The expression on her face was earnest, her gaze sincere. Indecision warred within Kieran, a foreign and unwelcome emotion. His people lived and died by his decisions.

He stepped closer. "How do I know I can trust ye?"

The flickering light sent shards of gold sparkling through her exotic eyes. "I have not told you a single lie since we met."

His derisive snort echoed off the cold walls. "Ye expect me to believe that?"

"No." Her back stiffened. "But it's the truth."

He could think of no proof to support or disprove her claim. She had deceived him and made him believe she was someone she was not.

Regardless, the most pressing matter centered on Blair and Dougal's safety. If Mariel were unable to carry out her assignment, another assassin would be dispatched in her place. Kieran knew all too well the persistence of men.

"Will you allow me to join you?" she asked.

Her voice was soft and carried with it an intimacy that brought back memories he preferred to forget. He scrubbed his face in an effort to clear his mind and focused on his original purpose in coming to see Mariel. To discover the truth.

"I will agree to let ye come, but first I want ye to answer

my questions."

"You trust me to tell the truth?"

"Ye dinna lie, remember?" He searched her eyes, challenging what he wanted desperately to believe.

She did not turn away. "No," she replied with an earnest expression. "I do not lie. I'll answer any question you ask."

He pulled the chair from outside her cell door, settled it in the small prison and motioned to it. "Ye can sit if ye like."

"I'd prefer not to."

Kieran shrugged. "Ye mentioned a meeting point. Where is it?"

"There is a large manor on the outskirts of Inverness. The exact location is difficult to find unless you know where to look. The man who owns the manor, the man you will need to stop, is Aaron." She pursed her lips.

Was she afraid to say more?

"Is he the man you feared when I met you?"

"Yes." She searched his eyes. "He runs an operation of spies, assassins, and whores. People pay him, and he has his people carry out the tasks without ever getting his hands dirty. He's hard and ruthless. Had you not allowed me to join you, he would have killed Jack and probably me as well."

"Who hired him?" Kieran pressed.

"Given the instructions I received, I can only guess."

Kieran's body instinctively tensed. "What instructions?"

Mariel hesitated. Her gaze flicked to the sword at his side. "Remember our agreement. You can't kill me until after Aaron is defeated."

Fear rippled through him. "What instructions?" he repeated through clenched teeth.

She looked away, unable to meet his eyes. "They wanted to know where Blair and Dougal were hidden. If I couldn't discover their whereabouts within three months, I was to kill you."

A chill tingled at the base of his neck. She had been sent after Blair and Dougal, not him. Kieran heard himself roar. He clenched a fist at his side and stared at Mariel in horror. Rage twisted dark and ugly within his gut. If she were a man…

Mariel shook her head. "I didn't know, Kieran. I thought they were grown men when I took the assignment, political refugees."

Kieran unfurled his hand and then balled it into a fist again, focusing on the action in an effort to control himself. "Ye dinna ever consider they were a woman and child?"

"What would you have thought?" she demanded, turning a hard gaze on him. Her expression softened. "You're angry and you're hurt. If striking me will make you feel better, do it. I can take the hit."

Her invitation caught him off guard, as did the subtle shift in her weight as she braced herself for the blow. He had never intentionally hit a woman in his life, and he refused to do so now.

He moved back a step, but her body did not relax.

"Was the attack from the MacLeods part of Aaron's effort to get to Blair and Dougal?"

"No, Aaron is far too subtle for that."

Kieran took another deep breath to calm himself before he asked the question that weighed heaviest on his heart. "When did ye send word to him of Blair's location?"

Mariel's chin lifted. "I never would do that." A look of pain crossed her features and the words trailed off. "I knew you would sacrifice everything for them and so I thought to..." Tears sparkled unshed in her eyes. "I couldn't do it."

She had meant to kill him.

Kieran hardened against her tortured look lest it pierce the stoicism necessary to handle the situation.

Manipulation would not work on him. Not again. He was fool enough to fall prey the first time. He was not so much a fool that he would fall for it again.

He wanted to slam his fist into the wall until the mortar sprinkled from the cracks like powder. He wanted to rage at her and make her understand his hatred for her lies. But he was a warrior and emotion never won wars.

"They dinna know," he murmured, reminding himself of the most important thing. As of now, Blair and Dougal were still safe.

God, he hoped she had been right about not lying to him.

If this were a lie…

His stomach churned with disgust. "How could ye agree to something like this?"

She drew a slow breath. "In exchange for my cooperation, I would have Jack's freedom and mine as well. Were I to decline, they would…" She sucked in pained breath. "They would kill him."

Kieran's brow furrowed. "Yer freedom? I dinna understand."

·   ·   ·

Mariel studied Kieran carefully, waiting for a reaction of some kind. He had listened without speaking while she recounted how she had been left as Jack's sole caregiver and how she'd been tricked into working for Aaron. Kieran crossed his arms over his chest, his face expressionless.

Her throat ached from speaking for so long, but she could take his silence no longer. "I'm not proud of what I've done," she said. "Were it not for Jack, I would have let myself slip into the gutter and never emerged. But Aaron would not release Jack unless I paid back the coin we had cost him. Little did I know the training he gave me, the clothes, the tutors—all of that added to the amount I owed. When I realized that, I wanted to give up, but I couldn't. Not when I had to be strong for Jack. If I were gone, he would have no one. He's too young to survive on his own, too weak."

He still showed no reaction. Instead he motioned toward her. "What happened to yer back?"

Such a simple question to ask. If he only knew the pain that question would dredge up, he would never have asked. She regarded his cold stare. Or perhaps he would.

Her knees turned soft and her weight became too much to bear. Perhaps the chair was a good idea after all. She sank down onto the smooth wooden seat. "Please don't ask me to relive that."

"Ye said scars were secrets and those on yer back are exceptional. There are no secrets between us now, aye?" His voice was almost soothing, as though he were trying to coax a response from her.

The musty cell suddenly felt colder and its damp chill pressed into her. Mariel pulled her legs to her chest and wrapped her arms around them. Though she felt the weight of Kieran's stare heavy upon her, she could not look at him.

A chip in the rough stone wall drew her attention, and she fixed on that as she heard her voice echo in the tiny room. "Toward the end of my training, Aaron wanted me to learn how to kill a man." She hesitated, anticipating the rush of memories with dread.

Kieran's voice sounded far away as he spoke. "Go on."

The foul odor of tallow candles choked her. There were no candles like that in the castle, and yet she could smell them, *feel* them as the smoke burned down her throat. Mariel closed her eyes, and the room around her melted away. Her heart raced. God help her, she did not want to go back…

She sat in the semidarkness, trying to breathe in the heavy air. A candle sat on a small table in the center of the chamber.

"They put me in a room with no windows. There was a man tied to a chair in the corner. He was frightened. I could see it in his eyes. I didn't know what they wanted me to do, but I think somehow he did."

Clear blue eyes darted anxiously toward her. The door creaked open, and a puddle spread beneath the chair as he urinated on himself.

"Another man entered the room. He was large and he smelled…horrible."

Sweat and death emanated from his swollen flesh, his chest wheezing with labored breath.

"He pressed a blade into my hand and ordered me to kill the man in the chair. I refused. He pulled a whip from his belt and ordered again for me to kill."

The coil of braided leather swirled to the floor with a sharp slap. A slow, menacing smile spread over the large man's face, revealing several missing teeth.

"I understood the threat and yet again, I refused. That's when he whipped me. He stopped after each lash and bade me kill the man. Each time I refused until I could withstand it no more."

Her dress hung in bloody shreds at her side and she swayed with exhaustion.

"No," she whispered and braced herself for the wrath of the whip. It fell against her and stripped away flesh that was no longer intact. She staggered against the pain, her knees buckling beneath her. The room rocked, turned hazy, and she slumped to the floor. She refused to accept her defeat and tried to raise herself. Her arms trembled with futile effort.

"My body wanted to die, but I clung to the pain. To feel meant I lived. No one would help Jack if I were dead. I heard the scrape of a chair and the frightened man was thrown next to me. His head was yanked backward and his throat slit. I couldn't close my eyes. If I did, I knew I might never open them again. I saw…everything."

The blade was soundless as it bit into tender flesh. Blue eyes bulged and blood gushed from the wound. It sprayed her with its slippery warmth and seeped into her dress. He gurgled and sputtered. His body jerked in the throes of final defeat before he fell still.

Bile rose in the back of her throat. The heat of the room, the coppery odor of blood, the metallic taste of it upon her lips, and the pain of her back. She could take no more. Lacking the strength to raise her head, she emptied the meager contents of her stomach where she lay.

"Aaron was furious when he learned I'd refused to kill the man. For my disobedience, he ordered…" She heard herself falter. "He ordered me to be locked in a closet with the body. For three days."

"That night at the inn, the nightmare ye had where ye felt my neck…" Kieran's voice startled her, calling her back from hell.

The air smelled of moist earth and the room was cold. There was no blood, no vomit, and no body.

Mariel hugged her legs tighter. Tears stained the black fabric stretched across her knees. "Please don't make me talk about this anymore."

Kieran took a step toward her and stopped. He was so close she could breathe in the scent that had once made her feel so safe, so loved. Her body trembled with want of that comfort.

His expression was softer, almost tender, and his hand reached toward her.

She waited, her body screaming for the slightest of touches, begging for reassurance and support.

But consolation did not come. His hand curled into a fist and dropped to his side. He turned away and walked from her cell.

"Where are you going?"

He faced her once more, his expression hard. Gone was the hint of kindness she had glimpsed only moments before.

"To tell the person this affects more than anyone else," he said. "Blair has a right to know."

Chapter Thirty-Two

Mariel did not move off the hard chair even after the door slammed overhead, announcing Kieran's departure. She hugged her legs and tried not to think about him waking Blair in the middle of the night. She tried not to imagine the disappointment, and the pain in Blair's gaze.

The door opened and footsteps clunked down the stairs. Mariel's heart pounded frantically. Kieran had returned. For the first time since she had peeled off that horrible mask, hope eased the knots in her stomach. Perhaps he had changed his mind. Perhaps he decided not to tell Blair.

"Mariel." The voice that spoke was familiar, but not Kieran's. Colin appeared before her cell door.

Disappointment left her reeling. Blair would still learn the truth, Kieran still despised her, and now Colin would witness her shame. Mariel squeezed her legs against her until her arms ached with the effort.

Her confession to Kieran had left her raw. Her spirit was battered, and she was exhausted. No longer did she possess the energy to keep her tears at bay or face the hurt of a friend's stare.

Her cell door creaked open, and she buried her face against the tops of her knees in a futile effort to hide. She could not face Colin. Not now.

A heavy blanket eased over her shoulders. Startled, she raised her head and found him gazing down at her, the expression on his face free of accusation.

His sympathetic smile showed the dimple in his left cheek. "Kieran said ye looked cold."

"Colin…" The lump in her throat choked off her words

and tears blurred her vision.

He eased her off the chair onto her stiff legs and said nothing as his arms wrapped around her. He asked no questions, demanded no explanation. He simply held her.

"I'll no tell anyone if ye cry," he said softly.

And then they came. Bitter tears coursed down her cheeks and melted against the smooth fabric of Colin's leine. Tears for Jack, tears for Kieran and the pain she'd caused his battered family, and tears for her own miserable, broken heart.

Colin's arms tightened around her as she sagged against him and wept for years of pain and humiliation.

She was too broken to fight.

．　．　．

Kieran studied Blair from across the table. Her hair lay against the blue velvet robe like a sable cape and her hands wrapped around a mug of hot chocolate. The rare treat had been brought back from the markets of London for her as a means of pleasure. He hated that it must now be used for consolation.

Not that Blair appeared to need much consoling.

He had expected many things in her reaction to Mariel's betrayal, but her blank look of nonchalance was not one of them. She had remained expressionless while Kieran repeated everything Mariel had told him, save the horrifying story of her back.

Blair gently blew a curl of steam and took a sip before speaking. "You don't believe her." It wasn't a question.

He straightened, irritated that his doubt was so obvious. "She lied to us. When she speaks, I dinna know what I can trust and what I can't."

Blair tilted her head to the side, studying him the same way their mother always had when she knew they were hiding something. "From what I understand, she did not lie, she just didn't tell the entire truth." She sipped her hot chocolate again and watched him over the rim of the mug.

"I dinna understand how ye can be so calm about this. She

was sent to report yer location to that bastard of a husband of yers. She tried to kill me. How can ye sit there as though nothing has happened?" His fist slammed the table and upset the warmed ale in front of him.

Blair righted the overturned cup and wiped up the spill with the same cool composure as she'd taken the news. "Mariel has known about my presence for a while now and has been free to come and go as she pleased. When you were gone, she did not rush away to reveal my location and send my husband to a partially defended castle. Do you know what she did?" Blair did not wait for his response. "She cared for the wounded."

"Ye're too trusting. She could have met with someone when ye werena looking."

Her lips pressed into a frown. "She slept in the rushes alongside the injured lest they need her." Blair grasped his forearm, her fingers warm from the mug she'd cradled. "What happened with Brennan was not your fault, Kieran. You were not the only one who trusted his killer." She stared directly into his eyes. "No one blames you."

Kieran snatched his arm away from her and stood so abruptly, the chair screeched against the stone floor. "Dinna speak of that."

How could Blair bring that up now?

She got to her feet and continued in a gentle voice. "If you stopped hiding, I wouldn't speak of it. I know the pain that man's betrayal causes you still." Her eyes shadowed with her own hurt. Brennan's murder had affected them all greatly. "You need to understand that you were not the only one fooled by him. Everyone was. No one had any idea what his intentions were."

Everyone had believed the spy to be a good man. But Kieran should have seen through the façade then, just as he should have seen through it now. If he could be so easily fooled, how could he protect his family? How could he be laird to the MacDonalds?

"Mariel is not the same. She is a good woman."

Rage coursed through his veins, fueled by past mistakes. "How can ye say that?"

"She had no choice. Can you not see? Look at what I did to free myself when Dougal was beaten." Blair sank down into her seat and motioned for him to do the same. "Let me ask you this. If Dougal and I were held captive and to free us you had to act as a spy and possibly kill a man you did not know, what would you do?"

Kieran sat heavily in the chair and avoided Blair's gaze. He knew exactly what he would do and so did she. "She should have told me," he ground out with great irritation.

Blair's eyebrow quirked up. "Did she not try?"

His mind flashed to the memory of Mariel standing in the moonlight, the air crackling with the frenzied pull of battle as she pleaded with him to speak to her. He had been fixated on the rush of men climbing toward them, and the danger her location placed her in. Something tightened in his chest at the image of her tear streaked face. Blair was right. Mariel had been desperate to talk and now he understood why.

"I'll be going back to bed now." Blair rose from her seat, but did not walk away. "I think you have some more talking to do with Mariel, aye?"

Kieran grunted again and tried to change the subject to more important matters. "I want a guard with ye at all times when ye are awake, and one stationed at yer door and Dougal's when ye sleep."

Mariel may be locked in the cellar and Blair may have faith in her, but Kieran was not about to take any chances.

"I will so long as you promise to speak to Mariel when I leave." She folded her arms over her chest, and Kieran knew the conversation was done.

He heaved a tired sigh. The women of Caisteal Camus would be the death of him one way or another. "Verra well."

After securing a warrior to guard Blair and Dougal, Kieran made good on his promise and trudged toward the cellar once more. He bit back a curse and pulled the heavy door to the stairs open. If it weren't for Blair, he would not be coming down to see Mariel again. Or so he told himself.

He reached the bottom of the stairs and stopped. Something

was wrong. The room was unnaturally still and Colin no longer stood guard. The cell door was open. His stomach clenched.

Mariel had fooled him again.

Kieran crossed the narrow floor, anticipating an empty prison.

Instead he found Colin sitting on the dirty floor with Mariel's head cradled in his lap as she slept soundly.

Kieran gritted his teeth. Colin had wasted no time laying claim to what belonged to Kieran.

What *had* belonged to him, he amended to himself.

"Colin, what—"

"Shh!" Colin gave him a sharp look. "The lass needs sleep. She is exhausted, and I'll no have ye waking her."

Kieran let out a low curse. "I dinna care how tired she is. She wouldna be here had she been honest from the beginning."

Did everyone take her damn side?

Colin opened his mouth to protest when Mariel shifted on the floor.

"How did I fall asleep?" Her voice was raspy with exhaustion. She climbed to her feet with Colin's aid.

An unexpected wave of sympathy washed over Kieran. She did look tired. Her eyes were red rimmed and swollen. His heart hardened. He would not be as weak as the others. He did not have that luxury.

"Colin, leave." Kieran stared directly at Mariel. "We need to talk."

Colin hesitated before brushing past Kieran. He stared down at Mariel and suddenly felt as tired as she looked. This had gone on too damn long already.

"Why dinna ye tell me before now? I told ye I would help."

The door at the top of the stairs opened once more. Irritation bristled along Kieran's back.

Mariel obviously heard the interruption too. Her voice dropped to a whisper, and she spoke in a rushed tone. "I tried so many times. But if you didn't believe me or you killed me, Jack would have no one. I finally decided to trust you but it was too late—"

Hamish interrupted her confession. "Laird?"

Kieran spun around with his hand on the hilt of his sword, making clear the threat. "What? What is it ye want?"

Hamish eyed the hilt and spoke in Gaelic, "There was a messenger on the coast earlier. Said he had a package for Mariel Brandon. I heard ye were awake and thought it best to bring it down here to ye."

"Where is he now?" Kieran demanded. Finally, he could have confirmation of Mariel's story.

Hamish shifted uncomfortably. "The guards, they dinna know about Mariel and so they let him go." He handed Kieran a smooth wooden box the size of a man's fist.

"Let me see it," Mariel said, in Gaelic.

Kieran turned to her, unable to hide his shock. Mariel spoke Gaelic. Did the level of her deception have no limit?

He frowned and rolled the box in his hands. Something inside *thunked* against the wooden walls.

"Oh God, please stop." The color drained from Mariel's face as she approached. "I know that box. It's from Aaron." She reached with a trembling hand. "Let me see it."

He hesitated at her request. The box was too small to hold a weapon of any bearing. Besides, she'd have to get through himself and Hamish first. An unlikely feat. With a shrug, Kieran dropped the parcel into her outstretched hand.

Mariel held it for a long minute, her eyes fixed on the harmless token. For someone so desperate, she certainly took a long time to open it.

She drew a deep breath and pulled the lid back. Her eyes went wide and her hands trembled. "No," she whispered.

The echo of her frantic breathing filled the room. "No," she said again and shook her head vigorously. The box tumbled from her hand and landed in the rushes, the sound muted by the howling cry ripping from her throat.

Chapter Thirty-Three

Mariel backed away from the box. Bile rose in her throat and choked off her cry.

The finger lying in the dirty straw was too small to be that of an adult.

Jack needed her. Now.

And she knew exactly what to do.

Her mind ticked through calculated points of her escape. The door to her cell stood open, but she would have to defeat Hamish and Kieran first. Based on what Hamish said earlier, very few people knew about her façade. That worked to her benefit.

Both men gaped at her in shock. She could use that to her advantage. While Kieran stood closest to her, he was stronger and would be more difficult to defeat. Hamish, however, was still young. His body was not yet honed with refined battle skills. Her decision was made.

She rushed Hamish and hit the young warrior under the jaw with her forearm. He slid to the floor as she rounded on Kieran.

Any hope she had at catching him off guard had been dashed by her attack on Hamish. Kieran lunged toward her, but she was faster than him and evaded his grasp by darting toward the back of the cell. He took the bait and advanced, thinking he had her cornered. She waited until he opened his arms to grab her before pitching forward into a somersault across the cellar floor.

By the time she stood, he was already in front of her again. Frustration threatened her composure. She hadn't realized he could move that quickly.

Her feet were light underneath her. She spun to the right

and feinted to the left in an effort to confuse him. The door stood open just three steps away. If she could manage to lock Kieran behind the door, she could escape toward freedom. Toward Jack. She was almost there.

Kieran's arms wrapped around her waist and lifted her against his chest so her feet dangled uselessly above the ground.

"Let me go," she hissed. She flailed in his arms, but no amount of squirming or writhing would loosen his grip.

Desperate for escape, she lifted her elbow and brought it down hard on his temple—a move that would send any normal man into unconsciousness. Kieran, however, narrowed his eyes and remained upright.

"Hit me like a man again and expect me to treat ye like one."

She pushed against his chest, anxious to be free of his viselike hold. No matter how hard she struggled, he did not release her. "Let me go." The words came out as a pathetic whimper. "He needs me. Please."

Helpless tears ran down her cheeks, but she did not care. If she could not escape in time, Jack would die.

"I said I'd help ye." Kieran's arms tightened further still.

Mariel shook her head miserably. "There's not enough time."

He met her eyes with an earnest expression. "The sun is almost up. Let my warriors break their fast while the lads prepare our horses, and then we'll leave."

He believed her. But for the first time since she met him, it mattered little. Nothing would replace Jack's finger or erase the fear and hurt he must have felt.

Mariel struggled against Kieran's grasp once more. "There's no time. I can travel faster alone. Kieran, he *needs* me."

A dark eyebrow lifted, and he regarded her with a look of skepticism. "And what would ye do by yerself when ye arrived?"

"I had a plan," she confessed. "I've had one since I came to Skye."

His stare hardened. "And why did ye no do it?"

She couldn't stand the accusation in his gaze, but still she didn't look away. "Because it was too risky. I would be going off the assumption that Aaron had Jack at the manor. And I would be one person against many. I thought if I found Blair and Dougal, I could somehow save you and save Jack at the same time. But after I realized who Blair and Dougal were…"

Kieran cocked his head for her to continue.

"If I left and proceeded with my plan, they would have no protection," she answered with a solemn tone that resonated in her heart. "I couldn't do that to them."

Kieran was quiet for a moment. When he answered, his voice was softer than it'd been since she peeled off her mask. "I dinna know if what ye were planning was stupid or brave, but I dinna recommend it. In two hours' time we will be ready to leave. Our ships are faster than anything ye could find resting on the shore, and our horses are better prepared for long distance than anything ye could steal. No to mention when ye arrive and find yerself alone, what would ye do with no army behind ye?"

Instead of waiting for an answer, he released her. The imprint of warmth his body left on hers immediately cooled in the damp chill of the cellar. The door still stood open, taunting her with impulsive freedom.

Her shoulders sagged. Kieran's words rang true. She had no plan, no army, and no equipment. Two hours seemed like a lifetime, but it was a sacrifice she had to make.

"Please get rid of it," she whispered and turned away from where the box lay on the ground. "I can't…look at it…"

His face softened, and he disappeared behind her. The lid of the wooden box snapped closed.

Mariel suppressed a shudder of unease. "It's a warning. Aaron is displeased with the length of time I am taking and wants me to know."

A groan sounded at her feet from Hamish's crumpled form.

The young warrior struggled to a standing position. His ruddy cheeks were a darker red than usual, and his glare was focused on her. She had wounded the pride of a boy just turning into a man. The days of his indifference were over.

Kieran, however, did not seem to notice or care. "Hamish, go tell the lads to get the horses ready for a long trip and gather nine of my best warriors. We leave in two hours."

The narrowed look of betrayal on Hamish's face furrowed into confusion. "Ye're helping her?"

Kieran gave him a stern look. "Ye have yer orders, now go."

Hamish kept his angry stare fixed on Mariel and trudged out of her cell in compliance with orders he clearly did not agree with.

Kieran turned toward Mariel with a shuttered expression. "Let's get ye some food before we ride out." He strode toward the stairs. When she did not follow, he returned to her cell once more. "Are ye no hungry?"

Mariel cast him a wary look and took a slow step forward. "Are you saying I can leave?"

"Aye, ye need to eat a solid breakfast before we ride." He paused and looked down at her. "I can trust ye?"

"You can," she said with conviction. "You definitely can."

∙ ∙ ∙

Kieran leaned against the rough bark of a tree and gazed into the heart of the clearing spread before him. The figures of his men were outlined against the shadows cast by the setting sun where they trained. The mock fighting was arduous after a long day of travel, but necessary. Witnessing Mariel's unique attack style made that evident.

Were it not for her instruction, Kieran's men would have been at a disadvantage during the attack, at least for the first several minutes. With an army of only ten, minutes made all the difference.

Soon this would be over. The threat against his life would be removed and once again his family would be safe.

In the distance, Mariel's lithe form arched backward in a neat flip in a successful attempt to avoid Hamish's blade. The lad still stung from the insult of being bested by a woman. A fact evident in the way he fought. His blade whipped in angry arcs toward her, powered by fury and the need to redeem himself. Lacking the finesse he'd been instructed to use.

Mariel avoided each swipe of the blade as though she were anticipating the movements. Inevitably, Hamish began to tire.

His sword lowered for the slightest second, but that was all she needed. Her foot caught Hamish's sword hand and sent the weapon to the ground. She wasted no time spinning behind him, and then pressed her dagger against his neck. Her hand on his shoulder signaled his defeat.

Kieran had to admit, he was impressed with her fighting skills. While unconventional, they were effective. The complicated rolls and tumbles she executed made her impossibly fast.

Not only was she a strong opponent, she also handled the men incredibly well. She remained patient as she explained maneuvers and instructed without fear or hesitation. Her energy was as endless as her patience, and she performed the same moves over and over again when requested. Most impressive of all though was the way the men responded to her.

Initially Kieran thought the men would bristle under the direction of a woman, especially once they learned the reason for her presence and the goal of their mission. However, over the last two days she had won over every man in the group.

He eyed Hamish stewing in the shade over his defeat. Almost every man.

Kieran himself had spoken little to Mariel outside of tactical discussions. Unfortunately, not talking did not mean he was not aware of her presence, particularly when she insisted on wearing the black men's clothing while training.

She did not appear to realize the way the fabric hugged the rounded curve of her arse and accentuated her long limbs. Certainly she had no idea the way her full breasts strained against the shirt or how evident her nipples were when they pebbled in the sharp spring air. Underneath, he knew, she was perfumed silk and creamy flesh. Despite all that had transpired between them, he could not stop his mind from the lustful thoughts, or his cock from rising hard against his belly.

In an effort to calm his desire, he shifted his gaze to where Colin and Alec were locked in battle. Even from her position several paces away, Mariel offered praise and instruction to the two.

There had been a dark change in her since their departure.

She joked with the men periodically and offered uplifting comments but was otherwise silent and kept to herself. The delicate features of her face were usually strained in a frown, and her brow furrowed while she stared into nothing, as though running through the battle plan in her head. She had the focus of a warrior.

No longer did he doubt anything she'd told him, yet it changed nothing. She was an assassin, and he was a laird protecting his family.

Mariel jogged to where Kieran stood and scooped a ladle of water from the pail beside him. Her chin tilted upward, and the milky expanse of her neck was exposed as she parted her lips and drank deeply. Her cheeks were flushed from the exertion of her training. A droplet of water clung to her lower lip and her tongue flicked out unconsciously to catch it. Kieran's groin tightened. The scent of roses caressed him and brought back a rush of memories he could not fight.

She was not looking at him, though. Like a good leader, she watched over the men as they fought.

"I have yet to train with you, Kieran," her voice was gentle, and her tone without malice.

He grunted. "Havena I already bested ye twice?"

She did not react to the barb. "That was on your territory. I think we should try on mine."

Things had been strained between them for the duration of their travels. Perhaps a good fight would help. Regardless, he was not about to ignore the challenge thrown at his feet. "I have no problem defeating ye again."

"We'll see." She met his gaze. God, she was beautiful when she looked at him like that.

She lifted the ladle to her parted lips once more. This time water spilled down the corner of her mouth as she drank. Desire slammed into him, leaving him hot, hard, and incredibly irritated. The ladle landed in the bucket with a hollow clunk, and Mariel ran back to the men without so much as glance in his direction.

Her bottom swayed side to side, and her long legs were graceful as one foot fell in front of the other. Kieran shifted his aching cock to a more comfortable position. If fighting in a gown weren't impossible, he would insist on it. How was he supposed to focus on the task at hand when the slightest glance at her made him throb with desire?

The sun was already going down and the nearby loch was exactly what he needed to cool his heated blood.

"That's enough, men," he called. "Let's set up camp before it gets too dark."

They would be sleeping in the forest surrounding the very field they practiced on. It was nothing his men were not used to. While the mission was different than any other they'd had before, the men had no problem adjusting.

Camp took only minutes to ready, and Kieran wasted no time finding the lake. He pulled off his clothing and stepped toward the smooth, mirrored surface. The icy water lapped at his feet with languid temptation. He dove through the surface in one fluid movement, pain needling his body as the frigid water enveloped him. The loch was far colder than he had expected, but the shock was a welcome one. He pushed forward and swam until his body went numb. His mind began to clear as he moved toward the center with smooth, steady strokes.

He swam back toward the shore until his feet brushed the pebbled ground beneath him. The final rays of the day's sun were enough to warm his clothes while he was in the water. His body was clean, his clothes were warm, and supper would be in his belly within minutes. Things were improving.

The feeling of satisfaction lasted a brief second before a branch cracked nearby. His senses flared.

Something was not right. Acting as though he had heard nothing, he discreetly slid the length of his dagger up his sleeve and pulled on his boots. He scanned the perimeter with his peripheral and saw nothing out of the ordinary, yet still unease tingled along the back of his neck.

No more sounds emerged as he walked through the forest, save the whisper of the leaves above. Though nothing further appeared out of the ordinary, he knew one thing for certain.

He was not alone.

Chapter Thirty-Four

Kieran surveyed the forest around him. The setting sun cast elongated shadows with its golden light, and a gentle breeze sent a wave of leaves skittering across the ground. Still nothing.

The tree above his head rustled. Before he could look up, a solid weight crashed down atop his shoulders. His body rolled forward on instinct, sending his attacker tumbling to the ground. Strength surged through him. He straightened and whipped the blade from his sleeve, ready to kill the person who dared assault him.

A heady rose perfume prickled his awareness before he saw the flash of violet eyes. Mariel. Her lips quirked in a half smile. She was obviously pleased with herself for having taken him by surprise.

They could drop from above. Lesson one learned.

He let the dagger fall from his grasp and lunged at her. She arched back into a flip and landed safely out of his grasp. Lightning fast, she dropped into a crouch and did a fluid sweep with her long leg that smacked against the back of his knees. While his feet remained on the ground, the impact upset his footing for a split second. She slammed her insignificant body weight against his chest. He caught his balance and stepped away, tensed for the second round of the attack.

He'd never trained with a woman and was not enjoying the experience thus far. When sparring with his men, he knew they could take full blows and deliver them back. But a woman, especially one as petite as Mariel, left him concerned with the possibility of hurting her.

In a halfhearted attempt to attack, he swung his fist in her direction. She caught his hand before he hit her temple and shoved him away with a look of disgust.

"Stop it," she said dryly.

He studied her movements, waiting for her to engage in an offensive maneuver so he could safely tackle her to the ground and end their mock battle. "Stop what?"

"Stop treating me like a delicate courtier and fight me like a man." Her leg swung at him.

Kieran palmed her firm calf and swept her standing leg from beneath her so that she fell into the soft soil. "Better?" he teased, his hand still fixed against the heat of her shapely leg.

Her eyes slanted up at him with the glint of a challenge. "Much."

Even in battle, her sensuality was not something he could ignore. His hands ached to slide up her smooth thighs, to elicit a soft whimper of longing that would push him over the edge.

Mariel whipped her free leg around, knocking his arm off her, and snapped up with a graceful flip.

Kieran gritted his teeth. *Focus.*

They recovered quickly. Lesson two learned.

Her face was smooth with concentration, her gaze intense, focused. How was it she wasn't even breathing hard yet? Kieran's body remained taut in preparation for her strike. But she didn't strike. She dropped unexpectedly and rolled between his legs.

Before he could see where she went, her arm wrapped around his neck from behind, and the warmth of her soft breasts pressed against his back. She tightened her grip and pushed his throat into the crook of her elbow. The wisp of a lass was trying to choke him into unconsciousness.

Kieran bent at the waist and pulled her arm over his back, rolling her to the ground once more. He waited for her to leap to her feet, and he caught her in an aggressive hug. Her arms were locked against her sides and her back pressed into his chest.

The curve of her bottom pushed against his throbbing erection. Fighting had always left him lusty, but nothing like this. He wanted to cover her with his body and explore the softness of her skin with his lips, his tongue.

A small foot flew toward his face and slammed into his forehead. The impact caught him off guard, and his hold eased for only a split second. That was all the time she needed to wriggle free once more.

They were flexible. Lesson three learned.

The tease of her lush backside squirming against his groin had been worth the pain of a kick to his face. Although now he understood why his men enjoyed training with Mariel as much as they did. The thought of them touching her the way he had made his stomach twist in jealous anger.

Her foot flew at him again and caught his jaw before he had time to dodge the blow.

Mariel's brow furrowed. "Focus, Kieran."

Taking the offensive once more, he flew forward and knocked her to the floor so that she was trapped beneath him. Her hand balled into a fist beneath his chest and something sharp dug below his ribs. What the hell was she doing?

The pressure turned uncomfortable and exploded in a pain that dazed him for one brief second. He vaguely felt the curves of her body grind against him, and then she was beneath him no more. Without the pressure of her hand, the sharp pain faded almost immediately.

They knew how to cause instant pain. But only for a moment. Lesson four learned.

However, she did not run. Instead, she crawled on top of him. The heat of her inner thighs cradled his hips and his cock strained to where she hovered over him, teasing him. Her warmth seeped against the plaid to where his desire pulsed.

Mariel braced her arms on either side of his head and leaned over him. Her hips arched back, and the temptation between her legs brushed the aching torture of his cock where it rose hard between them.

Her sweet breath whispered against his lips. "Captured."

His hands slid over her firm bottom. The fabric beneath his fingers was thin. One quick tug and they would shred away…

But no, the battle was not over. He still had yet to win. He grabbed her slender waist, but she did not fight back. Not this time.

Her eyes were stormy, her cheeks flushed in a way that did not stem from exertion.

He knew that look well.

Kieran rolled her beneath him and locked her arms to the ground with his large hands. Her nipples tightened beneath her shirt. His gaze fixed on her face, and he shifted his hips forward, pressing his cock between her legs. A moan escaped her parted lips. She wanted this as badly as he.

His resolve crumbled. No matter how hard he tried to distance himself, she always seemed to draw him back.

Mariel rolled her body against his, digging the ache of his cock against the center of her heat. He could take no more of her torture. With a groan, his mouth crushed down on top of hers, his tongue possessive as it swept into her honeyed depths. Her lips were softer than he'd remembered.

His fingers brushed against the damp fabric between her legs. She cried out and her hips arched forward. Yes, she wanted this. Very much so.

He peeled the trews off her shapely legs with one satisfying yank and skimmed his palms over her creamy flesh. Fueled by a mindless hunger, he gripped the hem of her shirt and pulled it off over her head. She was fully naked beneath him, writhing with need, her hands burning a restless path over his body, her tongue tasting, teasing.

The soft moan in the back of her throat was all the encouragement he needed. He skimmed her naked sex with the pad of his thumb and slid a finger inside her tight heat. God, she was so damn wet.

Mariel arched against Kieran's hand, squeezing her thighs around the delicious pressure of his fingers. Desperation wound tighter and tighter. She needed this release. No, she needed more than release. She needed the feel of his powerful arms around her and the unmistakable strength he lent her.

The dark hair of his legs prickled her skin when she slid her hand up his legs and wrapped her hand around the silky heat of his erection. With a tight groan, he spanned his hands across her inner thighs and firmly spread her legs. Everything within her pounded with anticipation.

His eyes focused on her, watching her. He positioned himself and shoved inside her with one hungry thrust. Shivers of bliss prickled her skin.

Having him within her once more, touching her, loving her…it was the first burning draw of air when she thought she would otherwise drown.

He ripped his shirt off and braced his arms on either side of her. The bands of his glorious stomach tightened with each thrust, his body taut from their mock battle.

Mariel wrapped her legs around his waist, drawing him deeper, reveling in the glorious feel of him filling her, stretching her.

His mouth slanted over hers as he lifted her off the ground and cradled her against him. He explored her mouth with the greedy stroke of his tongue and gently nipped her bottom lip. She curled her hips to meet each thrust until her body tightened with the promise of a heaven she had yet to only sample.

Kieran must have felt the change and increased his tempo with a ragged groan. She wound to the brink of ecstasy and cried out. The world around them shattered into a thousand lights that heated and tingled as all the chaos of her lost control centered on the inky depths of his stare. His bottom clenched beneath her heels as he roared his release.

They stayed like that for what felt like an eternity with their chests rising and falling as their frenzied breath calmed as one. His face was devoid of emotion, as expressionless and cold as it had been the previous two days, but his eyes were almost tender when he stared down at her. Mariel dared not speak for fear the delicate spell woven between them would snap.

Without warning, Kieran shoved off her and grabbed his leine from where it lay crumpled on the ground, his feelings apparent in the curl of contempt upon his lips.

Mariel grasped her shirt to her naked breasts with trembling fingers and choked down a sob.

What they'd just shared changed nothing.

Chapter Thirty-Five

The sun had not yet risen when Mariel's eyes flew open. Her stomach churned with excitement. Jack would be free today.

She threw off the heavy blanket of her bedroll and got to her feet, heedless of the sharp chill hanging in the air. Sleep would be impossible at this point, and she could use the extra time to prepare. She crept silently over the sleeping warriors surrounding her. Their rest was well-earned and necessary.

The last few days had been taxing on them all and left weary lines on their faces. Never once did they complain.

A tremor of unease coiled in her belly. Would two days of training be enough? Would the MacDonalds be ready for Aaron's mercenaries?

A shadow moved in the clearing as she approached. The waning light of the moon brilliant against the familiar bared back of a warrior with a proud stance. Kieran.

Mariel's breath caught in her throat and her step faltered. She did not want to be there, not with him. Not when he had wounded her as deeply as he had.

He turned in her direction, and his black eyes fixed upon hers as if he could see into the damage of her soul. "Mariel." His voice was low, husky still with the effects of sleep. He had not been awake long.

His body would be overwarm to the touch, the way it always was when he first woke. Her fingernails bit into her palms in a vain attempt to clear the thought from her mind.

"Kieran," she said in greeting. Her heartbeat thundered in her ears and heat flooded her cheeks. She was grateful for the cover of darkness.

She lowered herself to the damp ground and lay her chest against the length of her thigh, stretching the muscles necessary to ensure victory when the sun rose.

But no amount of focus or concentration could ease the pain burning within. Hearing his voice, seeing his naked back—all of it called to mind too many memories her heart could not stand to relive.

She did not blame him for what transpired between them. Not only had she not stopped him, she had wanted it as badly as he. While she was not fool enough to think he would forgive her transgressions afterward, she had not expected such blatant rejection.

The budding light of dawn cast an orange gold pallor on the silent forest and fell upon Kieran's powerful frame, illuminating the glorious chiseled flesh as he moved through his exercises beside her.

Her stomach knotted. This was the last time they would be alone. Too much had been left unsaid. She would be remiss if she wasted this opportunity.

"Kieran," she said softly.

He stilled, his sword extended in mock parry, his face trained away from her. "Aye?"

She wouldn't receive his undivided attention. So be it. She would speak her piece and remove the weight from her heart. "I want to thank you for agreeing to help Jack. I know he will look up to you."

He swung his blade and turned to the other side, focused on his efforts. "I dinna have much of a choice, did I?"

Mariel winced at the barb. "Neither of us had much of a choice in all this," she said. "I have not yet had a chance to apologize to you."

There was a pause before he extended the claymore in front of him with measured precision. His nonchalance would not dissuade her.

"The most horrible and selfish part is that I cannot completely regret my role in this heinous plot...because it led me to you." Her throat drew tight and she had to pause to regain her composure before continuing. "You are the only right thing that's happened to me since my parents died."

The blade of his sword caught the rising sun and reflected subdued rays in his shift back to the previous position. Every muscle in his body was visibly taut.

Mariel continued on before her courage expired. "I'm sorry for not confiding in you sooner."

Kieran stopped and drove his blade deep into the soft soil so the hilt thrust out from the earth like a cross. He bent down on one knee and bowed his head low as if in prayer. His prone shadow was outlined by the golden red glow of the sunrise. Still he did not speak.

"Kieran," Mariel said, her voice filled the tortured silence between them, then broke off in a husky whimper. "I love you. No matter what has happened between us or what can never be, I love you."

•   •   •

Kieran's fist tightened at his side and popped open the newly closed wounds across his knuckles. Her words of love resonated with conviction. He wanted so badly to believe her, and yet he could not still the doubt weighing heavily in his heart.

Why now? Why was she confessing this to him before battle? Perhaps it was another form of manipulation. Didn't she know he would help regardless?

He looked up and found she had left. The realization was met with a mixture of relief and disappointment.

Beyond where she had been, his warriors broke through the trees and stalked toward him with stoic determination. The sharp rays of the early dawn shone upon them, lighting their weapons with an ethereal glow. The boisterous group was now silent with focused concentration, and the cool morning air crackled with anticipation.

Kieran's blade would taste vengeance this day.

Chapter Thirty-Six

Kieran crouched low in the thick brush with his men. The chill of morning had not yet ebbed and crept up his bare legs to where his plaid rested against his thighs.

A great lawn stretched before them. The blades of grass were furry white with frost where the rising sun had not yet graced them. Manicured plants and trees like those he had seen at Hampton Court Palace lined a cobblestoned lane. The manor itself rose three stories high, pink with precious sandstone. Extravagant carvings of animals dotted the walls and lined the great arching entrance. Balconies rimmed the second and third floors.

The guards wore no uniform or livery as they stalked the perimeter with the disinterest of men who fought for gold. Mercenaries. Kieran knew all too well how they operated. He scanned the manor for Mariel's familiar form.

She had volunteered to quietly dispatch the guards so Kieran's men could enter the manor unseen to surprise the English bastards. Already the guards who once walked the lawn lay still in the shadows.

He glanced up to the balcony again, anxious lest the men there notice the absence of the mercenaries below.

Ordinary men would have gotten restless in their wait, but Kieran's men were warriors and remained as still as the animals adorning the manor.

Their patience was well rewarded when a dark shadow slipped over the wall of the third floor and slinked behind the lanky guard who stood unsuspecting with his back to her.

A dark arm wrapped around his neck, and he disappeared

into one of the many alcoves without a sound. Moving with the stealth and grace of a cat, Mariel crept down the prone form of a sandstone lion to where the final remaining man paced the second floor.

Once he turned his back to her, she stretched her body toward the underside of the third-floor balcony and vanished into darkness. As the guard did his second pass of the balcony, Mariel dangled her upper torso from the ceiling and caught him by the neck as she had the other man. She released his limp form with slow precision, and he slid to the ground. With a graceful somersault, she landed beside him, and he too disappeared into an alcove.

Not a one of Kieran's men spoke, but the glint in their eyes said it all. They were impressed.

Now she had to make her way into the manor undetected to secure a clear path for them to enter. To surprise or to be ambushed as Hamish had suggested. Regardless, there would be a fight and they would win. They had to.

Having Mariel in the bowels of the manor alone left Kieran on edge. Time ticked by in slow increments until it seemed to have stopped completely. He glanced at the rising sun, measuring her absence by its ascent. If she was not back before it met the juncture between two mountains in the distance, he and his men would charge in without her.

They would lose the element of surprise if they rushed in before she returned, but the sacrifice would be worth the protection it might offer Mariel.

The blood turned to ice in his veins. The profession of her love and the heartfelt apology had been said with purpose. What she spoke had been her final confession.

She did not plan to live through this day.

He glanced toward the door, all the more anxious to see her. Damn it, what was taking so long?

His body tensed with the preparation to order his men to attack when a side door eased open and a slender hand waved them forward. Kieran did a final visual sweep of the area, ensuring no remaining guards lurked. Mariel had done her job well. All mercenaries remained unconscious where they lay.

He nodded and his men moved silently across the grass and slipped into the door one by one until they were crowded in a narrow hallway.

The door closed soundlessly behind them and plunged them into darkness. As his eyes adjusted to the lack of light, Mariel stood before them with her hand pressed against the wall. It pushed in with apparent ease and revealed a hidden staircase on the other side.

He followed behind his men, bringing up the rear of their small group. The musty scent of disuse stung his nostrils, and the wooden floor groaned in protest beneath his weight. He trod lightly and curled his way down the winding stairs in an effort to keep them from making too much noise—a feat not easily done. From what he could see below, the stairs appeared to run abruptly into a wall. Another hidden door.

Mariel stopped and turned around to face them once more. Her face was serious, her mouth drawn in a tight line. Her sharp stare met his. *Ready?* She mouthed.

Energy shot through Kieran's body and his breathing intensified. He would win this fight and Mariel would remain safe. He gave a swift nod, and she shoved the trap door open.

Light flooded the small stairwell along with the heavy scent of fried eggs and thick slab pork. After days of oatcakes and hard cheese, Kieran's stomach loosed a frustrated growl of protest. He quashed his hunger. Food would come later.

The sound of clattering dishes and surprised cries swept into the stairwell as his men filtered out.

Kieran followed closely behind, dashing out into the brilliant chaos of a large dining hall. A long table stood in the center with its contents in total disarray, the diners locked in various stages of battle. Some were engaged in combat, some crouched beneath the table, and some already lay dead.

Though caught off guard, they were hardly defenseless. Blades were flicked out of hidden pockets and pistols were drawn from vests and belts. Of those still alive, Kieran guessed there were at least thirty men against his ten. Regardless, the battle would be quick against the poorly trained mercenaries.

Kieran disarmed a man beside him before the offensive weapon could be fired. The heavy weapon clattered uselessly to the ground, and the man was easily dispatched. As they all would be.

Mariel moved among his men, slowly distancing herself from the others. Kieran narrowed his eyes, keeping close watch of her.

She swung her leg at a short bald man's head, and he crumpled to the floor. She slipped something from her pocket and tucked it into the fallen man's mouth, her gaze locked on the wall opposite her. She flicked a glance around the room before she rose and slid silently against the back wall.

Kieran stalked closer. One final look behind her and she slipped inside a false door, leaving his men to fight her battle.

A low frustrated growl vibrated in Kieran's throat, all but choking him with the bitterness of disappointment. For all her heartfelt words, she had lied to them all.

. . .

Mariel crept along the hallway, her steps silent upon the lush carpet. How foolish she had once been to think herself fortunate to live in so rich a home.

A movement caught her eye and her heart leapt. Was it him? She forced down the frantic burn of hatred.

He had eased from the battle almost before it began, not that he'd be difficult to miss in his sunshine yellow silk suit. How like Aaron to be a coward to the end.

Today he would pay for the lives he'd ruined with his greed and manipulation.

Another movement flickered to her left around the corner. She drew a deep breath to calm her racing heart. Her hands trembled. She couldn't have that. No, she needed to be calm, focused. The blue silk wallpaper whispered against her back as she approached. She turned the corner, her body tense in preparation for what she must do.

A force slammed against her forehead and suddenly she was on her back. Her mind reeled in a fog of confusion. She tried to pull herself into a sitting position, but her limbs were too heavy. A meaty fist snagged the front of her shirt and lifted her so high her feet dangled above the ground. Pain squeezed her wrist and the dagger she held was easily plucked from her fist.

Then the smell hit her. Oh God, the smell of him...death and sweat.

Mariel felt the scream rip from her throat and heard it echo off the walls around her. Her clawed hands raked against him, but to no avail.

A grin spread over his rubbery lips. "I see you remember me." Laughter wheezed from his chest and crested into a thundering cough.

Her feet kicked against him, but his soft body absorbed the blows. Desperation and disgust fueled her need for escape and set her heart pounding. Her teeth sank against the grittiness of his hand until the putrid sting of his sweat on her tongue mingled with the taste of blood.

He howled in rage and loosened his grip.

She didn't waste time to see his reaction. Once her feet landed solid on the floor, she sprinted down the hall. His footsteps thundered behind her, but she dared not pause to look back.

She turned a corner and felt her foot yanked from beneath her. Her body slammed to the floor and sent her world spinning once more. A viselike grip caught her ankle, but she was still not done fighting. She turned toward the man who haunted her dreams and slammed her free foot against his face. The sickening crunch of his nose beneath her heel was a fleeting moment of victory.

Blood exploded from his nose and his grip tightened.

"You bitch," he snarled. "You'll pay for that when Aaron is done with you."

He grabbed her free foot and flipped her onto her stomach before he lumbered to a standing position. With a great tug, he pulled her down the hall toward a large door. Her shirt slid against the floor and rose up her back. Mariel's palms skimmed over the silky fibers of the rug with futile effort in an attempt to grasp at anything to still her forward progress. Her heart pounded erratically in her chest. She knew that door well and pictured in her mind's eye the overstuffed leather chairs and dark wood furnishings of Aaron's office.

The door banged open and the familiar, pungent scent of Aaron's heavy perfume hit her nostrils, bringing with it a wave of memories best left forgotten. Thick, soft arms wrapped around her and warmth ran down her shoulder where his broken nose trickled with fresh blood.

Aaron rose from behind a glossy wooden desk and opened his hands toward her as though he were welcoming an old friend. "Ah, Mariel…I see you've returned after all." He plucked a piece of fuzz from his brilliant yellow jacket and frowned. "Not only are you late, you've brought friends without asking. I would expect that level of rudeness from my whores, but never from you."

Mariel struggled against the solid grasp that pinned her arms uselessly against her sides. "Where is Jack? What have you done to him?"

Aaron ignored her question. "I hope you've at least brought me what I asked."

When she did not answer, he moved from around his desk and studied her with his cold gaze. But she was no longer a confused girl, helpless and broken. Her time on Skye had restored the strength she had once possessed, and she would use every last bit of that to fight back.

Aaron smirked. "Don't think yourself a hero for your silence, chit. You've brought Kieran MacDonald here. Once he is apprehended, I'm sure he can be persuaded to tell us everything we need. Your mission was still a success, all things considered."

"You were planning on killing him anyway, weren't you?" Mariel's cheeks were hot despite her attempt to curb her temper.

Aaron cocked his head, his expression one of boredom. "I figured you'd probably realize that eventually. It didn't matter if you knew or not, so long as you got the job done." A grin spread over his thin lips. "As it appears you did—in your own roundabout way."

He clasped his hands behind the small of his back and walked around her. "Perhaps it might interest you to know that the one who paid so handsomely for your time is here as well. And he's desperate to get his hands on the man you think yourself in love with."

Panic buzzed beneath Mariel's calm exterior. Aaron leaned forward, a smile hovering at the corners of his lips as though he could smell her anxiety. "Yes, I know all about your affection for the barbarian. Jane reported it well before you got rid of her."

"She was killed by an attacking clan." Mariel gave him a hard look. "She died in her service to you."

Aaron's thin shoulders lifted in a shrug of disinterest. "Many do." He leaned closer, and the heavy spice of his perfume assaulted her senses. "Would it please you to know that after all this time, you and your dear brother are under the same roof? I thought you would appreciate the comfort of knowing you were together before you died."

"No!" Mariel gasped and struggled in earnest against the man holding her.

He grunted as her elbow jabbed into his gut, but still he did not release her.

"His finger," she howled in wounded anger, no longer careful of shielding her emotions. "How could you cut off his finger? After all the money I've earned you, all the years I've been so compliant..."

"Don't be foolish, girl," Aaron said with obvious contempt. "Do you really think I'd remove a finger from my best pick pocket?"

Her stomach churned with rage as she digested what she'd been told. To have her brother's finger removed was a grievous act indeed, but to subject him to the darkness of a crime ridden life, to place him in harm's way...

Her body burned with energy, and she exploded from her captor's arms. All her focus honed in on Aaron's surprised face, and her fist connected with his brow. She would have landed another blow if the foul beast behind her had not managed to restrain her once more.

Aaron's hand flew to his face, cradling the injury. Blood trickled between his fingers and blossomed against the yellow silk sleeve of his jacket. "Kill her." Aaron said to the mass of flesh behind Mariel. "And I don't care what you do to her before you end her miserable life."

The large chest behind her rose, and an excited pant wheezed into her ear. Aaron burst from the room and slammed the solid door behind him. The man released his hold on her and let her fall onto the hard floor. Mariel choked in a mouthful of clean air and lunged for the door. The effort was futile, something her captor doubtlessly knew she would attempt. It was a game of cat and mouse, sick and twisted. Her fingers stretched toward the polished brass when a pressure gripped her ankle. She was jerked backward before she even had a chance to turn the smooth knob.

She kicked at him and managed to writhe free of his grasp. Desperation spurred her onward, forcing her to scramble up the shelves of books lining the back wall.

The hollow sound of a whip slapping free gave her pause. A low whistle filled the air and jerked memories from the pit of her mind. Her ears remembered that sound. Her flesh remembered its singeing bite. She clawed with a frenzy, desperate to reach higher ground.

Books fluttered to the ground below in her haste to remove herself from the whip's path, but her efforts were in vain. Pain ripped like fire around her waist where it curled her in its wicked embrace.

Her fingernails bent backward against the smooth surface of the shelves in her attempt to stay aloft. Despite her efforts, she succumbed to the second wrench and dropped into an uncontrolled fall before the hard edge of the desk cracked against the base of her skull.

His stench filled her nostrils and the world around her went black.

Chapter Thirty-Seven

A scream tore down the hallway and raised the hairs on the back of Kieran's neck. Mariel.

His footsteps pounded against the thick carpet as he sprinted down the corridor and slammed his shoulder against the door. He acted on foolish impulse, not bothering to form a plan or analyze what might lay on the other side. All he knew was that she was there and she needed him. Solid wood splintered beneath his weight, and the barrier between them flew open.

Mariel lay sprawled on her back, her arms bound over her head. A stout man knelt beside her and turned toward Kieran. A whip lay coiled at his side.

Kieran never gave him a chance to grab it. His foot connected with the man's stained shirt and sent him to the floor. Away from Mariel. Before the man could flounder to his knees, Kieran plunged his blade into the massive chest. A brilliant red stain spread against filthy linen, and the man's body relaxed into death.

Kieran pulled his sword free and knelt beside Mariel. The fabric of her shirt was torn around her waist and revealed tattered flesh beneath. Blood smeared the white carpet beneath her, but the wounds did not appear to be mortal.

Her gaze was bright and determined despite her pallid skin. She had offered her confession of love before the battle and like a fool he had denied her. No longer did she want his comfort.

She wanted revenge.

He loosened the rope that bound her wrists and eased her to a sitting position.

"I can still smell him." Her lip curled. "Are you sure he's…"

Her fingers rubbed against one another, their trembling subtle yet unmistakable.

He placed his hand atop hers. "He can never hurt you again."

"Thank you." She refused to meet his eyes as she pulled her hand from his and rose to her feet.

"Are ye well, Mariel?"

She drew a deep breath and pulled a dagger from the man's belt. Resolve lined the stubborn set of her mouth. "Lord Hampton is here. As is Jack. We've already wasted too much time." She moved as she spoke, darting into the hall. "I have a strong idea where to find Aaron, and I suspect the other two will be nearby."

Kieran followed her down a maze of stairs and false walls before stopping at a pair of polished doors. His grip tightened on the hilt of his blade until the worn leather burned his palm. Primal energy coursed through his veins and roared in his ears. Blair's wrongs would be righted with the edge of Kieran's sword. His family would be safe once more.

Mariel shoved the doors open to a smaller version of the lavish room they had come from. A man clad in yellow silk stood out from the rich, dark furnishings. There was a frown evident on his thin lips. His narrow shoulders and wiry frame were hardly a source to contend with, but Kieran had seen enough on the battlefield to know how deceiving appearances could be.

Mariel stepped forward with her blade locked in her hand. "Lord Hampton and Jack—where are they?"

The man dropped a fistful of coins into the leather satchel on the table in front of him.

"I'm unarmed." The man's voice was smooth, and a look of calm settled the initial shock in his gaze.

"I didn't ask if you were armed, Aaron." She caught him by the shirt and shoved him against the wall. "You told me they were here, now where are they?"

Kieran stepped forward and then stopped himself. Mariel had sought revenge for two long years. He would not take that from her. Unless, of course, the bastard didn't divulge Hampton's location soon. Kieran's muscles burned with his own need to exact vengeance.

"My guards will be here in a moment," Aaron said with nonchalance in an obvious attempt to brush her off.

Kieran stepped forward and raised the blade of his sword. "Yer guards are all dead. I suggest ye answer the lady."

The man's eyes widened, and he turned to Mariel as if seeking confirmation.

She pressed the dagger to his neck. "Tell me where they are."

Her body was rigid, her face smooth and expressionless with a cold gaze Kieran had never seen before.

A thin line of blood trickled down Aaron's neck as Mariel tightened her hold on him. "You have one last chance to tell me where Jack is."

He leaned away from her, his thin face twisted in a tortured grimace. "In your old room."

Mariel shoved him away from her. He backed into the corner with a hand to his neck, the beginnings of a bruise forming around his eye. "It doesn't matter what you do to me," he snarled. "He won't stop until he finds Blair Hampton." Aaron turned his pale blue gaze to Kieran. "The barbarian will be dead by then. Just like his brother."

Kieran's heart lurched in his chest. "Brennan." He hadn't realized he'd spoken the name out loud until Aaron's lip slid into a wicked sneer.

"Yes, your precious brother. He took almost a year to kill. When he was finally disposed of, we hadn't expected you to cease your barbaric ways and settle as laird in his stead. Not that your presence matters at this point. Soon you will join Brennan and your land will belong to that daft sister of yours once more. Your land is priceless, you know? Once Lord Hampton reclaims his wife, his newly inherited wife, he will have access to the wealth of your lands. You should hear how easy it was to seduce that bitch into marrying Lord Hampton in the first pl—"

A shot rang out and Aaron's head snapped back, his vehement words forever silenced.

●　　●　　●

Mariel stared in horror as blood pooled around Aaron's lifeless form. She had imagined him dead many times but had not actually thought to ever see it. His death did not elicit the surge of powerful victory she had once envisioned.

"Some people talk too damn much." A smooth, polished voice came from the other side of the room. The man's accent held an air of pretention that smacked of nobility. Lord Hampton had shown up for the fight.

Mariel turned in his direction as he exited a hidden door in the wall. He was far more handsome than she had assumed he might be. Dark hair curled just over the tips of his ears and his cheekbones were high beneath his regal brow. Sharp gray eyes glinted with hatred when they came to rest on Kieran. "So, we meet again, brother."

Kieran tensed. "Ye killed Brennan." He took a step closer to his adversary, his gaze intense. "Ye hurt Blair."

Hampton held his ground, his back straight with noble pride. "She was miserable in our marriage because of your actions. If you would have let me have the dowry I earned, none of this would have happened. With all your land and all your wealth, you refused to part with anything while I was forced to live on credit." Hampton spit out the last word, and his aquiline nose wrinkled in disgust. "A credit, might I add, that has run out. Do you have any idea how dangerous it is to owe the king taxes you cannot pay? I'd been given four months to pay what has been outstanding, and this street urchin consumed three of them with her lack of success."

He fingered the sword at his side, obviously not realizing the way Kieran's face darkened with rage. "Not that it matters. I'm pretty sure I can get her location out of you before I kill you. And once I reclaim my wife and her massive inheritance, the funds owed to the crown will be easily paid."

Kieran loosed a roar and charged forward with his claymore drawn. Hampton pulled an elaborate sword from its scabbard and parried with remarkable skill. Kieran lunged at him again, his heavy blade swinging through the air with enough force to split a man in two. Hampton narrowly evaded the blow.

Hampton feigned to the left and jabbed his thin blade at Kieran's shoulder. A small, red stain appeared against the stark white linen, but Kieran did not appear to notice. His black gaze remained focused on his target as he gripped his sword with two hands and swung.

The clash of metal on metal rang sharp against the rich walls. Both men grunted with effort and charged into a violent dance that would leave only one standing. Kieran was the more aggressive of the two and forced Hampton backward with powerful thrusts of his sword. The Englishman's heel bumped the wall behind him, and his confident smirk wavered. For every fatal blow Hampton attempted, there came the ring of failure as Kieran blocked the weapon's path.

"My men will be here soon," Hampton growled.

"No soon enough." Kieran plunged his blade into his opponent's chest.

Hampton's body jerked at the impact and blood bubbled from the wound. Surprise filled his cold, gray eyes.

"It is finally done." Kieran's voice was gravelly with emotion. He turned toward her, his face grim. "Brennan is avenged and my family is safe." His dark gaze locked on her with an unreadable expression. "Ye are safe."

Tears stung her eyes as the realization dawned on her. Over two years she had been under Aaron's control, forced to sacrifice a part of herself she would never reclaim. She was finally free. Jack was finally free.

"Jack," she whispered.

Kieran's hand touched her shoulder. "Aye, lass. Let's go find yer brother."

Mariel did not need further encouragement. She turned her back on the ugly past that lay in a broken pile of congealing blood and moved toward a future of promise and safety.

The complex twists and turns of the large home unraveled with simplicity as she followed the path she had traced so many times before. Each hurried footstep brought her closer to Jack until she was running down the darkened hallway.

Faster and faster she ran until it loomed before her, the

whitewashed plain wood door in a hallway of countless other doors. The room behind it was little more than a closet. She could see it perfectly in her mind's eye. The narrow bed, the barren walls pockmarked with scars of disrepair. Her knees went soft, and her hand seemed to drag through time as she reached for the key beneath the doorknob with trembling fingers. What if Aaron had lied? What if she found the room empty?

Her fingertips gripped the cool, unyielding brass, and her heart stuttered with fear.

Kieran's rough hand closed around hers, his warmth and strength lending her a quiet support as she turned the key. The door swung open with a familiar protesting squeal and revealed the blackness of a room without windows.

Her pulse raced. Was he in there?

"Jack?" Her voice trembled.

Naught answered her desperate call, but silence.

Chapter Thirty-Eight

Mariel stepped into the dark room.

"Jack?" Her voice strained with anxiety.

Kieran stepped beside her with a flickering candle in his hand. The flame illuminated the still form of a boy sitting on the bed, his dark head bent low.

He looked up with large, sapphire blue eyes.

"Jack." Her throat tightened and left his name thick on her tongue. She wanted to run to him, to scoop him into her arms, and cradle him as she had when he was younger. Her feet refused to move, so all she could do was stare down at the little boy who had been her reason for living.

His mouth dropped open and his eyes widened. "Mariel?"

Oh, to hear his sweet voice again, to see him alive. Emotion choked her. Two long years she had waited for this moment, and yet nothing could have prepared her for the rush of affection that ached within her chest.

She stepped toward him, her arms outstretched.

"Get away from me," he hissed. Contempt glowed in the beautiful eyes that once looked to her with unquestioning love.

"What?" The air grew thin and breathing became difficult.

Hatred glinted in his eyes. "Aaron told me about you," Jack said. "You could have come for me after I got better, but you never did. He tried to make excuses for you, but I saw through them." His little hands balled into fists at his side. "I waited for you."

"It wasn't like that," Mariel whispered. Her legs were no longer able to bear her weight, and she slowly sank to the floor. He thought she had *left* him.

Jack either did not hear her or did not care. "I know the truth. I begged Aaron, and he told me exactly where you had been. He didn't want to, but I made him. You became a whore and spent your days shopping for fine dresses and jewels and your nights on your back. He said that you didn't want...you didn't want your good fortune interrupted. He said you..." His voice trembled. "He said you didn't want me."

"No," Mariel cried and lunged toward him in desperation. If she could cradle him in her arms the way she used to and explain, perhaps he would listen. "No, that's not true. I wanted to see you—I tried to see you, but he wouldn't let me."

Jack leapt off the bed, away from her grasp. "More lies!"

"Aaron is the one who lied. He kept you from me, sometimes moving you in the middle of the night so I wouldn't find you. Everything I've done has been for you, to find you. Jack, please..." Her words shook, laced with a fear she'd never anticipated.

Hesitation crossed Jack's thin face. Regret lodged in the pit of Mariel's stomach for the little boy he had been and the years she had missed. She had failed in providing him with the happy childhood he deserved.

"Get away from me." The small tendons stood out around his neck. "I *hate* you!"

Large words for a little boy and spoken with such finality, they shredded the remnants of her marred soul. There was so much he didn't understand, so much he didn't know, and too much to say. Her death was imminent upon their arrival back at Skye. There would not be time to explain it all to him, to erase the years of hatred fed to him.

The energy drained from Mariel's body, and she sank back to the floor. A low keening cry rose from deep within her chest—the brutal sound of her heart breaking.

She had sacrificed more than she ever thought possible. Her pride, her morals, herself. Everything had been for Jack, and now the only thing she faced in her dark world was a traitor's death—one justly earned.

"Jack." A stern voice sounded from behind her.

Kieran filled the doorway, a firm gaze fixed on his face. "Come here, lad," he commanded.

Jack moved back as though unsure of what to do.

"I dinna ask ye if ye wanted to come here, I told ye to. Come here, Jack." The authority in Kieran's voice was unmistakable, undeniable even to Jack who skulked to the doorway.

While Kieran's efforts were appreciated, they would be futile. She would be dead before Jack would ever understand. He was lost to her forever.

The lad was a wee bit of a thing, no taller than Kieran's hip and doubtlessly weighed less than a child half his age. Dark blue eyes were set hauntingly wide in his narrow, peaked face as he stared up at Kieran.

Kieran crouched down next to Jack so he was eye level with him. "Ye've been through a lot, and ye've done it alone."

The lad stayed silent and kept an arm's reach away from Kieran.

"That's what men do, lad. It's no easy. I'll be the first to say that, but it's what makes ye a man."

Jack's eyes slid to where Mariel lay and shifted back to Kieran. Still he did not speak.

"A real man would do anything for his family. Steal, lie, even kill. Do ye agree?"

Jack nodded and shuffled closer.

"Yer sister did that and more for ye. Do ye know that since I met her, she has thought only of ye? Everything she's done moved her in yer direction so she could be with ye, to save ye from this life and give ye yer freedom. No matter who she hurt or betrayed."

Jack's brow furrowed. "She did?"

"Aye, she did. She had an opportunity for a new life in a beautiful land, surrounded by people who loved her, and she dinna take it. No when ye couldna be with her."

The boy narrowed his eyes with a wary expression. "How do you know all of this?"

Kieran looked past Jack's shoulder to where Mariel sat in dejected silence. "Because I'm the man who loves her."

Her eyes squeezed shut, and a tear slowly trailed down her wet cheek.

He spoke to Jack, but knew he reached Mariel. "Ye knew yer sister a long time ago, but I know her now and can say without a doubt that she isna the woman ye think she is. She is strong and caring, moral and honest." He met Jack's gaze. "If ye dinna believe me, look at her. The clothes she wears are those of a warrior."

Jack glanced at Mariel, and his small lips pursed in apparent confusion. "If what you say is true, why are they letting me go now?"

The lad was quick. "They dinna let ye go. We had to fight for ye. I've no ever seen a woman more brave or skilled in battle than her."

Jack cast a hesitant glance back to where Mariel sat upon the dirty floor. Her luminous stare was fixed on them with a quiet intensity. He turned his gaze to Kieran once more and squeezed his arms tighter against his chest as though preparing himself for a blow. "She didn't leave me?" he whispered.

"No," Kieran answered in a low voice, meant only for Jack. "She never stopped fighting for ye, never stopped loving ye."

The boy turned to where his sister sat. "Mariel?" he said, his small voice breaking.

Mariel did not wait for him to call again. She rose to her feet in a graceful movement and caught him in her arms. Her lips pressed against the top of his head and tears ran freely down her cheeks.

"Jack," she breathed.

Kieran fought the tug at his chest. Mariel had what she wanted.

He slipped back into the hall and waited for them to emerge.

· · ·

Mariel hugged Jack to her one last time. The manor always teemed with people coming and going. They could not stay any longer.

"We need to leave," Mariel said softly. The shoulder of her black shirt was wet with his sweet tears.

Jack's hand clutched hers, his eyes fixed on her as though he were afraid if he looked away, she would disappear.

Mariel smiled down at him and squeezed his hand. "Everything is fine," she assured him. "You will always be safe. I've made sure of that."

Kieran waited outside the door for them, his face solemn as they passed through the doorway. Mariel met his gaze and felt the unspoken understanding between them. There was much that needed to be said, but this was neither the time nor the place.

She led them through the house, purposefully choosing paths seldom used in an effort to decrease the chance of stumbling upon a guard or a body. She did not want to take a chance on frightening Jack any further.

There was so much he would have to adjust to already.

The warmth of his little hand inside of hers made her fingers stiff and her palms sweat. The sensation was one she wouldn't trade for all the jewels in London.

Kieran led them outside to the earthy scent of sun-warmed grass, the daylight brilliant. Never had there been a more beautiful day.

They slipped across the lawn and into the cool shade of the forest where they met with his men. Mariel did a quick count and released the breath she'd been holding. Every one of the warriors that entered the house had emerged, albeit peppered with a few cuts and nicks.

Colin grinned down at her brother. "Ye must be Jack."

Jack nodded. His eyes grew large as he looked from Colin to the other men around them. "Is everyone so tall?"

Mariel gave a carefree laugh, remembering having thought the same thing.

Colin chuckled as he knelt before Jack. "Aye, we are a tall lot. I'll let ye ride on my shoulders then ye can be the tallest of all if ye like."

Jack looked up at Mariel, his gaze questioning. She nodded,

and Colin carefully lifted Jack to his shoulders. A slow, tentative smile crept over her brother's face.

"Shall I run?" Colin teased, jogging in place. The cautious smile erupted in a wave of giggles, and Mariel's heart lightened at the precious sound. There had been too many days she had thought she might never hear that laughter again.

Colin hunkered his shoulders down with Jack settled securely atop them and lumbered through the trees like a crazed beast.

She glanced at Kieran from beneath the veil of her lashes. Jack would not be saved were not for him. His lies to her brother had been so convincing, she had almost believed them herself.

But she knew better.

She studied his serious profile and her heart turned to lead. He looked straight ahead, his jaw clenched.

He would never forgive her for what she had done. His silence following her confession that morning was answer enough to how he felt. Regardless of the love that would never be returned, she did not regret her words.

She shifted her focus to Jack. He would be happy on Skye.

Yet her joy was hampered by her own impending fate. The life she had been so ready to sacrifice for Jack's had increased in worth with his freedom. She would not see him thrive in his new home and never get to savor the victory of securing the bond time had loosened between them. Her throat tightened.

Kieran had upheld his end of the bargain for Jack's safe return. Now she would follow through with her promise and willingly face the public death of a traitor.

Chapter Thirty-Nine

Mariel cupped clear, icy water in her hands and splashed her face. Her lips stung with the sweat and grime that trickled down her chin to the rushing creek below. The few hours they'd traveled had felt like an eternity.

She scanned the surrounding trees once more. Jack had said he needed to relieve himself and though she had been hesitant to let him leave her side, she knew he required his privacy.

He had been gone too long. Perhaps she should have asked one of the men to accompany him.

A twig snapped behind her. "Jack, you certainly took your time. I was about to come—"

"Ye're lucky I dinna drop from a tree."

Mariel spun around and found Kieran standing several paces behind her. Her heart slammed in her chest.

He had cleaned up from battle and tied his hair back, away from his unshaven jaw. A familiar ache lanced through her as she stared at the man she could never have. The man she would never stop loving.

"Jack is with Colin." His black gaze met hers, and a warmth fluttered to life in the pit of her stomach.

"We need to talk," he said. "There is much to say."

He stepped closer, but she held out a hand to stop him. She had to speak now while she had the courage. If she caught the slightest whisper of warmth from his skin or breathed his comforting scent, her resolve would falter.

His dark brow rose, but he did not speak.

"First I want to say thank you for your help in rescuing Jack. You were right. Such a feat would have been impossible on my own. Whether you believed me or not, you risked your life and those of your best warriors to come here. Because of you, Jack is safe. I don't think I could ever thank you enough for what you've done for me." She swallowed thickly.

If she did not say it now, perhaps she would not ever have the strength to do so. "I want you to know that I am not afraid to uphold my end of our agreement. When we return to Skye, I will face my punishment without a fight." Her voice lowered. "I do not pretend to think I will receive anything better than a traitor's death and I am prepared."

Kieran closed the distance between them, standing so close, the top of his chin could rest atop her head.

He cupped her face, his fingers gentle and his palms cool against the heat of her cheeks. "I have no intention of having ye killed, lass."

She stepped away from him, refusing to allow any hope. "I'm a traitor," she said.

"Ye are nae a traitor. Ye dinna have a choice." He studied her for a brief moment before continuing. "I dinna know everything about yer past, but I do know ye've lived a hard life. Yet still ye persevered and stayed true to what is most important." The corner of his lip lifted in a slow smile. "I'm proud of ye."

Her pulse raced. Was he serious? He truly did not believe she was a traitor even after all she had done?

His eyes searched hers. "I meant what I said to Jack. My life is better for having known ye." He stepped in front of her once more and caught her chin between his thumb and forefinger. "I'm a better man because of ye."

"Kieran," she breathed, torn between wanting him to stop and needing him to continue. There could be nothing between them, not when she'd already hurt him so much. His words gave her a hope she did not deserve. A hope that would never flourish.

His thumb pressed against her lips, silencing her. "I dinna interrupt ye this morning when ye talked. Dinna interrupt me now, aye?" The pressure of his thumb brushed to a delicate caress. "I asked ye something once before and ye said no. At the time I dinna understand yer reasoning, but now I understand ye did what ye knew in yer heart was right."

Her breath quickened. Surely he didn't mean...

"This time I know ye as I dinna know ye then. I know yer faults that ye feel are great and that I feel are few. And I know yer strengths that ye feel are few and I feel are great. After hiding for years, ye finally have someone who knows ye, knows all of ye, and loves ye no in spite of it, but for it." He stroked her cheek. "I love ye, Mariel, and I would be honored if ye would become my wife."

She jerked back from the burn of his touch, unable to bear the torment of his closeness any longer. "How could you possibly wish to wed me?"

Kieran's hands gripped her arms firmly, forcing her to return her gaze to him. "I was a warrior for years, do ye no think I dinna have to do things I dinna want to do? Things I was ashamed to do? I killed men who meant to kill me and stole food when my warriors were starving. It doesna matter the direction necessity forces ye to take in life, it matters which way ye go when ye have a choice."

Pain laced his words. He understood her far more than she thought possible. He knew the raw burn of survival and bore its wicked scars.

His lips pressed against her forehead, and the familiar spice of his scent enveloped her with memories that left tears in her eyes.

"Ye dinna have to sacrifice any part of yerself ever again, Mariel. Come back to Skye with Jack." A muscle worked in his jaw. "Ye dinna have to marry me if ye dinna want to. Regardless, ye will have a home for the two of ye." He paused. "But if ye do want to marry me, I promise to be a verra good husband."

He saw something in her she had never allowed herself to see and gave her permission to accept what she had done in the past, to move forward into a future she had never considered. While she saw only the bad she had done, he opened her eyes to all the good in her life.

She could begin a new life. With him. A smile spread over her lips before she could stop it.

He grinned down at her. "Typically when a man asks a lass to marry him, it's polite to give him a response of some kind."

She gave a choked laugh. "You're exceptionally good at convincing people, Kieran MacDonald."

His eyebrows raised in a serious expression. "Is that a yes?"

"Aye," she teased, "that's a yes."

His arms wrapped around her, narrowly missing the whip's mark around her waist, and pulled her against the solid warmth of his chest. She melted against him and breathed deeply, allowing the memories to fill her heart with a joy she had tempered for too long.

"No one will ever hurt ye again," he whispered fiercely into her ear. "Ye're mine, and I'll no ever let anything cause ye unhappiness."

His heartbeat was steady and strong against her cheek. "I love you," she breathed into the warmth of his leine, not certain if he would hear her.

"And I love ye, my sweet Mariel."

•   •   •

Kieran stood at the front of the small, private chapel and tried to ignore the numerous sets of eyes on him. The thick stone walls held out the heat of the midafternoon sun while the large lead encased windows let in ample light. Small bundles of heather dotted the aisles with sprays of purple. Blair had outdone herself, and he couldn't help but smile knowing how it would please Mariel.

The glossy wooden door of the chapel, however, remained closed as they all waited for her arrival.

Kieran shifted from one foot to the other, and he caught the pungent aroma of rosemary he'd inadvertently crushed beneath his boot. He scanned the faces of his clan where they waited in eager anticipation.

Alec sat silent in the back with a rare grin on his face. Colin, who'd finally learned to keep his damned hands to himself, sat at the front. Even Hamish had arrived, wearing his best plaid for the occasion. Blair sat between Dougal and Jack with her arms affectionately slung around each boy. Tears glistened in her eyes, and the ceremony had yet to begin.

Jack and Dougal had not stayed out of trouble since they'd been introduced. Though Mariel and Blair acted exasperated with the antics, Kieran knew deep down they were glad to see the boys happy once more.

The doors to the chapel opened and Mariel swept in like a mythical goddess, ethereal with a halo of golden afternoon light framing her slender form.

Her long onyx hair tumbled down her shoulders to the simple blue gown she wore. She glided down the short aisle to his side. Her eyes sparkled up at him with a joy that lodged in his heart and swelled with pleasure.

There were so many things he wanted to tell her, so much to say that he found himself overwhelmed. She humbled him with her love. She made the warrior turned laird in a land never meant to be his suddenly feel right, and washed away the bitterness of his past with the warmth of her presence.

"Ye look bonnie," he whispered. Petty words that failed to cover all he wished to say.

He would take the time to show her his appreciation once the festivities came to a close and they were left alone in his chamber. *Their* chamber.

His blood heated at the thought.

The priest cleared his throat, silently chastising them with a stern look. Kieran reluctantly turned from his bride to face the old man who prattled on for what felt like an eternity before he finally addressed Mariel. "Do ye consent to this union?"

Mariel met his gaze and smiled radiantly. "I do."

"And do ye consent to the union?" the priest asked Kieran.

Kieran took Mariel's smooth hand in his. "Aye," he said in earnest, "I do."

Colin's voice piped up from the front pew. "Hurry up and kiss her before the priest starts up again, aye?"

The priest narrowed his eyes at Colin before giving them a gentle nod. "Go on then," he said and muttered under his breath about youth and failing traditions.

Kieran paid the old man little heed. He tilted Mariel's face toward him and closed his mouth over the warmth of her lips. Finally, he would convey the love he'd repressed for so long. His tongue dipped into the sweetness of her mouth—a promise of good things to come.

A delicious shiver raised the hair on Mariel's arms as Kieran's tongue brushed hers, none too discreetly based on the lewd applause of those watching. He grinned up at their audience, and the priest grumbled beside them.

"Kieran," she chided with a laugh. "You're wicked!"

"No nearly as wicked as I intend to be later, wife," he breathed into her ear. A fresh wave of heart pounding excitement washed over her. The expression on his face was not one of lust, but one of love. His dark gaze was tender.

He caught her hand in the crook of his large arm, and together they made their way down the aisle to exit the chapel. Jack scampered to his feet and ran beside her with a wide smile. She folded his sweaty hand in hers. Dougal wouldn't be far behind.

Caisteal Camus rose from the large hill before them, no longer a cold, ominous fortress. The castle had become her home, filled with those she loved.

Kieran brushed a kiss against her ear. "Welcome to yer new life, Lady MacDonald."

Mariel breathed deep Kieran's scent and basked in the warmth of his solid body against hers as she considered his words.

A new life, one filled with kindness, honesty, and love.

And blissfully free of deception.

Acknowledgments

I always thought the 'there are too many people to thank who made this moment possible' line was just a note of drama in an exciting moment. Now that I'm there, I realize exactly what they mean. There are always so many inspiring, amazing people to thank with each book written, but I think a debut requires an even longer list. First of all, I want to thank Laura Bradford for believing in me. Next I want to thank Randall Klein (and Sarah, Mary, Eliza, Hannah, Brielle and all the other awesome people with Diversion Books) for being so wonderful.

Thank you to my amazing beta readers who helped me with brutal honesty and made me giddy with genuine compliments (and holy Scotsman are y'all some fast readers!): Alli Searle, Sandy Martins, Katie Couch and Amanda Sumner. Thank you to Hillary Raymer for being the best critique partner ever and a wonderful friend—Wine Wednesday forever! Thank you to April Smith for the countless hours of e-mails and encouragement and for being so excited to read each chapter as soon as I wrote it—you motivated me more than you'll ever know. Thank you to Shelby Reed for being there for me (as a fellow writer and stoic friend) through the start of the book all the way to the finish (and all the chaos in between)—you inspire me.

I also want to thank First Coast Romance Writers for the incredible knowledge gleaned and friends gained. Thank you to the Fire Breathing Flamingos for the mentoring and encouragement and constant availability for questions and to the Lalalas for always being such a huge support network—I love you ladies. Thank you to Donna MacMeans for her rooting interests lecture and the way it revolutionized the way I write.

Thank you to Margie Lawson for encouraging me to write fresher than I ever realized I could.

Thank you to my loving parents for their nonstop encouragement and support all these years. And a final, special thank you to my beautiful daughters (the minions) who are my biggest, cutest cheerleaders ever and who only ever go to bed without a sound when they know my agent is going to call.

Thank you to anyone I may have missed in this incredibly long list. I'm a fortunate woman to have my dream come true and all the more fortunate for all the love and support surrounding me.

Available Now!

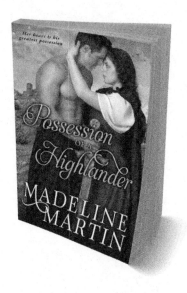

KEEP READING
FOR A PREVIEW OF

Possession
OF A
Highlander

Chapter One

Angus, Scotland - June 1606

Brianna Lindsay's time had run out.

Soil caked the undersides of her rounded fingernails and creased her palms like black sin. There was still much to do.

The sun burned high overhead, baring her deeds to all. Reminding her she could be discovered at any moment.

She plunged her hands into the cool, moist earth. But she mustn't delve too far.

She didn't know how deeply they'd buried him.

Her body clenched around another dry retch. There was nothing left for her stomach to give.

She could go no further. The gouged hole would have to do.

The rosebush at her side stretched away with twisted limbs, and its leaves quivered in the wind. Did it seek another way out as she did? Did it feel the looming threat?

"We all must make our sacrifices." She spoke under her breath in a soothing tone that would fall deaf upon wicked thorns.

It mattered not.

She had no other options. None, except this or surrender.

And there were too many lives at stake.

A pearl of sweat tickled a path from her brow to her chin. She swiped it away with a dirty fist.

The moisture upon her cheeks should be tears.

Edzell Castle had lost its earl the day before. No one could find out, most especially her uncle. Not until she figured out an alternative.

Bernard, her Captain of the Guard, had left hours before with a letter tucked safely in his vest.

This would all be over when he returned from Edinburgh. She hoped.

She grasped the hearty base of the rosebush and cradled its roots. With reverent care, she transplanted it into the freshly turned earth, beside the other three. Only two more remained to be sown into the ground.

Together, they would cover the makeshift grave in a tangle of fragrant blooms and barbed vines.

At least he lay in consecrated ground.

For the countless time, she willed the tears to come. For the countless time, still, they did not.

She winced beneath a slice of regret.

No matter how callous he had been, no matter how cruel a position he had left her in, surely Brianna should mourn the death of her own father.

• • •

Colin MacKinnon quickened his pace through the maze of curling ferns. Sunlight cut through the trees overhead and flickered around him, hastening his sense of urgency. The rich scent of soil rose from underfoot and mingled with the copper odor of blood.

He locked his arms beneath the battered old man he carried. As it was, the man's breath grew shallower by the moment. He would not last long.

"Do ye see the castle, Alec? Are we close?" Colin asked. He would run if necessary.

Alec strode several paces ahead, his large body clearing the forest's heavy growth from their path. "Aye, I see it just ahead."

"We're almost there," Colin said through gritted teeth. "Ye're almost home."

The man's mouth moved, and a weak exhale gasped through thin, bloodied lips.

Colin ducked beneath a veil of thin branches and found

himself bathed in the warmth of dazzling sunlight. Lush grass stretched before him, lining his path. Beckoning.

Edzell Castle rose at its center, nestled like a rare pearl behind walls tinged pink with precious sandstone.

Colin glanced over his shoulder to where a small white building sat against the forest. A servant knelt in the dirt beside a row of rosebushes, her long brown braid thrown over her shoulder.

Before either he or Alec could call out, her head snapped up. She tensed. The narrowed look on her comely face was not one of welcome.

"Who are you?" she demanded, her voice sharp. Suspicious.

Colin turned, and her gaze dropped to the man in his arms. "We seek Lady Lindsay."

All hostility drained from her widened eyes. She lurched to her feet and staggered toward them in a frantic run.

"What have you done?" Accusation screamed from her wild gaze. Soil smudged one flushed cheek.

"I seek Lady Lindsay," Colin said again.

The man stirred, and a low moan croaked from his throat.

"He's alive," she gasped. "What's happened? Who has done this?"

His patience waned. The dying man did not have time for the servant's lamentations. "Damn it, lass, listen to me. He is badly wounded and requests Lady Lindsay. All questions will be answered later. For now, I demand to see the lady of the castle."

Her generous lips fell open, but no words emerged. She dropped her gaze to the man, and her brows knit together. "This way." She motioned toward the white building and sprinted ahead, her thick braid bouncing against her back with each hastened step.

The structure was cool inside, a reprieve from the heat of the noonday sun. Costly stained glass windows lined either side of the walls and shot streaks of reds, yellows, and golds across the rows of wooden benches. A church. The location was fitting for a man soon dead.

Colin glanced down at the man, Bernard, in his arms, and

found his face had gone white beneath the streaks of blood. A bad sign.

The lass pulled a length of embroidered white silk from the altar and spread it on the ground. "Lay him here," she said.

Colin hesitated. The workmanship on the fabric was incredibly detailed in its depiction of the Garden of Eden, each leaf and flower crafted with obvious care. He glanced up at the servant. She would be whipped for using so costly a cloth for a dying man.

"Lay him here," she repeated, her voice strained with desperation.

Colin sank to his knees. "He is bleeding heavily."

"I understand." Her tone had lost its edge and was soft, somber. "Please." She motioned to the altar cloth once more with trembling fingers tinged black and dirty.

Colin eased Bernard to the silk-covered ground. The old man was finally home.

The furrows of pain on the man's weathered face smoothed into a smile. "Thank you." The words rasped from within his chest. He was still alive. There was still time.

The woman fell to the ground, her head bent over him. "What's happened to you?" Her voice broke in a way that would tug at any man's chest. Colin was no exception.

"Brianna?" The dying man squinted up at the servant.

"Yes," she whispered. "I'm here."

Colin cleared his throat, an inadvertently loud interruption in the silence of the church. "He needs Lady Lindsay," he said one final time.

"What?" The woman looked up at him from where she sat with her rough skirts tucked under her legs. "You don't understand." She pressed her dirty hand to her chest. "I *am* Lady Lindsay."

CPSIA information can be obtained
at www.ICGtesting.com
Printed in the USA
LVOW03s2305290318
571737LV00001B/165/P